Eleven Days

A NOVEL OF THE HEARTLAND

Eleven Days

A NOVEL OF THE HEARTLAND

Donald Harstad

DOUBLEDAY / New York Toronto London Sydney Auckland

PUBLISHED BY DOUBLEDAY
a division of Bantam Doubleday Dell Publishing Group, Inc.
1540 Broadway, New York, New York 10036

DOUBLEDAY and the portrayal of an anchor with a dolphin are
trademarks of Doubleday, a division of Bantam Doubleday Dell
Publishing Group, Inc.

All of the characters in this book are fictitious, and any resemblance
to actual persons, living or dead, is purely coincidental.

Book design by Donna Sinisgalli

Library of Congress Cataloging-in-Publication Data

Harstad, Donald.
    Eleven days: a novel of the heartland / Donald Harstad.
—1st ed.
        p.   cm.
    I. Title.
    PS3558.A67558E44   1998
813′.54—dc21   97-15515
                                                          CIP

ISBN 0-385-48894-7
Copyright © 1998 by Donald Harstad
All Rights Reserved
Printed in the United States of America
September 1998
10 9 8 7 6 5 4 3 2 1
First Edition

To my mother.

Acknowledgments

Writing this novel was a project that involved many people in many ways. I needed all of them to complete the process.

I would like to especially thank Mary and Erica, who put up with so much, not the least of which was me. My thanks also to Jerry Z., my agent, who believed in the project; Dan W., who also believed and provided much needed moral support; Rae and Nick, who ran with the ball; and Shawn, who helped as only an excellent editor can. I would also like to express my thanks to the men and women in law enforcement in northeast Iowa, with whom I worked and shared many memorable experiences over twenty-five years.

Inspired by Actual Events

Eleven Days

A NOVEL OF THE HEARTLAND

1

Friday, April 19, 1996
23:52 hours
The call came into County Communications from an unidentified source, believed female, possibly under fifty. No callback number was given and no further contact was noted.

"Sheriff's Department."

"My God, my God, help us here, help us here, please . . ."

"Who is calling and what is wrong?" The dispatcher was Sally Wells— no extra chatter at all and very calm. She was new and part-time, but she learned fast.

"Help us, they're killing everybody! Help!"

"Where are you and who is calling?"

"Just get help"—indecipherable—"killed Francis, he killed him, help us here!"

"Where are you?"

"The Francis McGuire farm! Help!"

"Where is the farm?"

"Jesus Christ, help us up"—indecipherable—"didn't mean it. Oh God, oh God, I don't know, please help. Please . . ."

"Stay on the line!" Sally held fast and with the phone to her ear contacted the available patrol cars.

"Comm, three and five . . . 10–33 . . . Possible homicide. Francis McGuire, I think that's the farm near William's Hollow. I, uh, think it's in progress, subject on line. Repeat, this is a 10–33."

"Comm. Three. Which side of the hollow, north or south?" I said in as soothing a voice as I could manage.

"Three, stand by," Sally said with relief. "Ma'am, are you north or south of the Hollow?"

"Jesus God, I don't know. *I don't know! Help!*"

"One moment. Hold tight. Three. Unable to advise."

Five, Mike Conners, came on. "I think they're on the south side, just before the bridge—about five miles out of Maitland, second or third gravel to the right."

"10–4, five. Comm, check the caller." I made the turn to take me to the Hollow.

Sally went back to the phone, and it became apparent that the complainant had heard the radio traffic.

"It's the second turn, the second turn, oh God, hurry!"

"She says the second turn, three."

"Tell 'em to hurry!" (Indecipherable) "told me"—indecipherable— "again! He's just dead. Can't—" With that, the line went dead. I was only about ten miles from William's Hollow, while Mike was about twenty-six miles out. Unfortunately I was north, and the directions were from the south.

"Comm, three. I'm in from the north. Find out from what location is the second or third gravel, or which gravel after I cross the bridge going south."

"10–4, three."

"And look the farm up in the phone book and call it back."

"I'm doing that," Sally snapped.

While she got better directions from Mike in car five, I continued south on the county paving. The roads in our part of Iowa are only twenty feet wide and are exceptionally curvy and hilly. They've managed to pack about 1,300-odd miles of them into the county's 750-square-mile border, and with no sign of a spring thaw, I could count on slipping and sliding the whole way.

"Comm, three. Get 10–78 going." 10–78 was the backup code. If we had a multiple homicide in progress, two duty officers on highway patrol could only do so much.

"10–4, three. For your 10–43, I'm getting no answer at the McGuire residence."

Mike was going to have to travel about nine miles on gravel roads that had the consistency of crushed ice before he would even hit the frozen paved ones. I would beat him to the scene by fifteen minutes or more. The backup in this case meant the one city officer on duty in Maitland, who was between Mike and me. I figured another fifteen minutes response on his side. Anybody else was going to be in bed. I hoped we didn't need them.

Mike and I were both running with lights at full beam and with sirens blaring, both to alert anyone on the scene that we were on the way and to frighten away any deer on the road in front of us. Hitting a two-hundred-pound deer at over a hundred miles per hour might not kill you, but you would be wasted at the point of impact. The manual says to go to a serious crime "as fast as possible, considering the conditions." Which means that if you wreck the car, it's your butt, buddy, not the county's. If I went by the book on this one, I'd hit the McGuire farm a week from Thursday. I made the first nine miles in just under six minutes.

"Comm, three's at the bridge. Confirm that it will be the third gravel on my left."

"10–4, three. Third left past the bridge. Also, three, the hospital received a call like ours and they've dispatched an ambulance."

"10–4, comm. Be sure to tell the paramedics to wait to come in until we've cleared them."

"10–4, three. As soon as they're in the unit."

I was going to acknowledge, but I was skidding past the third left turn. I softly nudged a snowbank, backed up about twenty yards, and made the turn onto the slushy gravel road.

"Comm, how far down this road?"

There are 2,200 farms in the county. I couldn't possibly know where they all were.

"Three, this is five, second farm on the right, it's down a long lane. I don't think there's a name on the mailbox, and you have to go over a little hill before you can see the farm from the road. I've been there about, uh, three times . . . think the house is on the right of the drive, bunch of other buildings on the left, and they're pretty close together."

My "10–4" was a little strained. I was just going over the knoll that cut the view from the roadway.

"Comm, three is 10–23." I was actually still about a hundred yards from the house, but didn't know if I'd have time to say anything from there on in. In those last hundred yards, I reached down and turned on my walkie-talkie, turned off my siren, unbuckled my seat belt and cleared it from interfering with my personal gear, and unsnapped my holster. By that time I was skidding to a stop. I grabbed my flashlight and got out of the car as quickly as I could. The house was on my right.

It was a frame house. Two stories. Needed paint pretty bad. It had a front porch and what appeared to be a back porch and just about every light in the house was on. No sign of movement inside.

They tell you at the academy that if you'll need it, the only place for your weapon is in your hand. I drew my revolver, a .44 magnum, and pointed it down and to my right as I approached the house. There was a bluish yard light, similar to a streetlight, illuminating the yard in a roughly circular pattern. My car was behind me, and without remembering doing it, I had correctly pointed the headlights toward the scene. The beams cast my shadow on the front porch, distracting my attention from cataloging what I was up against. My heart leapt every time I picked up my own movement, so I started with the left, at the barn and a couple of outbuildings. Interior light in the barn. The others were dark. No movement. Neither good nor bad. If there's nobody there, there's no movement. If somebody is aiming a shotgun at you from concealment, they probably won't move, either. I put that possibility out of my mind and proceeded toward the house, careful not to slip on the uneven sheets of ice that led to the front porch.

"Twenty-five, comm."

On my walkie-talkie. It scared the crap out of me, as the speaker was just by my left ear. I turned it off. Twenty-five was the Maitland backup officer, Dan Smith, and since I could hear him on my portable, he was probably within two miles of my position.

I made it to the landing of the screened porch and was able to see into the kitchen at about chest level for anyone standing in there. Nobody was. I would have to go onto the porch to look into the house. I didn't really want to do that. But I did. I stepped up onto the second of four steps and opened the screen door. The interior of the porch was a real mess, cluttered to the point that I was not sure I could negotiate a path. Garbage—empty boxes, broken glass, tools, tires, a chain saw—surrounded a small dog to my left who just sat there staring. He didn't move or make a sound. It was the first thing that really worried me.

"Police officer. Anybody in there?"

No response. I said it as loudly as I could without yelling. Tried again. Nothing. I approached the door, stepping as carefully as I could over the mess. I could see through the right-hand window, into the kitchen. Also a wreck, with a table tossed in a corner, its broken leg doubled back underneath. Several chairs were overturned, the refrigerator was dented and at an angle and the top freezer door was open. But no people.

I stood to the side of the front door, put my flashlight in my belt, and knocked as hard as I could.

"Police officer! Is anybody home?"

Again, no answer and then headlights coming down the lane. Twenty-five. I had to turn my portable back on and use my left hand to key the mike.

"Twenty-five, that you?"

"10–4."

"Okay, I'm on the porch. Park behind my car, and stay back until I can get in the house."

"10–4."

Dan Smith was an experienced officer. I felt a lot better. A few seconds later, I heard him jack a round into his shotgun and I didn't feel quite as confident. I hoped he kept the safety on.

I navigated across the porch and tried the kitchen door. It opened about an inch and then hung up. I pushed it harder and it gave a little with a gentle scraping sound from inside, and then a fairly loud thump, like it was blocked by a hundred-pound sack of potatoes. I pushed a little harder, and it opened about two feet to reveal the open mouth and staring eyes of a man who was obviously dead. I stepped back.

"Twenty-five, I'm going to have to try another entrance—this one is blocked by a body."

"10–9?"

10–9 means you should repeat your traffic, as the message was not understood. Or, in this case, believed.

"I've got a body blocking this door. I'm gonna work my way around the house to the left, here."

"10–4."

"Three? Five."

"Five, go."

Mike was close. Even better.

"Wanna wait till I get there? Only a minute or so."

It was tempting, but I was too exposed to stand still.

"No, just cover the right side of the house when you get here. I'll be around the left and coming right unless I can find a way in."

I gingerly backed down the steps and went to the left, toward the back of the house, to what appeared to be the back porch. The dog still hadn't stirred. Keeping my head below window level, I made my way to find that the back porch was actually an addition to the house with a separate entrance. The upper half of the door was glass.

The door was locked, but I could see through to the body in the kitchen. There was something sticking out of his chest or abdomen, but I couldn't make out what it was. The broken table was obstructing the full view. Then a noise.

"Three has movement inside!"

No reply. I heard running footsteps coming up from my right. Mike ran past me to the other side of the doorwell and put his back against the wall. We were both very quiet for a moment and heard the sound again. Like something dragging and then a bump. We looked at each other and nodded at the same time.

I kicked the door. It didn't move. I kicked again and the panel cracked. The third kick slammed the door back where it hit the interior wall and broke the glass, causing one hell of a racket. Mike flew by me into the house and stopped just as he hit the entrance to the living room. I moved behind him, but he was frozen, so I nudged him and stuck my gun around the corner of the door frame and pointed it to where he was looking.

"Jesus."

There was a German shepherd crawling across the floor toward us, dragging his hind legs. His mouth was bleeding, and he had a bloody wound on his head. His eyes were glazed. To the left, the TV was on, but no sound, playing a rerun of *Ensign O'Toole*. There were, as they say, signs of a struggle—magazines all over, overturned lamps, one stereo speaker knocked over, a houseplant in a broken pot lying on the floor.

"I don't want to kill him." Mike said what I was thinking.

"We have to."

"Who would leave an innocent animal like that?" Mike mumbled.

"Twenty-five," I said over my portable. "There will be a shot fired. We have to shoot a dog."

"A dog?"

"Yeah."

I aimed as carefully as I could, cocked the hammer back, and very gently squeezed the trigger. We waited a few seconds, our ears ringing, stunned by the shot and the strangeness of the situation. Then we slowly made our way to the kitchen.

"Twenty-five?"

"Go."

"We're in."

"Copy you in the house?"

"Yeah. Both of us."

"Okay. Two's on the way."

"Good." Two was the county's chief deputy. Although he was in charge of the night shift, he'd had the evening off. Sally must have called him in when Dan reported the body. I had my portable on single-channel mode and wasn't able to hear the other radio traffic, but Dan was still by his car and would relay our reports to those on the way.

We looked carefully around the kitchen. The body by the door was supine, his legs bent at not quite right angles. The object in his chest was a knife with an ornate handle, made of silver or stainless steel. His right hand was gone, the stump pointing toward the tilted refrigerator. But there was very little blood. He was nude, except for a pair of white socks with yellow toes. They were half on, half off his feet, and dirty. I turned to Mike.

"Didn't dispatch say that a female called?"

"Yeah." We'd been at death scenes before, but there was something about this one that had us both spooked.

"Well, let's look."

I hated to go stomping around a crime scene, but we had to see if the woman or the killer was still in the house. We crossed to the bedroom, the only other room on the ground floor. Nobody there. It was a mess, but it looked to me like from being lived in, not from a struggle or burglary. The lights were on and there was a fairly large painting above the bed, not framed. It was a star, point down, in a circle, with red eyes near the center. Not well done. Primitive.

I looked at Mike. "Let's do upstairs first, then the basement. Anybody gets out from the basement, twenty-five has a good chance of picking them up as they come out."

Mike headed for the stairs. I let him go up about five steps, then followed. The stairwell was only about thirty-six inches across, and the steps were so narrow that I had to put my feet down sideways. They creaked, adding to our tension, which in my case was at critical mass. I figured we'd find the caller, but that she would be dead or dying. I also thought we had a chance of finding the perpetrator, or of him finding us. On those stairs, he could have got both of us with a pellet gun.

Mike hit the top stair and started moving to his left. "Okay, Carl, we got doors both sides, all open," he whispered.

"Right." I took the right side of the narrow hallway as I topped the stairs—three small rooms, two left, one right. No one in any of them. Each room seemed messier than the one before it. Each one was dusty, dirty, and cold and piled high and deep with boxes of junk. I was amazed at how much garbage this guy held on to.

Then we carefully moved to the basement, down another set of small, rickety steps. I went first this time, exposing my body to whoever might be waiting. The basement was as dilapidated as the rest of the house, but I noticed a small, partitioned corner with a blanket tacked up that separated it from the rest of the mess. I cautiously pushed the blanket aside with my magnum while Mike covered me.

Nobody there. But four knives similar to the one stuck in the body upstairs were hanging on the wall. Next to the knives was a painting of Jesus on the cross that was desecrated with a happy-face sticker placed on his face. On the other side was an ink drawing of a small heart that appeared anatomically correct with a dagger in it. Below was a small workbench with several burned-down black candles. There was also a calendar and a rather seedy black robe hanging against the sidewall. We turned to find an inverted cross hung opposite the crucifixion painting.

"What in the hell is going on, Carl?"

"I don't know," is all I could come up with.

2

We left the house, closing the entry door as well as we could on the way out. We would now stay away from the crime scene until the Des Moines Division of Criminal Investigation mobile lab team arrived. It would take them about six hours to make it to Nation County. We would use the time to search the outbuildings and take some photographs through the windows.

Mike and I both lit cigarettes on the way to the patrol cars. The chief deputy, Art Meyerman, was waiting for us with Dan in the yard.

"What have you got?"

I took a deep breath. "One body, male, looks like he's been stabbed in the chest. His hand has been cut off. Oh, and a dead dog. We had to put him out of his misery. Nobody else."

"What about the woman?"

"No sign of her," said Mike.

"You killed a dog?"

I nodded. "Yep, had to."

"How'd you kill it?"

"I shot him," I said.

Art shook his head like he was dealing with a green recruit out of the academy. "We'll need a report on that. Better give me good reasons, too. You can be suspended if the owner finds out about it and complains."

"Unless this guy's middle name is Lazarus, I don't think that's gonna happen."

Art gave me another smirk, but let it go. He had a tendency to be an asshole under stress. Actually he was an asshole under normal circumstances, too. He stomped back to his car to use the radio and warm up. Mike, Dan, and I stayed in the cold and listened.

"Comm, tell one to keep coming and tell the ambulance to slow it up a little. It's not 10–33 for them."

"10–4, two. Do you want me to request 10–79?"

"When I want the coroner, I'll tell you."

Art was also rude. I resented his "I'm in charge here" attitude. Sally had done a fine job, and the notification of the coroner was the next logical step. He was just pissed he hadn't thought of it first.

I grinned at Dan. "Someday . . . you see Art crawling across the floor, and he looks hurt, call me."

We were still chuckling and pulling on our cigarettes when Art came back over.

"Cut the chat and get the buildings searched. Let's do it now."

We flicked our butts and split up. Mike took the machine shed, Dan took the garage, and I had the barn. Art, of course, stayed central and observed. I couldn't help but give him a dig.

"Art, don't you think we could use the DCI lab team? Might as well get them coming."

He didn't say anything. I'd been in the department about four years longer than he had and he was jealous of my record and resented my relationship with the sheriff.

We found nothing of particular significance in the outbuildings, and the ground was still too hard and icy to have any tracks in the yard. We surveyed the rest of the area, looking at the scattered patches of snow for traces of prints or tire tracks. There was nothing that stood out and nothing that appeared to be fresh.

One, Sheriff Lamar Ridgeway, came barreling over the knoll in his four-wheel drive, nearly leaving the ground. He slid to a stop and got out. We met him near his vehicle in a tight little clump and gave him a brief rundown—the body, the search, and the dog, of course.

"You shot it?"

"Yeah," I said.

"You had to. Glad you did."

I gave Art a look.

"Can we see the body from the outside?"

"Yeah, let me get my camera."

Lamar and I went up to the front porch, and he held the flashlight while I focused my 35mm through the window. The reality of the scene kicked in when I began clicking the shutter. With the zoom lens, I looked right down into the victim's mouth and nasal passages. I noticed something brown on his teeth and in his nose.

"Looks like he was a tobacco chewer."

Lamar nodded, bent down, and scooped up the frightened little dog on the porch.

As I took establishing shots of the kitchen, I noticed that the telephone was on the wall and seemed perfectly normal. Lamar had Art check the line entrance and he confirmed that the phone was in working order. Sally had told me that in the middle of the call the phone went dead, but when she called McGuire's minutes later, it rang but no one answered. The caller must have been on another extension and her line ripped out of the wall. I didn't remember seeing any other phone jacks, but I made a mental note to ask the lab to give the house a more thorough look.

A grinding sound in the distance announced the arrival of the ambulance. They had probably slowed down and were having trouble negotiating the icy lane. I'd learned long ago never to slow down on an Iowa farm lane before summer. The icy gravel was sure to hold you up if you did. They must not have made many trips this deep into the county, especially not in these conditions.

I was having a hard time holding the camera steady. The temperature had dropped to about twenty degrees and my adrenaline was running thin. I finished up and Lamar and I headed back to the patrol cars, where Dan was filling in the ambulance crew. We still didn't know anything and he shouldn't have been wagging his tongue. Being from a city of fifteen hundred, though, makes it hard to keep things to yourself and Dan was chatty to begin with. He looked suitably guilty upon our arrival and the paramedics tried to cover for him by shuffling around doing bogus EMT things.

"Fill 'em in, Dan?" I ribbed him as I helped Lamar clear a space for the dog in the cabin of his car.

"Oh, Carl, I don't really know much."

I just shook my head and grinned. "Thanks for coming out."

"No problem."

The radio in Dan's car blared. "One, comm."

Lamar picked up the mike in my car. "Go ahead, comm."

"One, I-388 is en route from Albion, ETA about thirty minutes. They want to know if you need the mobile crime lab."

"10–4, comm. We will."

"What the hell is an I-388?" I asked Lamar.

"A state special investigator. It's policy now. If you want the lab, you have to take the suit. I guess good old-fashioned small-town police work doesn't cut it with homicides anymore. The state doesn't want a bunch of bumpkins botching murder investigations." Lamar was pissed, but I knew he wouldn't take it out on the guy coming in. He'd suck it up and treat him fair and square.

While the five of us waited for I-388 and eventually the lab, we lit up and went over everything we could think of. We had no sign of the woman. Where was she? Did she leave the scene voluntarily or was she abducted during the call? We had a telephone line that was intact, but had somehow gone dead during the emergency call. I racked my brain trying to remember another extension in the house, but couldn't think of one. Neither could Mike. And we had a bunch of creepy shit in the basement and that strange painting in the bedroom that indicated that someone had some weird interests, probably the owner. Which brought us to a crucial question that we had stupidly forgotten to even answer.

"Is the body Francis McGuire?" Lamar asked.

I looked at him for a second. "Shit, I don't know. I never saw the man in my life."

Mike grinned. "It's him. I wondered when you'd get around to asking."

"Okay, smart-ass," I said, "anybody else live here?"

"Nope. No wife, no kids. He was married to a girl from Waterloo, but they split up about five years ago."

"How do you know so much about him?" Lamar chimed in.

"Wife's third cousin. She didn't like him. Can't say I did much, either.

Helped him clear some stumps in his fields a couple times. No thanks, no nothin'." Mike had relatives all over the county and knew something about just about everyone.

We kicked it around some more. What was the point of the missing right hand? It was too great a wound to be defensive, and even if it had been, it would be lying on the floor. Unless the dog dragged it away. The lab would figure that one out.

"Not very much blood around, was there?" More of a statement than a question from Mike.

I agreed. "Especially considering the severed hand."

"Somewhere else?" Lamar asked of no one in particular. "Somewhere else in the house?"

Mike and I shook our heads.

"Maybe he clots well." Dan smirked.

Lamar sighed. "I just wish we could find that woman."

"Well," Art finally broke in, "we'd better get somebody out on the main road so we can guide I-388 in. He'll never be able to find us." A real team player, our Art. Maybe we did need I-388.

3

After Special Agent Hester Gorse (I-388) arrived, we briefed her. There were a couple of smirks about her being the head of the investigation and Art said, "Just what we need. A female trying to be a cop." I didn't say anything. Lamar did.

"She'll be okay." End of discussion. At least for then.

We left Art to guard the scene until a reserve officer could be contacted, and Lamar with his new mutt, Mike, and I headed to the office to begin the reports. We only have two typewriters, so it was a little hairy at first. After a serious crime, we always try to get everything written down as soon as we can so that the day shift has something to go on, and more important, so that they don't bother us when we're home sleeping. I made a special effort to see Sally to tell her she'd done a good job.

Jane, the next dispatcher on shift, was with her. Sally had called her in early to help with the media calls. Murders are rare around here, and I guess a bunch of cub reporters had their scanners tuned in to the radio traffic. Sally handed me the typed-up radio logs, along with all of the transmission times and the content of the radio messages. They'd be needed for the reports.

"I-388's a woman, isn't she?" Sally had been toying with the idea of applying for a job as a deputy and was very interested in hearing about the life from female officers. I nodded.

"Got the radio logs done?" Art interrupted.

"Yes, we do."

"Got the phone logs?"

"Not yet. Just the radio logs."

"Get with it. Don't sit on your ass while we have officers on overtime waiting for you to get your work done." And he stomped out.

"Asshole," said Sally with what was nearly a hiss.

I went around the dispatch console. "I'll relieve you for a few minutes. You have time to hit the head and have some coffee."

"Thanks."

I got off at 07:45 and went directly home. My wife, a junior high teacher, had left for church, so I had three Oreo cookies, some milk, and went to bed, not much better informed than I had been fifteen minutes after I got to the scene. It took about an hour to go to sleep, and I was still thinking about our little case when I dropped off.

The phone rang at 11:58.

I remember saying "Hello," although I'm not sure Jane could understand me. I didn't have any trouble understanding her, though.

"One wants you to come back out. Right away. They've just found three other bodies."

"How could they, we searched the area really well . . ."

"They're at another farm. Lamar thinks they're connected."

The second scene was at the Phyllis Herkaman residence, a farmhouse but not a farm, located about eight miles southwest of the McGuire house.

Herkaman worked at the local hospital as an aide, and had been late for work. She had an estranged husband, who was on the violent side, and her coworkers got worried. Called us, but we had no one available. We requested that a state trooper be sent, and one was eventually dispatched to the Herkaman house. He discovered the body of an unidentified female in the front hallway. The other responding officers (we freed everybody up pretty quickly after he told comm about his discovery) located an unidentified male body, and the body of Phyllis Herkaman, both also in the house.

When I arrived, Lamar and I-388 were there, as well as our office day-shifters, Ed and Norris. Theo, our investigator, was on his way, but had been delayed at the McGuire scene.

We have eight officers, including the sheriff. Divided between three eight-hour shifts, and at seven days a week, we sometimes only have one or two available. It looked like everybody was going to miss a lot of sleep.

As it turned out, the lab team had just arrived at the McGuire house, and it would take them about six to eight hours to process the scene. I was being assigned to I-388 to assist in photographing the crime scene at Herkaman's prior to the arrival of the mobile lab. In an effort to preserve the essence of the scene, Lamar and I-388 made the decision to photograph the bodies before the lab team arrived and tramped everything down. I hoped that wouldn't come back to haunt us in court, but I kept my mouth shut. The bodies were still in the house, and virtually nothing had been disturbed. We'd have to be very careful.

There is quite a difference between doing a quick preliminary set of snapshots of a crime scene and doing one for real. We were going to do this one for real, and it was going to take some time. I already wished I hadn't put on my uniform, and had put on some clothing with lots of pockets. Also, you can't smoke at the crime scene, in case you deposit some "evidence" where none existed before. I'm a heavy smoker, and that always exasperates me. And, usually, the other guy at the scene doesn't smoke at all, so he's a little reluctant to take a smoke break. You also can't eat at the scene, for the same reason. I, of course, am also a heavy eater. Same problems. Being short of sleep, there was a good chance I'd get pissy before we were done. It turned out that I-388, Agent Hester Gorse, didn't smoke. Thin and stringy, it also looked like she didn't eat, either.

While I got some establishing shots of the exterior and took a photo of a broken twig that I-388 thought of some significance, we had to send Norris into Maitland to get film. The department usually makes you use your own camera, but at least they buy your film. They pay you by the print. Cheap, but that's the way it is. I also asked for a second set of gloves. The department issued us one pair, cream-colored latex, one size fits all. Or nobody, depending on your point of view. I couldn't help noticing that Agent Gorse was putting on a pair of double-thickness green gloves. Which she got from a box of one hundred. Is it any wonder we in the boonies sigh a lot?

It took us three hours to do the shots, recording camera settings and descriptors, and timing each shot. I taped my comments on a pocket recorder (provided by the department, who also, by God, provided the tapes; you had to buy your own batteries). Agent Gorse wrote descriptors and made sketches. I had never worked with her before, and it turned out that we both had an interest in astronomy. Discovered this when we found a small telescope in the house.

The significant evidence was as follows:

The body in the front hall was that of a white female, approximately thirty years of age, blond, about five feet five and 110 pounds. She was partially clothed, with blue jeans and a bra. Cause of death not known at the time, but might have had something to do with the red cord used as a ligature around her neck. Facial features were grossly discolored, and there appeared to be some signs of lividity on the belly, which we could see without turning her over. We were unable to identify her at that time.

The unidentified male was in what I'll call the master bedroom, as this house was considerably bigger than the McGuire home. He was on his back, legs secured to the bed with black cord. He had been castrated, and what appeared to be black wax had been poured into his eyes. His tongue was missing, and this time there was blood all over hell. There were also fresh lacerations on his chest and abdomen, one of them being "666" and another being what appeared to be three characters of unknown origin. There was a substance around his mouth which looked like dried super-glue.

When we were photographing that, Ms. Gorse said, "You don't suppose they tried to glue his tongue back on, do you?"

It was then that I knew that I was going to like this woman.

The body of Phyllis Herkaman was in the basement, in what appeared to be the laundry area. She was curled in the southwest corner, with her head pointed, as it turned out, north. She was lying in an enormous pool of blood, which was beginning to clot. There was sort of a skin on top of the pool, which was beginning to wrinkle as it clotted. Serum had separated at the edges of the pool, so what it looked like was a very large lump of pudding surrounded by a yellowish fluid. She was nude, supine, the curl being from left to right. Her right breast had been removed, and the cause of death appeared to be centered around the vaginal area, from which protruded a long, wooden shaft. She had been handcuffed behind her back, and a long red nylon cord was strung between her arms and her back, in a loop, which was secured to a two-inch drainpipe. There was what appeared to be a hatpin thrust through her left nipple. Again, there was a considerable amount of blood around and on the victim. There were no unusual markings on the body. There was, however, a circumscribed star, the circumscription being in the form of a snake eating its own tail, dangling from an overhead pipe directly over the body.

We also discovered a small silver jewelry box in the basement, in a wooden cabinet. It contained several silverlike items, including a small crucifix. The link for attaching the crucifix to a chain appeared to be on the wrong end.

"I'm going to go out for a smoke, Hester. Feel the need."

"Oh, sure," she said. "I would, too, if I still did. Quit four years ago."

She went up in my estimation again—at least, she *had* been a smoker. A redeeming trait if there ever was one.

When we got outside, she endeared herself to me again. Reached into her purse and pulled out two Snickers bars.

I remembered not to hurt her as I snatched one and tried not to injure myself as I unwrapped it. Very, very hungry.

We stayed just outside the back basement door, and could see the body inside as we ate and I smoked. Had sort of a picnic with Phyllis. I was too tired and too hungry to be grossed out. And very pleased that Hester had turned out to be an eater, after all.

I turned the film over to her and went outside to go home. Mistake. The media were finally there. They had gotten excited about the McGuire homicide, of course, but the news from the Herkaman house had them in a frenzy. Network newspeople were there. *Des Moines Register* reporters, two of them, and a photographer. TV teams from Waterloo and Dubuque. Some of them had traveled two hundred miles for this. They wanted a story.

There were also about thirty civilians, mostly neighbors, parked in a harvested cornfield across the highway from the Herkaman place. They stayed well back, except for two or three neighbor ladies who were talking to Norris.

Lamar, by the way, hates the media. Understandable, as we have had several stories screwed up by them over the years, and they have on at least two occasions failed to respect off-the-record remarks. Doesn't sound like much, but in a small, rural Iowa county, you only have a media event about once every three years. Zapped on the last two, Lamar was understandably leery of them.

By this time, the Herkaman house being located on the main highway, it being daylight, and a total of three bodies being found inside the house, we had also attracted a lot of other attention. There were six state troopers keeping the media back, three troopers securing the house, and a sergeant and a lieutenant in attendance. I was impressed. I walked over to Lamar and a Lieutenant Kainz.

"Howdy . . . seem to be getting a lot of attention, don't we?"

Lamar said something about "those sons of bitches," and Lieutenant Kainz began to laugh. Lamar is sort of cuddly when he's pissed off. Wouldn't think of shooting them, or anything effective like that. But he fumes in the background while he tries to think up a news release that will tell them absolutely nothing about what is going on. He's gotten really good at that over the years.

"Lamar, you talk to the press yet?"

"Yep."

"What you tell 'em?"

He handed me a sheet torn from a legal tablet. It said, "More than one body was discovered at the Herkaman residence this morning. Identities withheld pending notifying next of kin. Cause of death unknown. Incident under investigation."

"God, Lamar, that's a lot for you. Ever think about a journalism career?"

"Fuck 'em!"

I went home and sat at the dining room table, eating about two dozen Oreo cookies and drinking milk. And thinking about the day so far. I am the department intelligence officer and for that reason had a file on Satanism. Not that we'd had a case before, but I was just curious about it, and I knew some officers in the metro areas who had dealt with it before.

There was no doubt that the Satanic overtones were there. Overtones, hell. It was like somebody had used a how-to book for Satanic ritual killings. But this just didn't make sense, as far as I could tell. Satanists were into ritual sacrifice, on rare occasions, but this was a massacre. Not a ceremony, at least not one that I could match with anything I'd ever heard about. We had everything except a flashing neon sign saying "Satanic Cult Homicide."

I knew that Satanism attracted psychopaths, but so did many things mystical or unsocial. Satanism was both, of course. It attracted its share of sociopathic personalities, as well, for that very reason. But not like this. It didn't fit the pattern at all.

I went to bed, slept about four hours, and managed to hit my patrol car at 22:56. I was sent directly to a car wreck, with an unruly drunk driver. I was done with him by 01:10. I was then dispatched to a domestic dispute, arriving at 01:22. That took almost three hours to sort out, and by that time I was too tired to think.

I got home at 06:00 and prepared to enjoy my day off. I went to bed and slept till 17:00.

My wife, Sue, was home, and was going through her usual response in these instances: concern, frustration, concern, anger, concern, anger, anger, anger. By the time we got to the fourth anger, supper was long done, my digestion had gone to hell, the office had called twice, and she had gone to bed to be by herself.

As a result, I had plenty of time to think. Not exactly what I wanted, but better than being too tired. When you do a homicide case, it tends to bother you a lot until you figure it out. In this particular instance, we didn't even have a suspect.

One of the calls from the office was Art, telling me that the telephone at the McGuire residence had been out of order for three days prior to the murder and that there was no way the unknown female could have called from there. Oh, swell. He was pissed off at Sally, assuming that she had screwed up somehow. Not logical, as it was at the McGuire farm that we found the body. I told Art I wanted to talk about a possible dope connection, and he said to come up to the office in a couple of hours.

It was a little after midnight, Monday, April 22, and as our office is in Maitland, and I live in Maitland, I wandered up to see Sally and listen to the tape of the phone conversation.

She had already transferred the tape to a cassette, because she was outraged at the unfair suggestion that she had made a mistake. I listened to the tape. McGuire was the name, all right. I didn't recognize the voice.

"Okay, kiddo, what did you think about her?"

Sally thought for a second or two. "She was telling the truth, I think. She was really scared."

Sally is one of those rare dispatchers who have a natural way with people on the telephone. And who have an instinct for judging what they say. It would be a mistake not to use her in the investigation.

"So where is she?"

"If I was her, you'd never find me again . . . if I was alive."

Another problem. So far, the second female at the Herkaman residence hadn't been identified. There was a chance that she could have been the caller. Mike's wife also knew, or had known, Phyllis Herkaman, and had listened to the tape along with several hospital employees. The voice didn't belong to Phyllis.

But if the unidentified female was the caller, how did she get from McGuire's to Herkaman's, and why? The way she was dressed indicated that she might have been unclothed prior to her murder and had possibly dressed in anticipation of flight. Or, of course, that she was undressing and got surprised. Time of death would tell. Maybe.

"When you undress, what order do you take your clothes off in?"

"You'll never know."

"No, seriously."

"Oh, top, then bottom. Then underwear. Why?"

I told her. She considered things for a second, then said, "I think she was undressing and got caught. If it had been the other way, she wouldn't have put her bra on."

"But could she have slept with it on?"

"Like a support bra, you mean?" She grinned. "Big boobs?"

I thought for a second. "I don't think so . . . no, I suppose average or smaller, I guess. It's hard to tell, like that, but no . . ."

"Nope."

"Why not?"

"Not necessary. Too uncomfortable, if you don't really need to do it. Was it a regular bra?"

"Well, it was lacy, and pink."

"Then she was undressing."

No hesitation. Mild, friendly contempt, for having to state the obvious to someone of lesser wit.

"Thanks. Don't tell Art I asked."

"Of course not."

Art hated Sally, ever since she had refused to inform on one of her friends. He had been trying to get rid of her ever since, without success. He didn't trust her, and would have had a fit if he knew I discussed any part of the case with her. She was also the best-looking dispatcher we had, by far. He hated that, too, as he always thought that she would tempt us or something. Not that she couldn't. Just that she wouldn't. Our loss.

Art came back into the office, and we went into the back room.

"Do you think there's dope involved here?"

He looked at me for a long moment. He absolutely hates discussing anything to do with his dope cases unless he is forced to do it.

"No."

"Well, it's got to be something other than what it looks like."

"Why don't you let DCI get on with it? They'll handle the case. Just don't let it bother you. It's been turned over to State. Let them handle it."

Art is like that. Any opportunity to get out from under responsibility for something difficult or complex, and he will jump at the chance. Even if it means that the case is screwed up as a result. After all, it won't be his fault. He has turned it over to proper authorities.

"Look, Art, there's a lot that DCI doesn't know, and never will. They don't live here. And if there's not a break in the case in a week or two, they move on to something else. Besides, they don't 'take over' a case. They assist us. You know that. This is going to be our baby."

"What makes you think there's not going to be a break?"

"Just the way it's shaping up."

"Well, don't be too sure."

Art gets cryptic like that for two reasons: either he has some information that he won't give me, or he doesn't know at all.

I went home, couldn't sleep, of course, and ended up riding around Maitland with Dan. We talked about the homicides. He wanted details, as he had not seen any of the bodies. I told him a little, not much. Dan was a good guy, friendly, personable. A little too personable, in fact. Maitland was a small town. Dan was well liked, and loved to sip free coffee. Buy him a cup, he would entertain you for it. Like a medieval minstrel. Buy him a sandwich, he would outdo himself. And if you were curious about a homicide scene, you would begin to get details that shouldn't be public knowledge. If you bought him dessert, it was a case of "film at eleven." Get him really relaxed and happy, and if he didn't know the answer, you could get him to speculate. Unfortunately he wasn't always too specific about when the speculation line was crossed.

"Got any suspects, Carl?"

"No."

"God, who could do something like that? You know, guy? Really, who could do that?"

"Beats me, I just know somebody did."

I was forty then, and Dan was twenty-eight. I felt that I had to play the role of the cool, older cop with him. Wasn't always hard, but it had left Dan with the unfortunate impression that I was always sure of myself. Making him think he had to be sure of himself, too. Since he seldom was, he tended to feel a little inadequate. Eager, therefore, to impress and provide information. That was never my intention. It did prove helpful, though.

"You know," said Dan, "I don't think it could be local. Honest, nobody around here could do that."

Local meant Maitland to Dan. He was originally from Cedar Rapids, but had adapted so well to Maitland that he had considered it home from the first week he was here.

"I'm not so sure, Dan."

"Yeah, but, well shit, Carl, there just isn't anybody . . ."

"Well, nobody leaps to mind, Dan. That's for sure."

As we had been riding around the two square miles of Maitland, I had noticed that most of the homes had lights on. Unusual.

"Lot of houses lit up tonight."

"Yeah, I noticed that earlier."

"Natives are a little nervous."

There were about 250 residences in Maitland, not counting about thirty apartments above Main Street stores. I had noticed that several homes were dark—maybe ten or so.

"Do me a favor, Dan. Make a list of the houses that are dark, would you?"

"Why?"

"I want a list of the people who aren't nervous."

"Okay, guy."

He let me off at my house. It wasn't dark, either.

It was 01:30. I was wide awake, there was nothing on TV, and I hadn't been able to find a good book the last time I'd looked, either at the bookstores in Dubuque or in the local library. I made some coffee and went into my little office area, turned on my PC, and called up the database program that contained everybody we had ever arrested for possession or sale of dope. Or had good reason to suspect of same. I had no specific search criteria, of course, so merely browsed the list.

In a county of some 22,000 people, I had amassed some four hundred names over a period of a year and a half since I had begun the project. I had been really restrictive in establishing the criteria for inclusion in the list, and sort of wished I had been a little more liberal.

I cross-indexed the names, after looking at the whole list, and came up with those who had been involved in violent acts. Reduced the list to about three hundred. Dumped the index and did one for those involved in burglary. About seventy-five. Made a new index and did those suspected of occult involvement. Went down to about forty. Cheap database program, could only open one index at a time. Had to buy it myself, along with the computer and all the other software. Office bought me some printer ribbons. Once.

So now I had a list. Of suspects? Why not, you had to start somewhere. I hadn't printed the lists out, so went back and did each index again, dumping them to the printer. Nine pin dot matrix. Loud. Woke up my wife, could hear her stomping into the upstairs bathroom. Damn, I hated it when I did that. She was a light sleeper, and I was a little less than quiet, especially when I was trying to be. This time, for example, I had put a blanket over the printer, to deaden the sound. I made a mental note to either find a thicker blanket or get some foam.

My printer is a little slow, as well as a little loud. She woke up halfway through the first list. I drank coffee and waited about half an hour before printing out the second list, to let her get back to sleep. I looked for another blanket and couldn't find one without going into the bedroom, so I put two seat cushions from the couch around it. Printed the second list, the one with the burglars. Couch cushions interfered with the paper feed—had to do it three times before I got a complete list. Occult was last, so I waited with some anticipation, until I was sure she was still sleeping, then printed that one out.

So now I had three lists. I had to go through them manually, making marks by the names that came up on all the lists. Thirteen. Much better. Thirteen possible whos, no possible whys. Had to start somewhere.

It was now 04:45, and I went to bed. Too much coffee, and I couldn't sleep. Got back up, watched CNN, and saw myself leaving the Herkaman residence. Must have been a slow day for news. I observed that I didn't look all that impressive on TV. Looked a little overweight. I'm six three, weighed about 250 at the time. I consoled myself with the well-established "fact" that TV put on ten pounds.

Went to bed about 05:30. Slept poorly.

4

The phone woke me. Special Agent Gorse wanted to see me. They sleep at night. I brushed my teeth, drank one cup of coffee, grabbed my lists, and drove to the office. In my personal car, not the patrol car. That way, Lamar couldn't send me out on some dipshit call. No uniform, either. Same reason. I did wear a gun, but that was department regulations.

We do have, by the way, our own investigator on the department. Name of Theodore Zieman. Likes to be called Ted, we call him Theo. Theo originally came to us from out of state, I believe Ohio or Indiana, or somewhere like that, maybe Illinois now that I think about it. He probably had a case of burnout from a larger department, although I didn't do the confidential profile, so I couldn't know for sure. Anyway, he had ended up in Maitland, working for the PD for a couple of years. He was hired by the Sheriff's Department and made investigator because Lamar wanted somebody with energy and stamina, who could run all over the county doing interviews and taking pictures. And who didn't have the independence or the imagination to want to do the cases by himself. A lot of rural sheriff's departments didn't have people assigned specifically to investigations, because of the size of the departments, and it showed. We had one, and it showed, too. Same way. But Lamar had his gofer, and that counted for a lot. Especially with Lamar. All Lamar wanted Theo for was to keep people off his back by showing up at every petty theft and burglary and throwing fingerprint dust at everything. That he does. Unfortunately Theo tends to fail to make that leap from evidence to arrest—and is almost dyslexic besides. Honest. He's usually about three months behind on his reports, so he keeps the folders with his scratched notes in his car, so nobody can look at them and discover how far behind he is. Also tends to claim he has sent the file to the county attorney, and the CA is sitting on it for some obscure and mystical reason.

Lamar is bighearted and can't bring himself to fire Theo. Besides, it's Lamar's fault we have him in the first place. The rest of us don't want him on the night shift, so he can't really transfer him out of investigations. It makes it a little difficult for us, though, because Lamar won't trust him with an important case. At least, not anymore.

I got to the office and met with Lamar, Art, Mike, Theo, and Hester Gorse. I was finding her to be extremely efficient and free with her opinions. Which were usually right. She doesn't have that disturbing feminine trait of deferring to men, or to officers of experience. A definite asset.

I handed my list to Hester, who looked at it and raised her eyebrows.

"I'll explain that a little later."

She nodded and put it under her briefcase.

"Well," said Lamar, thereby bringing the meeting to order, "let's get started. Sorry to wake you guys up, but you know how it is." He paused. "We gotta get the son of a bitch who did this, and we gotta get him quick."

Lamar looked at Hester. "You want to start it off?"

She produced a legal tablet that looked like it was about three-fourths full, and began to summarize the progress of the case to date.

"Okay, let's start with the bodies. All four have been taken to Des Moines for autopsy by the state medical examiner. We should have the results within seventy-two hours. They will include, but will not be limited to, the following: (a) type of death (natural, unnatural, violent), (b) pathological diagnoses, (c) probable cause of death, (d) gross description, (e) laboratory procedures (but probably not all of the results), (f) body diagrams, and (g) summary and comments. This is standard autopsy stuff, but it should pin down time of deaths."

She also said that the one female remained unidentified at this time, and that a search of fingerprint and dental records was being started up on her.

"Oh, and Carl? The dog was apparently struck in the back with a blunt instrument. Possibly the back end of an ax. We found one, at McGuire's, and think his hand was cut off with it, too. It's on the way to the lab. The vet who posted the dog said they'd have had to put it to sleep, anyway." She smiled. "Just thought you'd want to know."

"Yeah, thanks." I looked at Art. He was writing something on a note-pad, so I wasn't able to give him a look.

She looked back at her notes. "That leads me to believe that his hand was cut off at his farm. We just haven't found where yet. And since there was not a lot of blood anywhere, it may have come off postmortem." She flipped the page. "We'll get back to that later."

She then went on to a general description of the crime scenes, paying particular attention to the occult paraphernalia found at both scenes. They had discovered several items I had not been aware of, particularly in the little boxes in the McGuire basement. Little crystal cylinders, purpose unknown. A shoe box full of letters from the state penitentiary at Fort Madison, apparently written by a prisoner, detailing Satanic practices and requesting McGuire to obtain several Satanic books for him. Also containing many homosexual references—some veiled and some obvious.

"Were you all aware that McGuire had done time for forgery?"

We all sat dumbly.

"About nine years ago. Did a year and a half at the reformatory at Anamosa."

She leafed through her notes. "This other guy, who only used his nickname of Mystic Fog, or the initials 'MF,' is believed to be one John Allen Zurcher, who was in Anamosa at the same time as McGuire. He was transferred to the Fort when he was convicted of molesting a child. He was under investigation by the Johnson County sheriff when he was convicted by Iowa County on two burglary charges, so the sex abuse charge was filed, and he was tried and convicted while in prison for the burglary."

Interesting.

"The correspondence covers a period beginning shortly after McGuire was released, until the present. We are assuming that McGuire answered some of the letters, because Zurcher refers to them in his letters to Mc-Guire. We also found almost all the books that Zurcher requested from McGuire at the Herkaman residence. Not the same copies, necessarily, but the same titles."

She flipped some more pages. "Oh, yeah. We also found thirty-seven hits of LSD at the Herkaman residence. They were in a small metallic box, like a little snuffbox, that was in the closet of the master bedroom."

She looked at Art. So did I. Did he know about this last night? "Any suggestions as to who might have sold the acid to them?"

Art thought for a second. "If they were bought local, maybe six or seven people. What were they, microdots?"

"Yes."

"At least six or seven, depends on the level of the connection. Probably didn't pick 'em up on the street corner—too wealthy to do that. Probably home delivery. I'll check it."

"Okay. Speaking of wealth, it appears that Herkaman's first husband died about four years ago, an accidental death in Bremer County. He was working at a grain mill and suffocated in a bin full of corn. She got a lot of money from the insurance, went back to school, ended up working at the hospital. One kid, nineteen, is at the community college in Cedar Rapids . . . what do they call that one?"

"Kirkwood Community College."

"Yeah. Anyway, he's clean, but we've got the CR office doing an interview with him today. And her 'estranged' is currently in jail in Bettendorf."

So Mr. Herkaman one was dead. And we'd eliminated the "estranged husband" as a suspect. Well, we knew it wasn't going to be easy.

"We have identified the male subject at the Herkaman residence—one William Randall Sirken, DOB 9/12/49. Petty criminal record, at least four convictions. Driver's license indicates a residence in Coralville, Iowa, and they advise he was employed at University Hospitals in Iowa City, as a maintenance man, and that he was also a part-time student at the university, with a major in psychology. Took about one course each year, not doing particularly well. Wanted to get into counseling, particularly for disturbed women."

Just doing research, your honor. For my term paper.

"We don't exactly know his connection to Herkaman, but they may have met in Iowa City when she went back to school. We'll check that out."

She looked up. Even after only working with her for a few days, I knew Hester wouldn't mix her words. "I feel sorry for you bastards. We don't really have shit at this point." She smiled. "Except, Carl, the 'chewing tobacco' you saw in McGuire's mouth wasn't. It was feces."

"No shit?" Sometimes I amaze myself.

She grinned. "Yes, shit."

"We don't know if it was ingested or not. The autopsy will tell us that." She wasn't using notes much at all. I liked that.

"As long as we're on McGuire, we'll take him first. Very little blood at the scene, so we think he was killed elsewhere and taken back home. Like I said. He was, we think, from a couple of faint traces on the door you found him at, in a sitting position, or possibly bent into a kneeling position, postmortem. The lividity was mostly on his stomach, indicating that he was in a prone position for some time after death. It also looked to me like the knife was stuck in him postmortem, but we'll have to wait for the autopsy for that one, too. I'm not qualified to determine the cause of death, as we all know. But I'd bet it was from asphyxiation." She looked up at us. "If that is the case, and it wasn't at his house, then there's a good chance that the telephone call came from the location where he was killed, and not where he was found."

She glanced at the ceiling for a second or two, then continued.

"At the Herkaman residence, let's take the bodies from the front door on in. The unidentified female appeared to have been strangled. It looks to me like she was surprised while she was undressing, and attempted to flee the residence, toward the front door. Or maybe she was dragged, with a possible motive of removing the corpse from the residence, and the perpetrator was either interrupted or changed his mind. No signs of a struggle anywhere that would point to her. The red cord around the neck was a ligature, and bit pretty deep into the tissues. She had abrasions on her knees that appeared fresh, and what looked like a possible fresh wear point on the right knee of her blue jeans. There was a little blue jean fabric, about six or seven threads, stuck at the bottom of the door frame of the second bedroom, in that metal strip where the tile met the carpet. Position indicated it might have been placed there by the main fabric as the fabric was moving toward the hall. There was some tissue, I think, under her nails on both hands—lab will ID those—and she had a cut on her lower lip that looked fresh.

"It looks to me like she may have been the first victim in the Herkaman residence."

She paused again, then went on.

"The male subject, now known to be Sirken, was pretty obviously castrated. I think that is the cause of death, as there was a whole lot of blood on the bed. The whole mattress was soaked. By the way, we're shipping that to Des Moines, too, Lamar."

Lamar winced. A bite out of the budget, as a king-sized bed wouldn't fit in the trunk of a patrol car. Gonna have to rent a truck.

"He appears to have been tortured, and the ligatures around his wrists and ankles made some severe abrasions, indicating he struggled. The cords are nylon, and it looked to me like he might have pulled his right arm free at one point, because that cord looks like it was retied. You know how cheap nylon cord retains kinks?"

She was asking nobody in particular.

"Anyway, I would prefer duct tape or something like that, so I think that the killer might have used the cord for a particular purpose or reason. The marks in his chest were mostly fresh, but it looks like the first 6 in the 666 was old. No ideas about that one. Also, it looked to me like the last two 6's were done in a different hand, although that could just be that they were done from a different angle."

Hester was nothing if not thorough. She had to be considering the critics in the audience, I guess.

"We should remember that, just because he is the second body discussed, he may not have been the second to die. We can't tie that down until the autopsy comes back. Maybe not even then."

"Any signs of a struggle with him?" I asked. "I mean, before he was tied up?"

"Not really. But there are a couple of interesting marks on his throat that could have been made by a sharp object, indicating a knife was used to make him cooperate. Or he could have cut himself shaving. Anyway, he also had a couple of burn marks on his dick, and the pubic hair on the rear of his scrotum was burned off, with reddening of the adjacent tissue."

Winces went around the room.

"You guys a little sensitive to this stuff?"

"No, that's okay, Hester. Always wanted to know how you checked out a date."

"Thanks . . . Mike, isn't it?"

"Yeah."

"I'll never forget you. Anyway, that's about all on the Sirken dude. It could have taken him anywhere from twenty minutes on to die, depending when the testicles were removed. *Oh!* The most fascinating part . . ."

A groan went around the room.

"You guessed it, guys. No nuts at the residence. At least not so's you'd notice. But there is an interesting bit of debris and bloodstain in the blender in the kitchen."

"You've got to be kidding." That was from Lamar.

"Nope. Just a possibility for now, but it looks to me like it's a good one."

"Jesus, Hester. You gotta be a little weird just to think of that."

"Nonsense. I'm a gourmet. But don't gross out too much—his tongue was missing, too, and still is. Also, the stuff that Carl thought was super-glue around his mouth looks like semen. We'll check that, too."

"Yucch," from all around.

"Anyway, let's get to Herkaman. She's pretty interesting, and is the most tortured of the three victims in her house."

Hester looked at the ceiling again for a minute. I found myself following her gaze, somehow thinking I was going to see crib notes or something.

"Let's see . . . Phyllis Irene Herkaman appears to have had her wrists handcuffed behind her back, Peerless brand. She then had the cord thrust through the space between her shoulder blades and her arms, forcing the arms to the rear, and making sort of a sling. Appears to be the same or similar cord as used on the other two. Her legs and ankles do not appear to have been tied at any point. There are marks about the mouth indicating the presence of fabric at some point, possibly a gag. There was a white dish towel approximately seven feet from her body which may have been used for that purpose. It will be analyzed to see if saliva from Herkaman is present. Anyway, the immediate cause of death appears to have been the shaft inserted into her vagina—the amount of blood is quite significant. The shaft was not removed by the lab team, and will be by the autopsy team. It is of note, though, that there was a rake inside the basement, behind the washer and dryer, with the shaft broken off at about the three-foot mark—a ragged break, leaving a sharp end, so that it is possible to assume that the same condition would exist on the missing end. It is similar to the shaft found in her, and I believe that is where it came from."

I noticed that the joking or bantering tone was missing from Hester's voice altogether now. I guess talking about your own sex's parts is harder than talking about the other's. She spared no detail, though.

"The right breast is still missing. The pin that was thrust through the left nipple is an antique, I think, with a small ruby centered in a five-sided mounting. Significance unknown. There was a pentagram, apparently sterling silver, a circumscribed pentagram, with the circle being a snake eating its own tail, hanging from a pipe above the body. There was also a stub of a black candle on the water heater about three feet from her.

"Carl and I apparently missed that. That's why the lab team makes the bucks. Just how long it took her to die is not certain, but from the amount of blood, her heart was working for a while after the instrument was inserted in the vagina. Autopsy will reveal what organs were affected, and that will give us a better estimate. I also feel that the breast was removed postmortem, as there is very little blood in that area.

"Found in the master bedroom was a copy of the *Necromiton,* a copy of the *Satanic Bible* by Anton LaVey, several books on witchcraft and the general occult, and a large amount of personal correspondence in a dresser drawer which will be read and printed. We haven't actually looked at any of the documents yet. There was also a small Gerber-type dagger, with a steel skull welded or soldered to the end of the handle. Ceremonial, I think. Plus several candles of various colors, including black and red, yellow, and, I think, green. A red robe with a hood in the same drawer and a white one in the closet. The one in the drawer was synthetic, rayon and something else. The white one was terry cloth and would be classified as a standard bathrobe, I think. There was also a small box in the upper left dresser drawer containing some nine hundred dollars in cash. None of the drawers appeared disturbed, except the one that held the candles, which appeared in a state of disarray, compared to the other drawers."

She paused for breath. "The labbies have got the whole scene on video camcorder, and Carl and I took four hundred 35mm stills." She looked at me. "We need yours labeled, so I'll get them back to you as soon as they're developed."

There was a long pause. "I'm done, I guess."

"Thanks, Hester," said Lamar. "Okay, gang, let's talk suspects."

5

Suspects. A more difficult proposition. There was a prolonged silence in the room. Finally I raised my hand.

"I don't suppose they had a butler?"

Broke the tension a little. Not much.

We went through all the obvious avenues to develop a suspect—cars at the crime scene, for example. At McGuire's place, only his car was present. At the Herkaman residence, her car, Sirken's, and a car belonging to a neighbor that was up on blocks in the garage. He worked on it on weekends.

Relatives . . . weren't known for sure, but we had a partial list. McGuire had a brother in Iowa Falls, worked in a hardware store. He would be checked out by Iowa Falls PD, but nothing there so far. No parents, both dead. No other siblings. Several cousins, all of whom lived in our county, and we'd go for them. But none of them were out of the ordinary, so no obvious suspects there.

None of us—not even Mike—could think of an enemy McGuire might have had. He was pretty clean, only the bad checks years ago. Not a particularly upstanding individual, and he had been known to drink to excess in the past. Nothing unusual there, either.

Herkaman was pretty well liked at the hospital, had been working there for three years, no known enemies. No known friends, either, but she was very good with the patients. Tended to keep to herself, but not obsessive about it. Thought to be pretty responsible, always on time for work.

No known vices, at least not before her murder. Two sisters, one brother, all from the Omaha area. Straight. Her activities at the university would be checked very thoroughly. Obviously, we hadn't known about Sirken, and we didn't know what other connections she had had there.

The unknown female remained just that, all the way around. We needed to know who she was, and if it would somehow be possible that she was the unidentified female caller who first reported McGuire.

Sirken was being looked into pretty thoroughly by Coralville and Iowa City. Coralville is a virtual suburb of Iowa City, and their respective police departments got along very well. Almost as one unit. They would come up with a lot, if there was a lot to come up with.

Which left us with a generic suspect or suspects. Not a good place to start.

Hester brought up my list, and I explained why I had done it that way. Lamar wasn't pleased, as Lamar had no time for computers in any way, shape, or form. He thought that relying on them to do too much made people lazy. Maybe. But it gave us a list of suspected Satanists in the county, and we could start with interviews with them, to see what they knew about the departed.

We went down the list and found that not one of them could be linked to the known dead. Either we had many more Satan worshipers in the county than we ever dreamed of or this group was getting their influence from outside our little part of the world.

We went on, and decided to profile the suspect/suspects. There was nowhere else to go, and it would be pretty valuable if we could get enough information from the bodies and the scene.

I had a primitive profiling program in my computer, but thought I'd better tell Hester later. Lamar would have a fit.

The discussion finally got down to whether or not we thought that the perpetrator was a Satanist. I thought not, but maybe Satanically informed; Lamar and Mike thought it was a Satanist, and Art was noncommittal. Hester, the most rational of us, simply said that she didn't have enough evidence to form an opinion.

Theo came up with an original thought. "Well, we know they're violent."

He was, of course, serious as hell. There was a stunned silence, and then, to his everlasting credit, Art said, "That's right." With a straight face.

We decided to break for lunch, which meant that we got the Maitland PD to go get a bunch of hamburgers from the local restaurant. Two other agents were out at the McGuire farm and were expected shortly, so we thought we'd eat and wait for them to show.

The meeting adjourned to the little kitchen, in the jail area of our building, which was furnished like a 1950s church basement, with brown metal folding chairs and tables.

As far as I could tell, the stumbling block to my theory that the perp wasn't a Satanist was the semen on Sirken's mouth. I talked with Art about that while we ate.

"You know, I can make all of it fit with or without a Satanic motive, with one exception."

"What's that?"

"The semen on Sirken's face. Or mouth, I guess."

"Hand me the salt—thanks—that does seem to be a problem."

Hester was about to comment, but had her mouth full and had to chew quickly. We both grinned at her and watched her intently.

"You gotta learn to chew your food slowly—more healthy for you."

"Sure. About that semen . . . I agree, that's a hard point to overlook. Most of the murders I've worked up, I've only seen that in a sex crime, you know?"

We nodded. Respectfully. Hester had probably worked a hundred murder cases . . . we had worked four or five. And she hadn't been with the law nearly as long as we had.

"And," she continued, wiping her fingers on a piece of brown paper towel, "I haven't seen any on male victims. I mean, if Sirken was a female, it would be explained, or explainable, but even the gay murders I've been on, you know that one in Cedar Falls last year, I mean they're vicious and really nasty sometimes, but I've never seen that."

She took a long gulp from her Pepsi bottle. "But I think that's the main clue we have anyway, for the perp, you know. I mean, he's either gay or has a real sex hang-up, not just nasty with sexual overtones or into dominance, you know?"

I noticed the room had become very quiet.

"Think so?" asked Art, chewing.

"Yes, I do."

I suppose he was concerned that a woman, who was essentially a technician, was leading men, who were essentially street officers, in the investigation of a murder. And he obviously hadn't thought it through that thoroughly himself. Not yet. Probably not ever. And if he did, we'd all remember that it was Hester who was pursuing that line of thinking first.

"Well, that's a hell of a thing to say about somebody. I don't think we should guess about the perp's sex life. We don't have the evidence . . ."

Art? I thought he must be inspired by the audience. What was he afraid of, a libel suit?

"Besides," he said, aware of how he had sounded and quite pleased with the effect, "that makes the perp sound like a psycho. I don't think he's psycho."

Embarrassing. Art, the department analyst.

He had moved down at the other end of the table from Hester, and I don't think he could see her lips move. When she mouthed a silent "lots of evidence." Or, a moment later, when her lips formed "fucking idiot." I did. She glanced up just as she said it and saw me watching. Her face reddened, and she looked down at her Styrofoam plate.

She just smiled and took another bite of her hamburger. It did define the relationship between the Sheriff's Department and the DCI, though. They would always defer in public to anything the sheriff said. Swallow their professional pride and then collar the sheriff later and explain some things to him. And, being the lone DCI agent in the room, Hester had to swallow just a bit harder. But I didn't think I wanted to be around when she and Lamar had their next meeting.

The other two DCI agents came in while we were still eating. They were hungry, too, so we sent Maitland PD out for more. We reconvened the meeting at the kitchen tables and continued to discuss suspects.

It was decided to interview those on my list, to see if they had any connection with Phyllis. The assignment was given, of course, to Theo.

"Okay, Theo," said Lamar, "why don't you interview those people . . . and you might want to tape the interviews."

"Sure."

The other two agents, fresh from the scenes, had a few requests, too. One of them, Hal Greeley, knew Theo from a previous series of safe burglaries.

"Why don't you and I do the interviews, and let's, uh, do them here in the office. That way they can be taped on a good machine."

That was in reference to Theo taping a series of interviews about a year ago and not realizing that his batteries had run down.

"And then we can get written statements, too."

When he'd realized his batteries were gone, he had also realized that he had no written statements to back him up.

"Sure, yeah. Okay. As many as we can."

Hester looked around the room. "You night people, you might keep an eye on both crime scenes. Sometimes a perp will actually return . . ."

We all said that we would.

"And I think we should assign photographers to all four funerals. Shoot the crowd. I want to know if anybody shows up at all four . . . or three. We still haven't ID'd the one female, have we?"

We hadn't.

Lamar came through again. "Right. I know that McGuire is going to be buried here, the Lutheran cemetery in Maitland. Sirken has had a brother request that he be cremated, and the ashes sent to him. He lives in Tacoma, Washington, and won't be back for the funeral, and asked us to have a ceremony wherever Phyllis is going to be buried."

Good. Two sets of photos for the price of one.

"Phyllis's kid wants her to be buried here, because he wants to live here in the house. Cheaper."

Better.

"I don't know what we're going to do with the unknown woman."

"Thanks, Lamar," said Hal.

"I do what I can for you guys. Cooperation is what we want."

Lamar had to run next year. Starting early.

Hester cleared her throat. "I've checked with LEIN, General Crim, and Narcotics, plus our intelligence analysts, and we have nothing similar to this anywhere. Also went through MOCIC, and nothing there, either."

We really hadn't expected anything. LEIN was the acronym for the Iowa Law Enforcement Intelligence Network, and MOCIC is the Midwest Organized Crime Information Center, a federal group.

"We gotta solve this one," said Lamar. "The people are getting really upset about this."

"I'm sure they are," said Hester.

On that note, the meeting started to break up. I grabbed Hester on the way out.

"I have a suggestion. Meet me in the parking lot."

She looked at me quizzically, but agreed.

I went to the lot and stood by my car for about ten minutes, when Hester finally came out.

"Look, there are a couple of people on my list that I would like to do the interviews on. Theo can't handle them."

"You'd better talk to Hal."

"Sure, but you're the case officer, and I wanted you to know about it."

I went back in, trying to find Hal. I did, but he was talking to Theo. I left, because I was tired, and I had to work at 20:00. And because I was getting sick of the devious ways we had to use to get around Theo and his incompetence. It was always the same, and when we were working with an outside agency, it became doubly hard, because they were understandably reluctant to get involved in our interdepartmental hassles. I'd been through all this before, many times. Lamar was unapproachable on the subject of Theo, and Art just buried his head by saying that Theo was investigator, and that was that. As a direct consequence, our last homicide had been pissed down the sink. I was determined that it wouldn't happen on this one, but how to avoid it I just didn't know. But if Lamar thought that "the people" were getting upset now, just wait until Theo blew the case . . .

I got home, but at the thought of Theo stomping through the case, I was too wound up to sleep. I sat around for a while, listening to some music and trying to think of a way around him. I had said several times that, in an ideal world, I would murder Theo, and he would be resurrected to handle the investigation. I was only half joking.

I had about six hours to shave, shower, eat, and get eight hours' sleep. I went upstairs to the bedroom, started to undress, and the dog threw up on the carpet. Cleaned it up, booted him out, and shaved. Let him back in and went to bed. Couldn't sleep. Got up, bathed, went back to bed, and couldn't sleep because I was hungry. Ate a TV dinner, refusing to share with the dog, and went back upstairs to go to bed when my wife came home from school.

"Are you up?"

"I'm up, Sue, but I don't want to be . . . Had a meeting most of the day." I put on some sweatpants and schlepped downstairs.

"You don't have to go to work tonight, do you?"

"Yeah, I do."

"That's silly. You haven't had any sleep."

"Yeah, but I have to go to work."

"Why don't you call in sick?"

"I can't do that."

"Well, I think this is the most stupid thing I ever heard!"

"Well, it's been quite a murder, you know. We need people out at night, and besides, I want to get to an interview before Theo does and fucks it up."

I was standing just inside the kitchen, and Sue was pouring some Pepsi.

"I don't like to hear you use that language."

What do you say to that? She brushed by me, on her way to the living room.

"Fred threw up on the rug."

"Oh, no. Poor Fred!" Fred, knowing he was the object of sympathy, but having absolutely no idea why, went to Sue and put his head on her lap. She scratched him behind his ears.

"He probably did it on purpose."

She looked into his eyes. "Oh, Fred, you wouldn't do a thing like that, would you?"

"Yes, he would." I turned toward the stairs. "Look, I'm going to try to get some sleep."

"Do you want to get up for supper?"

"No, I have to go in at eight, so I'll just grab something after I get up."

"Well, I don't think there's going to be much. I'll just fix a couple of eggs for myself."

"Okay, get me up about seven, will you?"

"I might forget. Set the alarm."

"Yeah." I went back upstairs. She was upset, I was upset. As usual. I kept thinking that it wasn't me she was mad at, just the situation. Unfortunately I was the target. I lay down again and finally slept. Woke at seven-fifteen. I had forgot to set the alarm, and Sue hadn't remembered to wake me.

6

Tuesday, April 23
20:00 hours

Since I started at 20:00 hours, half my shift was on the 23rd and half was on the 24th. It was routine most of the night, which meant that I simply drove through six towns and stared at empty stores, dark residences, and sparsely populated taverns. We always had to do one round right away, to check on the status of the various potential burglary targets, such as convenience stores, implement dealers, etc. Then maybe a break at the office, and a second round. There are very few eating places in the county that are open after 22:00, and those that are happen to be taverns. Nothing wrong with taverns, except I hate to eat with somebody who's slightly intoxicated trying to explain to me why his second cousin shouldn't have gotten a ticket for speeding in another county. And especially now, with the sensational case we had, there would be a lot of questions. Always eat either in the car or at the office.

I hit the office at about 00:45, where I met Mike and Dan. We went to the kitchen and opened our sandwiches. Conference time.

It was accepted among the three of us that we were going to have to try to solve this case in spite of Theo's efforts. Since we had been the first officers at the McGuire home, we sort of felt that we had a special interest.

I was the only one of the three of us who had been at the Herkaman residence, so I started off by filling them in on what I had seen. We agreed that the Herkaman house victims were probably involved in Satanism. We also agreed that it looked like Satanism had been a motive in the killings.

Somehow. But they agreed with me that it seemed a little too obvious and heavy. Something was wrong, but we didn't know what.

The department was putting on heavy pressure to identify the unknown woman at the Herkaman residence, and all the officers in the county had been contacted, given a physical description, and asked to nose it around. Nothing. Photographs of her face would be available by noon on the 24th, and they would be passed around, too.

Dan, of course, thought he had seen her somewhere. This is a fairly typical police officer's response, particularly when you haven't actually seen the victim. What it means is that you are trying to visualize the person, and are comparing him or her to several people you know, to complete your visual picture. In the process, you are subconsciously identifying several people, none of whom are the one in question. So you "think I've seen her, but I can't remember where."

The Herkaman house was in the zone Mike normally covered, and he was trying to think of any activities in that area that had really caught his attention. He finally scored.

"Wait a minute. Do you remember, oh, six months or so ago, that 10–50 out on C 23? The one where the gal tried to miss a deer and got the cluster of mailboxes?"

We didn't.

"That was Phyllis Herkaman!"

"Okay."

"No, no, there was a passenger in the car—a female, with a little cut on the bridge of her nose! She was with Phyllis. I know she was, and I bet it was the unknown woman."

We checked. The first step was to go to Sally and have her run Phyllis Herkaman's driving record. This had already been done, of course, to obtain her date of birth. But the copy had been given to Theo, so we'd probably never see it again. It was a chance to get the date of the accident, to help us find the accident report in the files. We are, thanks to repeated efforts of Lamar Ridgeway, decidedly low-tech. We were going to have to go through a stack of some six hundred accident reports, covering that period, which were rather loosely organized. Which means that they are put in as they are received, but even that order is disturbed when they are sifted by somebody who needs a copy of one of them. We needed a date.

Mike couldn't remember if there had been more than five hundred dollars' damage, which meant that if there hadn't been, the state wouldn't have gotten a copy of the report, which meant, in turn, that there would be no record of the event in the state computer.

We three had rushed out to Sally, who had caught the excitement. An actual lead, for God's sake. The adrenaline rush came to an abrupt end.

"The state computer is down."

A collective "Shit."

Sally was encouraging, though. "It'll probably be back up in an hour or so."

We went to the main office and grabbed all the accident reports, divided them into four nearly equal stacks, gave one to Sally, and started to go through them.

Thirty minutes later, we had nothing.

"Mike, you sure you didn't give Phyllis a ticket?"

The ticket stack was considerably smaller than the accident stack.

"No, there was a little deer hair on the car. No violation."

We average about five hundred car vs. deer accidents a year. Nothing unusual about it, and tickets are never issued, because the deer have a tendency to try to hit the car, not vice versa.

We exchanged stacks and tried again. Still nothing.

Mike was getting even more frustrated than the rest of us.

"Damn it, I know that it was in November or early December, when the deer are so thick."

"Well," said Sally, "I can go back through the telephone logs, to see when it was reported . . ."

"No," said Mike, "that won't be any help. I drove up on it just after it happened. There was no report." He paused. "You might try the radio logs, though. I had to call it in."

Sally sighed. "Okay, you have a time?"

"Probably between 23:00 and 01:00."

"One of you want to watch the radio while I go to the basement—all last year's logs are down there."

Being gentlemen, Mike and I went to the basement. The old radio logs were kept in cardboard boxes, most of which were labeled. It took about thirty minutes. The one we wanted was labeled, but the label was facing the wall. Figures.

Sally finally found the correct entry, at 00:19 hours on November 20. Mike called in that he was going to be out of the car at a motorist assist, called back a few minutes later, said it was a car vs. deer, and that he would be 10–6 for a while at the scene. Gave a plate of MKQ339.

The state computer was still down, but we did a manual lookup of Q339 in our own files, and found that it was on a yellow '82 Dodge, registered to Phyllis Herkaman.

"Well, we got it."

"Now all we need is the damned report . . ."

Armed with a date, we went through the reports again. Zero.

"Goddammit! It's got to be here somewhere."

It wasn't.

We sat there in the dispatch center, defeated.

"Well," I said, "somebody's got to have it."

The unstated implication was that Mike might have forgotten to make out a report.

"Was she hurt bad enough to go to the hospital?" I asked.

He shook his head. "No, and besides, I remember Phyllis saying that she would take care of it. They won't have a record."

"How about her insurance agent?"

"Possible, Dan. I suppose that could be checked out in the morning." I was getting more disappointed. We wanted to present the day shift with her name, not with more work.

"Just a minute," said Sally. "Wasn't that the one where the farmer reported the mailbox vandalism the next morning, because he didn't realize it was an accident?"

Bingo.

Back to the basement, to find the complaint report of the vandalism. Easy. Then to the case files, and there it was. Theo had apparently taken the accident report from the accident file and included it in the mailbox vandalism case file. Too lazy to make a copy.

Her name was Peggy Keller, and her age was given as thirty-one.

Sally announced that the state computer was back up. We ran Peggy Keller and got a driver's license. The DL indicated that she was five feet four inches tall and weighed 117 pounds. With blue eyes. I wasn't sure about the eyes, but she was blond, so that was a fair guess. We had our victim, we were sure. And her address was listed as Iowa City.

I looked at my watch: 01:58. Just about seventy-two hours after the first homicide was reported, we had identified the fourth victim. Not exactly breaking any records. It was tentative, to be sure, but I felt that we were right.

There was an air of mild euphoria in the dispatch center.

"Shit," said Dan. "Let's not tell anybody, and see how long it takes the rest of them to ID her."

We all laughed.

"Sally, be sure to have the next dispatcher call Lamar and tell him we have a tentative ID on the fourth victim."

"Come on, Carl, shouldn't I call Theo first?" She was grinning.

"Send Theo a letter."

1

Wednesday, April 24
02:20 hours

After identifying Peggy Keller, tentatively, of course, we all went back out on the road. I went directly to the McGuire residence and drove into the yard. Spooky. It was one of those Mary Shelley kind of nights . . . a light mist, patchy fog, with the trees still bare and stark. The kind of night that seems to eat your headlights, with everything just a little darker than normal, but with an uninterrupted sight distance—like it was all receding from your plane of reality a little bit.

McGuire's house was dark, of course, but the yard light was still on.

"Comm, three."

"Three?"

"I'll be out of the car at the McGuire residence for a minute or two. I'll have the walkie."

"10–4, three's out of the car, 02:23."

It's been my experience that, while it's the criminal who's always supposed to return to the scene of the crime, it is a lot more likely that you'll find an officer going back. There's a feel to the scene, somehow, that sometimes helps to focus your thoughts. Not always consciously, of course. Frequently you're just sort of drawn back to it.

I wasn't looking for anything in particular. Just sort of wandering around the yard and then up to the porch. It was very quiet, only the muffled sound of my car running in the background. An occasional faint rasping sound from the police radio in the car, which was picking up traffic my walkie-talkie wasn't.

I shined my flashlight into the machine shed. Mostly rusty farm equipment, with a fairly new tractor. Lots of steel and iron pieces lying around, most of them in pretty sad shape. I went in, knowing that I wouldn't find anything of substance, as the lab team had already been through it very well. Especially Hester. But I wanted to get a feeling for the type of person McGuire was, and since this was where he worked, it was worth just being there for a few minutes.

I left the machine shed with the impression that McGuire, while a farmer, wasn't particularly enthusiastic about it.

I went toward the house, walking around the corner toward the door we had entered two nights ago. I saw something reflecting in the beam of my flashlight, something affixed to the door. I stepped closer. An expensive-looking crucifix, wooden with what appeared to be a silver Christ. It had been nailed to the door.

I went back to the car, for my camera, and to call Mike as a witness.

"Comm, have Mike work his way out here, would you? Not urgent, but within the next few minutes, if he can."

"10–4."

"And I'll be out of the car again."

I rummaged around in my backseat, got out my camera, attached the flash, and went back to the door to photograph the crucifix. I was holding the camera to my eye, with my flashlight tucked under my arm and pointing at the door, to let me see well enough to focus the camera, when I heard somebody running on the back side of the house. Sounded like they were running on wet carpet.

Well, when the clarion call sounds, you always think you'll be ready. Here I was with my wife's camera, fumbling for a good grip on my flashlight, thundering around the corner of the house, not able to draw my gun without dropping the light or letting go of the camera, and totally unprepared to tackle a suspect. But I was there. Just in time to see a figure disappear into the pine trees that formed a windbreak on the west side of the house. Running at an angle, which would bring him or her out either on the road or at the next farm. And running fast.

I ran back to my car.

"Comm, I have, I see, a subject, on foot, running west, get five, up here, I'll be in pursuit . . ." I was breathing pretty hard.

"Three, 10–9?"

Repeat. Breathing harder than I thought. I put the camera in the car, got behind the wheel, and picked up the mike again.

"Comm, I have a suspect on foot, running northwest from the residence. Get five here quick."

"10–4, three."

I drove back down the lane, almost losing control on the little hill. The lane was greasy. Got out to the gravel, turned left, and went down the road about three hundred yards, to a high point where I would be able to see fairly far. I turned on my spotlight, pointing it back toward the McGuire lane and lighting along the roadside fence line. I pointed the car about forty-five degrees right, shining the headlights into the area the suspect was heading. I got out of the car, locked it up, and went across the barbed-wire fence and into the field. I ran down into the field, out of the light from my car, and then squatted down to listen.

The field was very rough, with the remains of last year's cornstalks sticking up about a foot or so. Hard to travel through, and I should be able to hear someone running pretty easily. I was hoping I had got to my vantage point well ahead of the suspect, and he would think I was in my car. I waited.

"Three, five?"

I always keep the mike-speaker of my walkie-talkie clipped on my left shoulder. You can keep the volume down that way and still hear. Unfortunately, in situations like this one, it always startles you.

"Go ahead, five."

"Three, five?"

Great. With a walkie-talkie, in open terrain, it is not unusual for you to be able to receive far better than you transmit. The case now. He couldn't hear me, and I couldn't get to the car to use the main radio.

"Comm, three?" Softly, because I didn't want my voice to carry into the field.

"Three? Your signal is breaking, try again."

"Tell five to come west of the house, and he'll see my car. I'm out in a field to the left."

"Three, try again?"

Shit. I stood up, unclipped the walkie-talkie from my belt, and held it up over my head, increasing the antenna height.

"Comm, you copy?"

"10–4, three."

"Okay, comm, tell—" Something hit my left shoulder, very hard, from the rear. Pushed me forward, I lost my footing, and went down on my right side.

Again, this time in the middle of my back and on my left arm. I tried to roll to my left, away from the blows, but was up against a frozen furrow ridge and couldn't get over it. I tried to get to my feet. Again, on the back, and down again, this time on my hands and knees. Again, on the right side of my head, and I was out of it altogether. Aware, but unable to get arms and legs coordinated enough to get back up. Or to scratch my nose, for that matter. I was dimly aware of heavy breathing and then the sound of somebody running away to the left.

I shook my head. No pain. Numb in the head and shoulder. It must have taken three or four seconds to stand, and that was a mistake. Dizzy, nausea. I knelt down, steadying myself with my right hand. Slowly blossoming lights, in pretty shades of red and blue. Okay, Carl, deep breaths. Slowly.

A few seconds later, I stood up again. Slowly. Not so bad this time. I looked for my car, and it didn't seem to be where I had left it. Disoriented, Carl. I reached for my mike, on my shoulder, and couldn't find it. Okay, dummy, it fell off. Follow the cord. No cord. Right, I had been holding it up in the air. My flashlight was still in my pocket, so I shined it around for a second and saw the walkie-talkie lying a few feet from me. I picked it up, saw the pretty lights again, and reached for the mike. Almost cut my hand, as the plastic casing had been shattered. I had to fumble with the attachment, disconnect the mike, and use the side switch to talk. Finally got that done.

"Five, three?"

"Three, go ahead!" Loud, and with some anxiety. Good, I appreciate anxiety about me.

"Yeah, five. Whoever it was got me with a club or something. He went west, on foot."

"You okay?"

"Yeah, I think so. You see my car yet?"

"10–4, I'll be right there."

"Okay." Dizzy again, not as good as I thought.

Apparently five still thought I was in my car. I could see his car parked behind mine, and his voice was anxious again.

"Three, *where are you?*"

I pointed my flashlight at him. "Over here."

I started moving toward the road. "Five, he went west."

"10–4."

I became aware that my car had the road blocked. Five had come in from the east. My car was locked. Good move.

I got to the fence, and Mike helped me over.

"Jesus Christ, what happened to you?"

"Got blindsided. With something."

"Let's stop the bleeding."

Bleeding? My head. "Yeah, let's get it stopped."

We went to his car, and he popped the trunk, removing his first-aid kit.

"Five, comm?" Sally's voice, and she sounded very worried. My first thought was that something else had happened.

Mike answered. "I found him, comm. He's hurt, but I think he'll be okay."

"10–4, and twenty-five is almost there now."

Twenty-five? He couldn't be, it was eight miles.

"How could he get here so fast?"

Mike put a compress on the side of my head and lifted my hand up to keep it in place. "Fast? Shit, you've been out of contact for five minutes, at least."

Five minutes. Hummmm. "Head must be softer than I thought."

"Yeah."

"Twenty-five is coming from the east, too, isn't he?"

"Yep." Mike began winding some gauze around my head, freeing my right hand.

"We better get my car moved."

"Too late now. Whoever hit you's been gone for a good five minutes."

"Shit."

"Don't worry about it."

"Yeah, but I think it was the suspect."

"If it was, you're lucky you're not dead."

"Yeah, I guess."

"We better get you to the hospital. Want an ambulance?"

"No. Give me a minute, and a cigarette, and I'll drive in."

Dan got there about that time. I had just lit a smoke, and he came over and looked pretty wide-eyed.

"God, you're a mess."

"Thanks."

"Shit, he got you a good one in the head."

"Thanks, doc. I thought it was my foot."

"No shit, really. Don't you just hate the way those head wounds bleed?" Directed at Mike.

"You're a lot of help."

"Who did it?"

I just looked at him. "My assailant, dumb-ass."

8

The drive into the hospital was uneventful, except that Dan, behind me, had headlights that were slightly out of adjustment. They made my head ache.

At the hospital, I was checked over by a nurse in the emergency room. She decided I should see a doctor. Earned her keep, I guess. My good friend Dr. Henry Zimmer was on call. At 3:30 A.M. I wondered just how long the friendship would last.

Doc Z arrived in good time and decided I needed stitches in my head. Also X rays of head and upper torso. I had to take off my uniform jacket and saw how much blood was on it for the first time. Trashed one shirt, too. Blood had soaked through. The jacket was also torn on the left shoulder, where he had hit the mike. Damn.

My bulletproof vest was okay, and Doc Z was of the opinion that it might have saved me from a back injury. I was, too.

My right shoulder was really sore by now, but the X rays showed no breaks. Same on the left. I hadn't been aware of it, but my shoulder must have caught a part of the blow to the head. Henry was also of the opinion that, had that not been the case, I might have sustained a severe head injury. Again, I had to agree.

Lamar, who had been called by Sally when it had become apparent that I was dead, arrived at the hospital just as I was being stitched up.

He barged into the ER, looking worried and pissed off at the same time.

"You okay?"

"Yeah, I guess so."

"What the hell happened?"

I told him.

"And you stood up, and he hit you?"

"Yeah, I must have been almost on top of him when I knelt down in the field. Just didn't see him. He must have thought it was time to go when I stood up, and he heard me talking to another car. Figured we'd get him, I guess."

"Yeah. You able to get a good look at him?"

"No. Nothing at all, except I think he's about my height or so, but I'm not even sure about that. Runs like a deer . . . Not very patriotic, either." I couldn't resist.

"What?"

"The way I was standing when he hit me the first time—looked just like the Statue of Liberty."

Lamar grinned. So did Henry.

"Well," said Lamar, "from now on, at least for a while, we'll send two of you out to check those places."

"Okay by me."

Henry dropped the bomb. "Carl, it won't be you for a while. You get three or four days off."

I gave him a look.

"You have a mild concussion. With your history of two skull fractures and three concussions, we aren't going to take any chances. Are we?"

Silence from both me and Lamar.

"Good, I'm going to let you go home, unless you want to stay here. But no bright lights, and no exertion for a while. And if you become nauseated again, get right back up here. Understand?"

"Yes."

Lamar and I left and went to the office. I told him about possibly identifying the unknown body, and he seemed pleased. I had to do my report on the incident before I went home. Took about an hour. I was very surprised to note, from the radio logs, that I had been out of it for six minutes. Even longer than Mike had guessed.

Sally looked very concerned. It's hard on a dispatcher to have something happen to a cop and not to be able to do anything about it. She really thought I had been killed. Good dispatchers always assume the worst. At least I think that would have been the worst.

Before I left the office, Mike called in. He and the boss had just been to the Herkaman house. Crucifix there, too. He had gone out with Lamar, implementing our new two-man policy. Hester, who was staying at the only motel in town, was to be notified at 07:00.

I got home and had a little trouble backing the patrol car into the garage. Shoulder hurt, and my eyes kept changing focus when I looked back over my shoulder, focusing on the wire squares of the restraining cage. Weird, as the garage looked like it would jump toward me four or five feet each time.

I put my jacket into the tub, to soak, and trashed the shirt. I made a sandwich and drank a Pepsi. Then snuck upstairs, trying to be quiet and to get to bed without waking Sue. Didn't work, as I stumbled against the chest of drawers.

"You might as well turn on the light," came the sleepy voice from the bed.

"Okay, but before I do, you might want to know I have a bandage on my head, and it's not serious."

I turned on the light.

"My God."

"It's not serious. Just a couple of stitches."

"What happened?"

I told her.

"What did he hit you with?"

"I don't know. A board, or a handle, or something. Something hard, I know that," and I grinned.

"I'm surprised you're home on time."

"Hey, Henry says I get a couple of days off . . ."

"You won't take them."

"Yes, I will. This time."

"Sure."

"You want to know how many stitches?"

"No. I'm having a hard time handling this. I don't like your work, and I don't like what happens to you."

"Hey, it doesn't happen very often. If it did, I'd quit."

"I don't think you would. I think you like it."

And, with that, she turned over and appeared to sleep.

Like it? Hardly. She really wanted me to be in another, more dignified line of work. Where people didn't beat on me, and where I associated with a little better clientele. Well, in a way, I did, too. But the job was interesting most of the time, and hardly ever routine. I liked my work. Something I never thought I had to apologize for.

Phone rang at 08:45. You can't come to work, no reason not to call you. It was Hester, apologetic, but she wanted to come by to talk to me.

I put the coffeepot on, took off the bandage, as it was giving me a headache, and washed my hair. Shaved. Tried everything I could to wake up. After the second cup of coffee, I was getting mad at Hester for being late. If they're going to bother you, at least be on time.

She arrived about 09:30. Bearing gifts in the form of a thick envelope of developed photographs of the Herkaman crime scene, and my photos of the McGuire scene. With a note from Lamar, wondering if I could label them while I was off.

"I think I can get these done in the next day or so."

"Good. How's your head?"

"Still there."

"I'd like to talk to you about last night."

"Want a cup of coffee?"

We spent about an hour going over the events of the early morning hours, with her taping everything. I had already said it all in my report, and she seemed disappointed that we were uncovering nothing new in the interview.

By the time we were finished, I was beginning to wake up.

"Autopsy reports back yet?"

"Oh, yeah, they were relayed up this morning. Got 'em in the car."

They were quite interesting.

In the first place, the times of death placed the sequence as follows:

1. William Sirken at approximately 10:30 P.M.

2. Francis McGuire at approximately midnight.

3. Unknown (possibly Peggy Keller) at about 1:00 A.M.

4. Phyllis Herkaman at about 5:00 A.M.

The causes of death were equally interesting.

1. William Sirken, hemorrhaged, due to severing of the inferior vesicle artery and the anterior trunk of the right common iliac artery, caused by an apparent stab wound.

2. Francis McGuire, death by asphyxiation, larynx crushed and hyoid broken.

3. Unknown (possibly Peggy Keller), death by asphyxiation due to ligature around her neck.

4. Phyllis Herkaman, hemorrhaged to death, due to puncture of the left common iliac artery and vein, the superior mesenteric artery, the abdominal aorta, and the inferior vena cava.

McGuire was the only surprise.

Removal of McGuire's hand apparently occurred postmortem and explained the lack of blood, at least to an extent. The knife in the chest was also an apparent afterthought.

The murders occurred over a six-to-seven-hour time span. Great. Somebody was really freaked out, because to sustain a murderous frame of mind for that long was really unusual.

"Well," said Hester, "what do you think?"

"I don't know."

"Me either. Somebody sure was mad, though."

"Yeah. Or extremely dedicated."

"I'll go with dope."

"Well, it's either that or crazy."

"Or both."

"Or more than one person. Each with an assigned victim or two."

She thought about that one. "You think it's a cult, then?"

"No, not really. But it does seem like a lot for one man to do. Or woman, I guess."

"A team effort," she said, "would make it easier. Somebody will crack."

"Yeah. Sooner or later."

"Unless it's a cult, where there's no guilt involved to work on their minds."

"You know," I said, "one thing bothers me . . ."

"You mean 'one more'?"

"Okay. The lists I came up with? There's nobody there I can associate with any of the victims. Nobody."

We talked long enough to consume a second pot of coffee, and she left to have lunch with Lamar, Theo, and Hal. Theo and Hal were still plugging away at interviews. Hester, by the way, was pretty sure that the unknown woman was Peggy Keller, but we were going to have to wait for dental records to make sure. I was pretty sure, too.

I tried to go back to bed, but found that I was now up for the rest of the day. Combination of a headache, the coffee, and hunger. Plus a little excitement thrown in on the side.

I went back downstairs and cranked up my computer. I loaded in the profiling program and started to work.

I began with the victim section, entering everything I knew about the four people whose bodies we had found. There wasn't much, but at least it got my thinking going in an organized direction.

Three of the four were connected to a hospital in some way, and there was a good chance they had met each other in Iowa City. The fourth, McGuire, not only had no connection to any hospital, there seemed to be nothing he would have had in common with the others except an interest in Satanism. Easy to see how they could come together on that, but what the hell was he doing sticking his nose into that stuff?

And, even with a Satanic interest, how did he get involved with the other three? They didn't seem to have anything in common . . . not at all.

What I was beginning to think was, if McGuire got involved, so did somebody else. Maybe the same way. And if I could figure McGuire's connection, maybe there was somebody else I could come up with who had gotten into the group the same way. Unless, of course, McGuire had recruited the other three . . .

Insufficient data, as they say.

It was about 14:00, so I thought I'd at least get a nap. Went into the living room, had just lain down on the couch when the phone rang. Wonderful. It was Mike, and could he come over for a few minutes? Sure.

Mike, being a night person, was prompt. What can I say? Anyway, he hit the door about three minutes after he called.

He'd been talking to his wife and had found out that McGuire was gay. He'd also been talking to Hester, who had told him that she had just found out that Sirken was associated with a gay group in Iowa City. His wife had also said that McGuire had gone into a hospital in Iowa City for back surgery about two years ago.

Well, well, well. Mike was as pleased as I'd ever seen him.

"Pretty good, huh?"

"Damn right."

"Got any coffee?"

"Will have in a minute." I went into the kitchen, and Mike followed. "You say anything to Hester about this?"

"Yeah."

"What did she think?"

"She was pretty happy—so happy that she's going to Iowa City to talk to some people there, who're connected with the hospitals."

I poured the water into the pot. "Did she have a chance to talk to Theo?"

"I don't think so. Theo's out on interviews again today."

"Good."

"Oh, also, my wife said that there's a problem with the funeral for McGuire."

"What kind of problem?"

"The minister has heard about the Satanic shit and won't allow him to be buried in consecrated ground."

I leaned back on the counter and gave Mike a look.

"How did a preacher find out about the Satanic stuff?"

"I don't know."

Everything, of course, was supposed to be confidential, and nobody was supposed to talk to the public about the case at all. Someone always did, of course. I didn't really give a damn about McGuire being buried, but I wanted to find the leak. You just don't want details getting out, for three main reasons. First, you don't want a suspect to know what you know, and second, you don't want some flake "confessing" and providing a lot of detail. Screws up the case. Third, you don't want the case people distracted by having to patch a leak. Takes a lot of effort to locate it, and in the meantime everybody is under suspicion. Flow of information comes to a complete stop, and the group effort goes to hell in a basket.

"Which preacher is it?"

"Pastor Rothberg."

"The church on the south end?"

"Yep."

"He's always seemed pretty sound . . ."

I had talked with Rothberg several times, when he had come up to talk to our prisoners. He'd always given the impression of being levelheaded and rational about his belief. Concerned about the prisoners' spiritual well-being, not evangelizing. Doomed, as I always told him, to see his efforts with the prisoners come to naught. It was our little joke. But he'd never struck me as the sort who would refuse to bury anybody.

"I sure would like to know how he found out."

"Well, Carl, it's probably pretty common knowledge by now, what with Theo interviewing people all day. He talks too much, you know that."

"Yeah, but, shit, he has Hal Greeley with him. Hal wouldn't let him say much about the Satanic stuff."

"I dunno. You know Theo."

We stood around the kitchen, waiting for the coffee to brew.

"Mike, maybe we should talk to Rothberg . . ."

"Doesn't do much good to close the barn door after the horse is out."

"Yeah, but it's the sort of thing I just gotta know."

"Well, I'm game, if you are."

I called the church, no answer. I called his home, and his wife answered. He wasn't home, was making rounds at the hospital and the nursing home. I left a message for him to call me at my home.

We drank our coffee at the dining room table, and the conversation turned to the unknown female who had made the first call about McGuire. We still didn't know who she was, and the times of death sort of eliminated Peggy Keller, unless she called as she was dying. That didn't seem likely, because of the manner of her death. If she had been surprised at the Herkaman house, and it looked like she had, and had tried to flee and been overtaken and killed, which seemed likely, she sure as hell wouldn't have time to make any phone calls. And, besides, the caller had said that she was at the McGuire farm. On the other hand, if she'd called from there, and then returned to the Herkaman place and walked in on all the carnage, it would mean there was a second killer unknown to her, who happened to be killing as she was calling . . . Not what you'd call likely. Not what I'd call likely, either.

I called Hester. "Did we ever determine if McGuire was killed at his house, or someplace else?"

"We're assuming at his house, at least for now."

"Ever find his hand?"

"No."

"Look, is it possible that he was killed someplace else?"

"Anything is possible."

"Herkaman's, maybe?"

"Maybe."

"Before you go to Iowa City, could you call the lab and see if they found any clothing that could have been McGuire's out at the Herkaman residence?"

"Sure."

I went back to the dining room. The house is small. Mike had overheard the call.

"Sirken and McGuire were pretty close to the same size, weren't they?"

"Yeah. But different kinds of clothes, different style of clothes. But I'm thinking something else . . . I think it's a good bet that we have a survivor, and that she's the one who called, and that she's probably hiding somewhere."

"Pretty obvious."

"Thanks."

"Anytime. Got any more coffee?"

"Yeah. It's in the kitchen . . ."

While he was out there, I had another partial thought. I'm famous for partial thoughts.

"Hey, Mike, don't you think it's a good chance that she's from Iowa City, too?"

He came back in with a full cup. "Well, three-fourths of them had an

Iowa City connection by living there, and McGuire had probably met the others there . . ."

"You could have brought the pot. Well, then, isn't it likely that she would have gone back there? And that would explain, at least a little, why she might have thought she was at the McGuire farm when she was at the Herkaman house."

He thought for a second. "Unless the perpetrator is connected to Iowa City, too. Then she probably didn't go back there."

"I don't know about that . . . where else could she go?"

"Beats me . . . we'll have to ask her when we find her."

"If we find her. And if we find her before the perp does. She's a witness."

"It ain't gonna be easy to find her. Especially not on the night shift."

And the phone rang. Pastor Rothberg. He said that he would come down, since I was injured. I had almost forgotten that small fact and probably sounded a little stupid for a second.

Neither Mike nor I knew if Rothberg drank coffee, so we put on another pot just in case. At this rate I wouldn't sleep for days.

Mark Rothberg was also prompt. He came to the front door, which we hardly ever use, moving up the steps quickly and easily. He was about my height, but about 190 pounds, and pretty fit. He was also about ten years younger, which put him around thirty. Fit, intelligent, energetic. Never could figure out why I liked him.

He did drink coffee, though. Took some of the edge off. But he didn't smoke.

"I presume you want some background information on Satanism?"

"Well, no, actually. Hadn't occurred to us. But go ahead, Reverend."

"I'm always ready to help out the police."

I handed him a cup of coffee.

"By the way, Carl, how's your head?"

"Foggy, but then it usually is."

"I'm glad you weren't hurt any more than you were."

"Me too."

He laughed. "Good thing it was a head wound."

Mike, bless him, laughed, too.

"Thanks, group."

He took a sip of his coffee, leaned back in the chair, and asked, "What do you want to know about Satanic cults?"

Well, I had a few questions, and I know Mike did, too.

"Why don't you just tell us what you know, and we can ask questions as we go along?"

He began by telling us that all Christian churches tended to accept the existence of Satan, in one form or another. That they accepted the concept of evil, and that Satan was the personification of it. Given that, it was no surprise, according to him, that misfits and sociopaths would gravitate toward a Satanic cult, or Satanist teachings. "Outcasts" was the word he used to describe them. He told us that he didn't take them too seriously himself, but that he was very concerned about their influence on others, and the espousal of a philosophy that generally denied responsibility for your own actions.

I chimed in. "You're aware, I'm sure, that there are many other groups who have the same basic approach?"

"Of course. But the Satanist is specifically an abomination, because he directly opposes and ridicules Christ."

Oh.

He went on to discuss the Church of Satan, Anton LaVey, and other San Francisco–based Satanic connections. Michael Aquino, who particularly outraged him because of his U.S. Army connections. About the insidious approach they had, because they wouldn't actually promote violence, but ended up condoning it by their basic philosophy.

"It's so like them, you know. Fostering that attitude, and then innocently disclaiming responsibility for it."

"Satanic, sort of?"

"Yes, Carl! Absolutely."

He continued to describe their influence, especially among the young. Which got him briefly into heavy metal music, and then into the young people who had suffered, and some of them who had committed suicide, because of Satanic propaganda. He seemed controlled, of course, but very intense. I couldn't help thinking that, if he could keep secrets, this man might be a pretty good ally in an investigation of this sort. He would be in a position to take the community pulse, so to speak. If he would only agree to tell us about what he found.

"Reverend, if you don't mind my asking, how do you come to know so much about this?"

"In my former congregation in Ohio, we had a tragic incident involving Satanism. A very intelligent young man took his own life, and another very nearly did so. It was a close thing, I can tell you. Very close. I helped counsel the one who survived, and I had to do some pretty heavy research to give me the necessary background to talk with him and to counter their arguments."

I thought the conversation had reached a good level to try to find out what we originally wanted to know.

I smiled. "I'm curious, and you surely don't have to tell me if you'd rather not, but I would like to know just how you were aware that Satanism would be the subject we wanted to talk about today?"

He smiled. "Four Satanic murders . . . I didn't think you called to make a donation to our building fund."

"True. But, then, how did you know about the Satanic connection to the murders?"

"Oh, just about everybody in town knows that. It's a small community. These things can't be kept secret for long."

"Yeah, I know. But, just out of curiosity, when did you find out about it? How long did this little community take to get the word around?"

"Well, without mentioning any names, a good friend in our congregation called me the day it happened. He knew of my concern over matters like this, of the incidents in Ohio that I was involved in. He has a troubled family member, you see, and we have discussed this."

"Okay." I grinned again. "But, then, I guess I'd like to know how he knew about it."

"Relentless. Relentless." But he was smiling. "I can't say, because he told me in confidence. Of course."

"I respect that, I guess."

"Reverend," asked Mike, "did he get the information from an inside source, or did he know that these were Satanists before they were killed?"

"Oh, no! No, it was an inside source. Absolutely. No, he didn't know about the Satanic connections with these people. I don't think anybody did."

"I don't know too much about your confidentiality restrictions," I tried to ease him in, "but I'm going to assume that they're as stringent as ours, at least. Fair?"

"I think so, yes."

"Okay, what I want to know is this. Is there any way you can let us know if there are other Satanists in this area, if you were to hear about it? I mean, people are going to talk, and probably some of them to you. Is there any way you could get some information to us without compromising yourself?"

He thought for a moment. "I think I might be able to do that."

"And we'll feel free to do the same, okay?"

"You mean, pass information to me. Of a general sort?"

I nodded.

"All right."

"Reverend, I don't want to put you in an awkward position, but you can see the importance of this case . . . so the first thing I'm going to ask you is that you not let anyone know that you have 'official' confirmation of Satanic involvement."

"That's no problem."

"Good. Now the second thing might be a little harder . . ."

"Go ahead."

"I'd like you to try to find out just how Francis McGuire got involved with all this sort of thing."

"I believe I can tell you that now. Francis came to me almost a year ago. He was a very troubled man . . ."

I don't know why intelligence officers ignore the clergy. They shouldn't. It turned out that McGuire was in deep financial trouble. A lot of farmers were at that time, but he was in a little further than most. He and an unnamed individual had bought a considerable amount of land, and McGuire had mortgaged his three-hundred-acre farm, which he had owned outright prior to that time. He had hurt his back and was unable to work his own land, not to mention the new acquisition. So he'd had to hire the work done, and that had cost too much. Rented the new land then, and his renter hadn't paid him promptly, so he had a hard time with the interest payments and had to borrow more to make them. Vicious circle. Very.

"Well, that might explain some of it . . ."

"I'm afraid that Francis McGuire was also homosexual."

Okay, so we already knew, or at least suspected that. From the correspondence from the prison. The reverend was doing so well I didn't want to discourage him.

"No kidding?"

"Yes, I'm afraid so."

He then went on to describe the anguish McGuire felt about that, and how he wanted to make sure that God would forgive him for it. Mark said he thought his church had an enlightened policy regarding that, and told McGuire that it was all right in the sight of God to be gay, just so long as he didn't give in to the temptation to have physical relations with another man. That he had to fight it, and to resist the temptations.

"So what was his reaction to that?"

"He didn't feel that he could comply." Mark looked disturbed. "Sometimes I feel that we let these people down—that we are here to offer solace, and when they come to us, we can only give them restrictions. Sometimes I think we alienate them." He sighed. "I know we alienated Francis."

"So you think that's why he went for Satanism?"

"Yes."

"Did he ever say anything about Satanism to you?"

"No. Of course not. No, I was shocked when I heard about it, but I wasn't surprised." He looked at me with real anguish in his eyes. "Do you understand that?"

"Yes, I think so."

"I do," said Mike.

"Did he ever say how long he'd known he was a homosexual?"

"No, he didn't. But it was the reason his marriage broke up."

"I hate to ask this, but did he ever mention any partners?"

"No," in a quiet voice. "Never."

"As a suspect, you know."

"I know why you have to ask."

We were silent for a couple of seconds. I had been waiting to ask why he had refused permission to bury them in his cemetery, and, with what he had just said, it didn't really make sense. But I had to ask. That was why he was here in the first place, regardless of what he thought.

"Mark, we've been told that you are refusing permission to bury McGuire and the others in your church's cemetery . . . would you mind telling us why?"

"They are an abomination."

"But they're innocent victims . . ."

"They believed in Satan."

"How do you know that? They may have been murdered by a Satanist, but we can't know that they were."

"When I was told, that day, the one who told me said that there was a lot of Satanic material in the house."

"Well," said Mike, "there may have been, but we don't know who it belonged to."

"And," I said, "an interest doesn't mean commitment. Take yourself— you know a lot about Satanism, but you certainly aren't one."

"I feel they would defile church ground."

"You might want to rethink that a little . . ."

"Absolutely not. I am certain in my mind and in my soul."

He left a few minutes later, promising to stay in touch. We decided immediately to have Mike go to the courthouse and find out what land McGuire had purchased, and with whom. And for how much.

After Mike left, I took a couple of Tylenol for my headache, knowing I shouldn't, and lay back down on the couch. I had just covered my head with a pillow, to shut out the light, and decided that I was really going to get the son of a bitch who hit me, when there was a knock on the back door. I got up and answered it. Mike.

He had a Xerox copy of a deed. The land that McGuire had purchased included the land Phyllis Herkaman's house was on. As well as the adjacent land. His was the only name on the deed.

9

I woke and turned over on the couch to see my wife asleep in the chair across the room. Sue was frequently very tired when she came home from work.

I got up quietly, and her eyes snapped open.

"Are you all right?"

"Yeah, I'm fine."

"I was worried when I came home and found you on the couch. I didn't know to wake you, or what."

She stood, too, and I went over and gave her a hug.

"I'm just fine. How about you?"

"I miss you."

"Me too." I squeezed her again. "But I'm home for a few nights now. Look on the bright side."

She just sighed, and after a moment asked me what I wanted for supper.

"I don't know . . . hamburgers?"

She backed away a few inches. "You're pretty easy."

"Norwegian genes. Every time."

By the time we got around to eating, we'd missed the network news, so we watched local out of Cedar Rapids. The announcer told us that there had been a Satanic multiple homicide in our county and that there were signs of Satanic rituals. They got McGuire and Sirken mixed up, but had identified the Herkaman place as belonging to McGuire. And they quoted a "confidential official source."

I glanced at Sue, who seemed a little surprised to hear of the Satanic stuff.

"Shit." Said with a mouthful of hamburger, it loses a little of its impact, but she got the point.

"Really Satanic?"

"Sort of. But they got a couple of the names mixed up."

"At school today, they were talking about it. You know Seth Meyers . . . junior high math?"

Yes, I knew him. Emergency medical technician. Just happened to be with the ambulance at the McGuire home.

"Well, he said that there was some cult stuff in the house."

He'd been briefed by Dan. Of course.

"There was."

The phone rang. Sue answered it, and it was for me. Art.

"Hello, Art, it wasn't me."

"You saw it, too?"

"Yep."

"This shit is starting to get out of hand."

"Yeah, well, it could have been anybody."

"I know. But you know Theo . . ."

"Anybody see him giving an interview?"

"I don't know. When you coming back to work?"

"Tomorrow night."

"We'll talk then."

"Okay, any suspects yet?"

"Not so far as I know, but Lamar said something about Hal and Theo doing an interview tomorrow at the office. Somebody with some sort of information." Art being cryptic again.

I went back to my hamburgers. Sue was clearing her TV tray. She had a school board meeting at 19:00 and was about to leave.

"Who told, any idea?"

"No, but the smart money is on Theo."

"I'll see you when I get back. It shouldn't be too late."

I lay back down on the couch. My headache was coming back, with a vengeance. Fred came to the couch and put his nose next to my hand. I scratched his ears and thought about the case.

We were pretty disorganized at this point. I hate to blame Theo for everything, but in this instance, we were all working on the case without much coordination. We had to work around an incompetent investigator, and DCI was going to have to pull most of its people out eventually if there wasn't a fast, solid lead. And it didn't look like there would be one.

I still thought there was a female survivor, the unknown caller. Especially since McGuire owned the Herkaman house, she could have thought it was his place of residence. Which would have explained a lot, except that it meant that McGuire was at the Herkaman residence when he was murdered. Then taken to his own place.

No evidence of that. Evidence he had been taken home, but no clue as to where he'd come from.

If he was murdered at Herkaman's, why take him elsewhere? Especially when Phyllis Herkaman wasn't dead yet, and wouldn't be for five more hours? Did the perp just leave her there and take the time to move McGuire and then come back? Not too damned likely.

Two perpetrators? Or more? Possible.

If he was murdered at Herkaman's place, where was his hand? Actually, where the hell was his hand, anyway? Did somebody take a souvenir? Hester had said that there was some evidence in the blender, but a hand would have held up pretty well, with all the bone. Sirken's testicles, and possibly his tongue, were soft tissue. Also, where was Phyllis's missing breast? Blender? Not impossible, but that would be a lot of tissue . . .

The souvenir bit was appealing, in its way. It would sure explain the missing hand.

McGuire's body just didn't figure. The other three obviously died where they were found. And it looked like Sirken was dead before McGuire. Okay. If so, that meant the perp was in the Herkaman house and had killed Sirken before McGuire had bought it. Then killed Keller and Herkaman. In that order. But how could he have surprised Keller, in the act of undressing, if there had already been a murder in the house, and then a second one, and the second body had been moved several miles? And where was Phyllis all this time? Standing around waiting to be killed? Tortured and then killed? Was she already tied to the pipe?

There was another partial thought. Could Keller have come home after the other three were already in extremis? Phyllis's car and Sirken's car had both been there . . . Keller could have been away. Could have been.

Why move McGuire? If he really was moved at all.

It kept coming back to that. And the fact that he had been moved to his own home, and that he had been the first discovered. It just didn't add up. And, while we're at it, what the hell had happened to his dog, to hurt it like that, if the murder had taken place elsewhere? A dog wouldn't attack somebody bringing his master home, would he?

My head really hurt, and not so much from the blow.

Just before I dropped off, I thought about how close I had been to the bastard in the field. Damn, I must have been right on top of him when I stopped to listen. Not good. Really have to sharpen up, Carl. He could have killed you. If it was the perp, he sure had demonstrated an ability to do that sort of thing.

The phone rang. Again. I got back up and picked it up in the kitchen. It was Lamar.

"Hi. Just checking, how you doin'?"

"Okay, a little headache, but nothing else."

"Good . . . Anything goin' on?"

"Nope. Well, Theo and Hal came up with a little something about the murders. There was another girl staying with Phyllis Herkaman—was there most of the time the last few months."

"No shit? Who?"

"Well, nobody seems to know. Not her name, anyway. One neighbor lady, Mrs. Bockman, thinks it might have been Rachel, or something like that. But no last name."

"That's pretty good . . . I've got Theo working day and night on the interviews. He's talked to a hell of a lot of people on this, you have to give him credit for that. I bet he's interviewed fifty people in the last three days. He's really bustin' his ass on this one. He really is . . . I talked to Pastor Rothberg a few minutes ago."

Uh-oh. "Yeah, I talked to him today, too. We needed a little information."

"Yeah, that's what he said. Anyway, I told him about how we had to keep this stuff down, if we can. Public. Anyway, he said it was okay to have the funeral at his church. Said he'd thought it over and he's going to do it."

I kind of figured he might. But what else had they talked about? And was Lamar going to be pissed off because we were working without consulting Theo? That bit about how hard Theo was working was leading to something.

"You and Mike got any information for Theo?"

"Not much yet. Except that McGuire owned Herkaman's place. I think that Mike is going to get hold of Theo yet today . . ." Making a mental note to call Mike and get him to tell Theo.

"Good. I want you guys to cooperate on this one. Theo is going to type up his information and give it to you guys."

"Good, Lamar. Good. It's nice to see Theo getting into this one." He's gonna fuck it up . . . I know he is. And he'll never get fifty interviews typed, and we'll never get the information, and there won't be any real information there, anyway.

I looked at the clock in the microwave: 20:15. Lamar had called from home . . . probably. He tended to take care of the personnel stuff after he got off work.

I called the office, and Hazel Willis answered. She was one of our more senior dispatchers, pretty competent, but not particularly interested in anything but keeping her job. Made her reliable unless she thought she could fortify her position by snitching a fellow worker off.

"Hi, Hazel. It's three. Who's working tonight?" Now, I knew who was working, but this was Hazel.

"Let me see, uh, Eddie is out now, then it's supposed to be you? How are you?"

"Oh, a little woozy but not too bad."

"Well, I'm glad to hear that. Let's see, after you were supposed to come out . . ." I could hear the other line ring in the background. "Got another call, let me put you on hold . . ."

I said "Okay" into an already dead phone. It was too bad I just couldn't ask for Mike, but then it would be logged that I had called specifically to talk with him, and I didn't want Lamar to think that I was trying to get ahold of Mike to tell him to connect up with Theo. Which is what I was trying to do, of course.

"I'm back . . . Let's see, Mike comes out at ten. But he might be out a little early, since you're off."

"Okay, uh, you want to check the back office and see if he might be there now? I think he had some stuff to do for Theo before he came to work."

"Just a sec."

Mike came on the line.

"Yeah?"

"Hi, it's Carl. You talk to Lamar recently?"

"Oh, about twenty minutes ago. Rothberg agreed to have the funeral. I was going to call you."

"Okay. Look, it might be a good idea if you were to connect up with Theo and give him a copy of the deed."

"Yeah, I think so, too. Lamar ain't altogether happy about us talking to Rothberg."

"Right. You know about the other female who lived with Herkaman?"

"What other female?"

I told him what Lamar had told me. Mike said that Theo was still out, and that he would pump him about the new woman and would see what he could come up with. Theo was pretty easy that way.

A new lead—a third woman at Herkaman's place. Rachel . . . Rachel who? Who cares . . . we'll find out. But I was sure she was the caller we hadn't been able to identify. Our survivor. Our witness. The key to the whole thing. Now all we had to do was find out who she was, and where she was, and get her to talk. No problem . . .

10

Thursday, April 25
12:12 hours

I woke up a little after noon and felt pretty damned good. A little sore in the shoulder, but my head seemed much better.

After I had a cup of coffee and had taken Fred out for a little while, I called the office to see what was new. Shouldn't have done that. Everybody was in a restrained sort of tizzy. We had had five burglaries the night before. Theo was working one now, and Mike was still up, doing the last of his reports on the first two burglaries, which he had discovered.

Two of the burglaries had occurred in Maitland, and Dan was still up, working those.

That meant that one or two burglars had taken just about the whole local homicide team off the case for at least a day, maybe longer, leaving DCI to do the work. With Hester still in Iowa City, that meant that Agent Hal Greeley was the only one left in our county to do any interviews, and probably meant that the search for Rachel was going to be his main project, and he didn't know anybody in the county. That was crucial, because many of our citizens will be somewhat less than candid with any cop, but with a state agent by himself . . . not good.

I got Hal on the phone and offered to help interview. He was going to the Bockman house first. I had another cup of coffee, some peanut butter toast, and I was ready to go.

Or so I thought. I realized that I didn't remember Bockman's first name. Or her maiden name. I hated to do it, but I called the school and asked for Sue. She had to be called away from class, so she would have to call me back. She did in about two minutes.

"Carl, are you all right?"

"Sure."

"Oh, you scared me to death!"

Uh-oh. I should have thought of that. I was home on sick leave with a head injury, right? What would be the first thing she would think? Dummy.

"I'm sorry, dear, no, I'm just fine. Look, what I need is Mrs. Bockman's first name."

"Who?"

"You remember, was in my class in high school—a year behind you. Hefty gal, about five ten, was in extracurricular speech with us one year, then went to school in Iowa City for about one semester . . . then quit? Married that Bockman who lives north of town about three or four miles?"

"Oh, that would be Tammy Bockman's mother. Her first name is Helen. She was a Floyd, wasn't she?"

"Sure! Okay, thanks a lot."

"Did you have to call me out of class for that?"

"Yeah, it was important. Look, I'll tell you tonight, okay?"

"All right. I love you."

"I love you, too. See you around suppertime."

"You're going someplace?"

"Just a ride with one of the state officers, no big deal."

"Should you be going out?"

"Hey, I feel fine."

"I think it's stupid. Let somebody else do it. You're on sick pay, stay home and be sick."

"I'll be okay, and there's nobody else available."

"There never is, is there?"

"Look, I'll be all right. Nothing dangerous or anything like that. Just an interview I don't want to miss."

"An interview for a better job?"

I forced a laugh. "No, afraid not."

"All right," she said, sounding resigned. "I'll see you for supper, or whenever you get home."

"Okay, bye."

Now I was ready to go. Helen. Yes, good old Helen. Now that I thought about it, she had to leave the U of Iowa because her mother had a stroke, and her dad needed her at the farm. Her sister had been through law school by that time and had left the area for good. I remembered hearing that Helen was pretty bitter and resentful about that . . . probably with reason, because Helen probably could have done very well in school.

Hal picked me up, and I filled him in on Helen on the way out to her place. We got there about 13:25.

Helen lived about three-fourths of a mile from Herkaman's place, off the main road and west, or behind, the Herkaman house. The closest farm to Herkaman's, as a matter of fact.

Helen came out onto the porch to meet us. She looked like she had aged more than I would like to think I have, but still didn't look too bad. She invited us in, and I introduced Hal. It looked like Helen remembered me, which made me feel a little embarrassed for not remembering her name. She was very congenial, and offered us coffee and cookies, while we sat at a modern kitchen table. I looked around briefly and was impressed. The house was quite clean and tidy, and most of the interior appeared to have been remodeled, with the furniture being nearly new. Helen was doing well for herself. Then I remembered that her dad had died about three or four years back. She must have inherited a bit of money.

I was kind of surprised that Hal and Theo hadn't talked to Helen before this, but Hal took care of that for me by saying that they had started with the northeast neighbors and had let interview lead to interview. He was explaining to Helen just what he was doing there and why he wanted to talk to her. He went into how horrible it all was and what a terrible thing had happened at the Herkaman house. How we really wanted the people who had done such a thing and how they should be put away for a long time. He was talking down to her, and I hoped he wouldn't make her mad.

He explained a little about the murders, just enough to let her know that we didn't have a suspect, but left out the Satanic overtones. Then he asked her to tell us what she knew about Phyllis Herkaman and her guests.

"Well, not a lot," said Helen.

She then proceeded to tell us a lot about Phyllis Herkaman, her son, and some of the strange guests at the house.

Helen had known Phyllis Herkaman for about two years, it turned out. She thought Phyllis pretty friendly but sort of melancholy. Thought that there must have been some pretty tragic circumstances in her life, even more than the death of Phyllis's husband, which she knew about. She and Phyllis had coffee in the mornings about once a week, and Phyllis had said some pretty disturbing things.

"Like what, Helen?"

She looked at me with kind of a funny expression. "Well, Carl, she was pretty quiet, like I told you. But she was always saying things about freedom to be yourself. Not like your typical liberal, understand. Not at all. Much more freedom than that. She would tell me that it was all right to do virtually anything, as long as it benefited you. That it was all right if it hurt somebody else, because if they could be hurt by it, they didn't deserve to be protected in the first place. That sort of thing. Very determined. Not forceful, you know? But deep down convinced, and unshakable."

"Was this political," asked Hal, "or was it more like a creed, or a religion, or something like that?"

Helen smiled. "She was a Satanist, if that's what you mean," she said matter-of-factly. "Care for another cookie?"

It turned out that Helen and Phyllis had discussed Satanism on several occasions. Phyllis had apparently had a considerable amount of respect for Helen, telling her that she admired her intelligence and could understand all about the tragedies in Helen's background. Phyllis had railed against "fate" and the fact that women were constantly being taken advantage of. By men, and by society as a whole.

Helen told us that Phyllis had taken the death of her husband pretty hard, because she was intending to leave him in a year or two anyway, and that she felt guilty about that. She had tried to find somebody in her hometown to talk to who would understand. No luck. She had gone back to school in Iowa City and had come across some people there who not only provided sympathy but told her that she had no business feeling guilty about anything. They had introduced her to Satanism, a little at a time, until she finally began to accept it as her religion.

"Did she try to, uh, persuade you to adopt Satanism, too?" I asked.

"Oh," said Helen, "sort of. In her own way. She wasn't pushy, or anything like that. Just trying to share what she thought was a good philosophy."

There was a short pause, with the unasked question hanging in the air.

"No, Carl." She reached over and poured more coffee into my cup. "She didn't convert me."

"Well, good."

"But I have to admit, she made me think."

"I suppose she did."

She gestured with the pot toward Hal's cup, and he shook his head. "You said on the phone yesterday, after I asked you what had happened to Rachel, that you didn't know anything about her. Is that true?"

"Yes," said Hal.

"I find that a little hard to believe."

I grinned. "So do we, Helen, but there it is."

She looked at me with that funny look again. "What do you want to know about her? I worry about her, she is pretty dependent, you know, and I hope nothing has happened to her."

"Well, we'd like to start off with her last name, if you know it."

"Certainly. Rachel Larsen."

Things were definitely looking up.

It turned out that Rachel had started coming to the Herkaman farm about a year to a year and a half ago. She was a student in Iowa City, originally from Minnesota. Majored in speech pathology. About twenty-six or twenty-seven years old, had been married, but was divorced by the time she was twenty-three. He apparently beat her. She was a part-time student and worked at the bookstore at the student union. She was pretty shy and withdrawn, and was bisexual, her female lover having been Peggy Keller. She also slept with Phyllis on occasion.

Hal and I exchanged glances. Wonderful. All I could think was, that if this case ever got to a jury, we were going to have a little trouble keeping their minds on something as mundane as a murder or four. And with the lifestyle and religious preferences of this group, a jury just might feel they had gotten their just deserts.

"Does that bother you?" asked Helen.

"No," I said. "It doesn't bother me, but if we ever get the suspect to trial, it might bother a jury."

She seemed to collect her thoughts for a moment. But something was bothering her.

We asked her if she knew Sirken, and she said only slightly, but that he was something of a jerk, tried to be very dominant, but only came across as a pain in the ass. He worked at a hospital, that was all she knew. Except that:

"He was a janitor, and took about three hours a year toward his psych major. But he tried to tell strangers that he was a psychologist, sometimes a psychiatrist. Didn't know anything! Only a fool would have bought his phony act."

"But he and Peggy and Rachel were all into Satanism?"

"Yes."

"Do you know about Francis McGuire's connection with these people? I mean, how did he fit in?"

Helen snorted. "He provided some support, like with money. He was always trying to impress them with his devotion to Satan, but he didn't really understand the true philosophy behind it." She shook her head. "But all three of the girls screwed him, if you'll pardon my language. Just to keep him around."

"Oh."

"They told me that they thought he was sort of nice, and that they could do that for him. But they always laughed at him and called him the whore."

"They called him," asked Hal, "the whore?"

"Sure. After his surgery, he had to be on the bottom every time. You know what they say . . . a whore spends most of her time on her back?"

"Yeah."

"That's why they called him that."

She paused, and seemed to be trying to resolve a conflict. She looked at me again.

"Carl, would you answer a question for me?"

"I will if I can."

Her lip started to tremble. "Did you find the baby?" And she started to cry.

11

Thursday, April 25
14:10 hours

Well, Hal and I just about crapped.

Turned out that Rachel had a baby a short time ago and that Helen thought we had some information about it and were withholding it from her. It took her a few minutes to compose herself, and Hal and I just sort of sat there stunned.

Helen went into the bathroom eventually.

"Jesus Christ, Hal. This is just getting to be like a freakin' soap opera!"

"You got that right."

"You don't suppose we have a dead baby over there, do you?"

"I don't see how. She probably took it with her."

"I didn't see any baby stuff in the house, Hal. Nothing. Nothing at all."

"That doesn't mean much. She lived in Iowa City."

"Yeah, but if she is the one who called, she sure didn't seem like somebody who had the time to pack up the kid and all its stuff."

"Maybe. Listen, let's take Helen to the office and have her listen to the tape of the original call. She ought to be able to tell if it's Rachel on the phone."

I nodded.

"In the meantime, let me call Iowa City and see if we can locate Rachel down there."

Helen returned to the table. "I'm sorry."

"Don't be," said Hal. "Nothing to be sorry about at all. Could I trouble you to use your phone? It'll be long-distance, but I'll use my state credit card."

"No, go ahead. That's fine."

"Thank you."

Hal went to call, leaving Helen and me at the table.

"Carl, I'm sorry I got so upset. It's just that I thought you knew and weren't telling me."

"That's okay. Really. Happens a lot. People think we're deliberately withholding information that we don't actually have. Happens a lot. They always think we know more than we do. Sort of flattering, in a way."

"I just am so worried about the baby."

"So am I, Helen, so am I."

We could hear Hal in the other room, talking on the phone to Hester. He was telling her where Rachel worked, and to get down there and find her.

"I didn't see the baby, or any baby gear, in the house, Helen."

"Oh, I suppose not."

"You suppose not?"

"I haven't seen the baby for quite a while."

"Then why do you think something happened to it?"

"Because I've seen Rachel."

"Without the baby?"

"Yes."

"And?"

Her lip started to quiver again. "And I'm afraid something happened to her. That they did something to her."

Get in here, Hal. Please, get in here.

"Who's they, Helen?"

"That damned Sirken and the one they call Darkness."

"Who the hell is Darkness?"

"I don't know. Just that that's what they call him."

"Hey, Hal!"

He stuck his head around the corner, the phone to his right ear, and held up his hand for me to hold on for a moment, then disappeared around the doorway again.

"Helen, Hal should hear this."

She nodded. "The baby's name was Cynthia . . ." and started to cry again. "Excuse me," she sobbed, and headed back to the bathroom.

Hal came back to the table as she was disappearing down the hall.

"She crying again?"

"Yeah, listen, she thinks something happened to the baby a few months ago, and there is a guy named Darkness who is also in the group, and she thinks that he did something to it, along with Sirken."

Hal just stood there for a second. "Jesus Christ, I was only gone a minute!"

I lit my fifth cigarette of the interview and just closed my eyes for a second. My head was starting to ache again. Damn.

"Well, I sent Hester to find Rachel. She's going to call back as soon as she locates her. She'll call your office first, and if we're still here, I gave her this number. This is getting a little too complicated."

"Yeah, but it's good information."

He asked me, in a lowered voice, if I thought that Helen was involved more than she was letting on. I said that I didn't know.

"How reliable is she?"

"Pretty reliable, I think."

Helen returned to the table, apologizing again.

"That's all right, Helen," said Hal. "Just take your time, there's no rush here."

Hal led the conversation slowly back to Darkness and the infant, starting by telling Helen that Hester was looking into the whereabouts of Rachel in Iowa City, and that he was sure that she would find her. He also said that he thought the baby might have just been left in Iowa City with a sitter, that that was common practice, and that Helen might be worried for no reason.

She didn't agree. She'd talked with Rachel several times while she was pregnant, and twice after the baby had been born.

"She just thought of it as a sort of job she had to do. Like it was a burden that she had to bear. I asked her a couple of times if she was going to adopt it out, because it was pretty obvious she didn't really want it."

"What did she say about that?"

"She said that she couldn't."

"Couldn't, or wouldn't?"

"Couldn't."

"Why was that, you think?"

"I don't know. But she was just sort of, well, dull, if you know what I mean. Dull, no luster, no excitement about the child."

I was busy taking notes and had just written one to remind myself to check with hospitals to get the birth record of the child. Helen apparently could read at an angle.

"She wasn't born in the hospital, Carl."

"What?"

"Don't check hospitals, it won't help. She was born at Phyllis's house."

"When was that?" asked Hal.

"Just a minute, let me check my calendar. Sometime in late November."

She went to a kitchen drawer and came back with a calendar. Most of the date boxes had penciled-in notations, the ones I could see having things to do with the farm—veterinary appointments, farm supply dealers, etc.

"Here it is . . . November 24th. 'Rachel-baby.' "

Hal looked at the calendar.

"Now, Helen," he said, "what about this Darkness individual?"

Helen visibly composed herself. "I hate him. So did Phyllis."

"Why?"

She began to explain, slowly at first, and gaining speed as she went.

"He was behind it all, I think. The leader of everything. He made them do everything. He made the decisions for them, all of them. And they did what he wanted."

"Can you give us an example?"

"I can give hundreds." She thought for a moment. "He was the one who told Phyllis to come here in the first place."

"He did?"

"Yes. He told her to get a job in a rural area, anyway. Not to be employed in the city. It was hard for her, because there aren't as many jobs out here, you know. It took her a while, but that's what she did."

"She told you this?"

"Yes. A few months ago. I asked her why she had come here, because she didn't like it here, you know. Neither did her son, Gary. So I asked her why, and she told me that Darkness had made her do it."

"Did you know about Darkness before then?"

"Oh, yes."

It turned out that Helen had first heard about Darkness when she asked Phyllis once about why she was depressed. After Phyllis had hinted around to Helen that she participate in their little group. About six months ago, or around October.

Helen really had meant it when she said that she didn't know much about this dude. What she did know was that he was male, and a dominant personality. That he lived within a hundred miles, no further, of Phyllis's house. An interpretation gained from the fact that he would be said to be leaving wherever he was coming from on a Friday, for example, and would be there on Friday night. She had no idea what he did for a living, but said that the impression she got was that he was pretty intelligent. And very forceful.

"Did they ever refer to him and another at the same time?"

"I don't understand, Carl."

"I mean, did they ever say anything like Darkness and so-and-so will be coming. Like he was married?"

"I don't remember that . . ."

"Did you ever meet him?" asked Hal.

"No, I never did. I thought I might have seen him once, when I went over to their place. I tried to call first, because Phyllis was pretty private, you know, but the line was busy all morning, so I went over to ask her if she was all right. It was a Saturday, I remember that. And Rachel answered the door, and I saw a man inside."

"What did he look like?"

"I really couldn't tell. It was in December, and there was a lot of snow on the ground, you know, and it was a bright, clear day, and I could hardly see inside the house. But Rachel wouldn't let me in."

"What did you see?"

"Well, he was sitting down, in the living room. He looked pretty big, to me, for a sitting man. And he had a beard."

"What color?"

"I don't know."

"Light or dark?"

"Dark. And a turtleneck." She smiled at Hal. "Dark."

"Thanks."

"But Rachel was very nervous, and I just knew it was him."

"You drove?" I asked.

"Yes."

"Did you notice any unusual car at their place? One that wasn't theirs?"

"Oh, yes. I didn't tell you. Yes, he drove a big, black car, kind of like our old Mercury, but newer." She smiled shyly. "I suppose that was what made me think it was him, too."

"The car?"

"Yes. I knew not to go there when he was there, and I knew it was his car. When I drove in, I knew he was there then, I guess. But I was curious about him, I suppose."

"I suppose."

"And it made Phyllis a little mad. She really liked me, but she was upset the next time I saw her. She didn't say anything specific, actually. But I knew I shouldn't have done it, and I really felt bad about it."

"Why's that?"

"I got the feeling that he had been pretty hard on her for it."

"Just a feeling?"

"Yes. Just a feeling."

"She didn't say anything, or look like she had been abused, or anything?"

"No. But it really made me think yesterday, I'll tell you that."

"Yesterday?"

"Yes. He came back. Drove by Phyllis's place and turned around in our driveway."

"He was here yesterday?"

"Yes, he was."

By this time, it was all I could do not to jump up and look out the window.

"What time was this?"

"Oh, it was just after dark. About six-thirty or so."

We just sort of took a break then. By mutual consensus. Helen put on another pot of coffee. I looked at my watch, and it was 16:36. A little while, we'd be eating supper out here.

The phone rang, Helen answered it, and said, "Yes, he is, just a sec. It's for you, Carl."

It was Lamar. "What the hell you doing out there? We've been trying to call you at home all afternoon. You're on sick leave."

"Yeah, well sort of a guide and making introductions."

"Greeley could find it himself."

"Well, it's not too strenuous . . . How you comin' on the burglaries?"

"Not good. Don't change the subject. You having any luck there?"

"Oh yes, yes we are. Yes."

"Really?"

"You bet. Quite a lot."

"Fill me in?"

"Not just yet . . ."

"Before you go home and be sick, get ahold of me."

"Oh, yeah. No doubt there."

I hung up and turned to Hal.

"That was Lamar. He was a little pissy because I'm on the injured list, and he thinks I should be home."

"I meant to ask you about your head," said Helen. "What happened?"

"Oh, somebody hit me with something."

"It looks like it would hurt."

"It does. Sometimes."

"It wasn't Sue, was it?"

"No, it wasn't Sue." Helen was a lot more pleasant than I'd remembered her from high school.

The phone rang again, and this time Helen gave it to Hal. While he talked, so did we.

"How do you like your job, Carl?"

"It's okay, I guess. I wouldn't recommend it to anybody, but it's all right."

"I never would have thought you'd be a cop, back when we were kids."

"Me either."

"In fact, of all the things I ever thought you'd be, this is probably the last one I would have picked."

"That makes two of us." I took a sip of coffee. Helen made very good coffee. Strong. "The same for you, too. I always thought you'd end up a professional woman, a doctor or lawyer?"

"Well, these things happen."

"Yeah, they do."

"Did you get hurt at work?"

"Yeah. Kind of dumb. Like I always tell Sue, whenever I get hurt it's more than likely it's my fault."

She pushed the plate of cookies, recently refilled, toward me across the table. "You just don't think of cops getting hurt around here . . . it bothers me that you got hurt, you know. I think you're too nice to get hurt." She smiled.

"Well, there's at least one person who doesn't agree with you."

"That's obvious, isn't it? Who was it, by the way?"

Hal came back to the table. "That was Gorse. She's been busy." He sat down.

Rachel hadn't been at work since last Thursday. Would have been the 18th. Didn't work Fridays or the weekend, but was supposed to have shown up Monday afternoon. Didn't. Hester had also found out where she lived in Iowa City. She wasn't there, either. Not particularly unusual, and she might return any minute. Iowa City PD had a man watching her apartment. She was still checking into her background and would be doing interviews with her coworkers and any friends. Finding people in Iowa City is not easy.

The *putt-putt* of a tractor intruded into the dining room.

"That'll be Fred," said Helen. Her husband. "Please don't tell him what I've told you. He doesn't know about a lot of this, but he hated them up there."

"He did?"

"Yes."

"All right," said Hal. "But we do have some more questions . . . would you be more comfortable talking at the office?"

"Yes, I guess so."

"Why don't I call you tomorrow and make an appointment?"

The tractor noise was stationary, and pretty close. There was heavy stomping on the back porch, as Fred cleaned his boots. Then the back door opened, and he came in. He was wearing a dun-colored coat, with a hat with earflaps down over his ears. He was medium height, large but solid, with a florid face.

He didn't say a word, just looked at us.

"You know Carl," said Helen. "And this is Mr. Greeley, he works for the state." She turned to us. "This is my husband, Fred."

I said, "Hi, Fred."

Hal stuck out his hand. Fred took it reluctantly.

"You here about that business?" said Fred, gesturing toward Herkaman's place with his head. More of a statement than a question.

"Yes."

"I sort of wondered when you'd show up."

"Takes a long time to talk to all the neighbors," said Hal.

"I guess."

"What do you know about them, Fred? Your wife has been helpful, but she doesn't seem to know too much about them, at all."

"Not much, uh, Greeley, isn't it?"

"That's right."

"Just that they were the sort who kept to themselves a lot. Not real friendly." He turned to Helen. "When's supper?"

"Soon."

"Good, I'm starved."

"What do you think about all this, Fred?" I asked.

"I think you better arrest somebody pretty soon."

"So do we, Fred," said Hal.

"Can you tell us anything about them?" I asked.

He was still standing just inside the kitchen. He wanted us to leave.

"Not much. They were quiet. Different."

"You ever talk to them?"

"Just to say hello."

"Any idea who might have done this?"

"Nope."

Helen looked embarrassed.

"Well," I said, trying to help her out, "you're not any more help than Helen."

He didn't say anything.

"Well," said Hal, "we have to be going. If either one of you thinks of anything that could help us, we'd appreciate you getting ahold of us. The sheriff's office in Maitland will know where to find us."

"We'll do that," said Helen. Fred just grunted noncommittally.

12

Thursday, April 25
17:45 hours

Hal and I went directly back to the office, and I called Sue immediately.

"Hi, look, I'll be just a little late for supper."

"Well, I'm going to fix myself something—you'll have to fend for yourself."

"That's all right."

"You should be here—you're not ready to work yet."

"Okay. See you when I get home."

Lamar was still there, so the three of us sat down and discussed the interview. Took about twenty minutes to fill him in. When he was finished, Hal said:

"What do you think about old Fred?"

"What do you want to know?" asked Lamar.

"I want to know if he could be our suspect. His wife said that he hated the group."

"I don't think so," said Lamar, "but I guess we can't rule him out yet."

Hal nodded. "And this Darkness character?"

"I don't have any idea at all who he could be," said Lamar.

"Me either," I added.

"We'll find out," said Hal. "It is a damned shame he came back yesterday and we didn't know what the hell was going on."

"He sounds to me," I said, "like the leader of our little group."

"Yes, he does, doesn't he?"

"Aren't they supposed to have thirteen members?"

"I think you're right, Carl," said Hal. "We have a request in to San Francisco PD, they have a Satanic expert, and he should be calling here tomorrow. Also one in to New York PD. Same reason."

"Think they'll want to look at the scene or anything?" I asked.

"I don't know," said Hal. "Any problem there?"

"Just that I'm glad you called them."

"We thought it would be a good idea."

"No, not that. I mean, if they came at your request, you foot the bill."

"Oh."

"When do you want Helen in to listen to the tape? Tomorrow?"

"The sooner, the better."

"Carl?"

"Yes, boss."

"You're on sick leave."

"Yeah, but Helen talks to me."

Lamar glanced at Hal.

"That's right, Lamar. She does. I'd like to have Carl up here when she comes in, if that's okay."

"If it doesn't take too long."

"Sure."

"Boss, I just can't drive or anything. I can talk all right."

"You can always talk."

"Well, yeah."

"And eat, too. Tell me the truth . . . did Helen feed you out there?"

"You gotta advise me of my rights first."

"I thought so."

Lamar had to go, and so did I. After he left, I talked with Hal for a minute. About Helen, and hiding her testimony from her husband. I wasn't too uncomfortable about it, and neither was Hal, except I didn't want to have Fred get on Helen about it, and have her dry up as a source. We'd have to be careful.

Hal dropped me off at home. My in-laws were there, checking on my health. My mother-in-law had brought some of her chocolate cookies, and some leftover beef roast, for my lunches when Sue was in school. All right!

About seven or so, I sat down at my computer and began doing the photo labels. God, there were a lot of them. I made a generic label, with as much on it as I could cram and fake without having to actually look at the pictures and negatives. I wanted to wait at least another day to do that. I wouldn't be able to wait much longer, though, because Hester was going to want the photos back.

What I really wanted was the videotape Hester had made of both scenes.

Anyway, Sue didn't get too upset, because the computer did most of the work. While it was grinding out labels, we talked about Helen.

"What do you know about her?"

"Oh, her kid was a little bothered. She graduated about a year ago, I think. When Tammy was in eighth grade, I remember Helen and Fred coming in for a parent-teacher's conference. He didn't seem like he really wanted to be there."

"Anything remarkable about Tammy?"

"Withdrawn, I guess. Sort of a quiet child. Bright, I think, but never gave much indication of it."

"I didn't even really remember her. Or Fred."

"Fred was in my class." That would have been a year ahead of me. "Is she involved in this murder business?"

"What . . . no, I don't think so. Just knew some of the victims."

"Pretty horrible, wasn't it?"

"Well, it was. Yeah."

"I thought so, you've been pretty withdrawn since."

"Well, it was kind of a heavy day, with the two crime scenes, one on top of the other like that."

"Let me look at your head."

She stood on my right, parted what's left of my hair, and looked closely at the wound.

"It's still all bruised, but it's not red or anything."

"Good."

"When do you get the stitches out?"

"Tomorrow, I think."

"That'll probably help."

"Yeah. That's the side I sleep on."

"Speaking of that, have you been getting much sleep lately?"

"No, not enough. Maybe five hours a day, or so."

"And you're smoking more, and drinking too much coffee."

I grinned. "Well, at least I don't go out and hang around with the boys."

"The hell you don't. That's what you've been doing all day."

Well, sort of. She did have a point. Sort of.

Fell asleep in the chair, watching TV. Woke up about three-thirty, took a bath, and went to bed. Feeling not so much tired, as just kind of washed-out. And muddleheaded.

13

Wonderful. I was going to be going back to work in a day or two, and I was now waking up at the time I normally went to bed. Damn. Fifteen years of nights, you get into a routine. And when you break it like that, you get into trouble. Like sleeping on the road. Or missing something important. Or getting nailed by somebody because you're not alert. Although, come to think of it, I had been alert on Wednesday, when I'd gotten my head thwacked. Oh, well.

I puttered around the kitchen for a while and was finishing my second cup of coffee when Sue's alarm went off, and I could hear her stirring around upstairs. I didn't want to tell her that I was going to the office today. I wanted her to think that I was being good and staying home, recuperating. She would worry a lot less.

I got out the crime scene photos, the sheets of computer labels, my pocket tape recorder, the copy of Hester's notes on the scene, and spread it all over the dining room table. Took about five minutes to find a felt-tipped pen. Set out a couple of place mats for the coffeepot and a cup, and was ready to go to work.

Labeling crime scene photos is a chore. There were more than two hundred of them. A label for this kind of case would have to be real accurate, and look something like this:

CASE #85–03–16–01 McGuire Residence
Roll #2 Frame #16 POV: Ext Kitchen Door
35mm SLR 50mm lens ISA 400 Color

Showing state of Kitchen

CLH 03–16–85 02:19 Exhibit #_____

Two hundred would be a chore all by themselves, but you also have to go over the negatives to make certain of the frame numbers, because you frequently don't start with #1 on a roll. Then you have to examine the photos themselves very carefully, because you often have several showing almost the same thing, and you can't get the frame numbers mixed up or they will make a rather large deal out of it in court. It takes some pretty bright light, and occasional intense concentration. I usually like to do it, because carefully examining the photos will sometimes reveal little details you miss at the scene. But in this case, since the lab crew had done about the same thing after I did, it did seem a little redundant.

Sue passed through on the way to the kitchen, to make her breakfast. "You been up all night?"

"Nope, only about an hour."

"Labeling pictures again?"

"Yep."

I could hear her in the kitchen, rattling around as she got her bowl of cereal. She always ate while she moved around, in the morning. Lining up school papers and things, making an occasional phone call, locating books for students. I wanted to be able to do that someday, but I would have left a trail of food all around the house. Sue never spilled a drop.

She came back through, on some errand, with her cereal bowl in her hand.

"Looks like you should be home today . . ."

"Yeah, this should take a while."

"Good."

"Hey, you seen the magnifying glass?"

There was a mumbled "ungmmm" from the living room, and she came back a moment later, her mouth full of Cheerios. She pointed with a spoon as she passed, indicating the buffet.

"Thanks."

I got the magnifying glass out, and was in the bathroom, wiping our little niece's fingerprints off the lens, when she came in to put on her makeup. Still with the bowl of Cheerios.

"Say, does that light board I gave you for Christmas last year still work?"

"Of course. It's in the closet in our room. Behind the boxes of the summer clothes."

"Thanks. Mind if I use it?"

"Nope."

I went upstairs, rummaged through the closet, and brought it down. It would be perfect to backlight the negatives. I normally would just hold them up to a light, but there were so many of them this time.

I had to get out a couple of more mats, so the board wouldn't scratch the table, causing me to rearrange the whole conglomeration. By the time I was ready to go, so was Sue.

"Carl, do you get your stitches out today?"

"Yep."

"What time?"

"No specific time. I'll just drop up when I get some time."

"All right, dear. Just don't forget."

"I won't."

"And, if you get a chance, maybe you could empty the dishwasher and fill it up again?"

I nodded.

"There's some of that lasagna in the refrigerator, for lunch." The front door shut, and she was gone.

I opened the photo package and started to place as many of the negatives as I could on the board. Negatives and prints should be in the same general sequence, as long as somebody hadn't messed them up too much when they looked at them.

It took about thirty minutes to stick the labels on the back of all the prints, and then I was ready to go to work.

Most of the shots had come out rather well, if I did say so myself. Not like the time I did up a burglary scene and found it easier to focus without my glasses on. If you ever want a record of your astigmatism, try that. All blurred, the extent depending on the distance of the focus. These were much, much better.

There's nothing quite like matching the negative to the print, especially when there are multiple shots of the same subject, same point of view, slightly different magnification with a zoom lens; it forces you to examine the detail of each shot. I was sort of hoping that something would pop out at me from one of the prints, something that would give me an indication or a suggestion regarding the perpetrator. Anything.

When I got to the sequence of Phyllis Herkaman's body in the basement, I carefully laid six prints out that I had taken in an attempt at a panoramic view of the scene. They matched quite well, and I found myself looking at the whole north side of the basement. I sat back a little and just let the scene sink in.

I was getting a sense of horrible despair from the montage, a feeling of almost pathetic fear and suffering. Especially as I remembered talking with Helen, and her saying that Phyllis wasn't pushy about Satanism, but believed in it sincerely as a philosophy. It didn't make much difference if somebody got hurt by your actions, because if they could be hurt, they didn't really deserve your consideration . . . or something like that. I wondered how far her philosophy had sustained her in the last few hours of her life. Through Helen, I had gotten to know Phyllis just a little bit. Making it much more difficult to dispassionately view what had happened to her.

When I had originally been at the crime scene, I had been able to pull myself back and view everything like it wasn't quite real. Not really people involved, just objects. You learn to do that after a while. A survival technique. But having become acquainted with Phyllis, so to speak, I was beginning to lose that necessary objectivity. Not necessary so much because it would keep me objective in investigating the case, but necessary because it would keep my head from filling with the horror of what had happened and what I had seen. So it wouldn't bother me for months to come.

I quickly picked up my coffee cup and went into the living room, leaving the prints on the table behind me. I took a deep breath and lit a cigarette. Whoa, boy. Take a break.

I checked the time on the VCR: 11:10. Well, let's go get the stitches out. That ought to be a distraction, and there'll be people there.

I left everything in place and took special care to lock the house up tight. I didn't want the in-laws coming down and seeing the pictures.

When I got to the clinic, there were two people there ahead of me. Henry's nurse ushered me into an exam room, took my temperature and blood pressure, and left me sitting there. Thinking about Phyllis. Not what I wanted, exactly, but it was better than sitting there looking at her body and wondering how that would feel.

Henry came in eventually, his usual exuberant, solid self.

"Well, how's the old noggin today!"

"Okay, I guess. No pain."

"Probably because there's nothing in there to hurt."

He looked the stitches over, decided that it would be all right if they came out. Stuck his head out the door and called for his nurse. Checked my pupils with that damned little light.

"I was right," he said. "Empty."

"Thanks, Henry."

"Just a professional opinion. Any nausea?"

"Nope."

"Good. Headaches?"

"Oh, sort of. When I get tired."

"Good. If you'd said no, I'd know you were lying."

The nurse came in with a little stainless-steel pan. I hate those, too.

"Might be a little uncomfortable for a second, but I don't think so."

"Uncomfortable for who?"

"My prize patient." He picked up a tweezery sort of device, and I could feel a little tug on the right side of my head. "Oh dear . . ."

"What?"

"We'll have to use the hammer and torch."

"Very funny, Henry."

"All done. You want a sucker?"

"No, but one of those neat little Snoopy Band-Aids would be good."

"All out. Used 'em all on injured cops."

The nurse left, and Henry turned serious.

"You feel okay, Carl?"

"Yeah, I'm fine. Why?"

"Well, your BP is up, and you look a little pale."

"Oh, I'm just in the middle of labeling the crime scene photos . . . bothers me a little."

"Phyllis and company?"

"Yeah."

"I'm glad I missed that one."

Henry, along with every other doctor in the county, was an assistant medical examiner. Fortunately for him, he'd been gone last Saturday.

"It was a mess."

"So I've been told."

"Can I go back to work?"

"Do you feel like it?"

"Yeah, I think so. Tomorrow night . . . haven't had much sleep to-day."

"Fine."

I grinned. "I'd hate to miss anything."

"You're aware that the life expectancy of a career cop is about fifty-five to sixty?"

"I've heard that."

"Know what kills them?"

"Stress, I'm told."

"Stress from boredom. Go back to work. This case ought to add five years to your life."

I got home a little after noon, and the phone was ringing. It was Hal.

"Where you been?"

"Getting the stitches out."

"Oh, yeah. Hey, I talked to Helen this morning on the phone, asked her to come into the office after lunch, and she said that she couldn't make it. Not today. It didn't sound right, like she was real reluctant to come in."

"Her husband?"

"I think so."

"Damn. I'd hate to lose her."

"We won't lose her. We can always subpoena her in."

"Yeah, but she was so cooperative, I'd hate to lose that. You can miss so much if you have to pry it out of somebody, you know?"

"Yeah, I know. Tell you what, she knows you . . . could you give her a call?"

"Sure, but I don't guarantee anything."

"No, just give it a try. Set up an appointment for tomorrow, maybe? And see what you think is going on. Talked to Hester this morning, too. Rachel didn't show all night last night. No contact with her employer, either."

"Swell."

"Yeah. I've made some calls around, and nobody gets a ringing bell with the description of this Darkness character, either."

"I'm not surprised."

"And Hester will be up tomorrow, with all the lab stuff. NYPD is sending their officer out, and I'll pick him up at the Cedar Rapids airport this evening. We'll meet at your office tomorrow at 09:00. Will you have the pictures done by then?"

"Oh, yeah. About three-fourths done now."

"Good, bring 'em with you."

"They really sending a man out?"

"Yeah."

"Must be nice to have a big budget."

"They're spending our bucks on this one."

"Like I said . . ."

"Yeah. Look, as long as Helen isn't available, I think I'll go to Iowa City and talk with Hester this afternoon. Got to be down that way to meet the plane this evening, anyway."

I hung up, looked up Helen's number, and called her. By the third ring, I'd decided that if her husband answered, I'd better hang up. He didn't, she did.

"Say, Helen, I'm still on sick leave today, but could you come into the office tomorrow? We have some more stuff to ask you about."

"I don't think so."

"Well, how about Saturday, then?"

"No, we're going to Fred's sister's in Dubuque."

"Sunday or Monday?"

"I don't think I should."

"Why not, Helen? Is something wrong?"

There was a long pause. "No."

She sounded really quiet and subdued. There was something wrong, all right. Somebody get to her? Husband Fred? Was he the suspect?

"Helen, are you sure?"

Another long pause. Good, I thought. She does want to talk, this isn't her idea.

"No, there is something. Wrong . . . Is this being recorded?"

"No, Helen. I'm at home, still 'recovering.' " I laughed.

"Oh."

Another pause. I didn't want to say anything . . . let her talk. But the pause lasted too long.

"Helen, what is it?"

"Not on the phone. Can I see you . . . not at your office. I won't go to your office."

"Well, you could come here, I guess. You know where I live?"

"Yes. But don't have that other man there. Please."

"All right, Helen."

"I have to get groceries. I was just about to leave, anyway. I'll be there in a few minutes."

Well. I figured it was probably Fred, not wanting her to talk to the cops. Not wanting her involved. Not wanting anybody to know that his wife had been the friend of some "different" people. So Fred decided to shut Helen down. Mistake, Fred. Big mistake. I really didn't care if he liked or trusted me or not. No problem. But don't screw up the case, Fred. Don't even think about screwing up the case.

I called Hal back at the office and told him to sit tight—I'd bring him in as soon as I could. I did a quick once-through of the downstairs, making sure it was acceptable for company. The pictures were still all spread out on the dining room table. That wouldn't do, not at all.

I didn't want to put it all away and go to the trouble of setting it all up after Helen left, so I found a tablecloth and threw it over the whole mess. Taking a second or two to look at the montage of the basement with Phyllis's body lying there.

I won't let you down, Phyllis. No matter what you thought, you didn't deserve to die like that. No matter what . . .

I put on a fresh pot of coffee, and was trying to scrounge up something to eat, when Helen rang the doorbell.

She looked like she'd missed some sleep. She looked over her shoulder and then sort of slipped into the house.

"Can I take your coat?"

She shook her head.

"Come on into the living room . . . I've got some coffee on, but I can't find any cookies. I don't suppose you brought any?"

She smiled at that. "No, I'm afraid I didn't."

"My fault, didn't think to ask." I pointed to a chair. "Here, have a seat."

She sat down, and Fred, our dog, went over to her and began sniffing her blue jeans.

"Fred!"

She looked startled. No wonder. Same name as her husband.

"Sorry, Helen." I laughed. "That's his name."

"Oh . . ."

"Let me get some coffee," I said, and went into the kitchen. Grabbed two cups, the pot, and hustled back to the living room, half expecting to find her gone.

She was scratching Fred's ears.

I poured the coffee and sat across the room on the couch.

She was wearing a purplish quilted jacket, with a white scarf around her neck, blue jeans, and gray tennis shoes. Reeboks, I noted. Just a habit. She looked more fragile than she had yesterday, and appeared smaller, somehow.

"What's the problem, Helen?"

She drank a sip of coffee, looking at me over the top of the cup. When she put the cup down, her hand was shaking just a little.

"I'm sorry I told you those things yesterday."

"Don't be. It's all confidential." I held up my right hand, palm toward her, and smiled. "I swear."

"So is Fred. He's pretty upset about it."

"Why?"

"He just didn't like Phyllis and Peggy and Rachel, that's all."

"That's no reason not to tell us anything." She was really uncomfortable. "Helen, wouldn't you be more comfortable up at the office?"

"No!" Instantly, vehemently.

"Just thought I'd ask," I said, and smiled at her. "This is fine with me."

Silence, while she sipped some more coffee. Then she put the cup down with resolve and stood up.

"I'm sorry, Carl, I never should have come here, and I never should have said anything yesterday."

"Just a minute, Helen!" She froze. "Look, they were your friends. Something terrible happened to them. You owe it to them to help us find out who did it."

"Maybe I do, maybe not. I have myself to think of, too."

She didn't sound too sure of herself, but she started to move toward the door again, anyway. I was getting a little desperate. She obviously knew something more, something she thought was extremely important. Fred knew it, too. There was some momentum that had been building, and I didn't want to lose it now. So I took a chance.

"Okay, Helen, but before you go, I want to show you something."

She stopped.

"Come into the dining room for a second, will you?"

I went in there, and she followed me, looking a little unsure of herself.

"Come here," I said, motioning her toward the dining room table. She moved closer. I flipped the tablecloth back, revealing the panoramic shot of Phyllis in the basement. She looked, went pale, her eyes widened, her legs buckled, and down she went. I caught her under one arm and eased her into a chair.

"Helen!" Shit, I hadn't quite expected that much of a reaction.

I kept my hand on her arm, firmly, while I frantically reached over and tried to cover the photographs with the cloth.

She was breathing very hard, very fast. Hyperventilating. Damn!

"Helen, listen to me! Helen, put your head down between your legs."

She did. And all bent over like that, she started to get the shakes. I patted her on the back, feeling guilty as hell, and feeling that I had blown the whole thing and was probably going to get myself sued in the process. Damn, damn, damn. What an asinine thing to do.

It took her a couple of minutes, but she stopped shaking. Staying bent over, but not shaking.

"Are you all right, Helen?"

Her head nodded.

"Why don't you sit up, now?"

She did, and I kept my hand on her shoulder, pinning her gently to the back of the chair. I didn't want her to fall over. She had her eyes closed. After a second she took a deep breath and opened them. I couldn't read the expression in them, but whatever it was, it sure as hell was intense.

"You okay?"

She nodded.

"I hated to do that to you, Helen. But that's how we felt when we walked in there. That's what happened. You need to know what happened."

She nodded.

I'm bullshitting you a little bit, Helen, I thought. Not completely, it is valid, but just a little. Buy it, and you'll understand, though. Buy it and we can cut through the crap and get down to reality here.

She was looking up at me, and I still couldn't read her gray eyes. But the intensity hadn't diminished at all.

"Take a deep breath, kid. It helps. I know."

She did.

"Now another one, slow, and let it all out."

She did, never taking her eyes off me.

"I'll ask you to forgive me for that sometime, Helen. But not yet. Do you feel well enough to go back into the living room?"

"I think so."

I helped her back to her seat in the living room.

"Take a sip of coffee . . ."

She did, obediently. She looked up at me again, and her eyes reminded me of a sad puppy. Ouch.

"There, now just take it easy. You might want to unwind your scarf."

She did that, too.

"You sure you're okay now?"

She spoke for the first time. "You're a son of a bitch, do you know that?" Softly, but with feeling.

"Sometimes, Helen. Sometimes."

She closed her eyes. "Phyllis and I were lovers. You knew that, didn't you?"

Wonderful. Just wonderful. I really hadn't expected that.

"No, Helen, I didn't. Believe me. If I had known that, I never would have shown you the pictures."

She shuddered. "What do you want to know?"

"I want to know who killed her, Helen."

14

Helen sort of gathered herself, and I sat down in the adjoining chair.

"I don't know who killed her."

"I think you think you do."

Silence.

"Who do you think did it?"

She took a deep, shuddering breath and opened her eyes again. Accusing.

"I don't know. I'm afraid that Fred might have had something to do with it. But I don't know."

"Why do you say that?"

She seemed drained. "Because," she said, "he knew."

"Knew what?"

"That Phyllis and I were . . . were lovers."

That surprised me a little, but it sure explained Fred's animosity toward the group.

"He, well, he found us. Sort of."

"Sort of?"

She sighed again and closed her eyes tightly.

"He came to use the phone one morning. I thought he'd be in the field all day, but some machinery broke, and he needed a part. He came in, and Phyllis and I were in the bedroom."

"And he saw you?"

"No. He didn't see anything much at all. We heard him come in, and we came right out. But I suppose we looked like we were caught . . ." She opened her eyes. "Do you know what I mean?"

"I think so."

"We weren't naked, or anything like that." Her eyes shut again. "But I thought he could tell that we'd been kissing and things. I thought he could tell, and later, Phyllis said she thought so, too.

"So, that night, after supper, things were really tense with Fred. Really tense." She opened her eyes and reached for the coffee cup, took a drink, and set it back down.

"So I told him."

"You told him?"

"I had to. He didn't want to know, so I never finished what I wanted to say. I guess I should have said that I tried to tell him. He couldn't handle it, and I should have known that, I suppose. But, don't you see, I couldn't handle it, either."

"So what did Fred do?"

"He told me to shut up, and went in and took a shower, and went to bed. He told me that such things weren't meant to be talked about. That he could never love me again. That I made him sick to his stomach. That it made him sick. That I was crazy."

"That wasn't necessary." Well, we've got a motive here, but I don't think it's going to fly, I thought. Normal man would go after Helen, not Phyllis. Couldn't acknowledge Phyllis as the competition, for Christ's sake. Ruin his image.

"What wasn't necessary?"

"Fred saying you were crazy."

"Thank you." I believe she meant that.

"When did Fred and you have this discussion?"

"Oh, just before Thanksgiving."

"Toward the end of November, then?"

"Yes."

"Did you tell Phyllis that you told Fred?"

"Yes. That was a mistake."

"Why, did it scare Phyllis off?"

She looked at me hard. "You didn't know Phyllis, did you?"

"No, not at all."

"No, it didn't scare her off." She stared out the window. "On the contrary. I went to her the next day and told her all about what Fred had said. She thought it was funny, said he was a 'typical' farmer. Said he was just stupid."

"What did she think about you? Didn't she know how hard it would be on you?"

"I don't think she cared. She thought it would drive me toward her, I think."

"Did it?"

"Oh, maybe at first. She thought it was exciting, that Fred was mad. She'd sneak over to the house and try to make love to me, when she knew he was close. Once, she came over after ten, when she knew Fred would be in bed, and tried to make love to me in the living room."

"How did that make you feel?"

"Guilty." She looked at me defiantly. "It was the most intense orgasm I've ever had."

Whoa, Helen. "So your relationship with Phyllis didn't end when Fred found out?" She shook her head. "I see." Standard phrase when you need time to think.

"It ended just before Christmas." Helen looked back toward the window, and a tear started down her cheek. "I thought she loved me, you understand. I really thought she did. She said that she did, and I believed her. She said that I should believe her, because she never told anybody that, she said, and because she told me that I should believe her. But she said that I should join the group. Get in touch with myself through Satan."

I didn't say anything.

"I thought it would be spiritual. Really spiritual, and that it would help our love." Helen turned back to me. The look of defiance had been replaced by hatred and revulsion. "She had me make love to Peggy and Todd that night!"

It turned out that there had been a little meeting of the group, and that it had turned into something quite a bit more physical than Helen had suspected. And turned out to be nothing like what she needed from Phyllis.

This wasn't the time to ask "Todd who?" but I made a mental note to find out in a few minutes.

"I felt so used, so betrayed. She held me while they had sex with me. Held my head, stroked my hair, said it was all right!"

"And that's the night you broke it off with Phyllis?"

"Yes."

"Did you tell Fred about that?"

"No."

"What did Phyllis say about you breaking it off?"

"She was mean, said I wasn't ready for life, and that I wasn't able to free myself. She said she was disappointed in me, and that I wasn't as intellectually free as I thought. As she'd hoped."

"And since then?"

"I've just sat at home. Oh, Carl, I feel so cheap and stupid. I really do. When I think of what I did, what I felt, what a fool I made of myself." She wasn't crying, but it looked like she was about to. "And what's the worst of it all, a couple of weeks later I tried to get back together with her. I did, I really did. And she said that she wasn't 'comfortable' with me anymore."

"Cheap shot."

"Yes, it was." She didn't cry. Good for you, Helen.

"Let me get you another cup of coffee . . ."

15

Helen was pretty washed-out. I took her cup of coffee in and thought that it was about time for Hal to come up.

"You mentioned some 'Todd' a few minutes ago? I want to know who he is."

"Well, it's Todd Glutzman. From Decorah."

"I don't think I know him . . . Let me call the officer who was here yesterday. I want him to be here, if it's all right with you."

She was really wiped out. "I don't care."

I excused myself and called the office.

It turned out that Hal was on his way to Cedar Rapids, but Hester was back. Even better.

I told her Helen was really spilling over. She got there about five minutes later. I got her some coffee, and we all sat in the living room. Helen was a bit surprised a woman officer was here, but seemed pleased, and a little more relaxed. I filled Hester in briefly, emphasizing Helen's attending a group meeting at Phyllis's place, and naming Todd Glutzman. I would tell Hester about the other business later, but not in front of Helen. If Helen wanted to fill her in before then, it was her choice.

"Who all was at the group meeting," asked Hester, "when you were there?"

Helen sat straight, tilting her head back and looking at the ceiling.

"There was Todd Glutzman, and Rachel, and Kenny and Liz Mills, and Frank McGuire. And Phyllis. And me."

She looked up from her notepad. "Any others?"

"No."

"Is one of these the one they call Darkness?"

"No. He wasn't there. At least, not when I left."

"What did you do at this meeting?"

"Not a lot of anything. Everybody had a robe on. Phyllis had one for me, it was white."

"Were they all white?" I asked.

"No, Phyllis was in red, and so was Todd. Ken and Liz were in green. Rachel was in yellow, and I think that Frank was in black. Maybe dark blue."

"What happened?"

Helen said that when she got there, Phyllis kept her in the master bedroom for a while, and everybody else was in the basement. Phyllis left her, after she put on the robe, and came back a little later. They went to the basement together.

"It was dim down there. But there were lots of candles. Everybody was just sort of sitting around in their robes. She presented me to each one in turn. That's the way she did it. She would lead me to each one, and say, 'so-and-so, I present you Helen.' Just like that."

"She said their names, that's how you know who they were?"

"No, she didn't use their regular names. They all have a secret name, you know. She used those." She hesitated and then looked at us with a rueful smile. "I didn't have one."

"Do you remember any of those names?" asked Hester.

"Oh, let me see . . . I know that Phyllis was called Shade. And Rachel was Handmaiden."

"The others?"

"Well, I remember thinking that Frank's was really appropriate. They called him Benefactor."

Yeah, it was. Appropriate.

"Liz Mills was called Dusk. I thought that fit her pretty well, with her dark hair."

She thought for a minute. "I thought that Todd's was Nathan, but he kept correcting me. He said it was pronounced 'Nathayane' or something. It reminded me of 'propane.' "

"Yeah . . ."

"I really don't remember what Ken was called."

"All right. Then what happened, after you got to the basement and were introduced?"

"Presented."

"Yeah, I'm sorry, presented. Then what happened?"

She said that they were all drinking red wine, that the conversations she was involved in revolved about freeing the spirit from its shackles, nurturing the soul with pleasant thoughts and feelings, of experiencing intense emotions.

"Was Satan ever mentioned?"

"A couple of times, not all that often. Mostly when Todd was telling me that Satan was misunderstood, that he had been given a bum rap by the Catholic Church, and how amusing that was, because they were using Satan to keep themselves in business. But mostly we sat around and talked about our souls, and our feelings, and how much the world puts us down."

Hester finished up her note. "Helen, were there any drugs being taken that night?"

That seemed to take her aback. "No, at least none that I saw."

"Go on."

"Well, after an hour or so, we'd been drinking the wine like I said. Phyllis and Todd and I were on a couch together. Phyllis had her arms around both of us, she was in the middle. She was very intense . . . and she asked me if I would like to join them in the group."

"And you said?"

"I said that I thought I might. But that I didn't know. Not for sure." She looked at me. "I was afraid of what Fred would do if he found out. It all looked a little silly at first, but they were so supportive, you know? I thought it would be good to be a member of a group that looked like they cared about me. The real me, not just my cooking and cleaning."

"I understand that, Helen," I said. "I do."

"This Satan stuff made me really nervous, you know? I get nervous even when his name is mentioned in a normal conversation. We were brought up not to think of him—well, not to acknowledge him. Isn't that right, Carl?"

"Yeah, I guess so. Evil—don't speak his name lightly, right?"

"Yes."

"So, then, what happened?" asked Hester.

"When Phyllis said that she thought that she and Todd and I should have a private discussion upstairs, I went with them. I think I'd had a little too much of the wine, because I was dizzy, sort of. And we got up to the bedroom, and Phyllis took off her robe."

She stopped. Cold.

Hester looked at me quizzically. I shook my head.

"How long were you in the bedroom?"

"About fifteen or twenty minutes. I started to leave once, and she coaxed me back. The second time, I grabbed my clothes and ran into the bathroom. I was so embarrassed . . ."

I'll bet, I thought. From the spiritual discussion to "let us in your pants" in fifteen minutes.

"Did Todd try to stop you physically?" I asked. "Or Phyllis?"

"Phyllis did. She grabbed me by the arm and said that if I left she would be very disappointed in me."

"And you left?"

"Yes. Todd just said, 'Let the bitch go.' " Her lip was trembling. "Oh, God," she said, "I was so mortified!"

Helen looked at her watch. "My God! It's after two-thirty!" She stood up and rewrapped her scarf. "I have to get groceries yet. And if I'm not home real soon, he'll know where I've been!"

We tried to set up another meeting, as she hurried out of the house. It was left at "Call me." And she was gone.

Hester and I sat there for a little while, talking about Helen and what she had told us. We agreed that, while we were getting pretty close to naming all the members of the coven, or whatever, and getting leads that would surely have to give us the identity of Darkness, we weren't a whole lot closer to solving the murders. Unless Fred was our man.

"Fred had a motive," said Hester. "No doubt about it."

"That he did."

"Depending, of course, on how much Helen told him."

"Well," I said, "before you got here she told me that he knew about her and Phyllis. Sort of caught the two of them in Helen's bedroom one day. Apparently pissed him off and revolted him at the same time."

"We need Rachel. She'll know."

We both agreed to hold off on interviewing Fred for forty-eight hours. He wasn't going anywhere, and if he did, it would tend to confirm him as a suspect. And Fred wasn't the sort of person who would be too hard to find. Anyway, that would give us time to find Rachel.

"I think," I said, "Fred's strong enough to have done it all by himself."

"True."

"And he had a motive."

"True again."

"But I don't think he did it. It just doesn't seem to fit, quite."

"I know. But he sure is looking good."

Hester left, heading for Iowa City to meet up with Hal and to begin tracking down the group members that Helen identified. I called Lamar at the office, and he wasn't in. Left a message for him that I would be going back to work the following night.

It suddenly dawned on me that Fred might well have been the one who tried to crack my skull. I had been concentrating so much on *the* case that I had forgotten about *mine.*

I thought about it. Tried to remember Fred's reaction to me when Hal and I were at the Bockman farm. It seemed to me that it was the reaction of somebody who had a secret, but that secret was probably concerning Helen. Then, again, if he was the suspect, whacking me on the head was the least of his offenses, and might not produce a guilty reaction at all.

It occurred to me that I didn't like Fred, even before he had become a suspect. I was rubbing the right side of my head and caught myself in the dining room mirror . . . sitting there, with my hand on my head, a little smile in the corner of my mouth. I broke into a grin. I reminded myself of the little statues of the Darwinian monkey contemplating the human skull.

I picked up where I had left off with labeling the photos. I had to get that done. I felt pretty cheap, showing Helen the montage like that. Her distress level had been a lot higher than I had anticipated. How could I have known that they had been lovers? Rationalize, Carl. It had been cruel, anyway. True. But it had gotten her to talk. Thinking about that, I hoped that she wouldn't be in too much trouble with Fred, which we would have also caused.

I was feeling guilty, and that tends to screw up your head. I began to think about Fred being a strong suspect and began to fear for Helen's safety. After all, if he had done the murders, he should be quite capable of killing her, too.

Then, again, if I tried to contact her, or to check on her, I would just make him mad. Especially if she pulled off the "grocery" trip, and he was calm. Shit.

I had a physics course once. Didn't do all that well, but I remembered one section devoted to the second law of thermodynamics. As I recall, it stated that all things tended to go from an ordered state to a less ordered state. Disorder, or entropy, always increased. Always. In one way or another. If you tried to decrease the entropy of something, the energy you created by doing that was increasing the entropy in another area. Or something like that.

Anyway, cop work was like that. Take the four murders. They had increased the community disorder by an order of magnitude. Our efforts to decrease that disorder by apprehending the suspect or suspects tended to increase the disorder in other areas. Helen and Fred, for example. The coven members, soon enough. The displaced officers, getting less sleep, getting hit on the head; making more cases as we went. The burial controversy with Pastor Rothberg. And on and on. Entropy increases. Inevitably. All we can do, in the long run, is to try to direct or channel it toward our goals.

I'd tried to explain that little philosophy to my colleagues. Success meant a puzzled look. Usual reaction was boredom. And that was okay, too. After all, entropy increases ever so slowly when you're bored. A worthwhile goal in itself.

Which brought me back to the unlabeled photos and the chaos on the table. Better get this done before Sue comes home. She just might have plans for the dining room table. Like, supper.

I had just finished up the mess when the phone started to ring. First, my mother. Just checking on how I was doing. Then my mother-in-law, with the same basic question. Then our daughter, who worked in a bank in Cedar Rapids.

"Well, hi, Dad!"

"Hey, Jane! How you doing?"

"I'm fine. Just called to check the state of your head—outside only, please. I'm not ready for what goes on inside."

"Just fine. I get to go back to work tomorrow night."

"Congratulations."

"Yeah, thanks."

"How things goin' with the crime of the century?"

"Oh, slow would describe it pretty well. Very well, in fact. If we ever solve it, it'll be the arrest of the next century."

"That good, huh?"

"You know us. Slow."

"Speaking of Theo, Dad, is he the one who's got the case this time?"

She knew all about Theo. Living at home all those years, the mutterings and rumblings I made so often hadn't gone unnoticed.

"Sort of."

"Well, I'll be sure to keep that in mind. I don't want to be too hard on you."

"I appreciate that."

"And I'll stop telling my friends that you're involved. I don't want to embarrass myself."

"If anything happens, I'll put out a release identifying myself as Jane Houseman's father."

She laughed. "God, if you do that, just make sure you do something right."

I had no sooner hung up the phone than Dan Smith called.

"Carl, you know what you asked me to do the other night?"

"What?"

"You know, about the dark houses?"

"Oh, yeah."

"I've got a list."

I thought for a minute. Probably not of any significance, not now that we had a number of names from Helen, but I had asked him to do it, and he had done it for me.

"Great! Listen, why don't you drop up after 18:30 or so? We'll go over it then."

Sue came home, we had supper, and she was a little upset because Dan was coming over. Wanted to spend my last night on sick leave together, alone. Me too.

Dan came to the back door right at 18:30, with his list. He'd done a remarkable job. He listed over a hundred houses that he said were normally dark, or that had one dim light at most; all of them had been pretty brightly lit on Sunday night. They all were on Monday and Tuesday, too. With a couple of exceptions.

"Power company's making bucks on this one, Carl."

"Ah-ha! A motive!"

He grinned.

I told him my head was bothering me, and he finally took the hint. I tossed the list on top of my computer and went out to enjoy the evening with Sue.

16

Saturday, April 27
00:11 hours

I was lying in bed with Sue, listening to the soft breathing of her sleep, when the fire siren summoning our local volunteer fire department went off. It's less than a block from our house, and it rattles the shingles. Sue woke, and we both looked out the upstairs windows, to see if it was close. We couldn't see anything.

About five minutes later, the sirens on the trucks could be heard going up the hill out of town to the west.

"Good," said Sue. She always worried about her parents' house, which was about two blocks away. "I wonder where it is?" She got back into bed, and I kissed her good night. I wouldn't be able to sleep for a while, and she knew that.

"Going downstairs?"

"Yeah."

"Don't go to the office, and don't do any office work, okay? Take some time for yourself."

"I promise."

"Sure."

I went downstairs and waited a few minutes to call the office and find out where the fire was. Let the initial burst of radio traffic die down.

"Sheriff's Department."

It was Sally.

"Hi, it's three. You busy?"

"Not now, not for a few minutes."

"Good. Where's the fire?"

"You're gonna love this. It's Francis McGuire's place. House is gone."

"Jesus Christ!"

"I knew you'd like it."

"Whoa, we'd better get somebody to Herkaman's."

"Already been done, Mike's there now. It's all right."

Great, just great. I, of course, began to jump to conclusions and had to slow myself down. The house was vacant now, and it could have been something like a short, or the furnace, or a chimney fire, or almost anything. Didn't have to be an arson. Not at all.

The hell.

But we'd have to wait for the deputy state fire marshal to investigate it. And he'd have to be briefed regarding the whole case. If it turned out to be arson. If.

Another felony, probably, in a case already too crowded. Far too crowded.

Entropy increases.

I called the office back.

"We have somebody going to the scene?"

"Fire chief requested one about five minutes ago, and I'm sending Eddie. Mike wants to stay at Herkaman's for a while yet."

"Where's Eddie at?"

"He was about nine or ten miles south of town when I called him."

"Look, if he's not through town yet, have him stop at my place for a second, would you?"

"Sure."

I could hear her talking on the radio and heard Eddie say that he would.

"Tell him I'll meet him in the alley."

I knew he'd be in a real hurry, but he'd only been a cop for about a year, and it would have been much better if we could get an experienced man out there.

I went out and stood in the backyard, and Eddie came screeching around the corner and into the alley.

I opened the passenger door and stuck my head in the car.

"Look, take lots of pictures, okay? Anything that looks unusual or different. Ask the fire chief, he'll know what to shoot. And talk to all the firemen, see what they saw. Okay?"

"Yeah."

"Get out there, but take your time once you're there. We're looking for Satanic signs and symbols, all right?"

"Yeah, yeah."

"And you might let two know, and get him out there. If it looks like there's anything at all."

"Yeah."

He was so anxious to go he was fidgeting.

"Get going."

"Later . . ."

He threw gravel all over the alley, and my garage, as he left. I shook my head. He was going to make a good cop, but it was going to be a while. Too anxious. Too excited. Just like I used to be, I suppose.

I went back into the house, to find Sue in the kitchen.

"I was hungry."

"Me too. You find anything?"

"Chicken from last night. You want some?"

I shook my head.

"Who was that?"

"Eddie. He's on his way to the fire, and I had to talk to him first."

"You don't have to tell him everything, I'm sure he can handle it without you."

"Most of the time. But the fire is at the McGuire house."

"Oh, no."

"Oh, yes."

"This complicates it a lot, I'll bet."

"Well, maybe and maybe not." I grinned. "Should be some sort of evidence out there. You can never have enough evidence."

"Yumm rie um id um eeb," she said, munching on a mouthful of chicken.

"What?"

"I said, you try to get some sleep."

"Yeah, I will. I'll sleep most of the day tomorrow."

"Don't count on it."

She went back upstairs, and I sat downstairs feeling frustrated. Not enough information to do anything, and I had already made enough of a pest of myself for one night. I turned on the tube and was disappointed, as usual. Fussed around for a few minutes in the kitchen and then went into my little office area and spotted Dan's list. Well, why not?

The first problem with the list was that he hadn't included any addresses. I knew where a lot of them were, but . . .

Got out the telephone book and went to work.

Second problem was that he'd only kept a list of the lighted places. Wonderful. Were the others dark, or did he just miss somebody? It was something to do, though.

Six of the locations were crossed out, then written in again. Probably not significant, but he should be asked.

When I was done with the addresses, I went to my computer and made up a quick database, just names and addresses and dates. Typed them all in. Boredom will make you do little things like that. Now that it was all in, I had no idea what to do with it. I called the office again.

"Hi, there."

"You, again?"

"Yeah . . . is Dan working tonight?"

"He sure is."

"Busy?"

"Is he ever?"

"Why don't you have him come up to my place, will you?"

"Okay. Having trouble sleeping?"

"Yep."

"Why don't you come up here, I brought in a whole bunch of sausage and cheese."

"Sold."

I ran the list off, grabbed three bottles of Pepsi, and walked out to get in my personal car when Dan pulled up. Rode to the office with him.

Eddie was still at the scene of the fire, and he had called Art out to help him. Sally didn't know what they had, but the fact that they were still there was a pretty good indication that they had something.

She and Dan and I sat in the dispatch center, eating sausage and going over the list I had just typed. Dan was really pleased with the database—no reason, but it always made him happy to see his information in print.

I asked him about the crossed-off entries, and he said that there had been lights on, that they had gone off and come back on again, between rounds.

"Why did they do that?" I asked.

Sally started to laugh.

"What's so funny?"

"Six couples in Maitland had sex that night, dummy."

Neither Dan nor I could think of a better explanation.

I got Sally talking about what she had heard in the community and got an earful. She just told her friends that she had been working that night, and they would start off. Mostly with questions, and when there was no information forthcoming, they would begin to speculate.

Most of her sources seemed to think that there was a crazy group near Maitland, who was killing people for the enjoyment of it. That nobody was safe. Satan was mentioned about half the time. A lot of them thought that we were scared of the Satanists and would do nothing.

Names were brought up, mostly the usual crazies that nobody trusted but that everybody had tolerated.

And the macho dudes who hung around the bars were talking of going out and getting whoever it was, since we hadn't.

Mostly idle talk, of course. But the guys who were talking about taking matters into their own hands bothered me. They always do.

Sally gave us the names of those individuals, and we noted them. For the simple reason that if we found a local flake beaten or worse, we would have a suspect or two. Most of it was said for the purpose of scoring with local barflies, of course. But they could egg somebody on, and who knew what would happen . . .

The radio came to life.

"Comm, six?"

Sally swallowed her sausage. "Six, go."

"We're 10–24 out here, 10–76 to the SO."

"10–4, six and two 10–24. Three fifty-six."

I decided to wait around and talk to Eddie and Art when they got back in. I was a little disappointed—Art went directly home. Eddie, however, came to the office.

He was a mess, covered with mud splatters and soot that had fallen on him. And damp.

"Hi, Ed."

"Oh, shit, what a mess out there."

"What did you do, crawl inside the fireplace?"

"No, those fire trucks were moving pretty good when they sent the tankers back for more water, you know? And I was doing traffic control at the end of the lane, and the splash from the trucks, you know?"

I grinned. "Yeah."

"Those crazy sons of bitches don't even slow down! And then Art had me poking around after they left, all over the place."

"Get a little warm?"

"Warm! Shit, I melted the sole of my overshoe!"

He stuck his foot up, and sure enough, the sole of his rubber boot was melted through.

"What did you step on something that hot for?"

"Oh, Art kept saying, 'You gotta get close if you're gonna get good pictures.' "

"Yeah, well you sort of do. You forget how to use the zoom?"

"I didn't want to fuck up the flash. I don't know how to reset it, and somebody told me that if you like double the power, you only get half the light."

"Yeah."

He set his camera bag down and took out the camera. It was filthy.

"Look at this!"

"Jesus, Ed, how'd you do that?"

"I was getting in real close to the kitchen, and a piece of the wall fell out. Into the mud. Splattered me all over. Scared the shit out of me, too!"

"I'll bet."

"So Art had to use his camera to take the rest of the pictures. Boy, was he pissed off!"

"So what did you find?"

"Oh, it was arson, all right. The fire chief said so, said that it was pretty obvious that somebody had poured gas all over the place. Said that almost the whole house had started up at the same time. And there is a crazy-looking burn mark on the wooden floor from the kitchen to the living room—like it was branded or something. You know, like a hamburger on the grill?"

"Sure."

"Fire chief said that was a line where gas was poured from one room to the other. And you know how you asked me to look for Satanic signs?"

I did. I sort of held my breath.

Ed reached into his coat pocket and pulled out a little plastic evidence bag. Containing a silverish medallion.

"This was stuck to a tree in the yard. A fireman found it."

He handed me the bag. A small medallion, a circumscribed penta-gram, the circle being a snake eating its own tail. Just like the one that was hanging over Phyllis Herkaman in her basement.

I looked at it for a minute, wondering where it had been made. Sally asked if she could see it, and I handed it to her, still in the bag, of course. Dan looked at it, too.

Sally looked up at me. "You look a little strange."

"I'm thinking."

"Must be a pretty bad thought."

Dan, of course, said, "I know I've seen one of these before. I know I have."

"Where?"

"I can't remember."

Now, knowing Dan, he might actually have seen one before. Then again, he might not. Or he might have seen something similar . . .

"You know," said Sally, "so have I."

"Where?"

"You know Liz Mills?"

"Sort of." Not before yesterday afternoon and Helen Bockman's weird tale.

"Well, about a month ago, she was down in one of the bars, and she was wearing one just like that. I noticed because it stood out against that black sweater she had on. You know what she's like—always showing off her chest to all the men, and she always wears something tight and tries to use jewelry to make them notice."

"Actually, I don't."

"Oh, sure. She thinks she's pretty hot stuff. Lets everybody know that she's, well, available, you know? That long, black hair." She thought for a second. "Always showing those long legs off, too." Afterthought.

Sally was a redhead. About five feet tall. Slender. Nothing to sneeze at, herself, but she was small all over, and sort of sensitive about it. She would be very much aware of somebody doing what she thought Liz Mills did. And would pay very close attention to what she was wearing.

"She was really showing off, Sally?"

"Makes you sick, the way she's all over the men."

"What does her husband think of all this?"

"Oh, he's never with her, or hardly ever."

"He thinks that going barhopping alone is good for her?"

"She doesn't go alone, silly. She's always with that little slut who works for Human Services . . . oh, what's her name . . ."

"What does she look like?"

"Oh, small blonde, but overweight. Big butt. Mouthy."

"Oh," said Dan. "I know her. Uh . . . name begins with a 'Z.' "

"Right!" said Sally. "That's her, Hedda, I think, Hedda, Hedda . . ."

"Let's look it up in the phone book," I suggested.

Sally grabbed the book first. Not fair, it was closer to her. She found it right away. Only seven Z entries. H. Zeiss, like in the binoculars.

"Here she is."

"She single, Sally?" I asked.

"Of course. You'd have to be crazy to marry her."

"Why's that?"

"She screws anybody she can." Her face reddened. "And I mean any-body. She even hit on me once."

"You're kidding. How long has she lived around here?"

"About two years," said Dan. "Lived in the apartment above Summerman's store, then bought that house at the lower end of town. Her mom died up at the nursing home in Decorah, and she and her brother got a lot of money."

Sally, Eddie, and I all looked at Dan.

His face very slowly turned red. "Hey, I just talk to people . . ."

"And where do you talk to her, Dan?" asked Sally in a syrupy voice.

"No, hey, guys, really. She comes up to me when I'm sitting on the corner. She just likes to talk."

"Sure, Dan."

"No, really."

17

I went home and got to bed just as Sue was getting up.

I woke at 14:30, back on schedule and ready to go to work at 20:00. The phone rang at 15:15. We were having a meeting at the office at 16:00 and they wanted me there. The man from NYPD had come in with Hal, and Judd Norman, the deputy state fire marshal, would give us the rundown on the fire.

Got to the office early, of course. So did just about everybody else.

All eight of us, two DCI agents, the guest from New York, Judd, and a small man I didn't know, but who seemed quite at home with the state officers.

We didn't have enough room to seat everybody except the kitchen, and we had people sitting on the counter and the floor.

Lamar started it off by introducing the small man as Brian Nieuhaus, from the state attorney general's office. He would be handling the case for them. While he was being introduced, our county attorney, Mark Fueller, and his assistant, Mitch Hamilton, came in. We all had to shift, as guests get the chairs.

The presence of the man from the AG's office surprised me quite a bit, because that meant that we probably had a suspect. I didn't know who that might be. I mean, several names came to mind, but none of them were what I would think of as really good possibilities.

I nudged Art, who was on the counter beside me.

"We arrest somebody?"

"Not that I know of."

"I wonder. The AG usually doesn't send somebody up unless we have a suspect in custody."

"Nobody said anything to me. But that's not unusual."

Lamar restarted, by saying that Nieuhaus wanted to make a brief statement.

Nieuhaus stood. "Gentlemen," he began, "this is an unusual case." I noticed Hester bristle a bit when he failed to recognize her presence. He paused. If he's pausing for effect, I thought, it's wasted. We already know that it's unusual.

"My boss," he said, "and the governor are both very concerned about some of the ramifications in these murders. There has already been some national media coverage, and the local media here in Iowa are assigning people to cover the case in depth." He paused again. This time he had our attention.

"Now, I don't know how many of you have ever been the target of 'in-depth' coverage by the media, but let me assure you it can be a very unpleasant experience."

We had had some experience, but I couldn't remember any thorough coverage in the last fifteen years. Couldn't remember any "adequate" coverage, either, for that matter.

"Your first tendency, gentlemen, is to either be fully cooperative or to withhold everything."

Lamar grinned. So did I.

"In either case," he continued, "you will have a problem, and with the extreme sensitivity of this matter, my boss and the governor feel that there could be a panic reaction on the part of the public. There could also be," he said, "enough sensationalism to ruin the case." He paused again. "That, we don't want."

He gestured toward the NYPD detective. "I am very glad to see Detective Saperstein here today. He has handled this sort of matter before, and I am sure he will prove invaluable to us, both from the investigative end and from the media relations standpoint."

Saperstein nodded. He looked pretty cool, and very serious.

Nieuhaus went on.

"Attorney General Scholle has asked your county attorney here to handle all media relations regarding this case.

"He feels that the 'clearinghouse' approach to the media in this case is essential. With the small number of officers available, it was also thought to be a good idea to let you work the case, and not to take one of you off to handle the press."

In other words, we don't want one of you dummies talking to the media. Fine by me.

"Just for your own information," said Nieuhaus, "the *Des Moines Register* already has a two-man team in place in this county. They will probably remain here in Maitland for some time, gathering information and talking to everybody they can get their hands on." He paused again. I remember thinking that this guy might be pretty good in the courtroom. "A major network news team is also on its way."

"Not *60 Minutes?*" I said. "Please, not *60 Minutes.*"

We all laughed. Except Saperstein, I noticed.

"No," said Nieuhaus, "not *60 Minutes.* We haven't fucked the case up yet."

At least he said "We."

"I believe," said Nieuhaus, "that Mark has something to say."

Our county attorney stood up. Mark Fueller was a pretty good attorney, and was considered part-time as a prosecutor, mostly because the county didn't want to pay him a living wage. He was a sincere man, one who probably had had nightmares about this sort of case.

"Just refer all media inquiries to me. After they get used to it, we shouldn't have any problems."

He looked around the room.

"But don't go around shooting off your mouth. Not in restaurants, not in bars, not even at home. We want a lid on this, except through me or Mitch. Understand?"

We all nodded.

"I want to control all outgoing information. I *will* control it. I want that understood."

I nudged Art again, and whispered, "You think Theo's gonna move in with him?"

Art nudged back. A little harder than was absolutely necessary.

"Now, I know," said Fueller, "that there's already been a lot of speculation out there. It will continue. But absolutely nothing with an official stamp on it goes out unless it's through me."

I looked at Theo. He was nodding his head vigorously. You bet, Theo. He was the biggest leak we had. And probably would continue to be.

Fueller sat back down. Lamar stood.

"Okay, now Detective Saperstein wants to say a couple of things here. He'll brief some of us more fully later, but he just wants to say a couple of words to all of us." He turned to Saperstein. "Go ahead, Bill."

Saperstein got up and leaned against the refrigerator. He had very sad eyes, I thought. But also very intense.

"This is a lovely area here. I hate to see something like this happen in such a place." He looked around the room. "Anybody here ever been involved in a cult-related murder before?" No response. "Then it's safe to assume that you've never been involved in a Satanic-cult-related murder." He gave a smile that was more like a tic than a grin.

"The first thing you have to know is this: Satanism doesn't mean that there is a red-faced man with horns and a tail involved. There is no magic. There are no spells that work, no incantations that produce any mystical effects. Likewise, you aren't dealing with ignorant or markedly stupid people. You'll find that out when you interrogate them. These people are really dangerous, in a way, but not in the way most people think.

"The only way to get a conviction, to get an arrest, to even get a suspect, is to play it absolutely straight. Good police work, all the way. Don't get involved in the religious aspects, except as to how it directly relates to the case. Satanism is a legal religion in the USA. You can be a Satanist, that's all right. Don't forget that. But with Satanism, you are dealing with a whole different mind-set. That's the essential point. The mind-set."

He lit a cigarette. "Look at it this way. Most of you are Christians, of one sort or another. Even if you never go to church. I'm sort of Jewish." He snapped out a grin. "But we have all been brought up with certain standards of behavior drummed into us from day one. If we violate those standards, we feel guilt. If we feel guilt, we are vulnerable to all the standard investigative techniques and interrogation approaches. The guilt does all the work. The cops just have to ask the right questions."

He thought for a second. "What I've heard about this case on the drive up here, I think the odds are that it's not a dyed-in-the-wool Satanist who is your perpetrator. But I know that the crime is Satanic in origin." He put out his cigarette. "I'll explain that later. What is important is that you are dealing with people who are highly motivated, and who, on both sides of the homicides, aren't going to feel guilt as you and I understand the term."

He leaned back against the refrigerator again. "Satanism and its associated groups only produce a psychological effect upon the believers. The mind-set. They can do nothing you and I would consider wrong. Because to them, it isn't wrong. And, in this case, I suspect that the perp acted from what he or she considers noble and righteous motives. We've got a perp with a 'mission,' whatever the origin of the motives for the killings. The motive appears to be vengeance, judging from the methods used. There will be a twisted logic involved. You'll probably never figure it out until after the case is solved. Maybe not even then. But the motive is human, not supernatural. Don't forget that aspect, ever. These are people, even if they're a little less sane than most. Even if they don't subscribe to what we would consider normal standards of behavior. Even if they can kill and maim and torture without any shred of remorse. Sociopaths have the same human motivations as anyone else. They just don't feel sorry afterward, that's all. Satanists have the same 'advantage,' if you will."

He sat back down abruptly. It was very, very quiet in the kitchen. I was going to like this man.

Lamar broke the silence. "Okay, now I think Agent Gorse has something for us."

Hester didn't bother to stand. "Rachel Larsen is not in Iowa City, we're pretty sure. She's gone to ground, but we don't know where.

"All the lab tests from the crime scene are in." She took some sheets of paper out of a folder and started them around the room. "Take a look at these, and I'll explain them to you."

The sheets, and there were twelve of them, looked something like this:

EXHIBIT	ABO	PGM	EAP
Q bed sheet	B	1+2+	B

AD red cord	B	1+2+	B
AL pillowcase	B	iss	iss
AV bloodstain	B	1+2+	na

Every exhibit taken had been processed, and there were lots of exhibits.

"Now," said Hester with a smile, "this is what it means. All these are what they call independently inherited factors. Physiological fluids can be identified and traced this way to a specific individual. These genetic markers are what they refer to as polymorphic, meaning that they vary from individual to individual.

"ABO is the standard blood typing, with four types of blood found in humans: A, B, O, and AB. The PGM stands for phosphoglucocomutase, and that's an enzyme found in blood, semen, etc. That stuff is classified as 1+, 1−, 2+, and 2−. Everybody has two of the four factors.

"EAP is erythrocyte acid phosphatase, and that's a three-factor genetic marker with the three factors being A, B, or C, and everybody has one or two of those.

"The note 'iss' stands for insufficient sample size, 'na' signifies lack of activity, and 'inc' would stand for inconclusive results."

She stopped, and took a long swig of Coke. "Okay, that's how we tell whose blood is where. You don't have to remember all that, just so you know how it's done. The important stuff is that the blood that's identified, or the nail scrapings from Peggy Keller and Phyllis Herkaman that were analyzed, have shown some results. The contents of the blender have shown results. Those contents were, by the way, confirmed as being Sirken's testicles and his tongue."

The room grimaced and groaned.

"There was no blood or other tissue from Francis McGuire found at the Herkaman residence.

"There were tissue samples taken from the fingernails of both Peggy Keller and Phyllis Herkaman. They sort of match, but weren't sufficient for more positive results. Sirken had no nails to speak of, he apparently chewed them or something. Also insufficient, but even less sufficient than the others. McGuire had no tissue to speak of on his remaining hand.

"Sirken, McGuire, and Herkaman had LSD in their blood."

Art perked up.

"All four had blood alcohol contents varying from 0.198 milligram percent in McGuire to 0.03 in Herkaman. Stomach contents indicated that it was a red wine with McGuire and Sirken, probably the same with Herkaman. With Keller, it was schnapps, indicating that she possibly consumed her drinks elsewhere. Keller also had consumed a pizza within an hour of her death, while there were no indications of pizza in the other three. It is consistent with observed facts, as it was unlikely that Herkaman was given any wine during her ordeal.

"The red ligature materials were as nearly identical as they can be determined, given technological limits. McGuire's hand was taken off by a heavy wedge, either an ax or a very large blade. The tissue was compressed, as was the bone. Heavy blow, only one. Some missing tissue on the exit side of the wound, as well as the nature of the wound itself, indicates that the wound was inflicted while the arm was resting on a surface, probably wooden. The hand was definitely severed after death.

"There was hair at the scene that was not that of any of the four victims. It was human, and we have classified it pretty well. Dark brown, reddish brown, gray, and blond." She grimaced. "Obviously, either we have four perps, or it's just an indication that there have been other people in the house. Not much there.

"Fingerprints of all four victims were matched to items at the Herkaman house. Those of Peggy Keller were also found among items removed from the McGuire farm. We have found a large number of prints in the Herkaman house, size indicating female origin, which we feel are those of Rachel Larsen. We can't tell because, to our knowledge, Rachel has never been fingerprinted, and we won't get a match until we find her. There was also a large variety of partial prints, and some good ones, which are also not identifiable at this time.

"We also found some infant items of apparel in the Herkaman house, and a couple of Polaroid photos of an infant being held by Herkaman and Rachel Larsen. Examinations of both Herkaman and Keller indicated that Herkaman had had a child several years ago and that Keller had never had children.

"There's one hell of a lot more, but those are the highlights." She exhaled deeply, and was finished.

"Thanks, Hester," said Lamar. "Now let's hear from Judd about the fire."

Judd was very brief. He had to be, because there wasn't much to say.

"Well, it's a definite arson. Accelerant, probably gasoline, was used throughout the house. Trailed from one room to another. Probably started just inside the side door, it looks like a soaked rag was thrown in. We might have an injury to the arsonist, because the gasoline vapors were permeating the entire house, and there was a minor explosion upon ignition. Just depends on how close he was, and whether or not he had the sense to take cover around the door frame. There was a lot of hot gas came out that door, in a hurry." He looked at his notes.

"We've checked all the local medical facilities—nobody in with burns. If he was dumb enough to be curious, and stuck his head around the corner of the door, he's probably bald now.

"No footprints linked to the perp, but there were a hell of a lot of firemen around out there. Found a two-gallon gas can inside the house, about where the kitchen used to be. There may be another one, but I haven't been able to get to the basement yet. We aren't gonna dust the can here, we'll send it to the DCI lab and have them do it."

He looked up, sort of shrugged, and sat down.

"Thanks, Judd," said Lamar. "Any questions?"

Just about every hand in the room went up.

"Okay," said Lamar, "let's order some supper and eat here. You night guys might want to get some rest, but you can stay if you want to. Carl, Detective Saperstein wants to talk to you and Hal. Theo, Agent Gorse wants to talk with you. And the attorneys want to talk with all of us.

"We're gonna have to get real organized, people."

18

We all kicked in a couple of bucks and sent Eddie Heinz and Quint Shapley out for pizza. The "get organized" meeting would follow supper. In the meantime, we broke up into groups.

Art, Hal, and I went into the back office with Detective Bill Saperstein.

We three Iowa people were all about six to eight inches taller than Saperstein, who was about five five. As we shut the office door, he looked at us and asked what they fed us in Iowa.

We introduced ourselves to him, and he got the ball rolling right away.

"You gentlemen are in for a rough time."

We agreed.

He lit a cigarette. I liked him more and more, as he was one of the few people left who seemed to smoke as much as I did.

"Your state attorney is right about the media. They'll drive you nuts, because this is sensational stuff. Digging into a case like this, with a little luck, can make somebody's journalistic career. So they're gonna pry and dig, and talk to all sorts of people. And they're gonna piss you off."

"Some do already," said Hal.

Saperstein shook his head. "You ain't seen nothin' yet, baby."

"Hey," I said, "you don't think that the job was done by Satanists?"

"No, I don't think so. It's related, and strong in the motive, but I don't like to label any case as 'Satanic.' They don't come that way. There isn't any real, true Satanic religion—not that's established. They're all involved in putting bunches of their wishes into a bucket with a bunch of the parts of

Satanic belief that they happen to be fond of, and shaking the bucket. What comes out is tailored to the individual, or the small group. This is an unusual case. Like I told Hal on the way here, I was expecting to find that we had a ritual killing—or massacre, I guess would be more like it."

"The dope surprised me, a little. I work dope in this county," said Art.

"It's possible that your perpetrator interrupted something. With the LSD, it would be a lot easier to surprise the victims."

"What I want to know," I said, "is what the hell happened to Mc-Guire?"

"Beats me. You've gotta find his hand, or where it was chopped off."

"We've tried."

"I know. But that's what I mean about good police work. You've gotta do your homework and handle the case like a routine murder."

"Easy for you to say," I said. "We don't have routine murders—we have about one every three or four years."

Saperstein laughed and shook his head. "Must be nice."

"We like it," said Art, "but it shorts us on practice."

"Well," said Saperstein, "from what Hal said, what I think you've got is this. Somebody knocked off a large part of a group. The group was composed of individuals with a common purpose. The motive for the killings is not known, but I think we can guess at revenge. If I'm wrong there, then there could be an inner-group motive, and you could call that political.

"So somebody wanted them dead. Either did it himself or got somebody else to do it for him. Whoever did it was psychotic, at least at the time of the murders. Whoever did it stayed in a psychotic state for a considerable length of time. That means that, unless you have a crazy running around that you all know is capable of it, and in a small area like this you would probably know him, there are two possibilities. One, the killer is an import from an area far enough away that you won't know who it is, or, two, the killer was in an artificially induced state of psychosis. I think two is your case here."

"Sounds reasonable," said Art. "By artificial, you mean dope?"

"Possibly. But artificial can include extreme emotional stress, too. Maybe helped out by chemicals.

"Now," continued Saperstein, "your perp is obviously acquainted with

Satanism. Not necessarily involved in the practice, but he knows something about it. He may be using the Satanic-related things to cover his tracks, or he might be saying to the victims, 'Look, you live by the sword, you die by the sword.' "

Not to try to claim credit for what Saperstein was saying, but it all sounded like the echoes of incomplete thoughts I'd been having all along. Better organized, more concise. But they had been there for a time. The "ring of truth" sometimes simply consists of stating the obvious in a new way.

"All of which," said Saperstein ruefully, "leaves you where you were yesterday."

"True enough," said Hal.

"But," said Saperstein, "somebody knows. That's your key. And if this Rachel is still around, she is the one who'll open it up for you."

"If we ever find her."

"Oh, you'll find her. Maybe five years from now, but you'll find her."

"I think," said Art, "we'd better do better than five years."

"And," said the New York detective, "there's at least one other who knows, too."

"Right, the perpetrator."

"You got it, Carl."

"But why did he come back and burn the McGuire house?"

"Ah," said Saperstein. "Good question. Cleansing ritual? Likely, but it may not be your killer at all."

"No?"

"No, it could easily be another member of the cult, cleansing the place that's been defiled by somebody else. You'll probably have at least an attempt at the other place, too. You look into it long enough, and you get lucky, I'll be willing to bet that most of the really dark ceremonies took place at McGuire's."

A ray of light.

"We have some names of some other members," I said. "We'll interview them shortly, probably starting tonight."

Art looked at me sharply. "We do?"

"Yeah, I haven't been able to get ahold of you and didn't want to leave a note."

"Does Theo know?"

"No."

"Well, there's hope yet."

"Who's Theo?" asked Saperstein.

"Our investigator."

"What, you got a problem with him?"

"Oh, yeah, you could say that."

"What is it? He talk too much?"

"Well," I said, "that, too. He's a little heavy-handed, and he's not too swift."

"That's too bad."

"I'm being charitable," I said.

"How'd he get to be investigator?"

"Long story," said Art. Not wanting to air our dirty laundry in front of a stranger.

"Think of him like inflation," I said. "Just something you have to live with."

"He the only one like that you got?" asked Saperstein.

"Yes."

"It must be nice to work in a small department."

We could hear a small commotion at the main entrance. The pizza was arriving.

We all trooped back to the kitchen, via the dispatch center.

"Who's the little redhead?" asked Saperstein.

"Oh," I said, "that's Sally."

"Hummmm . . ."

I grinned at him. "That's just an impression. Actually, she's very quiet and well behaved."

"Yeah."

"And she has a lot of big brothers."

"No kidding? Large family?"

"No," I said. "Large deputies."

"Oh."

During supper, Lamar told us that we were now organized into teams, with specific objectives. Art, Hal, and myself were assigned to the Satanic group, along with Ed Yarnell, who worked day shift. Theo, Hester, and

Quint were assigned to work the general public, to gather information about associates and habits. I'd thought that had been done. Mike, Eddie, and Judd were assigned the arson, and the prevention task at Herkaman's, just in case.

The homicides themselves were assigned to a composite team composed of Hal, Hester, Theo, Art, and me. With the emphasis on Hester and Theo. Ouch. All information was to go through the county attorney or his assistant, and Lamar, of course.

In addition, Theo and Ed Yarnell were to cover the funeral of the victims, which was scheduled to take place tomorrow. They were told to take photographs of everybody they could get, both at the church and at the cemetery.

Each team would have a minimum of one member meet with Lamar and the county attorney every day, at 17:00, to report on their progress.

Lamar, who is about as nice a guy as you could find, was beginning to get a little pissed off. He wanted this case solved, and wanted it solved now. Getting it done before the media could screw it up was a pretty strong motive. So was the public feeling that the unknown killer could "strike again, anywhere, anytime," or some such bullshit as that. The public was wrong, but like they say, it's not the truth that's important, it's what's perceived as the truth.

The meeting broke about 19:15, which gave me forty-five minutes to get home, shower and shave, and get my uniform on so that I could start my eight-hour shift at 20:00.

19

When I got home, Sue was a little angry. I'd neglected to leave her a note about the meeting. Consequently, supper had turned out to be a problem. She'd taken care of it by making a taco-type soup, so it was still warm when I got there. She'd eaten.

I grabbed a bowl and sat at the dining room table with her while I ate it. I apologized for not letting her know.

She'd had a bad day, with the administration at the school playing musical chairs with special programs, trying to shift assignments and responsibilities, and trying to tell some of their better teachers how to teach. She and two other teachers from her department had been meeting at school for most of the day.

My mother had called, and was having trouble with her heart again, and had been admitted to the local hospital for observation. Damn.

Sue's brother Jack had called, too, and was coming to visit from Minnesota. Good! Jack was an attorney, and one of my favorite people. He would be in the next Saturday. I could talk the entire case over with him and he would never tell a soul. And he would offer excellent suggestions. Good deal.

I rushed through the shower and shave, and threw on my uniform. I called the office and told them that I would be up in a while, but that there was an individual at the hospital I had to talk to first. Didn't say who. It was best that way, because if they thought it was official business they would be less likely to bother me with little things until I told them I was back in service. If they knew it was Mom, on the other hand, they would feel free to call her room. I didn't want that.

Mom looked pretty pale. IVs, but no oxygen. Heart monitor going in the background. She was watching TV.

"Hi, there, kiddo," I said. "How you doin'?"

"Oh! Hello, well, you didn't have to come up."

"Just in the neighborhood. How you feeling?"

"Just fine."

"Obviously."

"Well, my heart has been doing funny things, but Henry says it's not too serious. But you know how I worry, after the heart attack."

"Yeah. You're looking pretty good."

"Oh no I'm not. My hair is a mess."

"Well, that's okay. It looks good to me, anyway."

We talked for a while. She was, of course, more worried about me and my tap on the head. I told her it was nothing, and that I was okay, and all that. She was worried about my job, and the dangers. I reassured her that there was no danger at all, and if there was, I would avoid it.

"You didn't raise any dummy, Mom."

She smiled. Obligatory. Didn't believe a word I said.

Then she asked about the case. I told her I couldn't say anything, and she said that she understood. Well, she might have understood, but she didn't like it. After all, what was the use of having a son in my line of work if he won't tell you anything?

"I can tell you that you're in no danger, unless you have a pact with the devil or something."

"Everybody's worried, you know."

"I know they are, Mom. But I don't think they have to be."

"One of them worked here, you know," she whispered.

"Well, everybody has to work someplace."

"But . . . come closer . . . maybe there are others," she hissed.

Now, here's a quandary, I thought. My mother, a heart patient, worried about Satanic nurses, with some grounds to feel that way. What can I tell her to make it all right?

I leaned back. "Don't worry. Really. I can't tell you why, but the rest of the staff here had nothing to do with it."

"Are you sure?"

"Yes. The rest of the staff here are really nice people, they really are. They were as shocked as anybody else, believe me. They had nothing to do with that business."

"Thank you," said a soft feminine voice from behind me.

I turned around. A small, dark-haired nurse, with enormous eyes, about twenty-five, was standing in the door.

"Well, uh, you're welcome."

She went to Mom and checked her pulse, asked if everything was all right. Mother, being a mother, introduced me. The nurse was named Lori Phillips, according to her tag. I didn't know her.

"You don't have to worry, Mom, until Lori here comes in a black uniform with candles in her hands."

Mom laughed. Lori didn't. It really hadn't occurred to me that the hospital would take a hit on this case, but I could tell that they had. Understandable. And in a small community, with a predominantly older population, that could be serious. Rural hospitals are always in financial trouble, anyway, and if the patients weren't comfortable, they could really get hurt.

Lori left as quietly as she came.

"I didn't see her," said Mom. "You were in the way, I guess."

"I didn't even hear her. Well, look, I have to be leaving, so take care of yourself. I'll drop up tomorrow."

"You don't have to, I know how busy you must be."

"Oh, I think I can find the time."

I kissed her on the cheek and left.

Nurse Lori collared me in the hall.

"Can I talk to you for a minute?"

"Sure."

"In here," she said, indicating a small room with a table and a couple of chairs. "I'll be with you in a minute."

It was the nurses' lounge, apparently. A sweater draped over a chair, plastic furniture, no ashtray. A coffeepot on a small stand, and a couple of travel posters on the wall. The coffeepot intrigued me. It was pretty clear that the nurses didn't like the hospital coffee, either. I made a mental note that, the next time I brought a victim in at 3:00 A.M., I'd check this place for coffee before trying the kitchen. They also had a Tupperware bucket of homemade cookies.

Lori came back with an older nurse in tow. Her I knew from a previous stay of my own. Nice, gave the impression of being very stable and levelheaded. About forty, stocky. Curly hair. Named Carrie something.

They both looked concerned and anxious. They shut the door.

"We have a little problem," said Carrie.

"What's that?"

They looked at each other. "It's about Phyllis," said Carrie.

"What about her?"

"Well, when she . . . when it all happened, we were pretty shook. Things didn't happen quite the way they were supposed to. Anyway, we remembered her locker, so, well, we decided to take the things out of it, and we thought that they should be turned over to the next of kin. It's not like we were snooping or anything . . ."

"That's fine. I'll just give you a receipt, and we'll take care of it."

"No, that's not it."

"What, then?"

They exchanged glances again.

"We found this," said Carrie, and reached under her cardigan and produced a spiral notebook. She handed it to me.

It was thin, the kind you find anywhere. Light blue cover, with the brand name on the front. And in black ink, very carefully drawn, was the word "GRYMNYAR." Below it was a star, point down, within a circle. Very finely drawn. On the lower right-hand corner was the name "Phyllis H."

I leafed through it quickly. It was a sort of a diary, with dates, events, things like that. A couple of sketches. Several pages appeared to be oaths, or something of the sort.

"I think I'd better keep this."

I went to my car and put the book in the trunk. I came back in, gave Carrie a receipt for the notebook, and obtained a written statement from both of them, detailing how it had come into their possession.

"Are we going to have to get involved in this?" asked Lori.

"You're sort of involved already. But, no, not really, I don't think. I don't know, though."

"Will we have to testify?" asked Carrie.

I grinned at her. "Not unless we solve this one."

Lori looked up at me with those enormous dark eyes. "Do you know who did it?"

"We have some idea," I said. What I didn't say was that we had it narrowed down to a human.

"I hope you get him soon."

"So do we." She looked pretty concerned. "Listen, if you're spooked or anything, just call the office. Ask for one of us to come up. If you have any cookies left, ask for me personally."

"All right."

"By the way, have you been interviewed regarding this case at all? Except now?"

"No."

"Well, I have the feeling you will be."

20

I went directly to the office, grabbed the notebook out of the trunk, and told the dispatcher that I would be a little busy for a while. I turned on the Xerox machine and put on a pot of coffee. My first task was to copy the notebook: it was going to have to go in as evidence, and I wanted to be able to read it at my leisure. I also had the feeling that, as soon as it was submitted, it would disappear into DCI and never come back.

We had a box of surgical gloves in the evidence room, to be used when dusting for prints—not so much to keep your prints off the surface being examined as to keep the damned dust off your hands. I put a pair on and Xeroxed the little notebook. There were only about fifty pages that had been used, out of about a hundred.

When I was finished, I put my copy in a manila envelope and took it out to my car. I came back in, called the motel, and asked for Hal. I told him what I had, and asked him and Hester to come to the office. He said they would.

Then I told Sally to get hold of Art on the radio and see if he could meet me at the office within an hour.

I kept my gloves on, and using a toothpick to turn the pages, I began to read the notebook. The first page was sort of a title sheet: "The Recording of the Progress of the Coven of the Dark Messiah." Oh brother. "The Second Book. The Chronicle of Our Journey to Become One with the Prince of Darkness, As Recorded by Shade, a Humble Servant of Your

Spirit. From the 11th Day of September to"—with no final date. That was understandable.

The second page listed the members of the group. Unfortunately they were listed by their coven names. They were: Darkness, Virgil, Shade, Dark Princess, Handmaiden, Soothsayer, Benefactor, Nathane, Mystic Fog, Shaman, Dusk, Mist Queen, and Dirge, in that order.

Darkness we already knew about, and since he was first, it was a confirmation that he was the high priest. Shade was pretty obviously Phyllis Herkaman. Eleven to go.

On page three, the chronicle began with the date of September 11.

"The preparations for the ultimate sacrifice continue. All will be complete by the anniversary of the birth of the ultimate fool and the great misleader. Handmaiden will provide. Darkness approaches communion. The Benefactor has achieved."

That's as far as I got when Hal, Hester, and Saperstein came in the door.

"You got something?" asked Hal.

"Oh," I said, "I believe so." I turned the book back to the title page and pushed it across the desk. "From Phyllis Herkaman's locker at the hospital."

I pulled off my gloves and lit a cigarette, while they read the first page and used my toothpick to turn to the second and third.

"We might need a translator," I said.

Saperstein looked up. "Not too hard. I would have expected it to be encoded—at least a different alphabet."

Hal indicated the first entry. "How about this?"

Saperstein looked at the page. "Okay, an ultimate sacrifice is a human sacrifice. The birthday of the ultimate fool is Christmas. Whoever Handmaiden is, is going to bring the victim. Probably use sexual favors to attract somebody and get them out to the scene of the sacrifice. Darkness is preparing himself to conduct the ritual, by meditation and secondary rituals. Benefactor has finally become a full-fledged member of the group, which means that he has participated in their final initiation ceremony. That would require, by the way, that all members be present."

He smiled at us. "Like I said, it's easy."

"Maybe for you."

Art came in. "What you got?"

I told him.

"They change shifts at the hospital at eleven?"

"I think so."

"We'd better get both those nurses," said Art, "and get an interview done tonight. At shift change."

"Good idea," said Hal.

It was 21:40. "I'll call them now," I said. "They may have to make arrangements and let their family know they'll be a little late."

I picked up the phone, then put it down. "Hey, I'll bet that the one called Benefactor is McGuire. Even money." I grinned. "Cause Helen told me so."

An aide answered at the hospital, and I asked to speak to Carrie. While I waited, Saperstein was reading another entry.

"Definitely a human sacrifice," he said to nobody in particular.

Carrie came on the line.

"Hi, Carrie, this is Carl up at the sheriff's office."

"Yes?" She sounded a little suspicious.

"Carrie, we'd like to see you tonight. After your shift is over. And Lori, too."

"Well, I don't know about Lori, but I have to be home right away tonight."

"An emergency?"

"I just have some things to do." She was using her official nurse voice, not about to brook any arguments.

"Just a second, Carrie." I put my hand over the phone. "Hey, Hal?"

"Yeah . . ."

"Our nurses are a little reluctant. Making excuses."

"We need them tonight?"

"I think so. How about you, Art?"

"Yes."

"Well," said Hal, "let me talk to her." He went to another phone. "What's her name?"

"Carrie. I already have a written statement from both of them."

"We'd better talk to 'em anyway. Hello, Carrie?"

I listened in on my phone.

"Yes?"

"This is Special Agent Hal Greeley, Iowa Division of Criminal Investigation. We have to talk to you tonight."

"That's out of the question, I'm afraid."

"I don't think you understand, Carrie. It's very important."

"I don't think you understand, Mr. Greeley," she said, and hung up.

I looked at him. "Gee, I wish I could do that."

"We've been to special classes," said Hester, grinning at her fellow agent. "Hal excelled."

"Shut up." He was visibly embarrassed.

Saperstein interrupted. "Hey, they have the first appearance of the victim on the 24th of November. She says that 'the sacrifice was revealed to us at last.' "

"Wonder who the poor bastard was?" I said to nobody in particular.

While Hal was explaining some of the details to Art, I went over to Saperstein and read along in the diary. Weird stuff.

"I can't wait," he said. "Let's look at December 25th and see if they got him."

He flipped several pages ahead. The pertinent entry was on December 26.

"Darkness has led us to the ultimate power," he read. "The power flows through us all. We are supreme. We are complete. We are accomplished. Handmaiden has given us the vessel for our advancement. She is elevated. The sacrifice is in the arms of the Master and is safe. The Nathane bites deep into the heart of the sacrifice, releasing the life force and enhancing us all."

It got pretty quiet in the office.

"No shit," murmured Hester.

"They did it," said Hal. "They really did it, didn't they, Bill? They sacrificed somebody."

"They did," said Saperstein.

"Jesus. I wonder who it was?" asked Art.

"Me too," I said.

"There's a little more here," said Saperstein. "Listen to this. 'A human essence has been given to you, O Prince, to prove to you our dedication.

You thrive. We thrive. O Prince, treasure your sacrifice, and treasure the Handmaiden who gave to you.' "

"Sounds pretty certain to me," I said.

"Me too," said Hal, "but I'm not sure it will fly with a jury, unless we have a corpse."

"Let me check with Sally, but I don't think we have any local missing persons. So it's probably somebody from out of the area."

I asked Sally to check, over the intercom.

"With the connections," said Art, "into Iowa City, you might have her check them for missing persons from there."

"Sally, check with Iowa City. Better include Johnson County, too, and see what they have for missing persons from December—and November— of last year."

"God," said Hester. "We're going to have to check missing persons reports from all over hell. Shit, shit, shit." She looked around the room. "We don't even have a description, for God's sake. We can't really check without a description, unless it turns out to be local."

Oh, yeah. That could take months and still come to nothing. But it looked like it was going to have to be done. Because we now had a fifth murder.

Entropy increases.

21

"I wonder," I said, "if we have the other diary volume."

"Pardon?" said Hal.

"The other volume. This one says 'The Second Book.' "

Saperstein flipped back to the frontispiece. "It does, doesn't it?"

"I don't know," said Hester.

"Let's check the inventory," said Art. "From the search warrant at Herkaman's."

"McGuire too," I said. "There was a lot of stuff in his little basement grotto."

The inventory from the search warrant at Herkaman's place was sixteen pages long. The one from McGuire was eight. Hester's handwriting, small, precise.

On the Herkaman sheet was the entry: "Exhibit AQ 1–7, seven assorted notebooks, four spiral, three loose-leaf, from bedroom closet."

On the McGuire sheet: "Exhibit AB, one notebook, from basement, small room."

One problem. The evidence had been taken by the lab team for processing. All the evidence was at the DCI lab in Des Moines. A mere two hundred miles.

"I'll get them to look first thing in the morning," said Hester, "and if there's anything there they'll copy it and relay it up."

A relay would be from cop car to cop car. It would require a lot of gas, but it was a hell of a lot quicker than the post office.

Saperstein spoke up, from the depths of the notebook. "These people have a goal here, but I don't know what it is."

"What do you mean, a goal?"

"They're planning something, or, at least, they were. She refers to their 'ultimate objective' at least twice, once before the sacrifice, once after."

"I wonder what the ultimate objective would be for a Satanist?" I was just thinking out loud.

"I don't think I want to know," said Art. "We have enough trouble here without that."

The intercom buzzed, and I picked it up. It was Sally.

"We don't have any missing persons at all, Carl."

"Good."

"Johnson County had fifty-three from November 15th to now, forty-two of which have been located."

"Leaving eleven . . ."

"You must have majored in math . . ."

"Yeah . . . Look, are they sending you the info on them?"

"They say they'll mail it, unless we need it in a hurry."

"Just a minute . . . Hal, we have eleven missing persons unaccounted for in Johnson County from the 15th of November to date. They say they'll mail the info, unless we need it right away."

"Have 'em teletype it now."

"Okay . . . Sally, tell 'em we need it now."

"Wonderful," she said. "They're gonna hate me."

"Tell 'em it's for a homicide investigation, and that the request is from SA Greeley, DCI."

"Will do. I hope they're not busy tonight."

"Now that we got some dates here," said Hal, "I really want to talk to those nurses tonight." He made a fist, put it up by his ear, and moved it in an arc toward the desk, snapping his fingers. "We're on a roll."

"We can get 'em if you need 'em," I said. "Material witnesses."

In Iowa, we can arrest and hold a material witness for forty-eight hours. Not done often. In fifteen years, I'd only done it once before. Really aggravated the witness, and he'd started a civil damage suit against the department and me. Didn't get too far, but it wasn't the sort of thing you took lightly.

"Let's see their statements first," said Art.

I opened my case folder and handed them to him. I leafed through my notepad, intending to write some of the night's events down, with dates referred to in the notebook from Phyllis. I was flipping through the pages when I saw 'November 24th,' underlined. From the interview Hester and I had done with Helen Bockman. It was the date Rachel Larsen had had her baby.

I just sat there for a second, stunned.

Art turned toward me and did a double take. "You all right?"

"Fine. But it was Rachel's baby."

"What?"

"The sacrifice—it was Rachel's baby."

It had already clicked with Hester. "My God . . . you're right."

"What do you mean?" asked Art.

"Helen Bockman told us that Rachel had a baby. Looked it up on her calendar, and it was November 24th when she was born."

"Let's have that part about the victim's arrival again, Bill," he said to Saperstein.

He didn't even have to look it up. "The sacrifice was revealed to us at last."

"On November 24th?"

"Yeah, first mentioned on the 24th."

"And then, later, about how they got it?"

"Just a minute." He turned some pages. "Okay, 'Handmaiden has given us a vessel.'" Saperstein shook his head. "It fits. It fits. Especially if Rachel was Handmaiden."

"And they killed her baby."

"Sure sounds that way," he said. "Satanists have been reported to have done just this sort of thing in the past. We had a couple of instances where it was alleged, but never proved."

"Why not?" asked Hal.

"No corpse. They say that they either scatter them or in some instances eat them." He shook his head. "Don't know if the cannibalism bit is true or not. But we've never come up with a body."

"Jesus."

"And if they're born at home, without a doctor in attendance, there's no record of the birth. No record needed of the death, either. Just like they never existed."

"How the hell could the mother put up with that sort of shit?" asked Art.

Saperstein just shrugged. "You have to know them, I guess. The cult is everything. It probably ain't easy or anything. But they do it. They do it."

I shook my head. "We should have guessed as soon as Helen said she was worried about the baby."

Hester leaned her back against the wall. "Maybe you did, sort of." She crossed her arms over her chest and looked toward the ceiling. "Just didn't want to believe it." She shook her head. "You didn't have a lot of evidence, either. Not then."

Nobody said anything for a second.

"Actually," she said, "we don't have a lot now."

"Not a lot," I agreed. "But enough to convince me."

"Yeah, me too." She arched her back, bringing herself upright again. "Let's get those nurses. And see what else they found in the locker, among other things."

"Don't let 'em hang up on ya," said Hal with a small grin.

Hal called Lamar and told him we had to talk to the nurses even if we had to arrest them. And tonight. Lamar reluctantly agreed.

Art called the county attorney at the same time and told Fueller what we were going to do. It was okay with him, too, until Art gave him Carrie's name. Her husband was the son of a very wealthy farmer, and Fueller was the dad's attorney. He started to waffle. Art got pissed—well, just extra firm, I guess. Fueller told him to call Hamilton, the assistant CA. If Hamilton agreed, it was okay with Fueller. But he didn't want any complications.

Hamilton agreed.

Art, Hester, and I hit the hospital about 22:45. We hung around in the lobby, getting stared at by the staff, for a few minutes. At one point I saw Lori looking around the partition of the nurse's station at us. She saw me and ducked back.

We didn't want to interfere with shift change. We also decided to use persuasion, and to arrest only as a last resort.

The four second-shift nurses were being replaced by three third-shift, and Sylvia Sukow, chief of nursing, happened to be pulling a night shift for an absent nurse. Sylvia, who Art and I had known for a long time, approached us.

"Can I ask you people what is going on?"

"Sure, Sylvia, we're here to talk to Lori and Carrie."

"You're disrupting my nurses. You're making them very nervous."

"Well, we're sorry about that. We just have to talk to them tonight, and didn't want to interrupt anything until the shift had changed."

"I appreciate that, Art. But I'll have to ask you to wait in the staff conference room. We have to have a little meeting of our own, to discuss a patient problem. They'll be available in a few minutes."

Nurses. "Okay," said Hester. But tell them not to 'forget.' " She showed her badge. "Division of Criminal Investigation. I'm very serious about this. If there's any chance of them 'forgetting,' you could be in some serious trouble yourself."

Sylvia's eyes got a little wider than usual. She was almost six feet tall, graying hair. She put her hands on her hips and stared down at Hester.

"My nurses don't forget, lady."

She turned on her heel and walked back to the nurse's station.

"We're supposed to wait in here," said Art, indicating a room off the lobby.

They kept us waiting for about ten minutes. Then the door opened, and Carrie, Lori, and Sylvia came in. Sylvia took the offensive right away.

"My nurses will talk to you, but I will be present. This is a hospital, and I will know everything that is going on. Do you have any criminal charges against them?"

Now, we'd been getting off on the wrong foot ever since I had talked to Carrie on the phone. It was going downhill fast.

"Just a sec," I said. "Hester, look, if it's okay with you, I'd like to talk to Sylvia for a moment. In private. I'll have to reveal a little, but I think it's warranted in this case."

She thought about it. She looked at the three nurses. Sylvia was becoming hostile. Carrie was actively hostile, and resentful. Lori looked a little concerned. We were going to get nowhere, at this rate.

"Okay, but keep it brief."

"Right. Sylvia, could we talk in your office for a second?"

She wavered. I believe she thought I was trying to get her out of the way so that Hester and Art could talk to her two nurses without her.

"For a second, Carl."

We walked down the hall and into her little office. Desk, desk chair, and one hard-backed office chair. I leaned my backside against her desk and crossed my arms. "Close the door, would you?"

She did, but reluctantly.

"Okay, Sylvia. This is about Phyllis Herkaman. You know that. And about some stuff that they found in her locker. You know that, too, don't you?"

"Yes."

"We have to have their cooperation, and we're going about it in the wrong way. I know that. But we need them tonight, and maybe you, too. And if they refuse to cooperate, they are going to be arrested."

"For what?"

"Not for anything. As material witnesses."

"I don't understand, Carl. Phyllis was a damned *victim*. She didn't *do* anything!"

"Not so. Not quite the case, Sylvia."

I looked around for an ashtray. No luck. "Listen, Sylvia, what I'm going to tell you is not to be told to anybody, under any circumstance. Fair?"

"Sure."

"The only people who know what I'm going to tell you are the three of us, and a New York PD detective."

"New York?"

"Right. And now there's going to be you. But I think you have to know."

"So?"

"So, do you remember that girl that used to hang around with Phyllis? Rachel Larsen?"

"I know of her, yes."

"You know that Phyllis was into Satanism?"

"I don't know that. There've been rumors, that's all."

"Not rumors. Okay?"

She nodded.

"Did Phyllis ever mention to you that Rachel was pregnant?"

"No."

"Well, she was, and she delivered in November. She was a Satanist, too. Fact, not rumor."

"All right. So?"

"We have reason to believe that the baby was sacrificed on Christmas Eve."

Sylvia stared at me for a few seconds. "You're crazy," she whispered.

" 'Fraid not."

"You're crazy," she said again, and shook her head. "No."

"Yes."

"How do you know?"

"It was in the book that your nurses found in her locker."

"They didn't say anything about that . . ."

"You really can't pick it up by just reading it through. That's what the New York detective is doing here. He's an expert on this. We read it tonight. He picked up on the sacrifice right away. Just didn't know who. Then we read the entry about the sacrificial victim making its appearance on the 24th of November. Rachel's baby was born at Phyllis's house on November 24th."

"No."

"Yes. And the code name they used to refer to Rachel was the one who presented the victim to them. I'm afraid it all adds up."

"Oh, God."

"And we think it's linked to the four murders that happened Friday night."

Silence.

"Now do you see why we've been acting a little heavy in this?"

She nodded.

"So, if you can give us a little support in this, we'd really appreciate it. Believe me."

"Yes."

"Good. Let's go on back to the conference room."

"I'll have to tell Dr. Zimmer."

"You're right, but let's clear that with the DCI later, okay? I think he's going to have to know, too, but just don't bring it up right away, all right?"

"All right."

We rejoined the group in the conference room. Carrie was still hedging, apparently.

"Carrie," said Sylvia, "could I speak with you for a moment?"

She took her out in the hall for what seemed to be a second or two. Carrie came back in alone. She walked directly to the conference table, sat down, and said, "What do you need from me?"

I never did find out what Sylvia said.

We began to question both nurses about Phyllis's behavior over the last few months. With the way the rotation system worked among the nurses, there was really no specific group who worked together on a particular shift. But Carrie and Lori seemed to have worked with Phyllis as often as anyone.

They both thought that Phyllis was a loner, but we already knew that. Carrie thought she was frequently abrupt with patients, especially the older ones who made up the majority of the patient population. Lori said that Phyllis would advise her about her love life, and it was always the same: don't commit yourself, try different things first. There was nothing wrong with sleeping around, so go for it.

Given what we knew about Phyllis, and the attractiveness of Lori, we were obviously interpreting things a little differently than she was. It looked like Phyllis had been subtly hitting on Lori for several months, but that the connection never occurred to her. Just as well.

Both women had noticed that Phyllis had perked up around Christmastime. Seemed to be more self-possessed, as it were—more content and self-assured than ever.

One thing of significance, and that came late in the interview. Phyllis had been picked up by a friend, after work, on several occasions in December and January. Because her car didn't work, she said. The friend was Elizabeth Mills, and Lori remembered that Phyllis had referred to her as Dusky, twice.

"I remember her saying, one time, something about 'You should try a

dusky brunette, instead of those blond Swedes you always go out with."
She blushed.

We were all scribbling furiously when Sylvia came back into the room,
carrying a brown grocery sack.

"These things," she said, "are all that Phyllis had in her locker. I
thought you might want to look at them."

"Thank you," said Hester.

"And could I talk to one of you for a moment?"

"Sure," I said. I thought we'd just go out in the hall, but she took
me to her little office again. This time she shut the door without being
asked.

She opened a grocery sack. There was something wrapped in a small
towel. She laid it on her desk and unwrapped it.

"What's that?"

"It's a bulb syringe. We do equipment inventories frequently, you
know. I did one on October 22nd, a Sunday. The next time was on November 26th. We were missing several incidental items, nothing to
speak of."

"Like what?"

"Like several hemostats, a box of surgical gloves, sterile tape and
sponges . . . and a bulb syringe."

"Like this one?"

"Yes."

"And you found this in her locker?"

"Yes."

"What would she want with that?"

"Carl, if I was going to deliver a baby, not here, those are the items I
would want to have."

She emptied the rest of the sack, displaying the contents on the
desktop. A bottle of perfume, a pair of nurse's shoes, a white cardigan
sweater, two lipstick tubes, three tampons, a small pack of Kleenex, and
three pencils. And a stethoscope.

I gave her a receipt, and we went back to the conference room.

I took Hester aside and told her what Sylvia had told me. She seemed
pleased. I did the same with Art.

The interviews were pretty well complete. It was after midnight.

"I'd like to thank both of you," said Hester. "We really appreciate your cooperation."

Sounded a little flat, considering. But what the hell, I thought, DCI doesn't get along with nurses, anyway.

22

We were back in the office, slowly tearing our hair out. We had a lot. We had nothing. We had a lot of work to do. Sally had been relieved by Deb Finney at the radio, and had volunteered to stick around and help. She'd already made coffee once that night, so Art and I tossed for who would make the second pot. I lost.

We had Sally in the kitchen, typing the contents of Phyllis Herkaman's book. We'd decided to look up Elizabeth Mills and her husband, and we wanted some dates and events concerning them to look over first. Helen had said Elizabeth Mills was Dusk. The way that the entries read so far in the little diary, her name was always preceded by that of "Shaman." She was never mentioned without him being mentioned first, and never appeared in the diary alone. Neither did Shaman. Yet there were several entries when they weren't mentioned at all. The inference was that Shaman was her husband, Kenneth. At least, that's what we were going to go with.

"How's it coming, Sally?"

"Not bad . . . almost done, I think."

"You make much sense out of it?"

"A little, I'm afraid."

I made the coffee, not wanting to slow her up. She should be getting paid overtime for this, but there was no guarantee of that, as this wasn't "dispatching." I didn't want her to spend any more of her time on this than was absolutely necessary.

Hal and Hester had called their boss in Des Moines and explained to him that we thought we had another murder, one predating the quadruple one, and possibly related, in a rather obscure way. Their boss was not pleased.

Art and I had talked to Lamar and told him what we thought we'd do. He hadn't been too happy, either, but could certainly understand the reasoning.

When we'd first got back to the office, we'd had a little discussion, which was summed up best by Hal.

"All we're doin' in this case is reacting. We ain't initiating anything at all. We gotta take the initiative!"

He was right, of course. But, so far, we hadn't had the information to really get going. Now, especially with the probable identifying of Dusk and the tentative ID of Shaman, we had something to at least begin with.

There was a further complication: too many people were getting involved, and the possibility of leaks and flight of witnesses was getting greater. The possiblility of somebody getting ahold of Darkness was also greater every minute. We didn't want that to happen.

We had called Mark Fueller, the county attorney, again, this time asking if he thought we had enough evidence to get a warrant for the arrest of Elizabeth Mills. We wanted a warrant before we went to the house. It gave us a lot more leeway with a search.

Fueller didn't think we had enough. We thought we did. He thought we could interview her in the morning, and if we got an admission from her, then either arrest her or go get the warrant then. He wasn't a bad county attorney, but he was a pretty lousy cop.

We finally got him to go along with it, as we explained that we had to take a chance, because we felt that otherwise we'd blow the case. He thought we were blowing the case, anyway, but, being sleepy, he was pressurable. That had been the information we called Lamar with. We didn't go into the details of the county attorney's discomfort, of course.

We'd pulled Mike in off the road, to accompany Hal and Hester to the magistrate's house. We'd had to wake him up, too, to get the warrant.

We weren't too popular that night, and we all had the nagging feeling that we'd better come across with something, or we'd never hear the end of it.

When Hester, Hal, and Mike returned, they said that the magistrate, it turned out, was more than happy to issue an arrest warrant for Elizabeth Mills. The charge: murder in the first degree. All diary indications were that Dusk had been present at the so-called sacrifice of the baby. So had Shaman.

Sally came back to the main office, with her typed pages and the original. Copies were Xeroxed, and we all got one.

Since we were going to arrest a female, I made a suggestion.

"Hey, as long as Sally's here, and in uniform, don't you think we ought to have a matron along?"

"Absolutely," said Hester.

There wasn't a female officer in the county. Furthermore, if we used Sally as a matron, she would be paid. And paid from the time she got off her regular shift. Which meant that she'd be assured of getting paid for her typing.

"Okay," Art sighed. Dispatcher's base rates went up when they did matron duty.

I had another idea. "Sally, raise your right hand and repeat after me."

She did.

"Do you solemnly swear to uphold the laws of the State of Iowa?"

"I do."

"With particular reference to Chapter 692, regarding Criminal History and Law Enforcement Intelligence Data?"

"I do."

"Good. You are now deputized for the duration."

"Was that really necessary?" asked Art.

"You betcha. If we get an interview, we have to have a matron present. And if we get an interview, I don't want any unsworn personnel present."

"Good point."

"Okay," I said. "Sally, do you know Elizabeth Mills?"

"Sure." She looked a little startled. "Runs the In Between dress shop downtown."

"What's she look like?"

"Oh, about thirty or so. Taller than me, dark hair."

"Everybody's taller than you."

Sally was exactly five feet.

"Yeah, yeah," she said. "Well, she's about five inches taller than me."

"How about her husband?" asked Hester.

"Oh," said Sally, "he's about five eight or so, about 150, I guess. I can get his DL for you . . . blond hair, I know that."

"I know him," said Art. "He runs an accounting business, does taxes, things like that."

"Oh, yeah," I said. "The gray Dodge four-door that's always parked in front of the pharmacy."

"Yeah. They live in one of the apartments upstairs."

"Originally from Cedar Rapids, isn't he?" asked Mike.

"Yeah," said Art. "Down there somewhere. Moved here about four years ago, I think."

The next question was a tough one.

"Do we need," asked Mike, "a Maitland officer with us on this one?"

Professional courtesy dictated that we at least inform Maitland PD and ask them to accompany us. Discretion indicated that we not do that.

"No," said Art.

"No," said Hal.

"No," I chimed in.

"No," said Hester.

"No," said Sally.

We all looked at her.

"Hey, I'm sworn."

Mike grinned broadly. "Well, I guess that settles that."

It was decided to take one marked car, Mike's, which would contain Mike, me, and Sally, the three uniformed personnel present. One unmarked, Art's. With him, Hal, and Hester. We would transport Elizabeth Mills in the marked car. If we arrested Kenneth Mills, he would go in the unmarked. If he was violent, we would summon the Maitland PD car.

Art picked up the phone and called dispatch on the comm line.

"Deb, look, all of us are going to be busy in downtown Maitland for a little while. Very 10–6. No radio traffic, but we will have a portable or two, if you absolutely need to contact us."

He paused. "Yes, her too." Another pause. "No, no traffic. And nobody is to know where we are, so if Maitland asks, just say you will contact one of us. Got that? Good."

He stood up. "Let's go."

It was about seven blocks to the pharmacy. Sally, who was in the backseat of our car, stuck her head through the plastic security screen and asked me what we were going to do.

"Arrest Elizabeth Mills. And, possibly, Kenneth too."

"I know that," she said petulantly. "What for?"

"Murder."

She withdrew her head into the backseat.

We parked in the alley behind the pharmacy, while the unmarked pulled up in one of the designated parking stalls in front. Mike and I got out, and I opened the back door for Sally. There are no inside door handles on the back doors.

Mike stayed in the alley to secure the back of the building. I went up the front stairs with Art, followed by the two DCI agents and then Sally. There were two doors at the top, of course. But we got lucky. The one on the left had a wooden plaque hanging on the front that announced to the world, "Mills Mill." Cute.

I knocked on the door. No answer. I knocked again, louder. No answer. I knocked the third time, really hard. Knocked the plaque off, which fell onto the wooden landing with a loud clatter. Then we could hear footsteps stumbling around inside the apartment.

"What!" came from inside. Male voice.

"Open the door, police!"

At that point, the door on the right flew open, and a man in a T-shirt and boxer shorts emerged. It was pretty dark, and the first person he saw was Art. Who was not in uniform.

"What the fuck do you want, asshole?" he said to Art.

I emerged from the shadow by the Mills door. I had my gun drawn, per department procedure when effecting a felony arrest. I was holding it pointing upward, about shoulder level.

"Get back in your apartment, buddy. *Now!*"

He slammed the door.

The little distraction had caused us to lose track of the noises in the Mills apartment. I listened . . . nothing.

I knocked once more.

"Open the door, police!"

There was a muffled *thunk* as a bolt slammed home in the door frame. Great.

I looked at Art. "Shall I?"

"Go for it." He drew his gun.

One kick. That's all it took. Old door. The door slammed open, and whitish fragments from the frame flew into the room. Art's flashlight beamed past me, and I could see a man turning around in the living room, holding something in his hand.

"Freeze! Police." God, I love to do that.

He froze. He appeared to have a cardboard tube in his right hand. He was wearing tiger-striped jockey shorts.

Art flew by me, further into the apartment. A woman screamed, "Don't shoot him!" and Art yelled, "Freeze!"

I couldn't see her, but her voice had come from what appeared to be the bedroom.

Hal flew by as I was pushing the male subject against the wall, and headed for the bedroom. Hester cuffed my man, while I held him at gunpoint.

As soon as the cuffs were on, I heard Art's voice.

"She's secure."

I turned toward the door and could see Sally's head peering around the corner.

"Hey, Sally? Wanna see if you can find the light switch?"

A second later, the overhead light came on.

"Are you Kenneth Mills?" I asked my prisoner.

"Yes."

Whew. I mean, it's always nice to know you're at the right place.

Art and Hal came around the corner, accompanied by a woman I prayed was Elizabeth Mills. She was wearing a red and white T-shirt, with the slogan "Best Head" in yellow letters. Probably not referring to her intellect. She was cuffed in front. She looked sleepy, and pissed off.

Art had a small, transparent sealable bag in his hand, with some white powdery stuff in it. He held it up for me to see and grinned all over himself.

"Look what she was trying to hide," he said.

"What is it?"

"Crystal."

Methamphetamine. Good deal.

"Is this Elizabeth Mills?" I asked of nobody in particular.

"You bet your ass, stupid," said Elizabeth Mills. "You better have a fuckin' warrant!"

"As a matter of fact," I said, "we do." I pulled it from my hip pocket. "Elizabeth Mills, I have here a warrant for your arrest on a charge of Murder in the First Degree, pursuant to Chapter 707 of the Code of Iowa. You have the right to remain silent, anything you say can and will be used against you in a criminal prosecution, you have the right to have an attorney present during questioning, if you cannot afford an attorney, one will be provided for you by the court. Do you understand those rights?"

Silence.

"With those rights in mind, do you wish to give us a statement at this time?"

"Yeah, asshole. Fuck off!"

"Thanks, ma'am." I smiled down at her. "I, too, find courtesy always helps in a tight situation."

"Piss off." Sullen. Good. She would be talking in a few minutes.

By this time, Kenneth Mills was getting his act more or less together and had taken a cue from his wife. He also was getting a little braver, because his name hadn't been on the warrant.

"Get your fucking hands off my wife!" He seemed proud of himself.

"Shut up," said Hester.

"I said, get your fucking hands off my wife!"

Hester leaned close to him and said in a soft voice, "What's the matter, can't Dusk take care of herself?"

"Better than you can, bitch! But she's my wife, and you can't treat her like that!"

Dusk, huh? Now, that's the sort of thing a defense attorney will try to have thrown out, because his client just made an idiot of himself, and they don't like that. Trickery, you know. My client couldn't be that dumb unless you helped him, you bad people. That kind of thing.

The newly revealed Dusk just about took his head off with a shriek. "Stupidfucker!"

"What?" He still hadn't realized what he'd said.

"Now, honey," said Hal in a sweet voice. "I can't have you talking to Shaman like that."

Startled silence. She, at least, was smart enough not to take the bait. But that was okay. Now they knew. Let them think about it.

"Okay," said Hal, inordinately pleased with himself. "Let's get organized. Call Mike, have him come up and secure the apartment. Get Maitland PD in here for that, too. Let's get these people to the office, and Art and I will get a search warrant based on the dope, and we'll come back and search the place." He turned to Kenneth Mills. "By the way, you're under arrest for possession of a Schedule One controlled substance." He advised him of his rights.

When he was done, he turned to Elizabeth. "You, too, sweetie. You've already had your rights."

She said nothing.

"Okay," said Art. "Let's get 'em to the SO."

We headed out as Mike came in the door. Art and Hal took Kenneth downstairs, after allowing him to put on a pair of blue jeans and tennis shoes and throwing a jacket over his shoulders.

Sally had to go to the bedroom with Elizabeth so she could put on her jeans in privacy. I was just around the door frame.

There was a muffled thud, and Sally hollered "Carl!"

I was in the door in an instant and saw Sally bouncing on the bed, with Elizabeth just starting to swing both fists at her. Sally caught the blow with her hands as I grabbed Elizabeth by the hair and jerked her head back. Hard.

"That's an assault charge, sweetheart."

She tried to spit at me but missed. Bad angle. Pissed me off.

I pulled on her hair slowly but hard. Lifted her up on her tiptoes. I half whispered, "I'm gonna tear off your head if you ever do that again."

I let her down and looked at Sally. "You all right?"

"Yes." She sounded a little pissed herself.

"What happened?"

"I leaned over to help her get her shoes, and she kicked me." She sounded thoroughly disgusted.

"Where?"

"Never mind where!"

"Okay." I turned to go, taking Elizabeth with me. No shoes. I turned to ask Sally to pick them up for me and saw her rubbing her backside.

She saw that I saw, and turned red.

"Have to get you a Kevlar billfold," I said.

Dirty look. I chuckled.

"What's so fuckin' funny, pig?" said Elizabeth Mills.

Back to business. "Just thinking of how long you're gonna be away, ma'am." I sort of lifted her by her arm and propelled her toward the door. I was getting a little tired of Elizabeth.

23

Back at the office, we started the booking procedures on both prisoners. Sally and I did Elizabeth, and we called Quint in off the road to book Kenneth.

When it came time to change Elizabeth's clothes from her blue jeans and statement shirt to an orange jail uniform, I was having second thoughts about sending Sally into the changing room with her. I needn't have worried. Sally wasn't about to put up with any more nonsense from Elizabeth. I left the door open, just in case. Sally was the only one I could see. She was standing with her hands on her hips, slowly raising and lowering herself on the balls of her feet.

Elizabeth came out in her orange uniform, glancing occasionally at Sally.

"Sit down, Elizabeth," said Sally. "Right there," pointing to the chair across the desk from me.

"I want to talk to my attorney."

"Fine," I said, "just give me his name and number, and we'll call him."

"I ain't giving you shit, buddy."

"Then you ain't talking to your attorney. We need his name and number. That's all."

"Screw you."

I pulled a three-page form out of a folder.

"Okay, Elizabeth, this is a booking form that we're gonna attempt to fill out. I'm going to ask you several questions, such as your date of birth . . ."

"I'm not answering anything until I talk to my attorney."

"Well, Elizabeth, all you have to do is give me a name and we'll call. You can do all the talking."

She thought for a second.

"All right. My attorney is Oswald Traer, lives in Cedar Rapids. I don't have his number."

We looked it up and placed the call.

"Oswald, this is Elizabeth. I've been arrested for murder! . . . Yeah, okay . . . No, I didn't do it . . . How could I kill four people? . . . I don't know, the bastards kicked in our door while we were asleep . . . Yeah . . . Yeah, the cop shop here in Maitland . . . Well, they got some stuff in a bag they think is dope . . . Can you come up—just a minute . . ."

She looked at me. "Am I being charged with anything else?"

"Other than what?"

"Murder, you bag of shit."

"Yep. Possession of a Schedule One controlled substance, and assault."

"Assault!"

"You assaulted a matron."

"Shit!"

She went back to the phone. "Oh, they're charging for dope and assault . . . No, I didn't . . . I don't know, just a minute . . ."

Back to me. "What's my bond?"

"Two hundred fifty thousand dollars. Cash only."

She sneered.

Back to Oswald. "Son of a bitch, it's two hundred fifty thousand, and cash only. Can you believe that shit? . . . Yeah, they want to talk to me . . . No, I won't . . . No . . . Sure, just a second."

"He wants to talk to you." She handed me the phone.

"Deputy Houseman."

"Yes, Deputy," said a suave, self-possessed voice. "My client has told me what she is charged with, and the bond. I've instructed her to say nothing to anyone until I can get there. I'm sure you understand."

"Yes."

"You are insisting on cash?"

"Policy, set by the court."

"I see. Tell me, Officer, if you can, just why she is being charged with murder?"

"Apparently there is sufficient evidence."

"I see. Can you tell me the name of the victim?"

"As a matter of fact, I can't. I don't believe the name of a victim is specified on the warrant." The truth.

"One count?"

"That's what it says here."

"Thank you, Officer. Now, if you could, is Mr. Mills in custody at this time?"

"Yes, he is."

"I see. Is he charged with murder, too?"

"Not that I'm aware of."

"Just the narcotics possession charge, is that right?"

"To the best of my knowledge."

"Thank you. Would you let me talk to Mrs. Mills again, please?"

"Before I do, would you please tell her to cooperate in filling out the booking form? The boss really wants those filled out."

"Of course."

I handed the phone back to Elizabeth.

We finished booking the two of them shortly after Art, Hester, and Hal came back in, having obtained their search warrant from the now sleepless magistrate. So far so good. I told them that good old Elizabeth's attorney would be up in about an hour. We decided that Hal, Hester, and Art would execute the warrant, while I and Sally and Mike stayed at the jail to handle the prisoners and their attorney.

The hour and a half that it actually took for Attorney Traer to get to Maitland from Cedar Rapids was a tense time. I was really beginning to worry.

It all hinged on the arrest warrant for Elizabeth Mills. Everything. The dope, her Dusk alias, anything that was found in the apartment . . . it could all be lost if, upon review, the district court found that we didn't have probable cause for her arrest in the first place. And that was looking a little shaky.

We had her ID'd as Dusk, secondhand, by Lori the nurse. Same for the connection between her and Phyllis Herkaman. We also had her ID'd as Dusk by Helen Bockman, but her testimony was possibly questionable. Not in content, but in getting her to repeat anything to a judge. Okay, though. We did have our notes.

Dusk being present at the homicide of the child was substantiated by the book Phyllis kept. If a judge would buy that. And it would have to be done without the presence of Saperstein, who would probably be back in New York by that time. An affidavit might not do it.

We needed a corpse. Kinda hard to prove that a murder happened without one. And even if we found the body of a dead baby in the Mills apartment, it would be discovered as a consequence of the arrest warrant, and couldn't be used to reinforce the grounds for the warrant.

Not that we expected to find the body, of course. The Mills apartment or anywhere else.

Well, we knew we were taking a chance on the arrest. Calculated risk.

And for all that trouble, we would solve one homicide. Maybe. And not even directly related to the four murders we needed to solve.

Oswald Traer arrived at our office at 04:09, and was logged in.

He was about six feet tall, dark hair, about forty-five, and looked like he'd just stepped out of *People* magazine. He was obviously in a casual mode, considering the hour and all. Gray slacks, blue sweater vest, white shirt with blue pinstripe. Navy pea coat. No hat. A briefcase that probably cost more than my home office.

We introduced ourselves, and he shook hands with all of us, including Sally.

"I appreciate being notified, Deputy," he said to me.

"No trouble."

"I really am concerned for my clients. I have dealt with them before, regarding investments. I trust them, and they assuredly aren't the type of people to murder anyone."

"Well, you know, Mr. Traer, nobody ever is."

"I would like to know more details, if you would, before I speak with my clients."

"Certainly," I said. "Mike, would you call Art and see if one of them could come up here and brief Mr. Traer?"

"Sure." He picked up the phone.

"Could I get you a cup of coffee?" asked Sally.

"Yes, please."

As she opened the second door to the kitchen, behind Traer, I could see Saperstein sitting at the table with several notebooks spread out around him. Good. If he was here for the interviews, if there were any, we were in good shape.

Mike hung up the phone. "Hester is coming right up."

"May I ask," said Traer, "who this Hester is?"

"Sure. Hester Gorse, DCI."

"She is, then, the officer who orchestrated this arrest?"

Wow. "Orchestrated." This guy was going to be aggravating. Just what he wanted, because he made you want to take the wind out of his sails. To do that, you would be tempted to reveal some things that you shouldn't. He was good.

" 'Orchestrated' may be a little off the mark," I said. "Maybe 'scored' would fit a little better."

Traer looked me up and down. Noting all the details of my uniform. No tie. Long-sleeved shirt, sleeves rolled up. Light tan splatters from the alley on my black shoes.

"Ms. Gorse must be quite the detective."

The temptation to go into an "Aw, shucks, Mr. Lawyer" routine was almost overwhelming. I resisted. I think.

"She's pretty good."

Sally came back in with the coffee. She offered one to Traer, and he thanked her. I got mine, and she had one for Mike, too. As well as herself. Traer looked at his cup.

"Interesting cup," he said.

We scam coffee cups from wherever we can get them, and they usually contain advertising. His said "Sherman Hog Flooring" in orange and brown letters on a white background on a yellow cup.

"Thank you," said Sally sweetly. With that, she picked up her cup, placed it to her lips, and looked charmingly at Traer. Her cup was blue, and said, in white letters, "I'm Bad With Names, Can I Call You Shithead?"

The electric lock at the main entrance buzzed, and Hester walked in.

"Hi," she said. "You must be the Mills attorney," and stuck out her hand. Traer shook it.

"Yes, I am, Oswald Traer."

"Pleased to meet you," said Hester. She did look pleased, too. Very pleased, in fact. "I'm Special Agent Gorse, DCI."

"I am given to understand that you're the case officer in this matter?"

"One of the case officers. I am the senior DCI agent present."

"I see," said Traer. "But you would have information concerning the arrest of my client?"

"Oh, I sure do," said Hester.

"Well, then," said Traer, "why don't we take it from the bottom up? In the first place, who is she supposed to have assaulted?"

"Her," said Hester, indicating Sally.

"Oh, my," said Traer. "I hope that isn't true." He looked Sally over pretty closely. "I must say that if it is true, you certainly don't appear to have suffered at all . . ."

Sally smiled, and lifted her cup again.

"As for the second charge," said Traer, ignoring Sally, "I am given to understand that there is an allegation concerning the possession of narcotics?"

"Right," said Hester.

"What sort of narcotics were my clients supposed to have?"

"Crystallized methamphetamine. They usually call it crystal, sometimes crank, sometimes other things."

"And where was this found?"

"In Elizabeth's hand." Hester made no effort to hide her grin.

"I see."

"We're executing a search warrant of their premises right now," said Hester. "That's where I came from. We also found nearly a hundred hits of LSD—microdots."

Traer looked from Hal to me and back to Hal. "An additional count, then, I suppose?"

"Yep."

Traer smiled at Hal. "Well, now that we have addressed the human failings of my client, I would like to know how you can accuse her of complicity in a multiple homicide."

"Multiple homicide?" asked Hester.

"Come now," said Traer. "I read the papers, Miss Gorse. You just had a multiple homicide in this county—four victims, I believe."

"Yes," said Hester, "we did. And I prefer 'Ms.' "

"Certainly. And you actually believe my client was involved?"

"No, I don't think she was involved at all," said Hester. "Do you, Carl?"

"No," I said, "never occurred to me."

Traer, who knew he was being played with, and was getting a little exasperated himself, sighed and said, "Then would you mind telling me why you broke into my client's apartment and arrested her for murder?"

"Sure," said Hester, and grew very serious. "Because she was an active participant in a ritual homicide of a thirty-day-old infant named Cynthia Larsen."

Traer visibly paled, and shook his head. He almost said something, caught himself, and then he smiled.

"And while I'm at it, Oswald Traer," said Hester, "I am now placing you under arrest for the same murder.

"Carl," said Hester, "I'd like you to meet Darkness."

24

I doubt if anybody on earth could have been more taken aback than Oswald Tracr at that moment, but Mike and Sally and I came pretty close.

He refused to say a word. Nothing. He was booked very quickly by Mike and me, while Hester typed out a quick complaint and affidavit.

He did, however, want to make a phone call to his residence, to speak with his wife.

That was allowable. He simply told her that he'd been arrested and gave her the details of the charge. Said that he'd be away for a while, but should be able to post any bond that was set. To expect to see him later on in the day. Pretty wishful thinking, especially for a lawyer.

He went into his cell quietly. Unfortunately I slammed the door a little hard and must have awakened Kenneth Mills. As I was leaving the cell-block, I could hear Mills say, "What the fuck!"

Hester met me at the end of the hallway.

"Was that Mills I just heard?"

"That was him."

"Well, hell, as long as he's up, get him out. We've got to arrest him for murder, too."

I did.

Mills was a little vociferous at first, but became progressively more quiet as the basic details of the crime were laid out for him.

That done, Hester called the Mills residence and asked Art and Hal if they were about done. Apparently they were, and she told them to come on up.

She finally told me what had happened.

"We found a roster of the members of the 'Coven of the Dark Messiah,'" she said. "Names, cult names, addresses, phone numbers . . . the whole nine yards."

"No shit?"

"No shit . . . and a lot of other stuff, too."

"All right!"

She pulled a slip of paper out of her slacks pocket. "I got ahold of the State Patrol lieutenant, and he's already getting his people together. We'll have arrest warrants out for Sarah Freitag, aka Soothsayer; Todd Glutzman, aka Nathane; Hedda Zeiss, aka Mist Queen; and Martha Vernon, aka Dirge."

"Good enough."

"Mister Traer, our prize." she smiled. "And we can confirm that McGuire was Benefactor, like you guessed, and Herkaman was Shade, which we knew, and Sirken was Virgil and Keller was Dark Princess."

I was impressed.

"Also," said Hester, "Rachel Larsen is Handmaiden. And they all were present at the Christmas ceremonies."

"Got 'em all?"

"All of them except one member, a John Zurcher, aka Mystic Fog, who's in prison at Fort Madison."

"Damn."

"Hal and I got to get movin', 'cause we're going to do a search warrant at Traer's house in Cedar Rapids as soon as we can get there and get things started. I called Dickman at the CR office, and he's getting the stuff together right now, including a surveillance of the house."

"Progress is a wonderful thing."

"Isn't it, though?"

We rejoined Mike and Sally in the back room.

"You know, though," said Hester, "we've got one big problem left."

"I know," I said. "We still have an unsolved quadruple homicide."

"That's right. And Rachel is still the only key I'm aware of."

"So," asked Mike, "where's Rachel?"

"The question of the week," said Hester.

"Can I ask a question?" said Sally.

"Sure."

"Well, from what I've overheard tonight, this Traer is the head of the group, right?"

"Yes."

"And he's powerful—I mean it, I can feel the waves he gives off. Maybe you can, too," she said to Hester, "being female."

Hester smiled. "I can't say that I can, but I've been distracted."

"Yeah," said Sally. "So, anyway, if I was Rachel, and if I was a witness, like you say, and all the victims were members of my little religious group, I'd go to Traer for protection."

"Yeah . . ."

"So don't you think that this Rachel would be at his place? For her own safety?"

Of course we did. All of a sudden.

Hester called CRPD and told them to make sure that nobody entered or left the Traer home. They agreed, but said that their marked car who was the first one at the scene had reported a female leaving the residence, in a small gray car registered to Traer.

"What time?" She tossed her hair, a signal of frustration or exasperation I was beginning to recognize.

She wrote on a scratch pad, pushed it to me across the desk.

"Check his phone call time," it said. I did. 05:17. I wrote it down and passed it back to her. She looked at it and shook her head. Hester thanked CRPD and hung up the phone.

"Female left the residence at 05:26. Nine minutes after he made the call. Nine fuckin' minutes."

"Rachel?"

"Probably. CRPD says the asshole isn't married."

"Son of a bitch."

I turned to Sally. "Thanks, though."

She smiled, and raised her cup. Point well taken.

Art and Hal came in, carrying bags full of items from the search. Including several notebooks and an address book.

Saperstein, who'd pretty much stayed in the background all night, glommed onto the books immediately. He was making Xerox copies of them before they were even out of Art's hands.

Hester brought them up to date, and they were as dismayed as we were about Rachel.

It turned out that they'd had to cool their heels for over an hour, waiting for us to tell them to come on up, and that they had passed their time reading some of Elizabeth Mills's writing.

"Apparently," said Hal, "quite a shock wave went through the group when the murders went down. She doesn't know who did it, but good old Darkness apparently does. He was supposed to reveal the perp's identity at the next meeting. Tomorrow night."

"Well," said Mike, "who gets to lean on Darkness?"

"We'd better go slow with that one," said Hester. "He's pretty sharp."

Just then Lamar walked in the room.

"What the hell you guys been doing?"

It turned out that Art had called him about the search. That Hal had called him when they discovered the identity of Darkness, and knew he was on the way up. That Mike had called him when Darkness was being booked. That Art had called the county attorney about Traer, who in turn had called Lamar. The question, it seemed, was rhetorical.

Hal told him about Rachel, and the arrests that were going to go down within the next few hours. To be made outside our county, which was a relief for Lamar.

"God damn," said Lamar. "I got three general executions for today, and a farm sale at eleven, and you keep me up all night with a simple little murder."

I grinned at him. "Life is a bitch."

"Yeah."

"But," said Art, "we thought you'd want to know."

"Fuck it," said Lamar, "I'm buying breakfast. Let's go downtown."

You never pass up an offer like that.

We hit Sheffert's restaurant en masse: Lamar, Art, me, Mike, Hal, Hester, Sally, and Dan from the Maitland PD. The radio traffic was a little confusing.

"Comm, one."

"One, go ahead."

"One, two, three, five, twenty-five, I-28, I-388, and Sally are 10–7 Sheffert's."

"Checking, one, that's one, two, three, five, twenty-five, I-28, and I-388?"

"And Sally," said one. "And Detective Saperstein, too."

"Sally and Saperstein?"

"10–4."

Deb sounded a little miffed, and jealous. She obviously didn't like the fact that Sally was along.

Sally, who was riding with me, grinned and giggled like a schoolgirl. "She's jealous," she said.

"True."

"Well, what the hell."

"That's right. You earned it last night."

We all trooped to the rear, past about thirty other patrons, about evenly divided between local businesspeople and local farmers. Plus about five or six people I didn't know.

We all sat at three tables, pushed together to make one. Art was going back up as soon as breakfast was over, to begin inventorying the seized property. Hal and Hester were leaving for Cedar Rapids. I was feeling a little smug, thinking I could go home and get eight solid hours of sleep. Wrong.

"Carl," said Hal, "could you get ahold of Helen today? She still hasn't heard that tape, and she should get a good look at Traer. She said that he had a beard, and he doesn't now."

There went the afternoon. "Sure."

"And," he went on, "Judd Norman from the fire marshal's office is going to be back out at McGuire's place today, going into the debris, if it's cool enough. Could you, or maybe Mike, go with him?"

"Hey, Mike?"

"Yeah!"

"Hal, here, wants a favor."

We were having a pretty good time, tired but happy, when a small man in an enormous blue down-filled jacket came to the table.

"Excuse me, but would one of you be Sheriff Ridgeway?"

"I am," said Lamar. "What can I do for you?"

"My name is Ross Foreman, with the *Des Moines Register*. I'd like to talk to you about some arrests I hear you made last night . . ."

You can't even eat in privacy.

25

I got home in time to see Sue rolling out of bed. She was concerned, as she properly should have been, about my not getting enough sleep. I should have been, too, but I was excited and too close to events to be entirely rational about it.

"I'll be all right."

"You are supposed to work nights, not nights and days."

"This is a little unusual, right now."

Hard to argue with that.

I called the office and left a wake-up call for 14:00. Didn't need breakfast, thanks to Lamar, so I went right to bed. Couldn't sleep. Of course.

I was worried about the Cynthia Larsen case. We really didn't have a lot, and we had just arrested an attorney who seemed likely to be a Satanic high priest. Sort of man you really didn't want to piss off. Especially if you couldn't make it stick.

I mean, I'd always jokingly considered attorneys in general as works of the devil. But now, for the first time in my life, I had one who actually could be. Tiger by the tail, and all that.

Then, too, I began to think about the main investigation, our four murders. Whoever had done that was still on the loose, unless it had been a member of the local cult, and I doubted that very much.

Our people who covered the funeral must not have seen anybody interesting . . . there had been no news from them at all, as far as I knew. Just a shot you had to take.

Traer knows, I thought. Especially since it looks like Rachel has been staying with him. He knows, but I wonder if he'll ever tell . . .

Only if it were to benefit him.

A plea bargain, of course. God, I hated to see that happen, and hoped that it wouldn't. Being the probable high priest, he'd quite likely been the one to actually kill the baby. Which got me thinking about that . . . and I shouldn't have.

I was still awake at 09:30 or so, so I went back downstairs and had a glass of orange juice.

I think I got to sleep at about 10:15.

The office called right at 14:00 and woke me. I had intended to talk to Helen Bockman about 15:00, but decided to let it wait till later, and went back to bed.

I got up on my own at 16:15. Put on some coffee, let good old Fred out, and called the Bockmans'. No answer. Good. I wasn't awake yet, anyway.

The first cup didn't seem to do the trick. I was about halfway through the second, and on my fourth cigarette, when I heard Fred barking in the yard. I went out to let him in and discovered Lamar petting him.

"Hey, how're things?"

"Pretty good." He stood up, with Fred jumping for his hand.

"Knock it off, Fred!" I grabbed him and scooped him in the house. "You want a cup of coffee?"

"Sure."

"What's up?"

"I thought I'd stop by and let you know it looks like we found the baby."

"You did?"

"Yep. The McGuire house. Fire marshall found it. In the mess, in the basement."

That figured, somehow. Finding it in the basement. Nobody was looking for a small body when we did the scene. I remembered the basement. It really wasn't very big, but it was pretty much unfinished, with more clutter than you could believe, including garbage bags full of old feed sacks, paint cans, fertilizer bags . . . and then, of course, all the debris from the house would have collapsed into it during the fire.

"Well, now we have the body."

"Yeah. At least I think we do."

"What condition was it in?"

"Not too bad, really. It's been cooked pretty well by the fire, but the debris from the upper floors kept it from being burned too bad. Didn't have a head, though. Saperstein thinks maybe somebody kept it."

"God."

"Theo's on the way to Des Moines with the remains, takin' 'em to the state medical examiner. Now all we got to do is find this Rachel and then find out who killed everybody."

"Still just about at square one, aren't we?"

"Yeah."

"Well, Traer knows who did it, I think. All we got to do is squeeze him hard enough."

"I hope so," said Lamar. "But I got a feeling that he's gonna be able to bond out pretty soon."

"No kidding?"

"Yeah, he's been making phone calls all day. Bond is five hundred thousand, but I think he can make it. He's been talking to somebody in real estate in Cedar Rapids . . . says he's willing to sell the house."

"Speaking of his house, how did Hal and Hester make out?"

"Okay, I guess. They say that they'll be back here after supper sometime."

"How about the other arrests?"

"Pretty good so far. Got everybody but this Vernon woman, and they think she'll be home today or Monday."

I poured him a second cup of coffee.

"Media's been all over my ass today," he said. "They want to know everything. They asked to speak to the folks in jail, and I told them they have to wait till regular visiting hours."

"That's this afternoon, isn't it?"

"It was, but I was out of the office. So was everybody else." He grinned.

"Isn't that a little dangerous?"

"Yeah. I told 'em to come back tonight after supper. I want Hal and Hester to talk to me first. So does the county attorney."

We sat in silence for a minute. We were both washed-out.

"You know," I said, "Traer is going to split, if he gets out."

"Probably."

"And even if he doesn't, he's going to be pretty hard to squeeze, since he's got what we want, and his case isn't far enough down the road yet so that we can pressure him with an assured prison sentence."

"Yep."

"We need Rachel."

Lamar left a few minutes later. Sue came home and told me that I looked like I was dead. I agreed.

I broke a rule of mine and sat her down and told her just about everything in the case. It took over an hour, and when I was done she didn't look much better than I did.

The rumors going around school apparently had it that we'd solved the case and were wrapping it up. Three arrests, four bodies. Figured. I wished they were right.

"So you don't think that this attorney did it?"

"The four, you mean?"

"Yes."

"No."

"But who else would have?"

"That, my dear," I said, in my best imitation of W. C. Fields, "is the essential question. And we don't know. Saperstein and Hester agree with me that it was, maybe, a revenge killing. Maybe by somebody with a Satanic background, maybe not. The best suspect would normally be Rachel, since they killed her baby. But she was apparently almost a victim herself."

"Well, who was the father of the baby?"

The things you tend to overlook. . . .

After supper, Hester called. They had a lot of stuff from Traer's house. The real things were still at their Cedar Rapids office, but they had Xeroxed some seized documents and had brought them back. And copies of several audiotapes and one videotape.

They'd taken Saperstein with them, and he had insisted they make copies and bring them back to show us. We were all supposed to meet at the office at 19:00.

No problem, I had to go to work at 20:00, anyway.

We were all crammed into the back office. It was possible for prisoners to hear conversations from the kitchen, and since we had Traer and the Millses in the jail, we couldn't use the only room that would accommodate us properly.

"Gentlemen," said Saperstein. "What you are about to see is a so-called Black Mass. You will also see all four of our murder victims, very much alive, and very much involved. You will see Mr. Oswald Traer in the leading role."

Black and white horizontal lines on the screen, then a little bit of color, and then there they were.

The first few seconds were taken outside. The camera operator was obviously walking toward a barn, preceded by several figures in colored robes. There was apparently only one light accompanying the camera, so almost everything was in either complete darkness or washed-out light. It was at night.

There was sound, but the initial stuff was just about as blurred as the video. Some sort of song or chant.

They reached the barn, and the cameraman turned around, pointing the camera back along his path. Facing a residence that, although dim, looked a lot like McGuire's place. There was a figure approaching.

"That's McGuire's, isn't it?" asked Mike.

"Yeah," said Art.

The approaching figure was more discernible, since the camera was steady. Black robe, with the hood pushed back. As it approached, the face of a man with a full beard was very plain.

"Darkness approaches," said a voice offscreen. Muffled but under-standable. Shit, it was almost funny.

"That's Traer. The high priest," said Saperstein. "You get to see a lot of him."

Traer walked past the camera, too close, as his image blurred and washed out. The camera followed him inside.

It was dark in the barn, at least to the video camera. Virtually no detail at all, with several lines of parallel streaks as the camera moved toward a bright area that turned out to be sort of an altar. A black cloth draped over something, maybe an old table. Candles on both ends, with a kind of candelabra in the middle. A benchlike thing in front of it. Big pentagram hanging behind the altar, looked like a dyed and painted bed sheet. Pretty well done, as far as you could tell in the miserable light. The candles were all black, or purple.

Traer stopped in front of the altar and said something I couldn't understand. The camera turned, and panned the area to the side of the altar and back toward the door.

The parallel lights, it turned out, were candles being held by the rest of the group. The camera panned slowly, and we had our first view of people we could identify. Phyllis, in red. Sirken in red, as were Keller and Elizabeth Mills.

They were saying something. Couldn't tell what.

Sudden static, and we were now looking at the altar from about fifteen feet. The operator had shut the camera off to put it on a tripod and then restarted it. The lighting was much better, so the tripod must have had a flood attached.

Saperstein backed up the tape.

"You may have noticed that the sound quality is poor—well, it's not as bad as you think, because they are saying things backward. The main chant is 'Natas,' which is 'Satan' pronounced or read backward." He paused. "We can ID most of the people for sure. Some of you might have recognized Sirken and Herkaman. The woman beside Herkaman is Keller. Three of our four victims. You'll see a lot more of Herkaman later on. In the background we have people we have tentatively ID'd as both Millses and Hedda Zeiss. Possible on Todd Glutzman and Martha Vernon. There is a figure in a red robe you will see in a moment. Not too good, but we believe that's Rachel."

He reran the portion we had just seen, and stopped at a frame near the end.

"There," he said. "The one to Herkaman's left, sort of hidden behind Sirken in the red robe. We think that's her."

A small, thin face, with eyes set fairly close together. Not too clear, but I was struck by a resemblance to the dormouse in *Alice in Wonderland*.

He let the tape run for a couple of minutes.

"The reason it's all so hard to understand," he said, "is that our Mr. Traer is reciting the Roman Catholic mass backward. In Latin. The most important thing to notice is that book on the altar. You'll hardly ever see him look down at it, but he turns the pages automatically."

We watched. The quality was about that of a normal home video—poor. But you could see what he meant.

"He's got it memorized, just like a priest has the mass memorized."

"Now, that's dedication," said Art.

A few moments later, a naked woman appeared from offstage left and approached the altar. Traer said something, she knelt and then lay down on the table before it.

"The naked woman is Phyllis Herkaman. She is playing the role of the so-called living altar. The rest of the ceremony will be conducted on her, as it were."

It was. She was difficult to recognize most of the time. Her face was just a little too far from the camera to be truly recognizable.

Saperstein fast-forwarded all of a sudden, wrenching me back from the mass and into the crowded room.

"Most of it is like that, with the people in the background sometimes coming forward to do some little chore . . . and, okay, here," he said, resuming normal speed. "Here we have the members of the cult having sexual relations with Phyllis . . . the formal end to the ceremony."

Despite our better impulses, we were riveted.

"You'll notice that Traer gets first shot—rank has its privileges."

Traer seemed to be devoting as much energy to this part of the program as he had all the rest.

"Now," said Saperstein, "this is interesting. Watch who's next."

A woman approached Phyllis.

"This is unusual, the women normally come last." Saperstein chuckled. "No pun. This woman's different. This one is our guest, Elizabeth Mills."

Elizabeth placed her head between Phyllis's legs.

"Now, watch Phyllis here," said Saperstein. "She was pretty properly religious with Traer . . ."

Phyllis, who had been lying quietly, suddenly jerked, and almost fell off the table.

"Lost her concentration, there."

Elizabeth stood, and backed off-camera.

"Now, this is Sirken . . . and from here on out, it's all pretty much perfunctory . . . Just a second . . ." and he fast-forwarded it again.

"Here," he said, "this is Kenneth Mills. He's the next man, and watch this."

There appeared to be much fumbling on-screen, lasting for almost a minute. Then Kenneth Mills turned his back to the camera and moved off into the darkness.

Saperstein chuckled. "Old Kenny apparently couldn't get it up."

"After my wife had done such a good job," said Hal, "I'm not sure I could, either."

"Hard act to follow," I said.

"The rest of it is just normal stuff," said Saperstein quickly. "Whoever was responsible for the camera forgot it at the end, because we have three or four minutes of the empty altar."

He began rewinding the tape, and the lights came back on.

"Now," said Saperstein, "this tape tells us a lot about the group. For instance, it's plain that Traer is the high priest. It's also apparent that Elizabeth Mills is rather high in the organization, and I would think she would fall just behind Phyllis, or maybe just ahead of her. Kenneth Mills seems to lack commitment."

There was some appreciative laughter.

"Sirken," he continued, "seems to rank just behind Elizabeth and was probably the number two male. In their order, then came McGuire, then Todd Glutzman, or at least, we think it's Glutzman. Hard to tell. Then the other women, with Rachel being last. You can't tell because of the robe, but the note on the tape says that it was made on October 14th. A Saturday. If that is the correct approximate date, Rachel was about eight months along, and may have been last because of that.

"I think," said Saperstein, "that Kenneth Mills is our weak link in the group. I think that he can be 'approached.' "

"We wanted to show you this tape," said Hester, "just so that you realize what we're dealing with. These people are serious. They're fanatic. They probably 'sacrificed' a baby in a ceremony similar to the one you just saw. We'd like you to think about that."

We were thinking.

"These people," said Saperstein, "are at the upper level of Satanic activities. Philosophically, morally, politically. They're totally committed, and will do anything they have to, to protect the group."

"If you think of the term 'fanatic,'" said Hal, "you're just scratching the surface. And they will obey Traer to the bitter end. Literally."

"Kind of like Charlie Manson?" I asked.

"Exactly," said Saperstein.

"Great."

"Whoever killed the four," he said, "is also that committed, and that fanatic. For what reason, we don't know yet. But I don't think he'll be satisfied with just four of them. I would think that whoever it is, is going to want Traer. At least."

26

Hester stood up, and looked around the group.

"Now I've got some bad news." She picked up a copy of the Des Moines paper. "We have some interesting reporting going on here."

She tossed the paper to Quint, who caught it.

"Anybody who wants to read it can," she said. "But basically it's a case where there aren't many facts for them to go on, so they interview the 'man in the street.' Who, in this case, appears terrified."

"Is *made* to appear terrified," said Hal.

"You got it right," said Hester. She sat on Lamar's desk, swinging her feet back and forth. We knew it was important now. Nobody sits on Lamar's desk.

"I don't know about the rest of you, but I've been spending a lot of time in this town lately, and I haven't talked to a 'terrified' resident yet." She glanced at the rest of us.

There was a chorus of nope's and not me's.

"Well, the AG's office reads the paper. The governor reads the paper. And they don't spend much time up here talking to the people. So that's what they have to go by, I guess." She stood abruptly, tossing her hair like she was really aggravated.

"Anyway, the AG's office has given us sort of an ultimatum. We don't make an arrest in the next few days, they're gonna task-force the investigation."

Silence.

"Now, when they do that, two things happen. Number one, they assign thirty or so people from DCI and the AG to work the case. I've been in on two of those. Once as a member comin' in, once as the original case officer. You get almost unlimited resources, and almost unlimited fuckups. People stumbling all over each other, going over all the previous case data, reviewing all the information you've already got. Driving you crazy, and doing the second thing that they do."

She sipped some coffee. "The second thing is that they effectively take you off the case. They break the chain of events and ruin your concentration. They talk to your witnesses so often that they never want to hear a cop again. They burn out the whole bunch. They confuse everything."

She had some more coffee.

"And then, typically, they leave. Because they've 'exhausted the resources' in the case. And there you sit, two or three weeks later, with a fucked-up case and all the responsibility for it." She sat back down. "And, while they're active, you're effectively taken off the case."

"So," said Hal, "we've got to get moving. Just a little added pressure. We don't want a task force. Period. So we've pulled a couple of strings. And we've got one advantage." He gestured toward Hester and grinned. "Hester here used to be an undercover narc officer for us, for those who didn't know. She also was sent to the FBI Criminal Profiling school and worked for our Criminal Assessment Unit for a year and a half, before being put back in General Crim."

Hester stood up and bowed.

"Anyway," said Hal, "Hester has profiled the four homicides. Cross-referenced the material from the . . . ." He looked at a slip of paper on Lamar's desk. "From the National Center for the Analysis of Violent Crime." He grinned. "That's all I know about it. Hester . . . don't let all this go to your head."

"At my age, Hal, I can't afford to let it go anywhere else." She looked around the room. "This is gonna get a little esoteric for a few minutes, so if you feel sleepy, just raise your hand and I'll excuse you."

Silence.

"Okay, here we go. By the way, if they task-force this, everything I'm going to tell you will be done again, by another agent. That's what Hal's talking about."

She opened her valise and brought out a stack of paper.

"This, gentlemen," she said, holding it up for us to see, "is a profile of the four offenses. MO information; victimology, as far as I could take it; physical evidence; and suspect behavior, again as far as I could take it. No surprises. As far as I can tell, the four were done by the same person or persons. I have done a personality profile on the offender—slim, let me tell you. But there is one major indicator we can tell for sure, and that is that he is a criminal psychopath. Possibly a schizophrenic, possibly a paranoiac one . . ."

"No shit?" From Mike.

We laughed.

"Yeah," said Hester, "no shit. Mike, isn't it?"

"Yep."

"The main value here, Mike, is that we are now dealing with a scientifically designated psychopath, not just our uninformed opinions. There's a difference."

"Okay," said Mike, relatively unabashed. Lamar threw him a hard glance. "I mean," said Mike, "I see the difference."

"Good," said Hester.

She leafed through her papers for a second. "Now, he's approximately six feet tall, plus or minus two inches. Left-handed. Strong. Size 11 shoes. Stride of approximately thirty-three inches, on average. Medium brown hair, we think. Probably over 180 pounds, maybe as high as 210. We found a little blood on Peggy Keller's jeans, by the way, that wasn't hers and doesn't match any of the other four victims. Blood was AO, 1–2–, B. Scrapings from under her nails gave insufficient in the ABO and EAP, but also were 1–2–. Nail scrapings from Phyllis Herkaman were similar, with no ABO but with a 1–2– and an EAP of B. There was also an AO stain on the gag that was used on her. So we feel, based on that, that his injury was on his hand, probably the left, and we feel that he's an AO, 1–2–, B, and a secretor."

She shifted her papers again. "We ran him through our own computer and came up with nothing." She held up her hand. "Not at all surprising, gentlemen, since we are a new program, and we only have eleven people in our system at this time." She smiled. "We got to start somewhere, don't we?

"Anyway," she went on, "I interfaced with NCAVC and have a partial match on the MO and on the physicals."

Well, well, well.

"Our matchup is from a multiple homicide which took place in Cleveland, Ohio, a number of years ago. It is partially solved, which is a surprise."

Hester picked up a different sheet. "The incident was a homicide involving three individuals, two men and a woman. It is believed they were members of a cult, with at least overtones of Satanism. One male was castrated. Mutilations in all three victims. Originally it was felt that it was a murder-suicide, because a male suicide was discovered two days later, with notes and a Polaroid photo of the crime scene in his possession. He left a note, saying how he had accomplished his purpose and had gone to be with the devil. That his life was complete. Open and shut, except that the forensic team had evidence of two perpetrators. Our boy was the second. He was never identified." She looked back at her notes. "Oh, before I forget . . . If you're having trouble, emotionally, with this stuff, don't feel bad. One of the cops investigating this case in Ohio actually got off on a psychiatric disability."

She looked up. "Now, the physical evidence is good. The general Satanic overtones are good. But there's a problem here. The first murders were apparently committed by Satanists. We feel, however, that our perp isn't necessarily one himself. What he does doesn't jibe with the activities of the group. I mean, it's almost like he's read up on this stuff. The victim group wasn't nearly as 'formal' about their practices as our perp is. We feel that the Satanic-related evidence at the scene was set up. To make it look Satanic, or at least, more Satanic. Anybody disagree?"

Nobody did. Nobody had the information to have an opinion.

"Yeah. Well, our guy pretty well qualifies as a serial murderer, by definition. Little problem with the textbook classification, due to the time gap between incidents. Quite a long while. Which indicates to me that there is a strong possibility that our man has been sidetracked. Possibly by psychiatric treatment, or even being institutionalized. In the interim period." She paused. "Am I ringing any bells yet? With anybody?"

No.

"Kind of hoped I would."

"Hester," I said, "if I heard any bells ringing, I'd sure as hell never tell *you*."

She smiled. Waited. Still nothing.

"The MO in ours indicates somebody either in a sustained rage or with sustained purposefulness. I go for purposefulness, because of the general lack of collateral damage. Take McGuire's place, for example. Most of the mess in the house, if not all of it, was created for effect. 'Signs of a struggle.' Yet McGuire was murdered elsewhere and brought to the house. No struggle likely there. Unless he was kidnapped, and the struggle happened then, and I doubt that, given his known association with Herkaman.

"The valid assumption is that all four were killed at Herkaman's place. There are no signs of a major struggle there. At least nothing to indicate what they call a killing rage. So we have somebody who is methodical. Somebody who is extremely determined. Somebody who can sustain that mind-set for several hours. Somebody very patient, who can torture a victim for a considerable time period. Somebody who, for a period of time in excess of five hours, gives us the emotions of a reptile."

She paused again. "Any bells ringing yet?"

None.

"What we have here is a fanatic, and I believe one with strong religious motivations. Maybe not from an organized religion. But a man with a 'mission from God,' so to speak."

"A Blues Brother?" I asked.

She grinned. "You would make that connection."

"Well, it's the only bell that's rung so far."

"Anyhow, and you're not gonna like this, Lamar, I feel that our boy is going to go for more members of our little cult. Especially Traer. Especially. And the security here is like Swiss cheese. From six P.M. until six A.M., ninety percent of the time the only person in this building, except for prisoners, is a female dispatcher. Who has the keys to the cells. Anybody can walk in here, and I know that for sure, because I did. I came in the back door, and nobody knew I was here."

Silence.

"And we now have three of the best potential targets for our perp locked in one small area of an isolated building." She looked at Lamar. "I know you have a budget problem, but I'm afraid you're going to have to have a minimum of two officers in this building at all times. A minimum."

"Yeah," said Lamar reluctantly, "you're right. I just don't know where I'm gonna get the people."

"I don't know, either," said Hester. "But they're going to have to be officers, they're going to have to be well armed, and they're going to have to be alert as hell. And you're going to have to secure all the doors in this place. Well secured."

"Yeah."

"You'd better start tonight," said Hester. "I'm convinced this guy is still around. He probably had as much trouble finding the other members as we did. We've done most of his heavy work for him, at this point. And the media have told the whole world where they are."

The intercom buzzed. Lamar took the call. It was Mary Quentin, duty dispatcher. "Helen Bockman is here, to listen to a tape?"

"Oh, yeah. I'll be right out."

"I'll take it," said Art. He left the room.

"Perfect case in point," said Hester. "Here we have a dozen officers in a room less than fifty feet from the dispatch center. Did anybody know that Helen was even in the building?"

Of course not.

The dispatcher had probably let her in through the electrically locked front door, which was equipped with a two-way speaker system. No security there. I doubted if a killer would announce himself as such. We'd been trying to get approval for a closed-circuit TV system, but hadn't had any luck at all with that. And the dispatchers were accustomed to letting members of the public in at all hours, when they reported accidents, fights, etc. Besides, there were four other doors in the building, none of which would stop a determined man. Or a talented one. Not good.

"Well," said Lamar, "none of our reserve officers has to go to work tomorrow. I'll get a couple of them to sit in the building tonight." He shook his head. "But I don't know what I'm gonna do tomorrow. Or the rest of the week."

Hal stood up. "Okay, people, I have a sheet here that's based on Hester's workup. General description, one suspect." He began handing them out. "We're gonna have to move on this."

The intercom buzzed again. Mary. "We have a two-car 10–50, with injuries, three west on 55. Ambulance has been notified. Bodies reported on the road."

Mike, Eddie, and I stood up. Sunday night was beginning.

27

Blasting through Maitland with lights and sirens going, it only took us a few minutes to get to the accident scene. It was a bad one, one dead for sure at the scene, four injured, with one of them pinned. We called back to comm for the Jaws and a fire department unit. We tried to keep one of them alive, but I think we lost her at the scene. The ambulance took her, anyway. We had called for a backup ambulance, too, and that took a little while. All volunteer, and it's hard to get two crews right away, especially on a Sunday night.

The scene was cleared of victims within thirty minutes. We ordered up a trooper, to assist in the investigation. Two cars, head-on. Driver of the westbound car appeared intoxicated at the scene, so I went to the Maitland hospital to draw blood for a BAC.

Organized confusion at the hospital. Nurses, aides, EMTs running all over, each with a task. Technicians arriving for X-ray and blood typing. Henry was already there when I got there. He was sort of a rock and stopped any confusion. He was always that way. He asked for his partner, Dr. Bill Crane, to be contacted. And ordered up the air ambulance out of Iowa City.

As soon as I heard that, I went to the parking lot and used my portable to contact the Maitland car. It was Dan.

"Twenty-five, three."

"Three?"

"We got Air Care comin' in about twenty minutes."

"10–4, be right there."

The chopper lands in the parking lot, and all the cars have to be cleared out and kept out.

"Comm," I asked, "were you 10–4 on that?"

"Copied Air Care in twenty?"

"10–4."

Good, Sally was back on shift. She would be their first contact and would relay any traffic they had for us until they got within five miles or so. Dispatchers, air controllers . . . you name it, they do it.

I wandered back into the ER area, and Henry saw me for the first time.

"You want blood?"

"Yeah, from the one in the blue jacket."

"It'll be a few minutes."

"That's okay."

I sat down on one of the chairs in a little waiting area and began filling out an implied-consent form. I saw Lori standing in the hallway, so went up to her and asked her if she could get me the driver's license from the blue-jacketed driver.

"Could you ask somebody else, please? That's my cousin."

"Sorry . . ."

I saw an EMT and asked him. He got it for me, and I sat back down, filling in the blanks.

Most of the victims were in their late teens or early twenties. They usually were. I completed my form and started nosing around the ER area, picking up the names of the victims. The girl we had tried to save was in an exam room, with a blanket over her face. Damn.

Parents and relatives began arriving. It had happened pretty close to town, and the information had gotten out even before the hospital staff had had a chance to call them. Their presence, while accepted by everybody as a right, did confuse and complicate things sometimes.

I noticed that Pastor Rothberg was among the arrivals. Not surprising, as clergy were frequently either notified by the hospital or requested by family members. That was good. The clergy help a lot in cases like this.

I waved at him and he waved back. We were too far apart to speak, and there were lots of intervening people.

About fifteen minutes later, I wandered out to the parking lot and pulled my baseball cap out of my car. Air Care would be getting close, and I would have to help Dan keep people back. The problem was, we'd had ice all over the place about two weeks ago, and they'd sanded the hospital parking lot. Heavily. That was the reason for the cap. We were going to get sandblasted when the chopper set down.

I talked to Dan for a minute, about the wreck. Three of the victims were locals, two were from Minnesota. It was the local who appeared drunk, and both the Minnesota people were now dead.

We heard Air Care before we saw it, because of the hills. Dan contacted them on his portable and advised the lot was clear. We turned on our top lights—one car at each end of the landing area, to give him an aiming point. The pilot was pretty concerned about the winds at ground level. We told him not more than five knots, from the northwest.

"Must be pretty windy up there," said Dan.

The chopper was an Alouette III, small but sleek. The pilot set it down gently, after taking the skin off my face with sand from the parking lot. The nurse jumped out and headed for the ER, followed by another one, while the pilot shut things off.

Dan and I were just standing there, watching to make sure no bystander screwed with the chopper, when I heard a voice behind me. It was Pastor Rothberg.

"A wonderful thing, a wonderful thing." He paused, and we both looked at the helicopter. "I was wondering, uh, how you're coming with that matter we discussed at your house the other day."

I turned to look at him. "Pretty well."

"Anything I can do to help?"

Something had been nagging at me since Hester had talked to us. Sort of working on me all through the accident and while I was cooling my heels at the hospital. I still didn't know just what it was, but I was getting the definite impression that Pastor Rothberg was somebody to talk with. Like I've said before, I'm famous for partial thoughts. And nagging myself.

"Look, when we're done here, why don't we just chat about it? I need to talk to somebody about some of these things, and you seem to know a bit about it."

"I'd be glad to. Just let me tell my wife, so she can get a ride home?"

"Sure," I said. He turned and went to an older station wagon. I'd never met his wife. She got out of the car, and I got a good look at her. A little above medium height, light hair, about thirty or so. Slender, with a woebegone expression. Thin face. Pastor's wives suffer, too, I guess, but in a different way. I walked over to them.

"I hate to take your husband away from you," I said.

She smiled. "That's fine. I'm used to it."

"Dear," he said, "I'd like you to meet Deputy Carl Houseman. Carl, my wife, Betty."

She extended her hand, and I shook it. Felt frail. Small hands.

"Carl, Mark told me he had quite a conversation with you the other day. Remarkable."

Remarkable how? That he'd had an interesting conversation with a cop? Remarkable that he'd told her? Or remarkable subject matter? How do you tell?

"Well, the most remarkable thing was probably my coffee," I said, smiling.

"Doesn't your wife teach?"

Subject effectively changed. Good. Maybe she was really discreet. That would be nice, if he had told her much about what we had talked about.

Small talk for a minute or two, and then people started to move from the ER to the chopper. First, the pilot, then the attendants, with a couple of EMTs and Henry pushing a gurney with a well-wrapped victim on it. IVs dangling, portable oxygen in a pack. We were all watching, but I noticed that Betty was even paler than before.

They loaded the victim, cranked up the chopper, and I had to go back to work.

The takeoff was neat, as we have high-tension wires all over the place, and this guy went straight up for about a hundred feet. Fun to watch them rotate about their vertical axis and then move off. I'd have to ask Lamar if I could have one.

One of the X-ray techs was leaving, and apparently knew Betty, because she had no difficulty in getting a ride.

Rothberg and I went back into the hospital. As I went by the ER, Henry told me he could get the blood now.

I went to my little rest area and picked up the forms and the Vacutainer kit and took it to him. Just took a few seconds to advise the suspect of his options under the implied-consent law and have the blood withdrawn. I put my package under my arm and went looking for Mark. He was near the end of the hall by the conference room door, talking to the mother of the guy I'd just taken blood from. As I approached, she gave me a dirty look. That's okay, lady, I thought. If he's drunk, and they're both dead, he's looking at a lot more than DWI. How do you think the parents of the dead feel? But I didn't say anything of the sort.

"Ma'am," I said. "Mark, if I could talk to you, when you get a minute . . ." Give him an out. Surprisingly, he took it.

We sat at the conference room table, and I liberated a couple of cups of hospital coffee. Yucch.

"Your wife seemed to be having a hard time with the victim," I said. "She know her?"

"No," said Mark. "We were at the driver's parents' for supper when the call came. We don't really know the girl. But it does upset her, seeing people hurt like that."

"I suppose so. Especially when it's so unnecessary."

"Yes, it's the innocent victims . . ."

"Well"—I might as well test the waters—"you should talk to the detective we have out here from New York. He knows a lot about Satanism, too."

"Oh?"

"Yeah, sort of an expert on it. He got here the other day, the state requested him. On loan."

"Oh. Well, you know, I've been hearing a lot about this case, from my congregation, mostly. Especially since the funerals. They're a little upset about burying the victims in our cemetery, of course."

They are, are they? I thought. Seems to me you were, too.

"I'm sure," I said.

"God's mercy is extended to all, even to those who may not think they're serving him."

"That's good."

"We're all God's children, Carl. Although even I tend to overlook that once in a while."

An apology? Possibly.

"We all do."

"Yes. But we're all his children. Even if we stray, or are taken over by evil. It may be against our will, at least at first. We tend to become occupied with the corporeal side and not be as forgiving as we should."

Henry walked in.

"Can I join this club?" He got his coffee and sat down.

"We were just talking about the murders, sort of," I said. "Mark here is something of an expert on the occult."

Henry raised his eyebrows. "Really?"

"Oh, no, not really," said Mark. "But we had an incident at our last congregation, in Ohio, where there were some Satanic overtones. I learned a little by counseling some people."

"Yeah," I volunteered. "Didn't you have some kid kill himself, or something like that?"

"Yes. It was tragic. He was a good young man, from a good family. I counseled a friend of his, who was also involved in the occult at the time." He looked at Henry. "That's how I know so much about it, I guess. I had to research Satanism, to argue him away."

Henry asked the next question for me.

"My little brother lives in Ohio, near Dayton. Were you in Dayton?"

"No," said Rothberg. "A small town called Elyria. Nice place. We were in Dayton, once, to the air force museum at Wright-Patterson. Have you ever been there?"

That got us all going on another tangent, as we were all interested in airplanes, and I've always wanted to go there myself. But before I got too involved, I wrote Elyria on the top of the implied-consent folder. Small letters. Like I was finishing up my notes.

28

It was a little after midnight when I got back to the office. Nobody around except two reserve officers and Sally. On the worst shift, of course. Hazel Willis was the chief dispatcher and made out the schedule. She hated Sally.

I went into the kitchen and put on a fresh pot of coffee. Stood around making small talk with the reserves. When the coffee was done, I got a cup, and so did they. I took a cup to Sally.

I hesitated. "Hey, listen, I'm gonna need something done, and I want it kept totally between you and me for now. Absolutely."

"Sure."

"Thing is, I'm not sure what it's going to be. Not exactly."

"All right." She looked bemused.

"But I want you to do a DL request on Mark Rothberg."

"The pastor?"

"That's right."

"Sure, got his date of birth?"

I grinned. "Of course not."

She turned to the teletype terminal. "Just give me a minute."

The reserve officers chose that moment to wander into the dispatch center. They were bored. All well and good, but I sure as hell didn't want them to know I was even checking on Pastor Rothberg. If I was wrong . . . Sally killed the screen, and the four of us talked for a minute. About the traffic accident, mostly.

I sort of herded them into the back office with me, to let Sally finish her checks. She called on the intercom a few minutes later.

"I've got that stuff from the accident," she said.

"I'll be right out."

The reserves, by this time, were firmly ensconced in the back room. Discussing the wrecks they'd been to in the past. They wouldn't miss me for at least a couple of minutes.

Sally had Mark Rothberg's DL information up on the screen. She handed me the hard copy.

"Need anything else?"

"As a matter of fact . . ."

I had her get all vehicles registered to him. That was quick, now that we had his DOB and operator's license number. Then I had her run a registration check on all three vehicles. One of them, the station wagon, was in his and his wife's name.

In Iowa, the Social Security number of each registered owner is attached to the vehicle registration information.

"Run his wife's SSN, get a DL on her. Then do an NCIC check on both of them, Triple I. Then do a check through Ohio, the state police, or whatever they're called. Let me know when you're done, and I'll have a little more." NCIC is the National Crime Information Center, and a Triple I stands for the Interstate Identification Index. Access to it is restricted, of course.

"What about the logging?"

A problem, if you wanted things kept quiet. The requirements were that all NCIC checks for criminal records be logged, with the name of the subject, inquiry date, and identity of both the officer requesting the information and the dispatcher who ran it. The logbook was at the console, and anybody who worked for us could look at it and see who had been checked on.

"Keep a log yourself . . . hide it here. I'll clear it with Lamar later."

"Well, all right . . ." She looked worried. If I screwed this one up, she could be suspended.

"Don't worry."

"Sure."

I went back to the reserve's coffee klatch and talked with them for a while longer. Just to keep them out of the dispatch center while Sally was working on my project.

A few minutes later, she called again.

"Yeah."

"Got it."

"Okay, anything?"

"Nope."

"Good. Listen, now run those names through the PD in Cleveland, Ohio. Administrative message, to their intelligence unit, if possible. And get a PBX number for them, would you?"

"Sure."

"Thanks."

The reserves were looking at me a little strangely. They were very much aware that that sort of teletype traffic had nothing to do with any accidents.

"DCI's got me running some routine checks on some people," I said. "Give it to the night shift . . . we're too busy to do it during the day," I mimicked.

They agreed. They'd seen that before. Good.

"Look, guys, I'm gonna have to go into Lamar's office for a while, to make those phone calls. Nothing personal, but you know how it is."

They did. They decided to walk around the building again, just to have something to do.

That was one thing about our reserves. They nearly always got the most boring duty we had, but they never complained. Not once. They were as dedicated as the rest of us, if not more so.

I went into Lamar's office and shut the door. Called Sally and told her that I was on a different comm line. To call me there, when she had my information from Cleveland.

Then I sat back in Lamar's chair and just thought about the ramifications of my line of inquiry.

There were two reasons for my secrecy regarding the checking. First, I didn't want anybody else to jump to conclusions before I was reasonably sure of what I was doing. Second, I didn't want to look stupid in front of the whole group if I was wrong. And what I seemed to be suggesting seemed a little outrageous. Even to me.

But . . . the Ohio business, the suicide, the Satanic connection, the counseling of the survivor . . . God, but if it didn't seem to be one hell of a coincidence.

I looked around the room and saw Lamar's road atlas. Looked up Elyria. Found it about twenty miles southwest of Cleveland. Probably a suburb. Too close. Too close.

When you stumble on something sensitive like this, which is what I most certainly had done, you start to get a case of "Why me, O Lord?" And I was having a bad time with that. I was excited, because I thought I was onto something. But I was down, at the same time, because, especially in a small community, if you go for an upstanding citizen, you have real troubles. Nobody will believe you. They'd jump at a rumor that he was stepping out on his wife. Oh, yes. They'd love that. But to connect him with a murder? No way.

Damn.

The intercom buzzed. Sally.

"Yeah."

"Well, you got somebody's attention . . ."

"Oh yeah?"

"Yeah." She was a pretty good mimic, too. "Got a response real fast from Cleveland PD. Intelligence unit. And a PBX number. Officer is there now."

"Well, good."

She gave me the number. I told her to record it on the log, just as a number, with no ID beside it, for now.

I called the number, and as I waited for all the clicking and whirring to stop, I found myself drumming my fingers on the desk. Nervous. Excited. Worried.

"Detective Calumus."

"Yeah, this is Deputy Houseman, Nation County, Iowa."

"Yes. We got your message a few minutes ago."

"Yeah. Uh, I'm checking on two subjects, a Mark Rothberg, he's a pastor, and his wife, Betty. You know 'em?"

"We have some information. Do you have a particular reason for checking?"

Okay, I thought to myself. Here goes nothing.

"Yes, as a matter of fact, I do. We've had a quadruple homicide here, and it seems to have Satanic overtones. Believed to be similar to one you people had a few years back."

"How do you know it's similar?"

"VICAP."

"We had three victims."

"I know."

"Main suspect committed suicide. Second suspect never identified. Satanic motive, revenge, some problem with two of the three victims snitching off some of the others. At least, they apparently thought they had."

"Okay."

"Bloody fuckin' mess, I tell you no lie. Really severely mutilated those people. Fucked my partner's previous partner up so bad he took a psych disability."

"That bad?"

"Was to him. So how does Rothberg fit into your case?"

"I'm not sure yet. But the connection is there, as far as I can tell."

"Well, we had him connected on the side. I've got the file right here." There was a brief pause. "Just a second here . . . By the way, my partner and his previous were the case officers, like I said, and this Rothberg broad was a big part of his ex-partner getting his disability . . . Here it is, yeah, Mark William Rothberg, and Elizabeth Frances Rothberg. Née Killian. It was her brother who committed suicide—Philip Killian."

"Her brother?" Jesus. "You sure?"

He was insulted. "Unless she lied. And it doesn't sound like anybody would claim the little shit unless they had to."

"Okay."

"My partner said she just couldn't believe it. Her husband could, but she couldn't. Hired a private dick to try to prove we set it up after they found his body. Because we wanted to solve the homicides, she claimed. Planted the evidence. Bullshit."

"Yeah."

"But she kept it up for three, four months. Regular pain in the ass."

"I'll bet."

"Got her uncle and her sister involved, too, I guess . . . whole fuckin' family is nuts. Anyway, my partner says she finally gave up. So you got her out there?"

"Yeah."

"Giving you any trouble? Hey, I read about your murders, I think. Our paper didn't say anything about Satanism, though. Sure I did. Last week, about?"

"Yeah. Well, we're trying to hold the lid on the Satanic stuff right now. Our local newspeople have hit on it, but there's not been too much on the national media, at least not yet."

"Well, just wait, buddy. Just wait."

"Yeah."

"Good old Betty giving you any trouble?"

"Rothberg? No, not at all."

"Well, don't let her get started. She'll bug you to death."

"Yeah."

"You want a copy of our file? I can fax it to you real quick."

"Uh, we don't have any fax equipment. Let me check with the state—they might have something that can be used."

"Okay."

"Your name is . . ."

"Detective Tony Calumus."

"Okay. Could I talk to your partner?"

"He's not here right now, but I think you can in about an hour or so. I'll have him call you." I could almost see the grin. "It's his favorite fuckin' case."

"Yeah, I'll bet. Well, okay, hey, thanks for the help."

"No problem. Maybe you can clear this one for us. I sure would like to get the son of a bitch who did it here."

"Me too."

"Well, good luck. Don't get discouraged. Keep at 'em."

"Oh, yeah. Too dumb to give up."

"Yeah."

I hung up the phone. Son of a bitch.

I went out to the kitchen to get some more coffee. It was all gone.

Reserves. I put on another pot, and while I was waiting, I sat down at dispatch.

"Something wrong?"

"Not really. Not at all, in fact."

"You look funny," said Sally.

"Maybe I do . . ."

"You're sure as hell distracted. Perk up!" She lowered her voice. "Is it about the Rothbergs?"

"Yes."

She didn't say anything. Neither did I.

"I put on another pot of coffee. You want some?" I asked.

"Yeah, I guess so, it's only one-thirty."

"Okay. And why don't you call one of the state agents at the motel— I'm gonna have to talk to 'em."

"Which one?"

"Better make it Hester."

When I came back in with two cups, she had her on the phone. And both reserve officers were standing at the console.

"I'll take it in the back room."

The first thing that Hester said was "This better be good." She sounded pretty sleepy, her voice very soft, but raspy at the same time.

I told her what I had found out. And how. Started with the how, and sort of let it build. I was pretty proud of myself, actually.

"You've got to be kidding?"

"Nope."

"Holy shit." There were muffled scrambling sounds in the background as she got out of bed. "We'll be in five to ten. Minutes. I'll call Hal."

"Okay."

"I'm gonna call Saperstein, too. Maybe you should call Lamar?"

"Will do," I said.

I sat back. Well, here we go again. Entropy. Increases.

I called Lamar and told him. He wasn't as excited as Hester, but he sure was interested.

"Just make damned sure, before you do anything."

"You bet."

"Art's off tonight, isn't he?"

"Yeah."

"Okay, look, if things start to happen, call him in."

"Okay."

"Good luck, dumb shit."

"Thanks, Lamar. Do I get a raise?"

"You'll be lucky if I keep paying you."

29

When the troops were assembled, they asked me to run it by them again. I did. Step by step.

"We better get that file from Cleveland," said Hal, when I'd finished.

"We have fax at the CR office," said Hester. "I can call down and get it ready."

"Okay," said Hal. "When you get it set up, let me know, and we'll call Cleveland. I want to talk to this Calumus myself. And especially his partner."

"Right," said Hester.

"And let's get somebody up at the lab. We need those blood samples today."

As a matter of routine, Hester had obtained subpoenas for blood and saliva samples of all the members of the cult we had arrested. Just to make sure that one of them hadn't killed the four. They weren't back yet.

"That ought to piss 'em off," said Hester.

Hal shrugged. "If I have to call the director, I will. If he has to call the governor, he will. You might tell 'em that."

Hester smiled. "I might have to." She slurped her coffee. "God, who made this shit?"

I confessed.

"Whoa, this is bad."

"Hey, it's guaranteed to keep you up for twenty-four hours."

"Sure as hell ought to."

While she called the on-call lab agent in Des Moines, who was at home, and began to convince him to go to the office to get the samples done, I made a quick trip to the rest room. Hester was still on the phone when I came out.

"No, today. By ten A.M. . . . That's right, today . . . Hey, Hal says he'll call the director if he has to. The governor, too . . . Yeah, he's serious. Dead serious . . . Well, if that's what it takes . . ."

She looked up at Hal, the dead phone hanging in her hand.

"You better be ready to call the director."

"Why?"

" 'Cause that's what he says it's gonna take." She smiled.

"Son of a bitch!" Hall picked up the phone and dialed a number.

"Sir, Agent Greeley, I'm sorry to bother you . . . Yes, sir, I know . . . Sir, we need something from the lab today . . . Yes, I know, that's true, but we need it today . . . Well, I think we may be able to conclude this case today or tomorrow if we can get that stuff from the lab . . . Yes, sir, I think we might . . . Yes, sir, just a moment . . ."

He gestured frantically at Hester. "Gimme that tech's number."

"Okay, sir, here it is," he said, and gave him the technician's home number in Des Moines. "Thank you, sir . . . Yes, okay, I will, as soon as I know . . . Thank you again.

"Well," he said, pleased, "we ought to get action now."

"You didn't tell him that if he couldn't get results, he was supposed to call the governor," said Hester. "I really wanted to hear that."

"Fuck you, Hester," Hal said without malice.

"You couldn't get that lucky, Greeley."

He shook his head. "Probably not. Your loss."

"That's not what your wife says."

"You got that fax set up yet?"

"Shut up—who am I, your secretary?"

She picked up the phone and made the call to the Cedar Rapids office.

"After I talk to this Calumus, Carl," said Hal, "we'll decide what to do about the Rothbergs. I'd like to talk to them, and as soon as we can."

"Good."

I looked at my watch: 03:50. "He should be up by seven, I'd guess."

Hester hung up the phone. "Fax is set to go. We'll work out a 10–5 with the troops to bring it up as soon as it's here."

"Okay," said Hal. "Let's call Calumus and get it coming."

He placed the call, and appeared to be receiving the same information I had, when the intercom buzzed. Sally wanted to know if it was all right if Traer could have a copy of the current Criminal Code and volume 4 of "Iowa Practice," covering criminal law and procedure.

"Now?"

"Yes. He says he can't sleep."

"Okay, I'll get them in a minute. Just be sure it's not a trick to get you back there—in fact, I'll give them to him, okay?"

"Very fine with me."

"Wait a minute," said Hester. "Traer is up now?"

"Yeah, sounds like it."

"Just a minute . . . I've got an idea," said Hester. "Just wait till Hal's off the phone."

We waited. I went into Lamar's office and got the two volumes Traer had requested and set them on the counter. Hal got off the phone with Cleveland, and Hester put the proposition to him.

"Look, why don't we get Traer back here and just tell him most of what's going on. No names or anything. But the general information. Maybe, if we tell him that he's got a killer after the whole group, and one who's done it before, maybe he'll let us know where Rachel is."

Hal looked surprised. "No way."

"I think it'll work," said Hester.

"He won't say shit," said Hal.

"May I say something?" Saperstein finally spoke.

"Sure."

"Traer's an intelligent man. Well, an attorney, but still . . . If you lay out most of the case against him regarding the sacrifice of the child, and let him know the details, and then ask his cooperation with finding the man who killed his group, and let him know that there is no evidentiary connection between the crimes, he might go along with it. He might."

"No," said Hal. "He'll never tell us about Rachel's location. She's his best contact on the outside, and hiding her has become a game with him. He'll never go along with it."

There was a moment's silence.

"Can I say something?" I asked. It was, after all, our case.

"Sure," said Hal politely.

"Traer's probably going to bond out tomorrow—he has considerable resources. We know that. Once he's out, he's vulnerable, and Rachel no longer has much importance, except to bolster his ego within the group by keeping her from us. But she's the key to his survival, if this guy is really after him. She can identify the killer. And he's the key to Rachel."

Silence.

"And," I continued, "after he's out on bond, we won't get another shot at him until the trial for the murder of little Cynthia. That could be as much as a year from now. And even if we ID the killer by interviewing the Rothbergs, if he doesn't confess, he walks. We have no compelling physical evidence except the blood chemistry, and the county attorney won't charge based on that alone. I know he won't. But if we have Rachel able to ID the killer, we can sure as hell hold him on that. And we can probably offer Rachel immunity on the murder of her kid, anyway. 'Cause you know as well as I do that she'll claim coercion by the group and that she'll play the offended mother who was duped."

That may have been a mistake, I thought. The bit about Rachel testifying against Traer. I should have kept my mouth shut there.

"I agree with Carl," said Hester.

Hal looked at her for a second. Then at me. "Well, it's your county," he said.

Meaning that he was going to oppose, and that if it didn't work, it would be my responsibility. Meaning that he was passing the decision "down," as it were, and challenging me at the same time. He probably didn't think that I'd be able to make the decision and that he'd win by default.

"You're right," I said. "I'll go get him. Hester, how about you and me and Mr. Saperstein doing the talking? If it's all right with you," I said, looking at Hal. He was the case officer, after all. If we were going to play little games here, we might as well go all the way.

"Okay by me," said Hal. No choice. "Good luck." He didn't mean it.

"Thanks." I didn't mean that, either. "Let's talk to him in the kitchen, near the coffee. Why don't I meet you in there?"

Hester and Saperstein went to the kitchen, and I walked back into dispatch and got the cell keys from Sally.

"We're gonna talk with Traer, as long as he's up," I said. "I'm going to be 10–6 as hell, so if any calls come in, give 'em to somebody else." I have to admit that I was also a little pissed about Hal talking to Calumus and asking the same questions that I had already asked him. The fact that I wanted to talk to the partner, and original case officer, also rankled. Then, again, I was pleased about him getting the same answers. It's always been a little problem, the state people not thinking that the county people are really competent. And this "county people" was currently hoping that they were wrong.

I got back to the cell area, and Traer was sitting at the table in the bull pen.

He got up and came toward me. "The little redhead afraid of me? Think I might corrupt her, or cast a spell?" He was smiling, but the question was serious. He probably thought he could.

"Nope." I unlocked the door, and his eyes widened a little bit. "Come on out, Oswald, my boy. I want to talk to you."

Traer came out, but he was suspicious. "What about?"

"Tell you when we get to the kitchen."

I stood aside, placing him in front of me. "Take the first left, and go where I say."

He didn't reply, but followed orders. It had probably crossed his mind that I could be taking him out to beat him up or something. If it had, he didn't let it show. I directed him to the kitchen, and I could tell by his walk that he relaxed just a bit when he saw Hester.

"Have a seat," I said. "This is Hester Gorse, Iowa Division of Criminal Investigation"

"How do you do, my dear?"

Hester just looked at him.

"And this is Detective Saperstein, New York Police Department."

Traer stuck out his hand. Saperstein shook it.

"What brings you here?" asked Traer. He appeared a little flattered and a little intrigued. He obviously felt that he was the reason for Saperstein's presense. He was, of course, correct.

"You," said Saperstein.

"I hate to disappoint you, Detective Saperstein, but I've never been to the Big Apple."

"We haven't missed you, Mr. Traer."

I finished stuffing a pillow into the small connecting port between the cells and the kitchen, where the food was passed in to the prisoners, and where they had been seen on occasion with their ears pressed, listening to conversations in the kitchen. "Coffee?" I asked all around.

Hester helped pour. Some indication of her intense interest, because normally I don't think she would have. She was beginning to play a role, I thought. It sure wouldn't hurt if Traer considered her a subservient woman.

We cozied up around the table. Since I was "in charge," I felt it would be best if I started the conversation in the right direction.

"Oswald," I said.

"Please call me Link," he said. "My middle name is Lincoln, and I prefer that."

"Okay, Link. We have some information, and so do you. We'd like to trade some data."

"I probably won't be able to help you, but go ahead. It should be interesting, if nothing else."

So far so good. "I know you're aware of your rights, but I'll tell you, anyway," I said. I recited Miranda.

"Very good," said Traer. "You do that well."

"Thank you. Let's start with this. You are a Satanist."

"Yes."

"As such, you are probably a pragmatist as well?"

"I like to think so."

"And, being a pragmatist, I assume you have an interest in staying alive?"

"Assuredly."

"Well, we have a partial ID on the man who killed Phyllis and friends."

"I would hope so."

"Yes. The interesting thing is, we don't know who he is. We just know about him. No positive ID."

"How unfortunate," he said. He was trying to suppress it, but his interest was showing. "I sincerely hope you're not all as inept as I've made out for the last few years." He smiled.

"Well, I do, too, Link. Now, I'll let Hester tell you how much evidence we have."

She did, taking him step by step through the lab ID process. I watched him very closely while she talked. We weren't taking much of a chance, even if Oswald had been the perpetrator. All this would be readily available on discovery, anyway.

When she'd finished, Traer said. "That's all very basic, of course, but you have done your task efficiently. My compliments."

"Now," I interjected, before Hester could take his head off, "Hester ran the descriptors through the VICAP system, to check to see if there was any other crime that fit this description."

"Oh?"

"And it turned out that there was."

His eyes widened again. I decided that that was about all the emotion he would ever permit to show through. He didn't say anything, but he leaned forward a bit.

"A few years ago, in Ohio. Nearly the exact MO." Okay, so I lied a little. He was a Satanist. All's fair . . . "We have information," I said, "That indicates that this unknown killer wants your whole group. Especially you."

I let that sink in.

"That's why we have two reserve officers here tonight, Link. To make sure he doesn't get you while you're our guest."

He had to have noticed, and the other two prisoners were bound to have told him that it was unusual to have the reserves wandering back into the cell area. He'd probably thought it was to keep him in.

"I see."

"We have a twofold interest here," I told him. "One, we don't want another murder or two in the county. Makes us look bad."

"I can understand that," he said.

"And, number two, we want to get the killer. Not getting him makes us look bad, too."

"We wouldn't want that."

"That's where you come in."

He sat back. "You want me to be the bait? If so, I'm sorry to disappoint you."

Hadn't even occurred to me. But not a bad idea.

"No, not at all. You see, the only person we know who may be able to ID the killer is Rachel."

"Ah."

"We have a lead that we're going to follow up today," said Hester. "A connection from Ohio to here. But the information won't give us enough to hold the killer, although we think that it will identify him."

"Yes."

"Only Rachel can do that," she said.

"I have one question," said Traer.

"Sure," I said.

"Who is this Rachel?"

30

"Cut the shit, Oswald!" said Saperstein.

"Pardon?" said Traer with an innocent look.

"You heard me. Rachel is your breeder and the mother of the sacrifice. Don't try to stonewall me, asshole. You know who she is and where she is. And trying to stall us, you're going to get somebody else killed."

"I'm sorry," said Traer, "but I'm afraid you're wrong."

"The hell I am," said Saperstein. "Your whole plan is shot now, anyway. The ultimate goal—the suicide of the whole coven, except for you. The enhancement of your reputation . . . You're gonna look pretty silly in the eyes of that other coven you have going. The important one, the one that's going to make you famous. The whole thing's been blown, with the killer stalking your group. You have no power to protect them, no power to stop him. Your reputation is going downhill. Been contacted by your other following yet? They laugh?"

I hadn't the foggiest idea what the hell he was talking about. But Traer did. He didn't say anything, but Saperstein was hitting home.

"You can only win by talking with us. And that's the only way you can. Your reputation can be enhanced by doing a little time for the killing of Cynthia Larsen. A few years you'll walk out, if not sooner. You know that. Walk right into an influential, rich coven and make the big bucks. You'll be famous. But your original coven gets knocked off, or worse, turns on you because you can't protect them—you're done."

Traer was thinking.

"Your ego strong enough to stand that? A second-rate Satanist, no high-priest status except with some teenagers? A little sixteen-year-old pussy once in a while? Shit, you can't even talk to her after you screw her—just a dumb kid. Impress her, impress nobody. And some young stud takes her away from you. You get no money, no high standard of living, preaching to a bunch of little kids in a three-room apartment. What you gonna do, drive a cab? Write a book on how you failed as a Satanist? Come on, Traer. We're the only chance you got for fame and fortune. You cooperate with us, give up Rachel, you got it made. Your rep is enhanced in the joint. Your important coven waits for you, like the second coming. You can write your own ticket. Make Anton La Vey look like a piker. You know it. We know it. Piss on Rachel and the rest of that group. But do it our way. Otherwise, you lose all around."

Saperstein stopped. He stared at Traer, long and hard.

"You know I'm right. The murder of Cynthia was a calculated risk, and you know it. That's why you made the tape. To show the other coven. You aren't a real Satanist, are you? You're just out to go up the scale, and this was the right way at the right time, wasn't it? You're an act, and you took the ultimate risk to get the bucks and the influence. You got caught. But you can still make your rep—unless you fuck up now, unless the other coven finds out that they can get killed, tracked down, and you're the magnet for the killer. They'll drop you like a hot rock." He paused for breath. "You're done unless you cooperate with us, and you know it."

I was amazed. So, apparently, was Hester. Saperstein had kept such a low profile the last few days . . . he must have been grinding this out all the time. And listening to him, I would have cooperated, myself. Impressive.

"I'm not quite certain I understand you," said Traer, but the conviction was lacking.

"Shit," said Saperstein. "You understand. You just hate to think that you can be outthought. Don't you?"

Silence.

"Your ego can't handle having a dumb cop get ahead of you, can it?" Saperstein's voice was heavy with sarcasm. "You with your little law degree from Iowa—an educated man."

Traer still didn't speak.

"If it's any help, I got my LL.D. from Harvard."

Surprised me. But it was apparently all the salve that Traer's ego needed to enable him to capitulate.

"I'd like some time to think."

"We haven't got much time, if we're gonna get the killer," said Saperstein. "We have to find Rachel right away. Otherwise, he gets away from us, and he's real good at hiding."

"Some time, just some. I have some things to consider."

"We'll give you ten minutes," said Saperstein. He looked at me. "You got someplace where he can be alone for a few minutes?"

I escorted Traer to a small cell we used for the occasional second woman prisoner or juveniles. Locked him in, told Sally where he was, so she could activate the surveillance camera in that area. She gave me a surprised look but didn't ask any questions. "Talk to me really quick, soonest, will you?"

"Now all right?"

"Yes." She lowered her voice. "Thought you should know. Hal called the boss."

"His boss?"

"No, ours. About as soon as you went to the kitchen."

"No shit . . ." Calling Lamar at this hour? Even if he wasn't happy with me, that seemed to be taking it too far.

"And Lamar looks like he's coming in. He came up on the radio about two minutes ago."

"Thanks, kid." I grinned at her. "I owe you."

I went back to Hester and Saperstein in the kitchen.

"Jesus, Bill," I said, "I didn't know you knew so much about him."

Hester shook her head slowly from side to side and chuckled. "You want to tell him?"

Saperstein grinned. "Sure." He handed me my coffee. "Sit down, Carl."

I sat.

"Pure bullshit."

"What?" I asked.

"Pure bullshit, I was guessing. Well, at least, for a lot of it."

"You're kidding."

"Nope. At least, the part about the other coven was a guess. The part about him walking in a few years was an outright lie."

"You're obviously pretty close."

"Yeah. Well, I have to admit, I've got him figured out. He's just not like the dyed-in-the-wool Satanist I've dealt with before. But I've met his type, too. Lucifer's flimflam man. There are lots of them out there." He sipped his coffee. "His con is no different than any other con. He just uses Satan as a vehicle instead of séances, or a cure for cancer or AIDS."

"How did you know?" asked Hester.

"The tape. Too many flourishes. What we saw was a practice session. I'm sure the tape where they killed Cynthia is around someplace. Not with this group, but with the other one. A practice session for good old Oswald. The rest of the coven was playing it for real."

"You think he'll tell us where Rachel is?"

"Sure. No doubt in my mind."

"I hope you're right."

"I used to work bunco for a while, before I got transferred to homicide. I'm right."

I shook my head. "But, to kill a baby just for that . . ."

Saperstein shrugged. "I'll tell you the truth. It was a chance he took, for sure. But he made it, didn't he? The only thing that exposed him was our killer. Nobody else knew about it. He figured that in a rural area like this, he could hide the fact forever. The cops aren't sophisticated, the courts wouldn't believe them if they were." He smiled. "Nothing personal."

I shrugged.

"The only people who knew were dedicated. To Satan, or to themselves. They all participated, so they all shared the guilt. Look at Elizabeth Mills—you think she'd crack? You think she'd let her husband slip up?"

"That gives him a motive to kill our four victims, you know."

"A motive, maybe, but that's not his style. Killing them like that wouldn't occur to him. Coercion is his strongest suit. If he thought there was a leak, Phyllis or Elizabeth would take care of it for him. The weakest parts of his group up here were Kenneth Mills and McGuire. Kenny was being handled well by Elizabeth, and McGuire was being taken care of by his own conscience and Phyllis and Peggy. He had it sacked."

"I hope you're right," I said. "He looked pretty Satanic to me."

"You want to meet a real Satanic individual," said Saperstein, "wait till you find our killer. There's a Satanic psychopath. In the flesh."

"Think so?" asked Hester.

"Know so," said Saperstein. "You profiled him—you know he's psychotic. I profiled him, too." He tapped his head. "Up here. This boy's a real Satanist. No mumbo jumbo, none of the trappings the showman uses. In fact, the supposedly Satanic 'clues' at the scene may not have been made to throw us off the track. They may have been a 'statement' by a Satanic ascetic. I think our killer really believes he works for Satan."

I thought about that. Could be.

I looked at my watch. "The ten minutes are up." I stood.

"Let him wait for a few minutes," said Saperstein. "He's had his mind made up for nine minutes already. Let him sweat. He's gonna get anxious now. He's gonna want to impress us with his decision. Let us know how smart he is. He's gonna be driven to tell us, by his own ego, about a lot of things. Give him another ten."

"You're sure of yourself, aren't you?" said Hester.

Saperstein leaned back in his chair and contemplated his coffee cup. He looked up at her. "Yeah, I am. About Oswald. I feel like I've known him for years." He folded his hands behind his head. "I'm savoring Oswald Traer, because I'm on firm ground with him, and I have him where I want him. Because when we're done with Oswald, we go for the killer. And he scares me to death."

"Why?" I asked.

"Because our Oswald here is human. I don't think that our killer is. Not in the way we define it. He's a vicious, methodical robot. When he's in this mode, his mind is clear, and so is his conscience. He's not going to be easy to stop. Or to catch."

He brought his hands down to the table and pushed his chair back. "Let's get him."

I brought him back into the kitchen.

"You want your attorney present?" asked Saperstein.

"That's hardly necessary. What I'm considering telling you has no inculpatory properties whatsoever."

"Good."

"I'm going to advise you of your rights again, anyway," said Hester. "It'll make me feel better."

"Whatever pleases you, my dear."

Having placated the goddess Miranda, we got down to business.

"Well . . ."

"Rachel is staying at the Willmont Hotel in Cedar Rapids, under the assumed name of Allison Crowley."

"How original," said Saperstein.

"She thought so."

"Can she identify the killer?"

"She says she can."

"Did she tell you what happened that night?" asked Hester.

"Yes."

"What did she tell you?"

He considered for a moment. "You should really ask her."

"We will," said Hester. "Why don't you tell us, anyway."

"Just a second," I said. "Let's get Hal."

"Who is he?" asked Traer.

"DCI agent, working the homicides."

"That's acceptable to me," he said.

I went to the back office, very pleased.

Hal looked up as I came in. So did Lamar.

"What did he have to say?" asked Hal.

"Hi, boss." I grinned at Lamar. "Glad to see you working."

"Uh-huh," grunted Lamar. Distracted.

You bet, I thought. Just the way he was when somebody of consequence pitched a bitch about one of us.

"Rachel is in the Willmont Hotel in CR, under the name of Allison Crowley. She can ID the killer, and she's told Traer what happened that night, and he's about to tell us, so I thought you might like to hear. And I think we ought to get ahold of CRPD and get her picked up right away." I grinned so hard it hurt.

"I'll be damned."

He picked up the phone and was telling CRPD where Rachel was when I headed back to the kitchen. Lamar caught up to me in the hall.

"Carl . . ."

"Yeah?" I stopped. The hall was about the only place at the office where you could have a private conversation these days.

"Good work . . . I'm taking Theo off the case."

I must have looked shocked.

He nodded. "Has to be done. But keep it quiet."

"He screwed up something important, didn't he?"

"Oh, not really."

"Then who has he been talking to?"

"He's just got to get off the case. Personal reasons. That's all there is. I may be able to tell you later. Not now." He shook his head, like he was clearing it. "I'll tell him when he comes in on his next shift, day after tomorrow. So don't let on, okay?"

I nodded. "Okay with me." It felt good to share a secret with Lamar. He doesn't say word one to most people, and admitting a mistake is not easy for him. It kinda got awkward for a second, though.

"You guys gonna do some more interviews in the kitchen?"

I took the hint. Hal caught up and followed me back.

"They should have her in about twenty minutes," he said.

Traer looked him over when he walked in. Said nothing.

We settled ourselves around the table, making Traer the center of attention. He appeared pleased.

"Okay, Link," said Hester. "Tell us what Rachel told you."

Traer settled back and began.

"Rachel came to me Sunday morning, about ten. She was very frightened, and had this story about Peg being killed by Satan. I didn't believe her, of course. So I called Phyllis and couldn't get an answer. I thought that strange, but wasn't too concerned." He looked around. "She did have a tendency to indulge on weekends, you know.

"Anyway, Rachel had this wild story about Satan being in the house when she came home. She and Peg. She said that the two of them had been in a bar in Maitland, that they'd left Phyllis and Bill and Frank at the house."

He paused.

"The three of them were, oh, otherwise engaged, or about to be, when the women left."

He paused again. Just like an attorney, I thought. Pausing for effect.

"They got home sometime after midnight, I believe she said. They didn't see anyone else at first. They didn't expect to, you know. The house was apparently rather dark, but there was a light in Phyllis's bedroom." He smiled wanly. "That was expected, too, you know? Anyway, apparently Peg went into the other bedroom, to go to bed, and Rachel went into the kitchen to get something. That's when she noticed the bloody mess on the counter and in the Osterizer."

He looked at the coffeepot. "May I have some coffee, please?"

I got it for him.

"She said that she didn't know what it was at first, but when she did, she got real terrified. She went to Phyllis's bedroom and quietly opened the door and saw Bill."

Another pause.

"It must have been horrible for her," he said. "She is a very sensitive girl."

So sensitive, she got pregnant and had a kid for you to kill, I thought.

"She said that she froze for a moment or two. That she ran to the other bedroom and screamed for Peg. She apparently had some difficulty communicating what had happened, because she said that Peg slapped her."

He paused again.

"She took Peg to the bedroom, where Bill was. Peg saw what had happened and ran back to her room to get her clothes. Rachel went to the front door and waited for her. That's when she said that she saw him—the one she thought was Satan."

Pause for effect. It was effective.

"He came up from the basement, she said. Very quiet, seemingly very slow, although I suppose that she was so excited it just seemed that way, don't you? Anyway, she said that he didn't see her but that Peg yelled to her to get the car, and he heard her. He went to the bedroom and went inside, and Peg was apparently still in there." He paused. "She never saw Peg again."

He looked at us. We looked at him. Five cops, all with burning questions. But he wasn't done yet. We didn't want to stop his tale here. So we said nothing.

"She went to the car and started it and waited for Peg to come out. She waited for some time, it seems. She said that it seemed like a very long time. But she eventually became convinced that Peg wouldn't come out. Then the door opened, and she saw him again. She backed the car out and drove away as fast as she could."

Silence. "Where did she go?" asked Hester. I was proud of myself—somebody else asked before I did.

"I'm not sure," he said. "I don't think she is, either. But she eventually went to her friend's house and called the police."

"What friend?" I asked, jumping in ahead of Hal by about a tenth of a second.

"The neighbor lady, the one who wanted to join our group—Helen."

"Helen Bockman?" I asked.

"Yes, I think Bockman is right. The one that Phyllis was playing with. Rachel knew her. One of the few people that Rachel knows in this area, I'm sure. And she had expressed an interest in us."

"Yes." Well, what do you know.

"She said that this Helen was very frightened and that she, Rachel, called the police from her house. She wanted to stay there, I think, but this Helen's husband woke up, heard part of the phone conversation, and came out and unplugged the phone from the wall, to stop her from saying where she was. He was quite angry and told her that she had to leave. That they didn't want to be involved at all."

"Did she know who this man was, the one she thought was Satan?" asked Hal.

"She said not." He thought for a second. "But I think she was lying."

"You think she knew him?"

"I'm sure of it. She'd been seeing this man, if it's the one I think it is, for a while. She'd said he communes with Satan often. That he has 'used' her for some time. Just the two of them used to go off together." He took a sip of coffee. "I think he was the father of the child."

"But you never knew him?" Hal.

"Never laid eyes on him."

"Did she ever say what he looked like?" From Hester.

"She said he was very dark, very large. That he moved like a cat, very swift."

"What does she mean by dark? Was he black?" I asked.

"No, no. Dark means evil. He was very evil."

"Oh."

"Do you know what she meant by very large?" I asked.

"Those aren't her exact words. You have to know Rachel. What she said was something like 'he was a tall dude,' if I remember correctly," he said dryly.

"No other description?"

"Well, yes, there was." Traer actually giggled. "She'd said that he had a big dick . . . and that she could see it that night . . ."

"What?" said Hester.

"A big dick. You surely know what a dick is."

"Yeah, I know. But how could she tell that?"

"That night or before?" Traer asked rhetorically. The look he got from Hester made *me* flinch, and it had missed me by a couple of feet. "I'm sorry, I must have forgotten to tell you. He was nude, you see."

I looked at Hester. I couldn't resist. "This could complicate a lineup . . ."

Traer looked at me. "You have a rather unique sense of humor . . . I like that."

"I try to control it."

"You shouldn't. It makes it easier to talk."

"So what did you do with Rachel, decide to hide her?" asked Hal.

"Of course not," said Traer. "I was trying to confirm the incident, and I was trying to decide on the best course of action for her."

"Big of you. Thinking of her like that," Hal said.

"Not at all," said Traer. "After all, I'm her attorney of record. I am constrained by my professional ethics to maintain a constant awareness of the best interests of my client." He smiled.

"Unless it interferes with yours," said Hester.

"What do you mean?" Traer asked.

"You give her up to help us get somebody off your ass."

"Not at all . . . It is obviously in her best interests for her favorite attorney to continue to stay alive." He grinned at me. "You'll appreciate that."

"I do," I said, grinning. And thinking, alive in prison, you dummy. For quite a while. It was fascinating to see this man manipulated by his own ego.

"One more question?" said Hester.

"Surely."

"What Rachel told you doesn't exactly add up with what we know." She looked at him for a moment, interested. "What makes you think she's not lying to you?"

"She wouldn't do that."

Hester grinned. "Don't be too sure. You middle-aged men are pretty easy."

31

By the time we got Traer back in his cell, everybody was looking tired, but nobody felt that way.

CRPD had notified us that they had Rachel Larsen in custody. Lamar had been notified and had decided to call Ed Yarnell out early and send him down for her. Ed would take his wife as matron. They would stop at the DCI office and pick up the fax of the Cleveland PD file. Things were falling into place.

We had found the key. Now it was just a matter of bringing her to the lock. Or so we thought. Everybody was sort of congratulating one another, and the mood was pretty euphoric.

"We're on a roll again," said Hal. "Let's talk to Pastor Rothberg and his wife. They've got to be up by now."

That settled things down a little. You have a tendency to set a sequence of goals in a case, and you sometimes get a little high when you achieve one of them. The reality of Rachel as a goal would settle out soon. She was just a step, but the only one we had been able to define for what seemed to be so long.

"Shouldn't we get the file from Ohio first?" asked Hester.

"No, I don't think so," said Hal. "We have our energy up now, and the file should be here within an hour or two. We can use the fact that it's coming to put a little pressure on him."

"True," said Saperstein. "We have most of the file data, anyway. Anticipation may well do us more good than the file itself."

I thought about that. Yeah. *The file is coming.* Might be even better than "the file is right here" . . . yeah. If it's coming, you don't know what's in it. When it's here, it's going to be a letdown.

"Lamar's on his way in," I said. "Let's let him call it."

That was reasonable, because hauling in a clergyman was going to be a sensitive sort of thing.

In the meantime, it was decided that I'd call the county attorney and explain it to him. I used the intercom to ask Sally to place the call, so it would be logged. Just in case. There was no answer at his residence. I knew he and his wife were joggers—may well be out. Good, maybe he wouldn't be back before Lamar arrived at the office, and then Lamar could talk to him.

I went out to the kitchen to get my umpteenth cup of coffee, and on my way back through dispatch, Sally flagged me down.

"Phone call for you."

It was Mark Fueller, county attorney. Sally'd left a message with his kid.

I picked up one of the phones in dispatch and told Fueller what was happening. This was the first time Sally had known much of the detail of the case, and I had her full attention, too. When I got to the part about interviewing Rothberg, I told Fueller all about the Cleveland file.

"Oh, my God. Are you sure?"

"About what?"

"About his connection," said Fueller. "With the killer."

"Well, as sure as we can be without talking to him."

"Carl, this is pretty sensitive. Can it wait?"

"We don't think so, but it will be cleared with Lamar as soon as he gets in."

"Oh, damn . . . let me think a second . . ."

I could hear one of his kids yelling in the background, and his wife admonishing to "get dressed or we'll be late." And here was Mark trying to make the decision to bring in the county's best-known man of the cloth.

"Can't it wait?"

"Jeeze, Mark, I don't think so. The word is getting around, and we don't want our suspect to get wise and skip. We don't even know who he is yet."

He thought for a few more seconds. "Okay, then, go ahead. But keep me posted. I'll probably drop over after I check in at my office."

He lived in a truly small town about fifteen miles from Maitland.

I went back to the main office, after swearing Sally to silence, and found that Lamar had come in.

"Well, the county attorney says go."

"He does?" said Lamar.

"Just talked to him."

"Well, then, I guess that's what we do." He turned to Hal. "Let me go with you in an unmarked car. Less attention that way."

"Right," said Hal. Lamar was in civvies. Monday is his day off, and he wasn't supposed to be in.

I, on the other hand, was supposed to have been home hours ago. The specter of overtime was looming over my head. Well, comp time, actually. We didn't get paid for OT.

"Okay if I stick around for this?" I asked Lamar.

"You bet," he said on his way out the door.

I called Sue and told her I was all right but that I would probably be pretty late. She asked why, and I told her it had to do with the homicides. Tacit approval.

Lamar and Hal returned very quickly, with the Rothbergs following in their car. I watched them from the main office window. The Rothbergs were both wearing jogging outfits, and he put his arm around her as they walked to the door. Mutual support, I thought. We'd have to separate them for the interviews.

When they got inside, Lamar had them sit down and offered them coffee. They declined. He indicated Hal and said, "This officer has some questions to ask you."

Hal was standing with his back to the filing cabinets, leaning against them. He looked long and hard at the Rothbergs and then began.

"We've got a lot of questions to ask you. A lot of them. First, I'm going to advise you of your rights according to Miranda."

He did, asking them if they understood at each step. They did.

"Now," he said, "I'm going to share some information with you before I ask you anything. I want you to think carefully about what I'm about to tell you, and not say anything until I'm done. Do you understand?"

They did.

"We've gotten information about a case in Cleveland, Ohio. About a homicide they had a few years back."

The Rothbergs exchanged glances. Both of them, but particularly Betty, began to tense up.

"The case where your brother, Betty, committed suicide? The case where they suspect he was one of two perpetrators in the murder of three people?"

As instructed, the Rothbergs said nothing, but it was hard.

Hal told them about the similarities between the crimes, about the possible matchup with the suspect in both the Cleveland case and ours. About Mark Rothberg "counseling" a man who had been close to the suicide, according to his own statements. About the file from Cleveland being on the way to the office. He didn't mention Rachel, or most of what happened with Traer.

"We believe the two suspects are the same man, and we believe that you know who he is, and where he is. We want to know."

Silence.

"Do you have any questions?" asked Hester.

Silence.

"Do you want to make any statements?"

"I think," said Mark Rothberg, "that we'd better talk to an attorney first."

"Sure," I said. "Do you have one in mind?"

"No."

"Then we'll just have to pick one at random," said Lamar.

"That would be fine," said Rothberg.

We had a list of attorneys posted on the wall. Lamar found the first one from Maitland, Edward Phelps. He called him.

"Mr. Phelps? This is Lamar Ridgeway, the sheriff. Look, we have two people up here that need an attorney right away . . . Yes, it's a criminal case . . . No, it's not like that at all . . . I know you don't usually, but right now you're going to have to . . . Yes, right away . . . No, not good enough. This is extremely important, and they need you right now . . . Thank you." He hung up the phone. "He'll be right up."

I offered them coffee again. They accepted. Hester went for it, her turn.

I watched the Rothbergs sitting there in complete silence, both very self-possessed. Damn, I thought, this could drag on till noon tomorrow. They aren't going to talk. They aren't going to say a word. We're going to bomb on this one for sure. Saperstein can't bail us out on this one. And maybe we're wrong. Maybe I'm wrong. The anxiety level was skyrocketing, and the acid in my stomach was about to burn through my ballistic vest.

Phelps drove up and walked toward the door. He looked like he was in a bad mood. Blue jeans and a plaid shirt. Jacket. No papers or briefcase. As he got closer, I could see his jaw muscles working. I opened the door for him.

"Good morning."

"I think not."

He stepped around the corner and saw the Rothbergs. "These people?" he asked, visibly astonished.

"The Rothbergs, yes."

"What's going on here?"

Hal told him. In the same detail he'd explained it to the Rothbergs.

"I'd like to confer with my clients in private."

"Sure," said Lamar, and opened the door to his private office. "In here. We have coffee, if you like, and I'm going to go get some doughnuts."

The three of them disappeared into his private space.

They were in there for a long time.

"You wanna go on home?" Lamar asked me.

"Oh, I think I'll stick around for a while, if it's okay with you."

"Don't forget you gotta work tonight."

"I won't."

Lamar went for doughnuts. The rest of us sat around, making small talk and waiting. Lamar came back. We ate. We waited, and then waited some more. The momentum was going out of the case fast. Fatigue began to set in with all of us, and boredom.

I finally sat down, put my feet on a desk, and leaned my head back against the wall and closed my eyes. The doughnuts were absorbing some of the acid, but I had popped some Rolaids, anyway. Relax, I said to myself. Just relax.

I must have dozed off, because I was suddenly aware of a minor commotion. Ed and his wife had arrived with Rachel and the fax file.

I'd never seen Rachel before, but she looked shot to me. She appeared very small, in a large green quilted jacket, with a red stocking cap on her head. Set off by handcuffs on her wrists, in front of her. Rumpled, disheveled, and very lonely. Our witness.

"Folks," said Ed, "I'd like you to meet Rachel."

"Hello, Rachel," said Hester. Nobody else said anything.

Neither did she.

Ed handed Hal the fax file and had him sign a receipt for it. It was thick. I couldn't wait to get my hands on it, but DCI had dibs.

"Why am I under arrest?" said Rachel. Out of the blue.

"Did you read the warrant to her?" Lamar asked Ed.

"Yes, I did."

"Then you know why," said Lamar.

"You don't know what you're doing," said Rachel. Flat, but convinced.

"Well, you just let us worry about that," said Lamar.

"I don't know where you got your information," said Rachel, "but somebody's lying to you. That's all I have to say."

Flat, again. Not angry. She was reciting.

Just then the door opened, and Attorney Phelps and the Rothbergs came out of Lamar's office. Rachel saw them and just exploded.

"God damn you, can't you leave me alone!"

Betty Rothberg looked like she'd been slapped. Mark's jaw actually dropped.

"You fuckers! I should have known it was you!" Rachel whirled on Lamar. "Get my fucking sister out of here!" she screamed. "Get her out of here!"

Pandemonium. Rachel turned for the door and tried to leave the building. Ed grabbed her, and she started kicking him. I went to help Ed, while Betty Rothberg started yelling, "Rachel, Rachel!" and came running toward us. Hal intercepted her, and Mark Rothberg was yelling at the same time about "whore, whore of Satan!" The fax file flew off the counter and onto the floor, Hester jumped up and spilled her coffee. Sally, who was just ending her shift, and was coming down the hall, jumped back as Ed and I went waltzing through with Rachel, who was doing everything she could to bite my arm. It was a very busy ten seconds.

I finally wrapped my arms around Rachel's waist from behind and just picked her up off the floor and carried her back to the office. Hester had her hand on Betty's chest, stiff-armed, and was backing her toward Lamar's office. Hester and Hal had turned their attention to Mark Rothberg and were shutting him down in the corner. Lamar grabbed Rachel's flying feet as I walked by, and we laid her down on the desk. Saperstein was looking very amused, and Attorney Phelps looked like he wished he'd been a lit major.

Ed reached around me and grabbed Rachel's hair, holding a large handful firmly on the desk surface. She went inert. Hester had pushed Betty back into a chair, and Mark was holding his hands at chest level, palms outward, and saying, "I'm sorry, I apologize."

A few seconds later, I realized that we were mopping up Hester's spilled coffee with Rachel, so I sat her up and told her to be quiet. She just nodded.

Everybody sort of caught their breath.

Sally cautiously poked her head into the office.

"You need anything else before I go home?" Big grin.

Hal picked up the fax file, straightened it out, and looked at Betty Rothberg. He was still breathing hard. "So . . . Rachel's your sister?"

Betty nodded, and tears began to run down her cheeks.

Rachel looked over at her. "That's it, cry, bitch." Back to her flat, nearly monotone voice.

Betty said nothing.

"You don't talk to your sister like that," said Mark Rothberg. "Not after what you've put her through."

"Shut up, you fucking wimp," said Rachel. "Keep your nose out, too, asshole."

Rachel, I decided, was not going to be an object of sympathy.

"Shut your face," I said.

"Fuck you, pig."

I looked her up and down, and gave her my best smile. "No, I don't think so . . . I don't want anything to fall off."

She tried to kick me, but Lamar caught her foot.

"Take these fuckin' cuffs off, pig, and we'll see who's tough around here!"

"Oh," said Lamar, "I think we'll leave 'em on for just a bit."

We regrouped. Hal and Ed took Betty back into Lamar's office, Hester and I took Mark Rothberg into the far rear office, and Lamar and Ed's wife booked Rachel into jail. Attorney Phelps, a little disorganized himself, divided his time between the two Rothbergs. They both wanted to talk, and he wanted to be with both of them at the same time. We had them sign waivers.

While I was out with Mark Rothberg's waiver, making a Xerox copy in the main office, the county attorney walked in.

"Well, anything happening?"

I started to laugh, and Lamar wadded up a piece of paper and threw it at him. Fueller was too surprised to duck, and it bounced off his chest.

"What did I say?"

Lamar was beginning to explain it to him when I went back into the interview.

The pastor had decided to talk. To "purge his soul," as he put it. Apt.

It began, he said, when Betty's brother Phil had turned to drugs. Why, he didn't know. He was a pretty good musician, according to Rothberg, with a promising future. The wrong crowd was blamed, as usual. It always is. Anyway, he drifted into a Satanic cult in Cleveland. They weren't, apparently, too advanced philosophically but were really into the trappings and what they thought were appropriate Satanic activities. Phil's involvement had deepened, and he had joined a second group. This time, the philosophy was more deeply understood and appreciated. This group included an extremely weird individual named John Travis, and, no, he wasn't sure if that was his real name. He was described by Rothberg as being a sociopath, a physical fitness enthusiast, with a military background of some sort, and a black belt in something. He was also described as being intelligent but machinelike. He became Phil Killian's best friend and confidant.

"Phil worshiped him," said Mark. "There was nothing he couldn't do, according to him. He had 'thrown off the shackles of society' and would do anything that pleased him."

"Anarchist?" I asked.

"More than that," said Mark. Much more.

He said that this Travis character was really into imposing his will on others . . . in various ways. Often, by sheer force of personality. Phil had been with Travis and his group for nearly a year when Phil's original cult friends had crossed swords with him.

"I was never exactly sure," said Mark, "but I think it began over a woman. Ownership of a woman. Travis wanted her, but the other group had her, I think."

The conflict escalated, and somebody in the group had threatened Travis with exposure. Exactly the wrong move, apparently.

Phil Killian had come to see Betty Rothberg one day, and the subject came up. Mark said that Phil had told him that Travis had actually had tears in his eyes when he talked about his woman. He also talked about killing his opposition. Phil apparently needed some money, he said, to leave the Cleveland area and start fresh. He said that he would renounce Satan and try to make a good home for this woman. He needed cash.

Mark and Betty were convinced. They didn't know who the woman was, but it sounded like Phil had seen the light.

Mark and Betty had given five hundred dollars to Phil, to help him get his act back together. His brother-in-law was then "overcome by Satan," according to Mark. He used some of the money to buy some dope, and he and Travis decided that they would go and take the woman from the other group. They tried, and that was when the three homicides in Cleveland had taken place. Phil had gone to the police the same night and confessed to his role in the slayings. Travis, predictably, didn't.

Phil apparently realized, a couple of days later, that Travis had intended to kill the woman all along. He couldn't handle it and committed suicide.

At that point, the Rothbergs became aware that the Cleveland police didn't know who John Travis was. Two detectives had approached them, asking for information. Phil hadn't said, and Mark told them that he didn't know John Travis personally. That was true. He told them what he had just told us about Travis, and said that the information all came from Phil. The detectives apparently searched Phil's things, but as far as Mark Rothberg knew, they found nothing.

Things were getting a little uncomfortable for them in Cleveland, so when the opportunity arose for the Rothbergs to move, they came to Maitland.

Phil had a twin sister, Rachel. She had gone to school in Iowa City, but they had remained incredibly close. He had introduced her to Satanism, and she had bought into it heavily. Mark and Betty weren't aware of that until sometime after Phil's suicide. Phil, by the way, had introduced Travis to his sister.

Real smart man, that Phil.

Mark had spent a lot of time trying to "save" Rachel. Rachel failed Mark's course. So he and Betty attempted to "deprogram" her, apparently the next and "ultimate" step in her salvation. That failed, too, as she got away from them. She'd moved in with Phyllis Herkaman, who defended her from the goodwill of Mark and Betty.

32

So far so good. As far as the Rothbergs were concerned, while Rachel was gone, they still had hope because she would frequently appear near Maitland and would sometimes call. Three or four times in the last year, she had actually come to visit, accompanied by Phyllis Herkaman.

As far as we were concerned, though, it seemed clear that Rachel was milking them for money, while busy turning out a victim for a ritual sacrifice. Depends on your viewpoint, I guess. I was beginning to get a little tired of all of this stupidity and cruelty.

The Rothbergs became aware that Rachel was pregnant and were apparently unhappy about it at first, but then took the optimistic view that this might bring Rachel around to their side. It didn't, of course.

After the child was born, they only saw Rachel once, and had the opportunity to see little Cynthia. Apparently Betty had picked the child up, and Rachel had a screaming fit, saying that Betty wanted to take the child away and would "contaminate" it. Oh brother.

We then asked him about his relationship with Francis McGuire. After McGuire had left the church for the coven, he had come to see Rothberg on one occasion. He told Rothberg about the planned sacrifice of a child. Apparently he was not aware that Rachel was Betty's sister. Rothberg was floored and torn between going to the police and keeping the confidence of his position. He pleaded with McGuire to stop the ritual and prayed that the man had enough conscience left in his soul to protect the child. To make matters worse, Rothberg was sure that Betty had overheard the session with McGuire. On occasion she had betrayed confessional details of members of the parish to Mark. He was positive that she wouldn't pass up an opportunity to hear what one of Rachel's new friends had to say in one of his private counseling sessions.

By early February, Rachel's evasiveness about the child caused a confrontation. She finally admitted that the baby had died toward the end of December. Coupled with McGuire's tale, both Rothbergs began to believe the baby had been sacrificed.

Shortly afterward, Betty lost it. He took her to a psychiatric clinic in Dubuque. She stayed there for three weeks, under the pretext of visiting her parents in Ohio, and when she came home she was, in his words, "a different person."

When pressed, he said that she was rather disturbed, still, but had a serenity he could only feel had come from God. She was not very communicative and didn't talk about the baby at all, except to say that the whole thing was in other hands now and would eventually be all right. I decided not to ask if she was on Prozac.

She came home about three weeks before the four homicides.

"What became of telling the police about all of this?" I could barely contain my anger.

"We were going to, eventually. But not right away. After all, the child was dead, wasn't she? I have to think about Betty, too."

"Did you ever find out what happened to little Cynthia? I mean, where she was buried?"

Rothberg shuddered. "Not actually. Francis told me that the . . . sacrifice . . . had taken place at his home farm, in the barn. He did say that he had been assigned to take care of the body. With somebody else—a man, I think. And that they'd placed the remains in a 'safe place.' He never did say where."

"Then what happened?"

Not much, according to Rothberg, until the four murders went down. He heard pretty quickly, as he'd explained to me at my house on Thursday. As soon as he'd heard some detail, he knew what had happened. Travis.

"I knew it was him, Carl. There was absolutely no doubt at all. I'm not a man who is inspired all that often, but I knew then."

"What did you do?"

"I was distraught. Frantic. I felt that I was responsible. It was the most horrible time I have ever experienced. It was terrible. I had to do something . . ." He looked at me again. Guilt was eating him. "I know now that I was, perhaps, a little unhinged. That doesn't excuse my actions, Carl. I hope you understand that. But that was the reason."

"Reason for what?"

"I wanted to cleanse the places of evil."

"So?"

"I was trying to atone, I suppose," he said, "for what I felt was my guilt."

This was getting frustrating.

"What did you do, Mark?"

"I took crucifixes to both houses and tried to bless them."

It took me a second. But just a second.

"That was you?!"

"Yes, I'm afraid it was." He looked down.

"You're the one who hit me on the head?"

"I'm so very sorry, Carl . . . so very sorry."

I started to laugh. He looked at me quizzically.

"I am truly sorry, but I couldn't be caught, don't you see? No one could find me there, or I would have to explain my presence . . ."

I stopped laughing. He'd hit me more than once.

"I was a desperate man." He looked at me again. "I suppose I'll be charged for that, won't I?"

"Oh, yeah. No doubt about it."

"So, then," asked Hester, "did you go back and burn the McGuire place down, too?"

"Oh, my, no. No, no, indeed not! No."

"Do you know who did?"

"No."

"Okay, Mark," said Hester. "Now, just where is Travis? Do you know?"

"I think so, yes."

"Where?"

"Back in Dubuque. A one-room apartment on Fessler Street. A little white house, he lives upstairs. A Mrs. Skayhill rents rooms. That's where he used to meet Rachel. The room is under the name John Quarrels."

"Fine." Hester jotted the address down. "Does he work anywhere?"

"I'm sure."

There was a pause. "Would you happen to know where?"

"No," said Mark. "I'm afraid I don't."

"Do you know if he has any friends around here?"

"None that anyone mentioned." He sighed. "I feel so dead inside," he said. "But I am relieved that it's all come out. I want to thank you."

"Yeah . . . You're welcome." I didn't know what else to say.

33

Monday, April 29
10:00 hours

Phelps asked what we were going to do with Rothberg. We talked it over for a few seconds. An assault charge, possibly trespassing. Concealing evidence in a homicide . . . he was a material witness. Concealing evidence in another homicide case. So that was obstructing justice. But he wasn't a threat to the community. At least not physically. Except to me.

I grabbed Fueller, who was still in the office, and ran it by him. Rothberg had to conduct a funeral service and only had a few minutes to get to the church.

We decided that Ed would go with him and bring him back at the conclusion of services. A decision forced by haste. Bond would be set in his absence.

Rothberg and Ed left in a hurry. Ed wasn't too pleased at having to go to church, but since his wife was along, there wasn't much he could say.

Betty Rothberg was still talking in Lamar's office. Fueller told me that Hal and Saperstein were with her. And just as he finished his sentence, Hal came out of the interview and we filled him in on Mark's statement.

"We're just about finished up in there, too. It looks like Betty got this Travis dude to do it. Indirectly. Told him about the baby. It was his, all right. He apparently hadn't known about the sacrifice, and Rachel sure as hell never told him. So Betty talked with this Travis about revenge. Can you believe that? 'Suggestions' all the way, but given her knowledge of his background, it was like pointing a gun."

He motioned me aside.

"Betty was screwing him," he whispered.

"Travis?"

"Yep."

"God, he must be able to persuade anybody . . ."

"Other way around."

"What?"

"Betty hooked him after she heard about the baby. She persuaded him to do it. Used him all the way. He doesn't know that. But that's what she did. Flattered his ego, conned him all the way. To get him to 'prove' to her that he was all-powerful as he said. She's done some weird things with him—she makes no bones about that."

"Does her husband know?"

"No. She looked the dude up when she was in counseling in Dubuque. Got the address from her sister a while before. But her husband has no idea."

"Well, I sure as hell don't want to tell him."

"Me either. I think she's gone off the deep end. For real. I don't want to do conspiracy here, but she did set him off. Well, we'll see . . . We're just going to have her summarize. Want to join us?"

Of course I did. We went back into Lamar's office together. Phelps had already joined the group. It was getting pretty crowded in there, and I started to leave when Saperstein announced he had something to do and graciously allowed me to take his place.

Betty Rothberg's "summary" was composed and matter-of-fact. Not emotionless . . . but the emotion that was present was mostly a quiet satisfaction with a job well done.

What it amounted to was this:

Rachel had become pregnant, and Betty had discovered this in about the fourth or fifth month, June or July. She was very pleased for Rachel and thought that this would be the opportunity to get Rachel's life straightened out. Betty made all sorts of plans, even going so far as to begin to rearrange her house to accommodate Rachel and the baby. Betty had arranged a little baby shower for Rachel in October, and Rachel had shown up with Phyllis.

Betty remarked that Phyllis seemed to be the one who appreciated it, while Rachel was sort of withdrawn and sullen about the whole thing.

"You know," sighed Betty, "I suppose it was because Phyllis was trying to get Rachel to be 'normal' about it. To try to hide what they planned from me." She winced. "Do you think that could be?"

"I don't know," said Hester.

"I think it was," said Betty. "I think it was."

Betty had passed it off as Rachel just being herself. I could understand that.

After the shower, Rachel moved out of Phyllis's house and had gone to be with friends in Iowa City. She'd told Betty that it was because she wanted to be near better hospitals for the delivery. Betty had taken this as a sign of Rachel's maternity coming to the fore, and thought it was a good idea.

Betty talked for a minute, again, about how the baby would give Rachel a chance to get her life "sorted out," and how the sisters could have become so close. It was sad. She started rambling a little, about events prior to November and the birth.

Hal let her go on for a minute or two and then said, "Betty, what happened after the little girl was born?"

Betty stopped abruptly. Frowned.

"I saw her once," she said. Her face brightened. "She was so adorable, so sweet, such little, tiny hands and feet . . ."

It occured to me that Betty hadn't any children of her own.

"Where did you see the baby?" asked Hester.

"Out at Phyllis's place, one Saturday afternoon," said Betty.

It turned out that she had taken to driving past the Herkaman place on weekends, just to see if Rachel was there. She'd seen the car that Saturday and dropped in.

"How and when did you find out the baby was dead, Betty?" asked Hal.

They'd already been over this, of course. Normally, the second time through, the emotion would have dissipated. Not so here.

Betty's face contorted, but her body remained relaxed. Damnedest thing I'd ever seen.

"John told me."

"John Travis?" asked Hal.

"Yes."

"How did he know, Betty?"

"He didn't know," she said, with the emphasis on "know." "He just knew."

"What do you mean by that, Betty?" asked Hester.

"He told me. Told me after I told him that I believed the baby had been sacrificed. But I didn't want to believe it, you know? I just said so. I wanted him to tell me that it was a lie. But he didn't. He said that he knew they had done it. That he knew them, and that they had done it."

"But," said Hal, "John Travis didn't know for a fact, is that right?"

"Yes."

"He just sort of guessed?"

"No. He knew."

"I see," said Hal. "And you believed him?"

She nodded.

"Is that a 'yes'?" asked Hal, for the record.

"Yes."

"Did John Travis know any of Rachel's group?"

"No."

"None of them?" asked Hal.

"Just Rachel." She looked up. "That's what he said."

Betty went on to explain that, once John Travis had "known," she had "known," too. The ring of truth. She had been horrified, and kept trying to contact Rachel, to see if the baby was still alive. She was frantic.

"I didn't know what to do," she said, her voice pleading, trying to make us understand.

"Did you discuss this with Travis again?" asked Hal.

"Yes, many times."

"Where?"

"His place, in Dubuque."

"Did he have any suggestions?" asked Hester.

"He had a solution."

"What was that, Betty?" asked Hal.

"He said that he could take care of the group. Stop them before they did it." She looked at Hester. "We weren't certain, you see. Certain that little Cynthia was dead. But we knew it had happened. We just knew that. John knew that. He really knew . . ."

"Sure," said Hester.

"Did you know what he meant by 'take care' of them?" asked Hal.

"I assumed he meant kill them."

"You did?"

"Yes."

"And did you ask him to do that?"

"I couldn't."

"Why not?"

"It wouldn't be right." Simple, matter-of-fact.

"Because you weren't sure that Cynthia was dead?" asked Hester.

"Well, yes, that's part of it." She looked at Hester for a moment. "I wasn't certain that John was right."

"And when were you certain?" asked Hal.

"When Mark said something about it. In February." Dead voice now.

"What happened when he told you?"

"I don't know." Betty looked around the room. "I mean, I don't know what happened. I've been told. But I don't know."

"What were you told?" asked Hester.

"That I was hysterical." She looked at the floor. "I don't believe that, you know."

"Could you speak toward the tape recorder?"

"I said," she said forcefully, "I don't believe that I was hysterical."

"Who told you that you were?" asked Hal.

"Dr. Klieneman. My psychiatrist. In Dubuque."

"And you don't believe him?"

"I don't know what to believe. I don't remember being hysterical . . . I don't remember anything at all."

"But you did spend time at a psychiatric clinic in Dubuque?"

"Yes, of course. I was an outpatient, though. I wasn't restrained or anything."

It turned out that, as an outpatient, Betty had been with John Travis a lot. At his apartment and in parks and Kennedy Mall. And, with the confirmed death of the baby, she had agreed with Travis that revenge was the option to pursue. She didn't put it quite that way, of course.

"I told John that he was going to be an instrument of the Lord. We had to eradicate this menace, before something even worse happened."

"What would have been worse, Betty?" asked Hal.

"I don't know."

"Just something worse?" asked Hester. "Nothing specific?"

"Yes."

It turned out that she and Travis had decided that Rachel was a dupe and that she shouldn't be harmed. But Betty was certain that God wanted the rest of them killed, to avenge the death of the baby and to remove an abomination from the earth.

"Did you discuss this with Mark?" asked Hal.

"No, of course not. He didn't know I was involved with John. How could I explain that to him? He's never even met him."

"But he knew what John was capable of doing, didn't he?"

"He knew what Phil had said about John." She sighed. "But I think he's afraid of him."

Hal looked her straight in the eye. "When did you become sexually involved with John Travis?"

"In Dubuque, in February."

"For the express purpose of wiping out the cult Rachel was involved with?"

"Of course. I was an instrument, too." She gave a small smile to Hal. "You probably don't understand, do you?"

"I'm not sure that I do," he answered.

"These people are evil," she said. "They have to be prevented from transmitting their evil to innocent victims like Rachel. I know this through God, and he was acting through me."

Hal was right. Betty was not "sound of mind." Not at all. It was pathetic, somehow.

The interview wound down from there. She'd used Travis, but Travis wanted to be used. And Mark had a feeling about it all along. Had she set Travis up, or had he set her? One interesting note:

"Betty, did you ever meet with John Travis here?"

"No, I didn't."

"Do you know who he associated with here?" pressed Hal.

"No one." Simple as that.

It turned out that she had never seen Travis anywhere but Dubuque, and he had no friends there, either. As far as she knew.

I left the interview room and bumped into Saperstein in the outer office.

"Interesting, isn't it?" he asked me.

"Yeah." I started to go to dispatch and changed my mind. "Bill," I asked him, "do you think she used Travis, or that he used her?"

"They used each other. He needed a source of information. She needed a tool to do what she couldn't."

"So which came first, the chicken or the egg?" I had to ask. Everybody lies to us, even when they seem to be getting something off their chest. Well, I'll be charitable. Sometimes they lie to themselves. We get it second-hand.

"He wasn't sure because she hadn't told him yet. She wasn't sure because she didn't know if she believed it or not. But she convinced him, and he convinced her, and that's what counts."

Damn.

I checked with dispatch, to find Lamar. He was on a minor accident about nine miles south of us. Told Jane to have him come back in as soon as he was done. Just as I turned to leave, she said, "Oh, did you see the teletype from Linn County?"

"What teletype?"

"Here," she said, handing me a small slip of paper. "Looks like Traer's house burned down a few hours ago."

"What?!" Well, that made the rounds in a hurry. To everybody but Traer. We really didn't know just what to make of it, except that we were going to have to get an exact time when they thought it started—just to see if Rachel had set it when she left. Would be nice, but I didn't think she had.

Then Fueller and I sat down and did the arrest warrant information. He started on the search warrant applications while I ran the information to the local magistrate, to have the warrant issued.

Magistrate Halloran lived in Maitland. He was a pretty good attorney in his own right. He really wanted to press for details, but didn't. I appreciated that. But I think he could tell from my attitude that we were wrapping it up.

"I'm glad you've got this one."

"So are we," I said.

"Do you want me to stick around today, for an arraignment?"

"Yeah, I think so. Also, we'll be coming down with a couple of search warrant applications in a little while."

"Fine."

"Hate to ruin your Monday."

"Not ruined at all, Carl."

I hustled the warrant back to the office. He'd set bond at $500,000, cash. Ought to do it. I went directly to dispatch and had her teletype the information to Dubuque PD.

"Better have 'em call us before they go on the warrant. He's extremely dangerous."

"Okay," said Jane.

I went back to the main office and found Betty being booked into jail. One count of conspiracy to commit murder. I showed the new arrest warrant to Fueller and Hal.

"Good," said Hal.

"I told 'em to call us here before they go."

"Good idea."

I glanced at Betty. She appeared very calm and self-possessed. Not bothered at all.

I finished the booking forms—they had to be signed by a deputy from our county. Took Betty back and put her in the cell with Elizabeth Mills. It was either that or put her in the juvenile cell with Rachel, and I didn't think that would be such a good idea.

Went back out and was told that Hal and Hester would be going to Dubuque as soon as the search warrants were issued. Saperstein as well.

"You want to come along?"

"No thanks," I said. Two reasons. I was getting really tired and had to go to work in about eight or nine hours. And I know "courtesy" when I hear it. Five is a crowd.

Saperstein seemed a little disappointed. "I wanted to tell you what we've found out about John Travis."

I sat down. "We've got a few minutes. I'm all ears."

"Let's go in the back room," he said. "I don't want to bother them."

Good point. Fueller was furiously typing the search warrant application while Hester and Hal were feeding him data.

We sat in the rear office, and Saperstein told me about Travis.

"He's a self-contained cult," he said, "and an ascetic as well. Satanic ascetic. Doesn't believe in most of the ceremonies, the trappings, the regalia. He has a tattoo of a pentagram in his right armpit. That's all. He doesn't have any symbols in his room, nothing like that."

"Hmmm." For want of anything else to say.

"He's the most dangerous kind of Satanic follower. Looks down on people like Traer and company . . . told Betty that they were 'Barnum and Bailey' Satanists. He considers himself the 'sword of Satan.' His words."

Saperstein shook his head.

"From what she said," he went on, "this man is a force unto himself. His only weakness is that he wants occasional rewards from Satan—like her, for instance. Appreciation. Not often, but he does need that sometimes. His only weakness, and she figured it out."

"Pretty smart."

"I don't know about that, Carl. If he ever thinks that he's been used, he'll kill her."

"You think so?"

"Yes. I really think that he shouldn't come to this jail, after we get him."

"That bad?"

"You don't know what you're dealing with here. This man is evil. No other word for it. And active, as well."

"I'll tell Lamar, but maybe you should talk to him, too."

"I will, if he gets back before we leave. If I don't get the chance, you tell him."

"I will."

"Carl," he said, "words fail me regarding this man. They really do. He kills without remorse. With a purpose. Efficiently, but with a message. I know him, I think. Like the Satanic symbols at Herkaman's place. Those were his way of mocking them. Using their little symbols . . . And he could have killed Rachel easily, I'm sure of it. He let her get away, maybe because she was Betty's sister, and he was supposed to let her go."

Ah . . .

"And that's why he took McGuire back to his own house, where the 'sacrifice' of Cynthia had been made. He has great disdain for killing a child, I'm sure. His idea of a 'sacrifice' is to take on somebody who is a little bit more of a challenge than an infant. Somebody who gives meaning to his efforts. I don't know, of course, but that's why, I think, McGuire had the feces in his mouth. He must have said something to Travis before he died, something about the child, or about being a Satanist, too. That would be Travis's style of symbol—direct and to the point."

"I'll bet," I nodded, "you're right. I'll bet you are . . ."

"I don't know if he'll resist the Dubuque cops or not—it should depend on circumstance—but they shouldn't take any chances."

"We'll tell 'em."

"But I think if he thinks that he is going to be brought back here, he might just go along with it. He isn't done yet, you know. He wants the whole group, with the exception of Rachel. When we were pressuring Traer, I wasn't sure. I am now."

"Another reason not to bring him back here."

"That's right."

"Lamar's gonna hate that—he thinks Dubuque County charges quite a lot to store prisoners."

Saperstein smiled. "Tell him it's going to be worth the investment."

"I will."

"I doubt that he'll talk to us down there, but if he does, I'll be very interested in talking to him. I think he's likely to be what they call a paranoid schizophrenic, and you don't get a real chance to talk with them very often. I've always wanted to do an interview if they were hearing a voice at the same time. Competing for their attention, as it were." He smiled a little bit, to himself. "What time do you go to work tonight?"

"20:00."

"Look, I'll find you when we get back and tell you what we've found."

"I'd appreciate that."

We went back out to the main office and discovered that Hal had gone to the magistrate. Lamar was back and Saperstein took him aside and told him about what he'd told me. I said my farewells and went home. Looked at the clock, but couldn't make out the numbers.

Last thing I remember, until I woke up about 18:00. Sue had covered me up.

34

I came stumbling down the stairs and found Sue in the kitchen. I could smell lasagna.

"Welcome back," she said.

"Thank you . . . Look, I'm sorry about this morning . . ."

"Don't be."

"Sure smells good in here," I said as I loaded the coffeepot.

"Lasagna."

"I could tell." I gave her a hug. "You're pretty good to me."

"Too good, actually."

"Well, that's true."

"But what the hell, you're all I've got handy." She smiled.

I chuckled. "Thanks a lot."

I picked up the phone and called the office. Checking to see if they had got Travis.

"Hi, Hazel. They get that guy in Dubuque for us today?"

"Oh, hello. No, I don't think so. They haven't said they have him, anyway."

Shit.

"Anybody else there?"

"Mike, he's in back."

"Let me talk to him.

"We get that Travis dude yet?"

"Nope."

"You're kidding."

"Nope. Hal called about half an hour ago. They haven't been able to find him. They don't think he's been tipped off or anything, just not there. Landlady says that he usually comes home about two or three days out of ten. They're waiting."

"They do the search of his place yet?"

"Didn't say."

"Anything else going?"

"Not much . . . I had to put Betty in the juvenile cell, and transferred Rachel into the cell with Elizabeth Mills."

"Why?"

"Old Liz kept screaming at Betty. Apparently knows her. And Betty just happened to tell Liz about what happened, and how she was involved. I was really afraid that Liz would try to harm her."

"Shit, I didn't think she'd tell."

"Well, she did."

"Wonderful."

"Yeah. Oh well, there's nothing else going on. At least, as far as I know."

"Okay," I said, "tell Jane I'll be out at 20:00."

I hung up the phone. "Damn."

"What?" asked Sue.

"They haven't got him yet."

"Who?"

Of course, I hadn't managed to tell her about the events of the morning. It's easy to miss connections on a weird schedule.

Now, just how much do I say . . .

"We have a suspect we're trying to find. Should have him later tonight."

"Will you have to get him?"

"No, not me. He's a little out of my jurisdiction."

"Well, that's good. Here, give me a hand with these, will you?"

I set the table while she finished the salad. That's always been about the extent of my kitchen expertise—setting the table.

I ate, relaxed with a cup of coffee for a few minutes, showered, shaved, and put all that clumsy gear back on. I fell into my patrol car at about five to eight.

I started the engine, tested the top lights, the spotlight, the outside speaker, made sure the little red light on the rechargeable flashlight came on, indicating it was charging, turned on the police radio and checked it by hitting the transmit button on my portable. All set. I recorded my start mileage, the weather, time, and car number on my daily log. Put on my seat belt, cinching it down. Checked the fuel level—about half a tank—made a mental note to get gas before I left Maitland.

"Comm, three."

"Three, go."

"10–41, mileage . . ."

Another enchanting evening in northeast Iowa was about to begin.

I made a quick stop at the hospital, to see Mom, who was getting better and about to be released in the next day or so, and then went to the office.

I met Mike, who was about to leave for a theft call. Two hydraulic cylinders from a farm, farmer last saw them about two months ago, not pressing. He and I went back into the office.

I told him I wanted to call Helen in and tear off her fingernails for lying to me. And brain her husband. He agreed, but thought I should clear it with DCI first. I agreed, but reluctantly. Then we talked about my getting thumped by a pastor—he thought it was really funny.

I had noticed a couple of extra cars in the lot and asked him about them. It turned out that we still had two reserve officers at the jail, all night, and that they'd be there until we had Travis in custody.

Mike left to check the hot leads on the missing cylinders, and I stopped at dispatch to talk to Jane for a second and let her know approximately where I intended to go.

"Just south?"

"Yeah, Mike's call is north. I really don't have anything to do that's special. I'll just be south at first. Then I don't know."

I stopped in the kitchen and talked to the two reserves for a few seconds. They had coffee going and a card game. They were two of my favorites, Harvey Jeffries and Kendall Harp. They both had to go to work in the morning and planned to alternate naps on a cot. I'd never known just how they managed, let alone why. But since they had fresh coffee, I knew I'd be back a little sooner than normal. Maybe I could pick up some rolls or something. Maybe I could have Dan do it.

I went back to my car. A light mist was falling, and I hoped it didn't freeze. Spring hadn't sprung.

There had been no news from Dubuque. That was my real reason for working south for the first part of my shift. I wanted to be in a position to intercept the DCI people on their way back to Maitland, if they got him. I was pretty anxious to find out what they had discovered.

I went out to the county maintenance shop to get gas and called Dan to meet with me.

I put in 12.3 gallons, hung up the pump, and recorded the amount in my log, with mileage. Dan drove up just then, so I put off going 10–8 for a few minutes, to talk with him about the homicides and see if there was anything going on in Maitland. We sat with our cars side by side for about ten minutes, while I explained why Betty Rothberg was in jail and why Mark Rothberg was at home. He'd heard about Betty, but nobody had told him exactly why.

Dan went to Rothberg's church occasionally, whenever the pressure from his wife reached a level where it was easier to attend than not. He had been there today for the funeral.

"Quite a sermon. I saw Ed there, and I thought something might be up. Pastor Rothberg talked about Satan, and the fact that he was alive and well, and in Maitland. No details, but he sure was disturbed."

"He was, was he? And at a funeral?"

"Oh, yeah. Said that Satan had entered his life more than once and that it had been a terrible struggle, but that he had finally thrown him out for good."

"I'm pleased for him."

"Yeah. Most of the people thought he'd had an affair, or had been hitting the bottle."

"Figures."

"Don't it, though. The mourners were a little surprised."

I just shook my head.

"You heard that we found the guy who tried to break my skull, didn't you?"

"No! Who is it?"

"Rothberg."

"Pastor Rothberg?"

"Yep."

He started to laugh.

"Dan . . ." I said.

"Yeah?"

"Fuck you."

He laughed even harder. "Maybe if you'd gone to church . . ." He couldn't finish. He made a cross with his fingers, holding them up in front of himself. "Don't hit me, I'm a Christian," and laughed even harder.

"Well, I gotta go . . ."

"Watch out for rabid clergymen . . ."

"Yeah . . ." I remembered. "Oh, Dan?"

"Yeah?"

"Want to pick up some rolls at the bakery in a while? Meet at the office for coffee?"

"Sure thing."

I pulled my car away and picked up the mike.

"Comm, three."

No answer. Probably a bathroom break. Dan pulled in front of me at the entrance to the shop and signed his cross again. He went north, toward the big industrial park near the Maitland city limits. I turned south, onto the main highway.

"Comm, three."

I had to call in my gas. If it wasn't logged, the books wouldn't balance at the end of the month.

Still no answer. Damn it, Jane. Well, maybe she was on the phone.

I turned at an intersection and was heading toward Maitland when I called again. I was getting a little testy.

"Maitland comm, car three!"

No answer.

"Twenty-five, three? You copy this signal?"

"10–4, three. You're 10–2 here."

Okay, Jane. I tried her on info, a separate channel into com. only.

No answer.

By now it had been a good six or seven minutes since I had first tried to call in my fuel. I had heard no traffic from the comm center at all during that period. None.

I spun the car around and hit the top lights.

"Twenty-five, three, go to the comm center."

I got a scratchy response I couldn't decipher. Great, he was out on door checks, on his portable. With the hills, he wouldn't hear me clearly until I was back in Maitland.

I stepped it up and hit the siren. I blew the stop sign at the intersection and worked it up to around 110. I was gonna feel real dumb if Jane was talking to the card players. I turned off the siren before my next call, just in case she had been doing that.

"Comm, three!"

Nothing. Absolutely nothing.

I was just about in Maitland by then, and Dan heard me. He also heard the roaring of the airflow around the car and through the partially opened window. He knew I was moving.

"Three, what you got?"

"Get to the comm center, 10–33!"

I hit the siren again as I entered Maitland, hurtling up the street toward the comm center. I went right by Dan, who was running to his car. I was still doing about 90, and the posted limit was 25. Blew around an old pickup, who dived into the parking lot at the supermarket. We'd hear about that one.

I shut off the siren as I pulled into the lot, and jumped out of the car, leaving it running with the top lights on. I always locked it, and I did so this time. I pulled my revolver out as I hit the steps. I pushed the buzzer for admittance. No answer. I fumbled for my key, realized it was on the set in the car, and ran back for it. Hit the steps again at a dead run, just as Dan was pulling into the lot.

I unlocked the door and stuck my head around the corner. Nothing seemed disturbed. All the proper lights were on. In dispatch, in the hall. But it was dead quiet.

I heard Dan on the steps and held my left hand up, pointing my revolver ahead of me as I slowly approached the dispatch center. Jane was pretty tall, and I could usually see her head from the doorway, behind the console.

Nothing.

With Dan right behind me, I entered the dispatch center. He went left and pointed his gun toward the kitchen, while I rounded the console to the right.

Jane was slumped over the console desk. There was blood on the log sheet and the notepaper. A little bit of tissue extruded from the left side of her head.

"Jane!"

No response.

"Watch out, Dan! She's been shot!"

"*Shit!*" he hissed, but he never looked my way, keeping his gun pointed toward the kitchen.

I tried for a pulse on Jane's neck, couldn't get one.

I picked up the phone, cradled it on my shoulder while I dialed with my left hand, keeping my revolver in my right.

"Maitland Hospital?"

"Get an ambulance to the sheriff's office, this is extremely 10–33! Right fucking now!"

I hung up and keyed the mike on ops.

"All cars, 10–33 at the comm center. Possible 10–32. We need 10–78!"

I backed away from the console and heard cars start to acknowledge.

I joined Dan. "Okay, let's take the kitchen first. Watch the door to the left, that goes to the cells. I'll go for the kitchen, *you watch that door.*"

We went through the little hallway, and Dan peeled off, facing the door to the cells. I continued into the kitchen.

Harvey was slumped over the table, the cards scattered onto the floor. Kendall was lying on the floor, on the opposite side of the table, his revolver in his hand. They'd both been shot in the head. I guessed Harvey first, as he was facing the open back door. Small holes. Probably a .22. I was getting so tense I thought I'd break the grip on my gun.

I backed up, looking around to see Dan staring at me. His gun was still pointed at the cell access door.

"Got 'em both. Back door is open. Don't know if he's left or not."

"Okay."

"Now we check the cells. You ready?"

"Yeah, I guess . . ."

"Don't guess, goddammit—you ready or not?"

"Ready."

"Okay, let's go."

I reached forward, turned the knob, and gave the door a little push. It opened freely, nearly all the way. I found myself looking into the women's cell. I saw a pair of legs, up to nearly the hips, on the floor in front of the cell door. I could hear a quiet whimpering, but I didn't know where from.

I had to go through a thick archway, with hallway going both directions. I stuck my head around to the right, toward the men's cells and bull pen. I could see part of the bull pen area, but saw nobody. I checked left, looking back toward dispatch. Nothing. I kept my revolver in front of me and slowly went toward the men's area. As I went past the juvenile cell, where Betty was supposed to be, I caught movement out of the corner of my eye. I looked in, and she was lying on the floor, making swimming motions, trying to hide under her bunk. I could see the lower half of her, and she appeared to be all right.

I motioned to Dan.

"She's okay. Let's go on."

We went all the way down the hall to the men's cell. I could see the floor of the bull pen when I was about five feet away. There was a body in an orange jail suit on the floor to the right, another one just beyond it. I couldn't tell who they were, but one looked like Mills. I went around to the left, where I could see into the cells. Orange-clad body in the third cell. Motionless, like the others. We had two prisoners in addition to Traer and Mills—a twenty-five-year-old for drunk driving and a fifty-year-old for bad checks. I needed one more.

"There should be one more, Dan."

I continued down to the end of the bull pen. The last area I could look into was the shower. I couldn't see anything.

"Anybody here?"

Silence.

"It's the good guys, is anybody here?"

There was a metallic thud against the wall near the shower.

"If you're alive, tell me, for Christ's sake."

"Is that you, Houseman?"

"Yes. Who is it?"

"Traer."

"Where is he, Traer?"

"I don't know!"

I had seen that the bull pen door was padlocked in two places, just the way it should be.

"Stay in there. You should be safe there for a while until we get more people here."

There was a muffled sound, which I took to be an acknowledgment.

"Okay, Dan, back out and let's do the rest of the area. He might still be here."

"Right."

35

We moved cautiously out of the cellblock area, Dan now in the lead. We got to the hall, and I began to feel safe. Whoever it was, and I was assuming it was Travis, was not likely to be anywhere around. I was just about ready to tell Dan to step on it when I heard a popping sound, and Dan's legs buckled instantly, spilling him on the floor. As he went down, I saw a man standing in front of me.

I fired without thinking and without aiming. I saw a spark, and he twisted around to his right and disappeared through the door into the kitchen.

I was momentarily stunned by the noise made by the .44 magnum inside the steel-enclosed hall. I must have hesitated for about two or three seconds before following him.

I had enough wits about me to stop, kneel down, and peer around the door frame from about waist height, to clear my path. He wasn't there. I hurried into the kitchen. That was a mistake, because there were several places there he could hide, and I thought about that after I'd gone all the way through and onto the back porch.

The porch was only screened, and I could hear a siren approaching. Ambulance or cop? I didn't know.

I went outside, into the rear yard and drive. There was an old car out there, a green '67 Chevy, and it started to roll forward and down the hill toward the roadway.

At the same time, Mike came rocketing up the drive, right past the old Chevy. Its lights weren't on, and it was moving so slowly he didn't recognize it as a possible fleeing vehicle. He jumped out of his car just as I fired at the Chevy.

Mike drew his gun and dropped to one knee, but obviously didn't know what I was shooting at.

I emptied my gun.

"Stop that fucker!" I screamed, and started to run down the hill after the car.

Mike looked at me with his eyes wide, turned, and fired six rounds at the back of the Chevy. It kept going.

Its lights came on, and it leaned hard as it rounded the corner, and went toward the main highway.

Mike and I were both reloading. "Get on your radio and tell anybody you can that the car is on the highway, and we want it, and he's killed everybody!"

Mike did even better than that, jumping into his car and screaming off in pursuit. I could hear him on my portable, giving the gist of my message to two troopers coming in from the south.

I finished reloading. Habit. Then I turned around and started back into the office. And froze.

I couldn't move. I just couldn't do it. I must have stood there for a full minute and couldn't get an inch closer to that bloodbath.

I took a deep breath and reached in my pocket for a cigarette, hearing sirens coming in from all over.

I lit it on the second try and decided that maybe, if I went around to the front door, I could go in.

As I came around the corner of the building, I saw the ambulance come up the drive, followed by the Maitland PD car.

The EMTs spotted me right away. They came running toward me as I went up the front steps. My keys were still in the lock. I started to open the door when one of the ambulance people touched me on the left arm and said, "Sit down."

"What?"

"You'll be okay, sit down."

"I'm fine, damn it. We have half a dozen people shot in there—you're needed in there," and I went in the door. I really don't know if I could have done it without the distraction of the EMT.

He followed me in. Jerry Foells, the Maitland cop, was right with me.

"Be careful," I said. "We've got shot people all over. I think the building is clear, but let me go first."

I walked back into the dispatch center. Jane had fallen off her chair and was in a lump on the floor. I got a little dizzy then, but took another drag off the cigarette and walked to the radio. I took a very deep breath, counted to ten, and keyed the mike.

"Maitland comm to all cars and stations," I said. "Maitland comm has been hit. We have at least three dead, several wounded. Suspect is a white male, about six feet, slender, driving an older model dark-colored Chevy, with possible bullet holes in the rear. Use extreme caution, suspect is armed and dangerous." I took another deep breath. "Maitland is clear at 20:42. This station will be 10–6 for several minutes."

There was a lot of babble on the radio, but I ignored it.

I picked up the phone and used the automatic dialer to call Lamar. I told him about what had happened. I'm not sure how clear and concise I was, but he got the message. I was about to call Art when I saw him come into the dispatch center.

He saw Jane first. Then Dan in the hallway.

"Sweet Jesus Christ."

I didn't say anything, just punched Sally's number up on the dialer.

"Hello?"

"Sally. Carl. We've had a hit at the dispatch center. Jane is dead. So is Dan, and Harvey and Kendall, and at least three prisoners. We're secure now. Get up here right away."

I looked up at Art, who had been listening.

"Fuck," I said.

"You been looked at?" he asked.

"No." I dialed the hospital. "We need the other ambulance here, right away."

"You better get that looked at."

"Get what looked at?"

I dialed the Maitland hospital. I told them to get both their ambulances coming.

Art went into the kitchen and came back looking very pale.

"What the hell happened?"

An EMT came in, asking for the keys to the cells, to get to the victims there. I reached into the drawer, and the EMT saw Jane for the first time. I couldn't find the keys and then noticed them on her belt. I gestured to Art.

"Could you get those?"

He reached down, almost being hit on the head by the EMT, who was just rising up.

"She's dead."

"Yeah, we know . . . Art, you might want to go to the cell with them. Traer is alive."

He went out. I stood up, dizzy again, and went out onto the front porch to get some air. I could hear the dispatch phone ringing. Somebody else would have to get it.

I watched the second ambulance pull up, damned near running over Sally, who had just gotten out of her car and was heading for the office at a dead run. Getting pretty crowded out here, I thought.

Sally stopped when she saw me. "Are you all right?"

"Yeah, but nobody else is. Jane's dead. I guess I told you that."

"Yes," she said. Her lip started to tremble.

"Look," I said as the second ambulance crew hustled by, "why don't I take you in? It's pretty gruesome, but we need a dispatcher pretty bad."

I took her by the arm and guided her into the center. Jane was still there, and the blood was on the counter.

"I'm sorry, Sally. We haven't had a chance to clean up."

Dumb thing to say.

She started to cry. Looking at Jane. I squeezed her shoulder.

"It'll be okay."

"Oh, God."

"Look, get busy, it'll make it easier. Call in another dispatcher right away."

She nodded.

"And I just think I'll sit down" I said as a wave of dizziness came over me.

An EMT came up to me, Donna Gorskey. "I'm going to look at your head now, whether you want me to or not."

"My head?"

"You've got a large cut on your head."

Well, what do you know about that? I thought.

It turned out that I'd been shot, just lightly grazed, by the .22. He'd fired at me, too. That must have been the spark I saw. I remembered him spinning, and the spark at the same time.

"Hey, Art!" I hollered. Him spinning. Him spinning. "Hey, Art!"

He came around the corner. "Yeah."

"Hey Art, I think I hit him. I shot inside the hallway, and I think I hit him. How's Dan?"

"He's dead."

"I thought so. He was right in front of me. We had just gone through the cell area, and I was ahead, then we came out and he was in front and he fell and that son of a bitch was shooting and I think I hit him."

It came out pretty fast. Sally was staring at me, and so was Art.

"Who is 'that son of a bitch' you're talking about?"

"Man named Travis. He did the Herkaman murders." Revelation. "Art, I know that guy."

"Who?"

"That Travis. I know him. I mean I recognized him."

"You've seen him before?"

"Yeah. Not his face, Art. His walk. The way he carries himself. I know him, but not by this Travis name."

Art waited as long as he could, maybe two seconds, maybe three. "Well, then, who is it?"

I looked at him. "I don't know, I can't place him." I shook my head. "Ain't that a son of a bitch?"

"Yes."

"Something else . . . but I can't put my finger on it. Oh. Did Mike get him? Mike chased him out of the back drive."

"Check with Mike," said Art to Sally.

I saw Lamar come into the dispatch center. He was pale. He'd evidently come in through the kitchen.

"What happened?"

I told him as best I could. I was getting a little confused myself at that point.

He listened, then said to Sally, "Start calling everybody who isn't on the radio. Start with Lieutenant Kainz, we're gonna need people. Then get the medical examiner. Then, Art, you call the reserves. We'll need to secure this place and the hospital."

"Okay. I can call Theo and Mike of our people."

"Do it. And Mike's out, I just saw him. Get as many people on the road as you can. If Carl did hit him, he might be out on a gravel somewhere. Dead, but I hope not. Not yet."

"We'd better call Dubuque," I said. "DCI is waiting for this guy down at his house. He might be going back there."

Mary Quentin, another dispatcher, came in. She seemed stunned. We all were.

My attending EMT, the soft-spoken Donna Gorskey, said, "You need a head X-ray." She turned to Lamar. "You better get him up to the hospital right away, we're gonna be awful busy here for a while."

"Right," said Lamar. Which, of course, would take him out of the picture at a critical time. He also didn't want to lose Art right now, either.

"Carl, we'll get you up there as soon as we can free somebody up."

"No rush, I'm fine."

I continued to sit in the side chair at dispatch. Under the No Smoking sign. I lit up. Who was that son of a bitch? I knew I'd seen him before. Often, to be able to say that. Looked awfully familiar. I tried to remember if he'd said anything. No, no voice. I was sure of that. But my head felt kind of thick. His moves. His build. What *was* it?

They came for Jane's body, and I thought that Mary Quentin was going to lose it right there. She got hold of herself, though, with little help from anybody. I was just about all helped out myself.

I caught a ride with the first ambulance to leave the scene, and sat in the hospital for a little while, as Kenneth Mills was hurt a lot worse that I was. But he was still alive. Doing better than Elizabeth.

I got my head X-rayed again, and Henry looked at it carefully.

"You'll be all right. No new cracks. How do you feel?"

"Oh, okay, I guess."

"You could be dead."

"Yeah."

I had already called Sue from the hospital and told her the gist of what had happened. She wanted to come up, and did. She fought her way through the crowd and was crying when she got to me. I put my arm around her and tried to get her out of the way when Dan's wife arrived. Too late.

Sue stayed with Alice Smith, and I hitched a ride back to the office with a lab tech.

I wanted Travis. And I was beginning to think I knew where he was.

36

Tuesday, April 30
00:07 hours
Tuesday was finally over.

I went into the dispatch center, looking for Lamar or Art.

Sally looked up. "How are you?" she asked with genuine concern.

"Oh, I'm fine. How are you?"

"I'll make it."

"Good. They find him yet?"

"Not yet. But they found the car."

"They did?"

"About half a mile out. Flat rear tire, I guess. Everybody just drove by where it went off over the edge by the vet's office. No tracks, I guess. State trooper found it when he was on his way into town."

"Where is it now?"

"I'm not sure," she said. "But there were two holes in the back of the car. One in the tire. You must have got it."

"Good." I sat down on the edge of the desk. "Where's Lamar?"

"Back in the cells, I think. He and Art are taking pictures before they move the last of the bodies." She glanced at the jail monitor screen. "Yeah, there he is."

I looked at the familiar shape of Lamar on the black-and-white TV screen. I was very tired, I realized. I'd talk to him later, when he was done. I sure didn't want to get dragooned into taking any pictures tonight. That should have been Theo's job, anyway.

"Theo should be doing this."

I shrugged. "I don't know. Don't bother with him, Lamar took him off the case. We don't need him, anyway."

She smiled. "The one good thing . . ."

I smiled back, glad for a bit of distraction. "Not enough."

I sat in the dispatch center, on the floor, leaning my head back against the wall. They were becoming enormously busy, with a tremendous amount of radio, telephone, and teletype traffic. I didn't realize it at the time, but I was seeing the beginning of the largest manhunt in the history of Iowa.

The noise was constant, but always the same, so to speak. I found it helped me relax, and let me think about what had happened. I had to think it through. I didn't know if I missed something or what, but I was getting the feeling that there was something I had to remember that I had forgotten. Who was it? of course.

There was a discordant note in the background noise, and I opened my eyes and saw Hal and Hester looking down at me, with Sally saying, "I think he's asleep."

"I'm not asleep."

I stood up. "You guys made good time back from Dubuque."

"Are you all right?" asked Hester.

"Fine."

"He keeps saying that," said Sally with considerable doubt in her voice.

"You up to giving us a statement?" asked Hal.

"Sure."

We went through the thinning crowd to the rear and into Lamar's office. The first thing they had me do was take a breath alcohol test. Passed with flying colors, of course. But you can't be too careful with defense attorneys. Standard procedure. They also advised me of my rights.

Then we taped my account of what had happened. I was really surprised at myself. It seemed to me that my rendition was clear and concise. I felt nothing. Nothing at all. No regret, no sadness, no feeling of loss over Jane and Dan, Harvey and Kendall. No anger, either. Nothing. I was reminded of a song of that name, from the show *A Chorus Line*. Except I didn't cry over feeling nothing. But it kept running through my mind. The song, that is.

I gave the best description of the assailant that I could, and of the car. As I was finishing up, I realized that I still didn't know the status of all the prisoners. I asked.

"Traer, Betty, and Rachel are all okay. Tommy Jenks is alive, but not expected to live."

Tommy was the twenty-five-year-old prisoner.

"Kenny Mills died about half an hour ago," said Hal. "His wife was dead on the scene."

"Except for Traer, it was a clean sweep."

"Yeah."

"Three troopers are taking him to the Linn County jail," said Lamar. "Better security. And we don't want that son of a bitch Travis coming back here."

"For sure," I said. "Except I'd like another crack at him."

"Now," said Hal, "Art says you recognize this guy?"

I sighed. "Yeah. Sort of. I think I'm familiar with his walk, or his build. I don't know who it is yet, but I know the son of a bitch."

"Think you'll be able to place him?"

I looked at Hal. "Sooner or later." I shook my head. "I wish I'd reacted better."

"From what Saperstein tells us about him," said Hester, "you did well just to stay alive, let alone hit him."

"Did I hit him?"

"We think so. There's a large bloodstain on the wall, right where he was when you shot."

"Good."

"Which reminds me," said Hal, "we're going to have to have your gun for ballistics tests." He held out his hand.

"You're gonna have to wait a few minutes," I said. "Where's Phil Daniels?"

Phil was a Maitland PD officer, and an avid gun collector.

"Don't know," said Lamar, "out there somewhere." He made a general gesture toward the exterior of the building.

I picked up the intercom and told Sally to have Phil come into the office.

I looked at Hal. "You can keep it in sight, but I'm not gonna hand it over to you until I have the replacement in my hand."

"Sure, sure . . ."

The only other handgun I owned was a two-inch .38, and I just didn't feel it was adequate for this situation. Not that I could reasonably expect to ever see Travis again. But I was a little less than logical right then.

"So what are we doing?" I asked.

"We've got almost a hundred troopers searching the roads in this and the adjacent counties," said Hal.

"And almost that many deputies and police officers coming in from all over," said Lamar.

"Any luck?"

"Not yet."

"How bad you think he was hurt?" I asked.

"Probably pretty bad," said Hester. "That cannon you carry probably nearly took his arm off."

"Good."

"We found the dent in the hall, where the bullet exited. It went through and through. What kind of ammunition do you use in that?"

"210-grain Silvertip."

"You heard a *pop* when he shot at you and Dan?" asked Hal.

"Very clearly. Loud *pop*, like a little firecracker."

"You think he had a silencer?"

"No."

"He must be a pretty good shot," mused Hal.

"Good enough," I said.

"I'm just thinking out loud."

Saperstein came in. "How are you?"

"Fine."

Phil Daniels stuck his head in the office. "Somebody want me for something?"

"Yeah," I said. "You have a .44 four-inch at home, don't you?"

"Sure."

"Can I borrow it for a while? They need this one to take to the lab."

"You bet, I'll get it right away. You okay?"

I nodded.

I was beginning to get a little tired of people asking me how I was. I excused myself and went to the john, remembering to hand Hal my revolver as I left the room.

I looked in the mirror and discovered the reason for all the questions. I looked like shit. There was disinfectant, that heavy orange kind, all over the right side of my head. Same side that Rothberg got. And on the right shoulder of my uniform shirt. Almost no blood, but a lot of disinfectant.

I went back to Lamar's office and called home. Sue answered right away.

"Hi, how you doin'?"

"Fine, how are you?"

"I'm just fine," I said, and forced a chuckle. "So many people have asked, I decided to look and see why. I got disinfectant all over my shirt. Could you get another one out of the closet, and I'll have somebody pick it up?"

"Sure. You're not coming home?"

"Not just yet, darling."

"All right."

"Why don't you go up to your folks' house for a while?"

"I think I'll do that."

"Good, I think that'd be a good idea."

"It's all over the news, and the phone was ringing when I came in the door. It was Jane. I told her you were all right. I was right, wasn't I?"

"You bet."

"I also stopped and saw your mother while I was at the hospital. I told her you were okay, too."

"Thank you."

"When are you coming home?"

"Later. That's all I know."

I dialed dispatch. "Hey, Sally, could you tell Phil to stop by my residence and pick up a uniform shirt?"

"Sure."

"Carl," said Hal, "let's go over what he was wearing again."

"To the best of my recollection, it was a dark sweat suit with a hood. Dark blue, I think, maybe black. That's all I know."

"And he didn't return fire when you and Mike were shooting at the car?"

"No. Why?"

"Don't know yet."

"There wasn't much of a blood trail," said Hester. "Blood on the wall, and possible tissue, where you shot him. A couple of drops on the kitchen floor, and a few drops on the asphalt on the back lot. I don't think any of it was yours—you don't appear to have bled much—but it might be."

"So," I said.

"Well, that happens sometimes, especially if the clothing is absorbing the blood. But, well, in a few minutes, why don't you and I walk it through?"

"Sure."

"Something I think you should know, though," said Hester.

"What's that?"

"We found a hand."

"I hit him in the hand?"

"No, Carl." She smiled. "It was somebody else's hand, from a few days ago."

"I'm not with you," I said. I wasn't.

"We think it's McGuire's missing hand."

"Wow." The only thing I could think to say.

"It was back in the cellblock, under the library table. Whoever he is, he must have dropped it."

I looked at her. "Why'd he bring it?"

She shrugged. "We don't know."

Phil came back, with my shirt and a duplicate of my revolver. I loaded the gun, went into the john, and replaced my shirt. I soaped most of the disinfectant off my face and neck and combed what was left of my hair down over the scratch on the side of my head. I looked almost presentable when I came out, and felt one hell of a lot better.

I looked at my watch and nearly fell over. It was 03:43. I must have slept for almost two hours out at the dispatch center.

I went back into Lamar's office and signed a receipt for Hal, for my gun. Put a copy in my pocket.

"Well, Hester, you ready for a walk?"

She was, so we went back into the cells, and she had me stand in the same spot I had been in when I fired the shot. She stood where Travis had been.

We reenacted the whole thing. Hester is five feet eight inches tall, and Travis was about five ten. Close enough, for our purposes. She spun to her right and almost fell through the door. Just like he must have. We did it three times.

While she was figuring out the patterns, she told me that they felt that Travis must have fired about sixteen to eighteen rounds. When he'd killed Elizabeth Mills, he'd shot her four times.

She wasn't sure how he'd gotten in. There were no marks of forced entry anywhere on the exterior of the building. She did know that he'd surprised the two reserves and had probably taken them out first. Then Jane, at dispatch. Then he'd simply worked his way through the cell areas, apparently recognizing and sparing Rachel and Betty. He'd then gone through the men's area, killing everybody he met, most likely because he didn't know which one was Traer. Or Kenny Mills.

They'd interviewed Traer, and he felt that Travis was aware that he'd missed his main target, and thought he'd come for him again. Traer remembered hearing a siren, which was probably mine, in the distance, and he said that the shooting had stopped abruptly. Good old Oswald Traer was apparently having a real fit, because he'd also told Hal that he'd gotten Todd Glutzman, aka Nathane, to burn the McGuire house. To cleanse it, he said. Said that he figured that the killer was going to go for Glutzman for doing that. Dumb, but Traer was scared nearly to death. Good.

Hester figured that Travis had hidden in the dispatcher's broom closet and had come in behind Dan and me when we were in the men's cell area. His timing was just a little off, she thought, because he'd probably intended shooting us from the rear.

She was probably right. I hadn't even thought about the little broom closet. I wondered if Dan had, and had deferred his own judgment because I was senior to him. God, I hoped not. It would be so much easier if we had both made the mistake.

Hester and I walked slowly out into the kitchen and then onto the back porch.

"Now, think, Carl. Did you see him here?"

"No."

"Okay, now look, here's a small smear, like he brushed the side of the door frame with his sleeve as he went out. See?"

I saw. Not much blood. Damn.

We went outside. There were five or six squad cars parked back there now, and a couple of officers I didn't know standing around. Security.

"Just where was his car?"

I indicated an area occupied by two police vehicles.

"Whose cars are these?" asked Hester.

One of the cops I didn't know said, "One's mine."

"Would you move it, please?"

He looked at her, decided she might have some authority, and agreed. He took it out onto the lawn. Rude. Lamar was proud of that lawn.

"Yeah, right about here, Hester."

We went over the asphalt between the kitchen door and where his car had been parked. There were three drops of blood, inside chalk circles, on his approximate path.

"These are the only ones we found," said Hester. "Where were you when you shot at the car?"

"Well," I said, "I started about here, shot probably four times, I think, yeah it must have been four, because then I moved to here and shot again, and then it clicked empty."

I was standing right on the chalk marks.

"Might be yours," she said.

"Yeah. Shit."

"And where was Mike?"

"He pulled up right over there, got out of the car, and fired at it as it went down the hill. I ran toward it but gave up real quick. We both reloaded, then he took off in pursuit, and I went back to the jail."

"The back door?"

"Uh, no, I sort of couldn't. Honest, Hester, I just couldn't go back in there right then. I had a smoke and then went around to the front."

"I can understand that."

"Good, I'm having a hard time myself."

Hester stood, looking around. There were two buildings behind the jail. One is an old barn that was converted into a two-story, three-stall garage; the other is a small garage slightly down the hill. Hester started toward the big one.

"Where you going?"

"Oh, just checking something out."

I went with her.

"You were only about two seconds behind him, weren't you, Carl?"

"Oh, maybe three or four, maybe a bit more. I waited at least a second in the hall, then took another second to clear the kitchen area, I think. Then outside. He might have had four to five seconds on me at that time."

"So you didn't see him get in the car?"

"No."

"But somebody was in it, weren't they? It left."

"Oh, yeah, there was a driver."

"I wonder," she said. "I wonder . . . could there have been two of them?"

"What, you think he's in here?"

"No, but he might have missed his ride. Hidden behind or in the buildings, then left on foot." We were at the big garage. "Is this always locked?"

"Never has been, as far as I know," I said, pulling my gun out. Oh, God, I thought. Don't let him be in here.

"Hey, you over there!" I shouted to the two strange cops. "Come here a minute."

They started over, saw my gun out, and Hester reaching for hers, and drew their own.

"One of you stay here with us," said Hester. "The other one go get some more people."

"He in there?"

"We don't know," she said, never looking at them.

"Just move it," I said.

One of them went flying into the jail and returned in a couple of seconds with about half a dozen officers, including Hal and Lamar.

We went through the building extremely thoroughly. Nothing. Good.

37

A search of Maitland was organized immediately. At least, that's what the official report stated later. Actually, it was thrown together in quite a hurry, and it was far from organized.

We had about ten squads running around the streets, checking out every Chevy, Buick, and Oldsmobile manufactured since the late fifties. Dispatch was going nuts running the registration checks. Station wagons, convertibles, four-door sedans, two-door hardtops, you name it. In every conceivable color. I remember hearing one that was on a car I knew was up on blocks, and had been for nearly a year.

One team of officers, about thirty or so, was going door-to-door, fanning out from the jail. Waking everybody up and having them check their cars. Pissing everybody off, unless they scared them to death.

About half the State Patrol TAC team from the Mason City office was there, with the rest coming, and we had them change into their tactical uniforms. If we found him, they were going in to get him. We didn't want to lose anybody else.

The rest of us, and there must have been fifteen or so, divided up into three teams, and went to the residences we thought he might be familiar with, and their neighbors. We searched just about every house and garage in Maitland.

Lamar, Art, Hal, Hester, and I went to the Rothbergs'.

The parsonage was located next door to the church. It was a very large frame house, built in the 1890s. Full basement, full attic. Lamar, Art, and I lived in similar homes. We were going to be on familiar territory.

Rothberg, of course, didn't appear to be home.

"He came up to the jail," said Art. "Talked to his wife. He might have gone with her."

"Gone with her?" I asked. "Where in the hell did she go?"

"Hospital, for sedatives and an examination. She was going hysterical as soon as she figured out what had happened."

Likely. From the juvenile cell, she wouldn't have been able to see much of anything. Just hear. To hell with her, I thought. She'd started the whole thing off in the first place.

We contacted dispatch, who contacted the hospital. Art was the last one of us who had been up there, and he thought there were about six or seven out-of-county cops there when he left. Looking at the nurses and trying to get free coffee.

Dispatch advised that Mark Rothberg, indeed, was at the hospital.

"Have one of the cops still there bring him home, comm."

"10–4."

"Right away."

"10–4, one."

We waited outside, Hester at the right rear, me at the left rear corner of the house, Art at the right front, and Lamar and Hal at the door. It was cold and damp. You could see your breath easily.

A squad car came poking around the corner. The driver was obviously unfamiliar with the area. It turned out to be a trooper from about fifty miles away. Rothberg was with him.

The parsonage was four blocks from the jail. It was quite possible that even a severely wounded Travis had been able to get there.

Rothberg said he didn't know if he was there or not, but that he hadn't seen him. He was talking in a loud voice and was obviously rather disturbed. Good.

Lamar and Hal had a discussion about whether or not to get the TAC team down for the search or to hold them in reserve until Travis had been located.

Compromise. There were five TAC officers in town. It was decided that two of them would go in with the search team and lead them through the house. The other three would be held in reserve.

"Comm, one."

"One," said Sally.

"Have about four officers meet us here."

Lamar decided that Hester and I weren't going to go in. I was "too personally involved." He didn't give a reason for excluding Hester, but he didn't have to. She was a woman. Even though Lamar thought women were just as good as men, especially Hester, he couldn't shake his basic gentleman's manners. He wouldn't apologize for them, either.

The four other cops, all of whom I didn't know, ringed Rothberg's house, while the two TAC officers, Hal, Lamar, and Art went inside. With Rothberg. I sort of felt that they should have sent him in first, but didn't say anything except to Hester.

Hester, who was as pissed as I was, wandered to the street and leaned up against my squad car. I lit a cigarette. She didn't.

"I don't know about you," I said, "but I kind of feel left out."

"Me too."

"But I think we should do something useful, don't you?"

"Like what?"

"Well, it occurs to me that he might be in the church." I took a drag of the cigarette. "For example."

She looked at the large, wooden church. Dark. Quite dark.

"Could be."

"I mean, with his little Satanic sense of humor, what better place to go." I ground out my cigarette. "I thought of that back at the hospital."

"Shouldn't we tell somebody?" She was smiling. "They might worry about us."

"No sooner said than done." I reached into the squad and punched the radio off ops and onto info. Info is tone-coded. Mobile units and portables can't hear one another on info.

"Comm, three."

"Three?"

"Agent Gorse and I are going to be going into the church, to look around. Keep us posted, will you?"

"10–4."

"There," I said, quite pleased with myself. I hung up the mike, grabbed my rifle and my flashlight. "Let's go."

We walked around the building first. No signs of forced entry. Didn't have to be, as none of the doors were locked.

We went in on the south side. I gave Hester my light and held my rifle with both hands. There's no place on earth quieter than a dark church.

We moved slowly through the small room we first entered, and came out on the altar, from the side. Nothing. Then Hester shined the light back the way we had come, to clear the rear before we ventured out, and we both saw the blood smear on the white wall. I froze, and my heart started pounding in my ears. I guess I really hadn't expected him to be here.

Hester cut the light, and we both ducked back into the small room and flattened out against opposite sides of the door to the altar.

"Whoa!" she whispered. "He's here."

The big question was, Does he know *we* are, too? No way to know, not for sure.

The obvious thing to do was to call for help. Mom didn't raise any fools.

"Comm, three!"

"Three?"

"We believe he's in the church. Get 10–78. We're just inside the south door, by the altar."

"10—4!"

"Wanna just stay put?" asked Hester in a whisper.

"You bet," I whispered back.

There was a muffled *pop*, and some wood from our door frame splintered.

We both squatted down instantly and adjusted back from the doorway.

"Think he knows we're here?" she whispered.

"Yep."

Pop, pop, pop. At least one of them went by my ear. From an angle. He was shooting into the room from an angle. I hunkered back along the wall, delighted not to have been trapped out there on the altar.

"No doubt in my mind. . ."

Pop.

This time the bullet could be heard striking the stained glass in the exterior door. He was changing position.

"He's advancing," said Hester in a normal voice.

"Great."

I pulled the cocking handle on the AR-15 back and let a round clack into the chamber.

"Let's see if we can get him to retreat," I said. I reached the rifle through the door as far to the right as I could. I'm left-handed, and I was on the right side of the door frame.

Five quick rounds, as I moved the barrel to the left. Trying to spread them out. I had no idea where he was.

Silence. Deafening silence, except for the shrill ringing in my ears. He could have yelled, and I don't think I could have heard him. And I had ruined my night vision in the dark church. I had, however, gotten a pretty good look at the church in the muzzle flash. Like a flashbulb going off. I hadn't seen him.

We waited for what seemed like a reasonable time, and I stuck my head cautiously around the door frame. Nothing.

"Police!" I yelled.

"No shit," said Hester.

Silence. Then *pop*.

It must have hit something inside the room, because there was a *clang* and something hit the floor behind us. But I had seen that muzzle flash. Like a spark, like in the hall at the jail.

"He's to our right, up on the altar," I said. "I think."

I was staring out into the interior of the church, pretty close to the floor, when Hester stuck out her leg and caught me in the shoulder. My heart about stopped.

"What!"

"I'm going for the pews," she said. She began to gather herself to move. "Just let me clear the door, and then crank off three rounds, okay?"

"You think that's a good idea?"

"Of course I do."

Dumb question.

"Okay. I think he's still to the right."

Without another word, she hurled herself out the door. As per instructions, as soon as she cleared the frame, I stuck the rifle barrel to the right and fired three quick rounds.

No response.

What about Hester?

I looked around the door frame again. I couldn't see her.

Pop, pop, pop. Nothing near me. I couldn't see her, but it sounded like he could.

I hadn't seen the spark this time. He wasn't pointing it at me.

I stood up and aimed the rifle at the altar.

Hester, I thought, why did you do that?

"Okay, you inept son of a bitch!" I yelled. "You can shoot women and people in cages. Come on, asshole. Try this."

No response. Good or bad? At least there were no shots.

I kept trying to think of what Saperstein had said about Travis. About his character. Ascetic. That's all I could remember.

"You really fucked up this time, dummy!"

Nothing.

I was trying to listen for sounds through the ringing in my ears. Movement. Anything.

The front door opened, letting in the orangish glow from the streetlight, and I saw a shadow come through and move to my left.

"TAC's in, Hester!" I yelled.

Another shadow through the door. Then two of them. So now we had four more officers in the church. With Travis. And Hester. In the dark. God, I thought, don't let him shoot at them. And if he does, don't let them return fire toward Hester.

I keyed my portable. "We have an officer in the pews at the front of the church. I think the suspect's up on the altar."

I hoped they heard me.

"You're in the wrong place now!" I yelled. "Satan can't help you here. You left him at the door, stupid."

Suddenly the lights came on by the main entrance. One of the TAC people must have found the switch.

"Shut off the fuckin' lights!" yelled somebody near the back of the church.

I went down in a crouch and looked toward the pews. I could see Hester, down on one knee, behind the second one. She was okay. I looked toward the altar. Nothing.

The pillars cast long shadows across the middle of the church, making it difficult to be certain you picked up on any movement. I saw one of the TAC guys slowly stand up at the rear of the church, pointing a shotgun. He had no target, you could tell.

I cautiously stepped from behind the door frame, making sure the TAC man saw me. He moved the muzzle of the shotgun away from me, toward his left. Slowly. Still no target.

I stepped onto the altar, hugging the wall. As I came around, I could see one of the TAC men crawling on the floor at the outside of the pews. He had a pistol in his right hand. Looking down each row as he went. I figured there was another one on the far side, doing the same thing.

I put my rifle to my shoulder, sweeping from about the middle of the pews toward the front, keeping the standing TAC man out of my line of fire. Still nothing.

Hester stood slowly, holding her badge up above her head as she got up. She was in a pretty bad position, so started to move to her left, never taking her eyes from the altar.

Travis chose that moment to rise up from the elevated pulpit, his pistol pointing generally toward Hester. I couldn't believe my eyes. Honest to God. It wasn't Travis. It was Theo. Travis was Theo.

"Don't shoot!" I couldn't think. "Theo, don't you shoot, either! Stay calm, Theo, stay calm." I raised my voice, for the benefit of the TAC team. "He's a cop, one of our people! Hold back a second . . ."

Theo looked right at me, then shifted his eyes to my right, toward Hester. No expression. Didn't say a thing.

"Drop the gun, Theo!" He didn't answer me. Didn't even acknowledge my existence. I still had my rifle at my shoulder from when I'd come through the door. I was afraid to lower it because the movement might set him off. I could see Hester out of the corner of my eye to my right, and she kept glancing at me. The old cop protocol: he's your officer, you do something.

"Drop it, Theo," I said, more calmly this time. "It'll be okay, man, it'll be all right, just drop—"

He pivoted at the waist, bringing his gun to bear on me. He fired, Hester fired, I fired, the TAC man in the aisle fired.

He whipped backward, striking the edge of the pulpit behind him, whipped forward again, the gun still in his hand.

I hit him hard.

He sort of came apart, a sizable chunk of his skull flying off to the rear. He disappeared, down into the pulpit.

We approached slowly. We needn't have. He was dead as hell. He was also somebody now. He was Theo.

There was an arm sticking out of the back of the pulpit as I came around. The rest of him was sort of stuffed down inside. Hester came up, her revolver held in both hands. Pointing at him.

His shirt was off, with part of it wrapped around his left arm. From where I'd got him earlier. He'd been shooting at us with his right hand, I thought. No wonder he missed.

"Jesus Christ," she said.

The TAC guys, as they were trained, were handcuffing Theo, even though he appeared to be dead to everybody including God.

"Theo." I looked at Hester.

"Damn," she said.

"Now I know why I thought I recognized him."

"I never shot anybody before," she said.

I wished I could have said the same.

Epilogue

It took us a while to get straight on everything. Years ago, we had all realized that there was a good likelihood that, because of the restrictions on the dissemination of Criminal History and Law Enforcement Intelligence Information, we couldn't share everything with each other. Need to know and all that. We had a doubling procedure in place to ensure a check and to make certain that critical information wasn't denied a case officer. That's all well and good, but it's pretty incredible that the stuff put into law to make an investigation go more smoothly ended up costing us so dearly. Big-city police politics.

As it turned out, Hal had found out during his telephone conversation with the Ohio officers that Theo had been the officer who got the psych discharge. Hal did the right thing and told Lamar. Even though Theo had been "cured," ostensibly, in outpatient therapy, Lamar didn't think he should tell every loudmouth in the station, like me, about Theo's past. It was confidential and Lamar felt sorry for him. That's why Hal was the only one to get access to the entire file from Ohio. But Hal had been too busy to read it. And if the file had been shared with everyone, I'm sure we would have been able to figure out that Theo had been a peripheral suspect in the Ohio murders, mainly because of his association with some of the victims and their friends. If we had all known, we would have started putting things together much quicker. Like how the department had been penetrated on the night of the last murders so easily. Jane let him in, of course. That's a real basic tenet of murder investigation. They're most likely done by someone you know. Hell, we knew that. What we hadn't known was that our dead personnel had known him, too. And that was why Theo had to kill them.

Lamar really hasn't been the same since it's all played out. I don't blame him for keeping Theo's secrets. Theo had been in his own little Satanic world for years. Meds had kept him in control most of the time. It looks like he was getting Haldol/Risperidone from a psychiatrist in Dubuque, and Prozac from a local doc. He paid for the Prozac himself, just to make sure our insurance company didn't put two and two together. Paranoid schizophrenic, I'm told. He did well on the drugs, I guess. I talked to a psychiatrist about that, and he said that sometimes they just get lonesome for the voices that the drugs suppress, and they stop taking the meds. At any rate, he became much craftier and a lot more aggressive than the Theo we all knew. How was Lamar to know?

Interestingly enough, because Theo lived about thirty miles from Maitland, worked plainclothes and in an unmarked car, Betty never saw him in a police connection. We asked her, and she never remembered seeing him in Maitland at all. But, of course, she started blaming us for the whole thing when she found out he was a cop.

One thing to say about Betty's family is that Rachel turned out all right in the end. She never did let the coven sacrifice Cynthia. We found the little girl later in Cedar Rapids. Good old Oswald stashed her with one of his cronies to keep up his reputation. Complete with papers. It still pays to know an attorney, I guess. The body at the farm turned out to be a headless dog. Yep. If you don't think you could make the same mistake, look at a dead dog that's been skinned, or its skeleton. Especially in a fire. Weird isn't the half of it. I don't know why Phyllis lied about the sacrifice in her journal, unless it was to perpetuate the myth that Traer was really powerful. People in cults do that sort of thing, I'm told. Should we have bought that at face value? I don't see why not. It wasn't like we could question her. At any rate, we were all too happy to admit to the screwup. The little girl alive almost put the entire nightmare behind us.

So Theo had found a home in Nation County, and a comfortable one, too. He was saved by the confidentiality requirements of our Personnel Policy. Jesus.

Anyway, Oswald Traer, Sarah Freitag, Todd Glutzman, Martha Vernon, and Hedda Zeiss had to be released. Needless to say, the community didn't jump for joy when they were sprung. After a couple of months passed, they were all out of the county.

Betty Rothberg was committed to a mental health hospital and never came to trial for her role in the mess. The prosecution team said it would cost the taxpayers too much money to try her. Mark Rothberg pled guilty to assaulting me and did a few months of time before being paroled. He's living near Betty now and praying for her soul, I guess.

We never did figure out where McGuire was killed.

I see Helen Bockman on the street occasionally. We don't talk.

Sally quit dispatching. Financial reasons. Went to a better job, where she can make eleven thousand a year. She's been making noises about coming back to us. I hope she does.

Dan Smith's wife left the area, but he's buried here. She's never been back, as far as I know.

Peggy Keller's family misses her a lot. Especially the three kids. Her husband is dating, but who knows?

I received one letter from Detective Saperstein, about a month after the events in the church. Wrote back, never an answer.

All the rest of us are still around, still doing our thing. But those eleven days come back to me pretty much every night around midnight.